NIGHTBRINGER

A SPACE CLEARED around the two warriors as battle continued to rage throughout the bridge. The shapeless forms around the alien's legs resolved into clarity and Uriel was horrified as he clearly saw the heaving mass of creatures that hissed and spat beside the alien leader.

Uriel extended his sword, pointing the tip at the alien leader's chest.

'I am Uriel Ventris of the Ultramarines and I have come to kill you.'

The alien leader cocked his head to one side before speaking. His voice rasped, unused to forming human words.

'You are nothing but a mon-keigh, an animal, and I shall feed you to the excrents.'

More Warhammer 40,000 from the Black Library

• LAST CHANCERS •

13TH LEGION by Gav Thorpe

KILL TEAM by Gav Thorpe

• GAUNT'S GHOSTS •

FIRST & ONLY by Dan Abnett

GHOSTMAKER by Dan Abnett

NECROPOLIS by Dan Abnett

HONOUR GUARD by Dan Abnett

• EISENHORN •

XENOS by Dan Abnett

MALLEUS by Dan Abnett

• SPACE WOLF •

SPACE WOLF by William King

RAGNAR'S CLAW by William King

• OTHER WARHAMMER 40,000 TITLES •

EXECUTION HOUR by Gordon Rennie

PAWNS OF CHAOS by Brian Craig

EYE OF TERROR by Barrington J. Bayley

INTO THE MAELSTROM
eds. Marc Gascoigne & Andy Jones

STATUS: DEADZONE
eds. Marc Gascoigne & Andy Jones

DARK IMPERIUM
eds. Marc Gascoigne & Andy Jones

DEATHWING
eds. Neil Jones & David Pringle

A WARHAMMER 40,000 NOVEL

An Ultramarines Novel

NIGHTBRINGER

Graham McNeill

To everyone who helped me realise this book.

A BLACK LIBRARY PUBLICATION

First published in Great Britain in 2002 by
Games Workshop Publishing
Willow Road, Lenton,
Nottingham, NG7 2WS, UK

10 9 8 7 6 5 4 3 2 1

Cover illustration by Clint Langley

A CIP record for this book
is available from the British Library

ISBN 1 84154 205 9

Set in ITC Giovanni

Printed and bound in Great Britain by
Cox & Wyman Ltd, Cardiff Rd, Reading, Berkshire RG1 8EX, UK

NIGHTBRINGER

PROLOGUE

60 million years ago...

THE STAR WAS being destroyed. It was a dwarf star of some one and a half million kilometres diameter and had burned for over six billion years. Had it not been for the immense, crescent-moon shaped starship orbiting the system's fourth planet and draining its massive energies, it would have probably continued to do so for perhaps another sixteen billion years.

The star generated energy at a colossal rate by burning hydrogen to helium in nuclear fusion reactions deep in its heart before radiating that energy into space. These reactions produced intense electro-magnetic fields in the star's core that rippled to the surface in seething magnetic waves.

A clutch of these surging fields erupted as a toroidal loop of magnetic flux some 200,000 kilometres in diameter, producing a dark, swelling sunspot within the star's photosphere.

This active region of magnetic flux expanded rapidly, suddenly exploding upwards from the star's surface in a gigantic flare, covering a billion square kilometres and becoming a bright curling spear of light in the star's corona. These powerful waves of electromagnetic energy and sprays of plasma formed into a rippling nimbus of coruscating light that spiralled a snaking route towards a rune-encrusted pyramid at the centre of the vast starship. Eldritch sigils carved into the ship's side blazed with the received energies and the hull pulsed as though the ship itself was swelling with barely contained power.

Every flaring beam of light ripped from the star that washed its power over the ship shortened the star's lifespan by a hundred thousand years, but the occupants of the starship cared not that its death would cause the extinction of every living thing in that system. Galaxies had lived and died by their masters' command, whole stellar realms had been extinguished for their pleasure and entire races brought into existence as their playthings. What mattered the fate of one insignificant star system to beings of such power?

Like some obscene mechanised leech, the ship continued to suck the vital forces from the star as it orbited the planet. An array of smaller pyramids and obelisks on the ship's base rippled as though in a heat haze, flickering in and out of perception as the massive ship shuddered with the colossal energies it was stripping from the star.

Abruptly the snaking beam of liquid light from the star faded and vanished from sight, the silver ship having had its fill for the moment. Ponderously it began to rotate and dropped slowly through the planet's atmosphere. Fiery coronas flared from the leading edges of the crescent wings as it descended towards a vast, iron-oxide desert in the northern hemisphere. The surface of the planet sped by below: rugged mountains, grinding tectonic plates and ash-spewing volcanoes. The ship began slowing as it neared its destination, a sandy dust bowl with a tiny spot of absolute darkness at its centre.

The ship's speed continued to drop as the shape resolved itself into a glassy black pyramid, its peak capped in gold. Its shimmering obsidian walls, smoky and reflective, were impervious to the howling winds that scoured the planet bare. Small, scuttling creatures that glittered in the burning sun crawled across its surface with a chittering mechanical gait. Runes identical to those on the orbiting starship hummed as powerful receptors activated.

The ship manoeuvred itself gracefully into position above the pyramid as the gold cap began to open like the petals of a flower. The humming rose to an ear-splitting shriek as the smaller pyramids and obelisks on the ship's underside exploded with energy, and a rippling column of pure electromagnetic force shot straight down the black pyramid's hungry maw.

Incandescent white light blazed from the pyramid, instantly incinerating the mechanical creatures that crawled across its surface. The desert it stood upon flared gold, streaks of power radiating outwards from the pyramid's base in snaking lines and vitrifying the sand in complex geometric patterns. The enormous vessel held its position until the last of its stolen energy had been transferred. Once the gold cap of the pyramid had sealed itself shut, the ship made the long trip back into orbit to repeat the process, its intention to continue ripping energy from the star until it was nothing more than a cooling ball of inert gasses.

The vessel settled into position before the star, the arcane device mounted upon its hull powering up once more.

An area of space behind the vessel twisted, shifting out of true and ripping asunder as the fragile veil of reality tore aside and a massive flotilla of bizarre alien vessels poured out from the maelstrom beyond.

No two ships were alike, each having its own unique geometries and form, but all had the same lethal purpose. As though commanded by a single will, the rag-tag fleet of ships closed rapidly on the crescent-shaped starship, weapons of all descriptions firing. A series of bright explosions blossomed across the mighty ship's hull, bolts of powerful energy smashing against the uppermost pyramid. The craft shuddered like a wounded beast.

But this starship could fight back.

Arcs of cobalt lightning whiplashed from its weapon batteries, smashing a dozen of its foes to destruction. Invisible beams of immense power stripped another group down to their component atoms. But no amount of losses could dissuade the alien fleet from its attack, and no matter how many were destroyed, it seemed there were always more to take their place. The faceless crew of the starship appeared to realise that unless they could escape, they were doomed. Slowly the ship began to rotate on its axis, a powerful, electric haze growing from its inertialess engines.

A multitude of alien weapons hammered the ship's flattened topside, tearing great gouges in its hull and blasting jagged chunks of metal from the vessel. Self-repair mechanisms attempted to stem the damage, but, like the ship itself, they were fighting a losing battle. Wreckage from the ship spun off into the darkness of space as its engines fired with retina-searing brightness. Time slowed and the image of the enormous ship stretched like elastic, the nearby gravity well of the star enacting its revenge on the vampire ship as it vainly attempted to escape.

With a tortured shriek that echoed through the warp, the crescent ship seemed to contract to a singular point of unbearable brightness. Its attackers were sucked into the screaming wake and together the foes were hurled into oblivion, perhaps never to return.

The star continued to burn and, far below, the glow emanating from the golden cap of the black pyramid faded until it was a dull lustreless bronze.

Soon, the sands obscured even that.

ONE

The 41st Millennium...

THE EIGHTEEN RIDERS made their way along the base of the frozen stream bed, their horses carefully picking their steps through the ice-slick rocky ground. Despite their caution, and the herd of nearly a hundred scaly-skinned grox they were driving through the snow, Gedrik knew they were making good time.

He twisted in the saddle, making sure the herd was still together.

Gedrik was lean and rangy, wrapped tightly in a battered, but well cared-for snow cape with leather riding trousers, padded on the inner thighs, and warm, fur lined boots. His head was protected by a thick colback of toughened leather and furs, his face wrapped in a woollen scarf to keep the worst of the vicious mountain winds at bay.

The green plaid so common on Caernus IV, Gedrik's home planet, was tied loosely across his chest, its frayed ends hanging over the wire-wound hilt of his sword. Hidden in his left boot, he also carried a slender bladed dagger. He had crafted both weapons himself from the Metal six years ago, and they were still as sharp and untarnished as the day he had forged them. Preacher Mallein had taught him how to use the sword, and they were lessons he had learned well; no one in the Four Valleys could fight as well as Gedrik.

To complete his arsenal he carried a simple bolt-action rifle slung across his wide shoulders. Gedrik knew they were almost home and he looked forward to a warm fire and the even warmer embrace of his wife, Maeren.

This last week on the mountains, gathering the herd for the slaughter, had been hard, as though the wind and snow had sought to scour the pitiful humans who dared their wrath from the rocky peaks.

But soon they would be home and Gedrik could almost taste the fine steak Maeren would cook for him once Gohbar had begun slaughtering the herd.

He turned as he heard a muffled curse behind him and grinned as his cousin, Faergus rode alongside him. Though Gedrik knew that 'rode' was a flattering term for Faergus's skill in the saddle.

Gedrik's cousin could only be described as a bear of a man, with huge shoulders and a thick, shapeless neck. His face was battered and lumpen, with a squashed nose broken in countless brawls and a thick, black beard.

His feet dangled almost to the snow and Gedrik could well understand his mount's desire to unseat him. He ignored his cousin's discomfort, content to simply enjoy the majestic beauty of the Gelroch Mountains as they travelled home.

The sun was an hour past its zenith when the snow-wreathed settlement of Morten's Reach came into view. Nestling in the loop of a sluggish river at the centre of a wide glen, the buildings of the community seemed to huddle together as though for shared warmth. Gedrik could see the inhabitants milling about the town square in front of the small stone-built temple to the Emperor, squatting on the slopes of the Hill of the Metal. Preacher Mallein must have just finished one of his sermons, and Gedrik smiled as he pictured his son, Rouari, telling him all about the winged angels and heroic deeds of the Emperor over supper. Mallein could spin a fine tale, that was for sure!

Smoke drifted from the forge and, on the near side of the village, Gedrik could see Gohbar the slaughterman preparing the iron-walled corral on the river bank for the grox.

Gedrik urged his mount on, fresh energy filling him at the thought of Maeren and a home cooked meal. Only the grox seemed reluctant to pick up the pace, but a few shouted oaths and well-placed blows from Faergus's shock-prod soon sorted that out.

Gedrik allowed his gaze to wander as he caught a flash of movement across the glen. He narrowed his eyes and raised a hand to shield his sight from the low, winter sun. Something had moved behind a thick copse of evergreens at the crest of the opposite rise, he could have sworn it. Automatically, he unslung his rifle and worked the bolt, chambering a bullet.

'Trouble?' asked Faergus, noting Gedrik's actions.

'I'm not sure. I thought I saw something,' said Gedrik, pointing to the dark tree-line.

Faergus squinted across the glen, drawing his own weapon, a stubby barrelled shotgun from its shoulder scabbard.

'I don't see–' began Faergus as a dozen, sleek prowed vehicles emerged from the trees. Wickedly angled with blades and curved barbs, the vehicles swept down the hillside towards the settlement, their open decks swarming with warriors. Black bolts spat from weapons mounted on the foredecks of the skimming craft, exploding with shocking violence amongst the buildings of Morten's Reach.

'Emperor's blood!' cursed Gedrik, raking back his spurs, all thought of the herd forgotten as he pushed his horse to the gallop. Without looking, he knew the rest of his men were behind him. Screams and the dull crack of gunfire echoed from below and hot fear gripped his heart at the thought of these terrible aliens in his home.

Heedless of the danger of such a mad gallop, Gedrik pushed his mount hard over the stony ground. Despite the horse's bouncing rush, he saw the alien vehicles begin to spread out, a group detaching from each flank to encircle the settlement while the remainder speared towards the heart of the township. Gedrik saw his people scatter, running for their homes or the sanctuary of the temple as the first skimmers blasted their way into the village, reducing building after building to rubble.

Closer now, the horse careering up to the outskirts of the village, he saw a woman clutching a child – Maeren and Rouari? – dash inside the church as Preacher Mallein was cut down by a flurry of lethal splinters fired from alien rifles. Whooping warriors in close-fitting armour of black and red somersaulted from the decks of their vehicles and sprinted through the township, firing long barrelled guns from the hip.

He shouted in horror as he saw the villagers gunned down where they stood, women and children running towards the church, their bodies jerking in the fusillade. Black smoke boiled skyward as more buildings burned and the screams of the dying cut Gedrik like a knife. Small arms fire blasted from a few windows, felling a number of the alien raiders and he knew the invaders would not take Morten's Reach without a fight.

His wild charge had carried him almost to the river, close enough to see old Gohbar run screaming towards a group of the alien warriors, a flensing halberd raised above his head. The aliens turned and laughingly despatched the slaughterman with a volley from their deadly rifles before disappearing into the smoke of the village's death throes.

Gedrik willed his horse ever faster as he thundered across the river bridge, beside the generator mill he had helped build with his own hands, and passed the convulsing Gohbar. The man's face was purple and distended, his tongue protruding from his mouth like a swollen black snake. The entire town was in flames, the heat and smoke intolerable.

Gedrik emerged into the settlement's square, stopping his horse violently. Two of the attackers' craft hovered before the temple, the alien warriors dragging screaming townspeople towards them. Their faces were exquisitely cruel and pale; humanoid, yet wholly alien. Gedrik stood forward in the stirrups and aimed his rifle at one of the red armoured invaders, placing its angled helm squarely between his sights.

He squeezed the trigger, punching the warrior from its feet, sending blood jetting from its neck. The others scattered and Gedrik yelled out, hammering his spurs into his mount's flanks. The horse leapt forwards and Gedrik fired twice more, pitching another two aliens to the ground before the rifle jammed.

The aliens turned their weapons on him, but the Emperor was with him and their whickering ammunition flew wide of the mark. Then he was amongst them and swung his rifle in a brutal arc, smashing an enemy's skull to shards. He dropped the gun and drew his sword. He caught a flash of red, before a bolt of dark light blasted his horse from under him.

Kicking his feet free of the stirrups, Gedrik jumped from the dying beast and landed lightly before a knot of the alien warriors and lashed out with his shimmering, broad bladed sword. The first fell with its guts looping around its ankles and the second died with Gedrik's sword lodged deep in its chest. Their alien armour was no protection against the preternatural sharpness of Gedrik's sword, which cut through it with ease. The third thrust with a smoking blade on the end of its rifle and Gedrik dodged backwards, losing his grip on the sword. The alien advanced slowly, emotionless behind its smooth-faced helm.

Gedrik snarled and dived towards his foe. He rolled beneath the alien's weapon, dragging his dagger from his boot and hammering it through the warrior's calf. The alien fell, shrieking horribly, and Gedrik wrenched the knife free, plunging it repeatedly through the alien's chest.

He saw Faergus following him, blasting two of the aliens to bloody rags with a thunderous blast of his shotgun. Faergus wheeled his horse as Gedrik retrieved his sword and shouted to his cousin.

'Get everyone you can inside the temple. We'll try to hold them from there!'

Faergus nodded, but before he could move, a flaring wash of violet fire blasted from one of the alien vehicles and engulfed him. Faergus screamed as the horrifying energies burned the flesh from his frame in moments. Slowly his charred skeleton toppled from the shrieking horse and Gedrik felt his stomach lurch at his cousin's terrible death. The horse toppled, a bloody gouge burned through the beast's flank where the alien weapon had struck.

Gedrik bounded up the steps of the temple, hammering on the door, shouting out Maeren's name. Splinters were blasted from the building as more aliens converged on the centre of the village, firing wildly towards him. He dived from the steps and rolled to his feet. He saw the surviving inhabitants driven before the aliens to their deaths and, watching it all, a slender, white haired figure in jade green armour atop the lead vehicle.

The figure slashed his huge axe impatiently through the air and Gedrik screamed as his people were shot down where they stood. He wanted to plant his dagger in the alien leader's chest, but knew he would be dead before he got close.

He ducked back, knowing that the people inside the temple could not risk opening the doors now and sprinted around the side, hoping that they had not yet barred the vestry.

Gedrik heard the bark of commands being issued and a deep bass rumble of a powerful weapon. He prayed that someone had managed to send a warning to the nearby communities.

The vestry door was just ahead and he cried in relief as he saw it was still ajar. He skidded to a halt before it and gripped the iron handle.

Before he could pull the door open, the temple exploded, roiling orange flames mushrooming skyward and blasting Gedrik from his feet. Pain like nothing he had ever known engulfed him as the blast smashed him into the hillside behind the building. He flopped like a boneless creature, shocked to his very bones by the impact. His skin burned, patches of his anatomy exposed to the elements by the unnatural flames.

He sensed cool snow upon his body, but could feel no pain. He knew that was bad. Pain meant life.

He rolled his eyes towards the smoking wreckage of the temple, timber columns poking upwards like blackened ribs. He couldn't make out any bodies, but knew that no one could have survived the explosion and grief swamped him.

Maeren, Rouari, Faergus, Mallein, Gohbar... all gone. Everyone was dead. Even him soon.

His breath rattled in his throat as he heard the low humming of the alien vehicles approaching and he tried to push himself upright, but his limbs would not obey him. Dimly he heard the aliens' sing-song voices, elegant but threatening, and tried to spit a defiant curse. But the voices passed him, climbing the Hill of the Metal. He watched as the green-armoured warrior pointed at the hillside and directed his warriors to spread out. He heard their voices chatter excitedly, but could not understand what they said. Was this the reason his community had been slaughtered?

For the Metal?

He heard the whoosh of flames and the hillside lit up, hissing as the snow flashed to steam. The aliens continued to work the flames of their weapons across the hillside, only stopping when a hooded figure wearing shimmering red robes climbed down from the nearest alien vehicle and raised its hand. The figure stepped forward to examine what had been revealed beneath the snow and a low gasp went up from the aliens as the steam dissipated.

Swirling like quicksilver, the exposed strata sparkled in the sunlight, its entire flank shining with a metallic sheen. Beneath the snow, a whole swathe of the hillside was formed from a smooth, silver metal. It rippled and twisted like a liquid where it had run molten under the heat of the flames, undulating like a living thing. Slowly it began reshaping itself, flowing with swirling currents into a smooth, glass-flat surface until it resembled a gigantic mirror. Gedrik watched as the hooded figure dropped to its knees before the metallic hillside and began chanting in rapture, the words rasping and artificial.

Moments passed before Gedrik realised that the figure's words were familiar to him. He did not truly understand them, but recognised the mantra from times he had spent working in the forge with Faergus.

It was a chant in praise of the Omnissiah. The Machine God.

The robed figure rose to face the aliens' leader and threw back his hood. Gedrik saw that most of the figure's face had been replaced by cybernetic implants. A brass-rimmed vox-unit nestled in the centre of his throat below his stitched lips, crackling with hissing white noise. Ribbed copper wiring curled from beneath his robes and plugged into his empty eye sockets, and meshed discs were sutured over the puckered skin where a normal man's ears would be. His flesh was pallid and grey, but despite all the deforming aspects of the figure's loathsome surgery, Gedrik could see that the man was clearly human, and the horror of such treachery made him want to cry with rage.

Cold agony began seeping into his body and he tried to scream, but unconsciousness swept over him and took the pain away.

TWO

THE AIR WAS chill as Captain Uriel Ventris of the Ultramarines made his way up the thousand steps to the chapter master's chambers. He carried his helm in the crook of his arm and his stride was sure, the servo muscles in his suit of power armour making light work of the climb despite the slight limp from the wound he had suffered on Thracia nearly six months ago. The steps wound their way upwards along the side of the valley of Laponis, site of the most magnificent structure on Macragge, the Fortress of Hera, bastion of the Ultramarines.

Constructed from great slabs of marble quarried from the valley sides, the vast body of the structure was a gigantic, columned masterpiece, its surfaces white and pristine. Graceful balconies, golden geodesic domes and slender glass walkways, supported by angled silver-steel buttresses, gave the impression of both great strength and light, airy weightlessness.

The fortress monastery of the Ultramarines was a wonder of engineering, designed by the Chapter's primarch Roboute Guilliman and constructed during the days of the Emperor's Great Crusade ten thousand years ago. Since that time, the warriors of the Ultramarines Chapter of Space Marines had dwelt here.

The fortress sat amidst the tallest peaks in the valley of Laponis, surrounded by highland fir and alongside the mighty Hera's Falls. Glacial water thundered over the falls to the rocks, hundreds of metres below, and glittering rainbows arced across the narrow width of the valley. Uriel stopped and cast his gaze towards the falls, remembering the first time he had seen them and the sense of humbling awe he had felt. A smile touched his lips as he realised he still felt it.

He placed his hand on the pommel of his sword, feeling the weight of responsibility it represented. As he took in the elaborate detailing along the masterfully carved scabbard, his mind returned to the carnage on the rebel world of Thracia where his company commander and trusted friend, Captain Idaeus, had presented him with the magnificent weapon before going to his death.

Tasked with destroying a bridge to prevent the traitorous soldiers of Thracia from flanking an Imperial army, Idaeus's detachment had become trapped in a desperate battle against a huge enemy contingent attempting to force the bridge. For a day and a night, the thirty Ultramarines had held nearly a thousand soldiers at bay until heretical warriors of the Night Lords entered the fray.

Uriel shivered as he remembered his horror at the sight of his comrades crucified upon the hulls of the Night Lords' transports, and knew he would carry their pain-filled faces to his grave. The Traitor Marines had come close to overrunning the Ultramarines' position, but thanks to a desperate gamble by Idaeus, one that had cost him his life, the bridge had been destroyed and the attack defeated.

The feeling of grief at Idaeus's passing rose once more in his chest, but he suppressed it quickly, continuing his journey upwards. It would not do to keep his lord and master waiting.

He climbed higher up the steps, their centres worn smooth by the passage of uncounted footsteps, and briefly wondered exactly how many had made this climb before him. Eventually, he reached the wide esplanade at the summit and turned to look back on the route his climb had taken him.

Snow-capped mountains stretched as far as the eye could see in all directions save one. To the west, the horizon shimmered a deep, azure blue where Uriel's genetically enhanced vision could make out the rocky coastline and the sea, far in the distance. The domed and marble roofed structures of the fortress stepped down before him, each step a citadel in its own right.

He turned on his heel and strode towards the mighty structure before him, passing beneath the many columned portico that led to the chambers of the chapter master of the Ultramarines, Marneus Calgar. Gleaming bronze doors swung open as he approached and two massive warriors of the First Company, clad in holy suits of Terminator armour and carrying long bladed polearms stepped through, their weapons held at the ready.

Even Uriel's armoured physique was dwarfed by the bulk of the Terminators and Uriel nodded respectfully to the veterans as he passed, emerging into the cool air of the vestibule. A servant of the chapter master, dressed in a plain blue tunic, appeared at his side and took his helm, pointing towards the central courtyard of the structure without speaking. Uriel offered his thanks and descended the steps into the sunken courtyard, his gaze sweeping around and taking in every detail. Gold-stitched battle honours hung from the courtyard's balconies above shadowed cloisters, and statues of Ultramarines heroes from ancient times ringed a gurgling fountain set in its marbled centre. Here was Ancient Galatan, a former bearer of the Banner of Macragge, and there was Captain Invictus, hero of the First Company who had died fighting the Great Devourer.

The fountain was carved in the form of a mighty warrior upon a massive steed, his lance raised to the heavens. Konor, the first Battle King of Macragge, his face artfully carved, fully capturing the man's fierce determination to do the best for his people. Another servant arrived, carrying a tray upon which sat an earthenware jug and two silver goblets. He deposited them on the stone bench that encircled the fountain and silently withdrew. Uriel nervously clasped the hilt of his sword, wishing that he felt worthy of its history.

'Konor was a giant amongst men,' said a voice laden with centuries of authority and power. 'He pacified the entire continent before his twenty-first year and set in motion events that enabled the Holy Guilliman to become the man he needed to be.'

Uriel turned to face the Lord of Macragge, Marneus Calgar.

'I remember well from my teachings at the Agiselus Barracks, my lord,' replied Uriel, bowing low.

'A fine institution. Guilliman himself trained there.'

Uriel smiled at Calgar's modesty, knowing full well that the chapter master had trained there also.

The lord of the Ultramarines was a giant of a man, even by the standards of the Space Marines. The lustre of his blue armour barely seemed able to contain his sheer dynamism and power, the bronze two-headed Imperial eagle on his right shoulder shining like polished gold. Black rings hung from the lobe of his right ear and his left eye had been replaced with a flat, gem-like bionic version, fine copper wiring trailing from its mechanics to the back of his skull. Calgar's venerable face appeared to be carved from oak, yet he had lost none of his cunning or insight. Over four hundred years old, his strength and vitality were the envy of warriors half his age.

'Well met, brother,' greeted Calgar, slapping both palms upon the shoulder guards of Uriel's armour. 'It is good to see you, Uriel. My pride and my admiration are yours. The victories on Thracia were honourable.'

Uriel bowed, accepting the compliment as Calgar bade him sit. The master of the Ultramarines lowered himself to the bench and poured two goblets of wine from the earthenware jug, offering one to Uriel. The goblet was absurdly tiny in Calgar's massive gauntlet.

'My thanks,' said Uriel, tasting the cool wine and lapsing into silence.

His aquiline countenance was serious and angular, his eyes the colour of storm clouds. He wore his black hair cropped close to his tanned skull and two gold studs were set into his brow above his left eye. Uriel was a warrior born, hailing from the underground, cavern world of Calth. His feats of bravery had earned him a fearsome reputation among the Ultramarines as a warrior of great strength and passion and his devotion to the Chapter was exemplary.

'Idaeus was a fine warrior and a true friend,' stated Calgar, guessing Uriel's thoughts.

'He was indeed,' agreed Uriel, placing his hand upon the tooled scabbard of the sword. 'He gave me this before he left to destroy the bridge on Thracia. He said it would serve me better than him, yet I do not know if I can do it the honour it demands or that I can replace him as captain of the Fourth Company.'

'He would not have wished you to merely replace him, Uriel. He would have desired you to be your own man, to make the Fourth Company your own.'

Calgar set down his goblet. 'I knew Idaeus well, Captain Ventris,' he began, acknowledging Uriel's new rank, 'and was aware of his more... unorthodox methods. He was a man of great gifts and true heart. You served with him for many years and know as well as I that Idaeus would not have bequeathed the sword he had crafted himself to an unworthy man.'

Calgar set his gaze in stone as he continued, 'Know this, son of Guilliman, the father of our Chapter watches over us always. He knows your soul, your strengths and, aye, even your fears. I share your pain at the loss of Brother-Captain Idaeus, but to dishonour his name with grief is wrong. He gave his life so that his battle-brothers would live and the enemies of the Emperor would be defeated. A warrior can ask for no better death than that. Captain Idaeus was the senior officer, and you were duty bound to follow his orders when they were given. The chain of command must not be broken or we are nothing. Discipline and order are everything on the battlefield and the army that lives by that credo will always triumph. Remember that.'

'I will,' affirmed Uriel.

'Do you understand all that I have said?'

'I do.'

'Then we will speak of Idaeus no more today, and instead speak of battles yet to come, for I have need of the Fourth Company.'

Uriel set down his goblet, anticipation surging through his body at the thought of serving the Emperor once more.

'We stand ready to fight, Lord Calgar,' stated Uriel proudly.

Calgar smiled, having fully expected Uriel's answer. 'I know you do, Uriel. There is a world some weeks distant from Ultramar that requires the force of your presence. It is named Pavonis and suffers the depredations of piratical activity from the accursed eldar.'

Uriel's expression hardened in contempt at the mention of the eldar, decadent aliens who refused to recognise the divine right of humanity to rule the galaxy. Uriel had fought the eldar before, yet knew little of their blasphemous alien ways. The indoctrinal sermons of the chaplains had taught him that they were arrogant beyond words and could not be trusted, which was enough for Uriel.

'We shall hunt them down and destroy them like the alien traitors they are, my lord.'

Calgar poured more wine and raised his goblet, saying, 'I drink to the battles and victories to come, Uriel, but there is yet another reason you must journey to Pavonis.'

'And that is?'

'The Administratum is much vexed with the planetary governor of Pavonis. They wish to take issue with her regarding her failure to deliver the right and proper tithes of an Imperial world. You are to transport an adept of the Administratum to Pavonis and ensure that he safely conveys their displeasure. I make his safety your personal responsibility, captain.'

Uriel nodded, unsure as to why this particular quill-pusher was to be accorded such protection, but dismissed the thought as irrelevant. That Lord Calgar had entrusted the man's safety to Uriel was enough of a reason to see that he came to no harm.

'Lord Admiral Tiberius has the *Vae Victus* ready for departure and your charge will be aboard on the morrow with more detailed information. I expect you and your men to be ready to depart before the next sunset.'

'It shall be so, Lord Calgar,' assured Uriel, truly honoured at the trust the master of the Ultramarines had bestowed upon him. He knew that he would die before he would allow that trust to be misplaced.

'Go then, Captain Ventris,' ordered Calgar, standing and saluting Uriel. 'Make your obeisance at the Shrine of the Primarch, then ready your men.'

Calgar offered his hand and Uriel stood, the two warriors sealing their oath of loyalty and courage to one another in the warrior's grip, wrist to wrist.

Uriel bowed deeply to Calgar and marched with renewed purpose from the courtyard. Calgar watched his newest captain pass through the bronze doors and into the evening sun, wishing he could have told him more. He picked up his goblet and drained its contents in a single gulp.

His enhanced hearing picked up the rustle of cloth behind him and he knew without turning who stood behind him in the shadow of the cloisters.

'That one carries a great responsibility now, Lord Calgar. There is much at stake here. Will he prevail?' asked the newcomer.

'Yes,' said Marneus Calgar softly, 'I believe he will.'

URIEL MARCHED ALONG the golden processional, between throngs of robed pilgrims, oblivious to the stares of wonder his presence garnered. Head and shoulders above those who had come to witness one of the most holy places in the Imperium, Uriel felt his heartbeats increase as he neared the centre of the Temple of Correction.

Like much of the Fortress of Hera, the temple was said to have been designed by Roboute Guilliman, its proportions defying the mind with the scale of its construction and the grandeur of its ornamentation. Multi-coloured radiance spilled from a massive archway ahead of him, light from the low evening sun shimmering through the stained-glass dome in gold, azure, ruby and emerald rays. The multitude of pilgrims parted before him, his status as one of the Emperor's chosen granting him hushed precedence over their desire to lay their eyes on the blessed Guilliman.

As always, his breath caught in his throat as he emerged into the awesome, humbling presence of the primarch and he cast his eyes downwards, unworthy of allowing his gaze to dwell upon his Chapter's founding father for too long.

The massively armoured form of Roboute Guilliman, primarch of the Ultramarines, sat upon his enormous marble throne, entombed these last ten thousand years within the luminous sepulchre of a stasis field. Gathered around the primarch's feet were his weapons and shield and, behind him, the first banner of Macragge, said to have been woven from the shorn hair of a thousand martyrs and touched by the Emperor's own hand. Uriel felt a fierce pride swell within his breast that his veins ran with the blood of this mightiest of heroes and warriors stretching back to the days of the Great Crusade. He dropped to one knee, overwhelmed by the honour his very existence brought him.

Even in death the primarch's features spoke of great courage and fortitude and were it not for the glistening wound upon his neck, Uriel would have sworn that the giant warrior could stand and march from the temple. He felt a cold, steel rage as his eyes fixed upon the scarlet wound. Beads of blood, like tiny, glittering rubies, were held immobile below the primarch's neck, suspended in mid air by the static time stream within. Guilliman's life had been cut short by the envenomed blade of the traitor primarch, Fulgrim of the Emperor's Children, his works undone, his legacy unfulfilled and in that lay the greatest tragedy of Guilliman's death.

Uriel knew that there were those who believed that the primarch's wounds were slowly healing and claimed he would one day arise from his throne. How such an impossibility could occur within the time-sealed bubble of a stasis field was a matter such prophets ascribed to the infallible will of the Emperor.

He could sense the presence of the silent masses behind him, aware of the holy esteem they held him in, and feeling unworthy of such reverence. He knew such thoughts marked him out from the majority of his brethren, but Idaeus had taught him the value of looking beyond the boundaries of conventional thinking.

The ordinary, faceless masses of humanity were the true heroes of the galaxy. The men and women of the Imperium who stood, naked and vulnerable, before the horrors of an infinite universe and refused to bow before its sheer incomprehensible vastness. It was for them that he existed. His purpose in life was to protect them so that they would go onto fulfil humankind's manifest destiny of ruling the galaxy in the name of the Emperor. Most would have travelled for many months or years across thousands of light years and sacrificed everything they owned to be here, but every one of them kept a respectful distance as one of the sons of Guilliman honoured his primarch.

Uriel dropped to one knee, and whispered, 'Forgive me, my lord, but I come before you to seek your blessing. I lead my men to war and ask that you might grant me the courage and wisdom to lead them through the fires of battle with honour.'

Uriel closed his eyes, allowing his surroundings to infuse him with its serenity and majesty. He took a deep breath, the scent of faded battle honours hung around the circumference of the high, domed ceiling filling his senses.

Sensations flooded through him as the neuroglottis situated at the back of his mouth assessed the chemical content of the air, redolent with the scent of alien worlds and crusades fought in ancient times. Memories came tumbling over themselves, one in particular reaching up from over a century ago. He had just turned fourteen, barely a month since he had first been brought to the Temple of Hera.

URIEL HAD BEEN racing uphill, his breath burning in his chest as his long stride carried him swiftly through the sprawling evergreen forests of the high mountain. Already his fitness was greater than most of the other recruits chosen by the Ultramarines and only Learchus was ahead of him now. Uriel was gaining on him though. Working the cavern farms of Calth and training at the Agiselus Barracks had kept his body lean and hard and he knew he had the stamina to catch Learchus before the top.

Only Cleander was close behind him, but Uriel could not spare a glance to see how near Learchus's friend was. Uriel was closing the gap on Learchus and only a few strides separated them now. He grinned as he slowly reeled in the larger youth, all his energy focussed on drawing past the race leader. Cleander's footfalls were close, but Uriel was too intent on catching Learchus.

Learchus threw a quick glance over his shoulder, worry plain on his exhausted features, and Uriel exulted. He could see the knowledge of defeat writ large on Learchus's features and pushed himself harder, arms pistoning at his sides as he drew level.

Uriel cut to the right to overtake Learchus, fighting through the burning pain in his thighs as he pushed himself to a sprint. Learchus glanced round as he caught sight of Uriel in his peripheral vision and slashed back with his elbow.

Blood sprayed from Uriel's nose and his eyes filled with water. Blinding light sunburst before him and he stumbled forwards, hands flying to his face. He felt hands seize his shoulders from behind and yelled as Cleander pushed him from the track. He fell hard, cracking his broken nose on the hard packed earth. He heard laughter and a terrible rage engulfed him.

Uriel groggily tried to push himself to his feet, wiping blood from his nose and jaw, but dizziness swamped him and he collapsed. Through the haze of pain he could make out other recruits passing him, loping after his attackers to the top of the mountain.

A hand gripped his bare arm and hauled him to his feet. Uriel blinked away tears of pain, seeing his squad mate Pasanius, and gripped his friend's shoulders as he steadied himself.

'Let me guess,' said Pasanius breathlessly. 'Learchus?'

Uriel could only nod, glaring up the side of the mountain. Learchus was far ahead now, nearly at the top.

'Are you fit to run?'

'Aye, I'll run,' snarled Uriel. 'Straight to the top and punch that cheating animal's face in!'

He shrugged off Pasanius's hand and set off once more, each thud of his bare feet against the ground lancing hot spikes of pain through his face. Blood ran freely from his nose and he welcomed the bitter, metallic taste in his mouth as his rage built. He passed runners, barely even noticing them, his head filling with thoughts of vengeance.

Uriel crested the top of the peak and stumbled to the cairn at the centre of the small, rocky plateau. He touched the column of boulders and turned to where Learchus and Cleander sat. Jagged black mountains stretched as far as the eye could see, but Uriel paid the spectacular view no heed as he marched towards the lounging Learchus, who watched him approach with a wary eye. Cleander stood to move between the pair as Uriel approached, and he caught a flash of annoyance cross Learchus's face. Cleander was younger than Uriel, but half a head taller, with great slabs of muscle across his sweat-streaked chest.

Uriel stopped and met the larger boy's stare, then punched him hard in the solar plexus with the heel of his palm.

Cleander sagged and Uriel followed with powerful uppercuts to his face and neck, finishing with a thunderous right cross. The larger boy dropped and Uriel stepped over his moaning form towards Learchus. The boy rose, backing off and assuming a boxer's position, fists raised before him.

'You cheated,' accused Uriel, also raising his fists.

Learchus shrugged. 'I won the race,' he pointed out.

'And you think that is all that matters? The winning?'

'Of course,' sneered Learchus. 'You are a fool to believe anything else.'

The pair circled, feinting with jabs as the last of the recruits reached the mountaintop.

'Did you learn nothing at Agiselus, Learchus? A victory counts for nothing if you do not retain your honour.'

'Don't presume to lecture me, farm boy!' snapped Learchus. 'You should not even have been there. I at least earned my place. I was not granted one by virtue of my ancestry.'

'I also won my place fairly, Learchus,' replied Uriel darkly. 'Lucian had nothing to do with my choosing.'

'Horse dung! I know the truth of the matter,' hissed Learchus, darting in and hammering a blow to Uriel's temple. Uriel rolled with the punch, reaching up to wrap both hands around his opponent's wrist. He spun, pulling Learchus off balance and dropped to one knee, throwing him over his shoulder.

Learchus yelled as he flew through the air and grunted as the breath was driven from his lungs on impact with the ground. Uriel wrenched the boy's arm backwards and felt the wrist break, hearing the splintered ends of snapped bone grinding together over Learchus's scream of pain.

Uriel released his grip and walked back to the cairn. He slumped against it, his exhaustion and pain returning with a vengeance.

A group of boys moved to help the fallen recruits and Uriel was suddenly filled with shame. Learchus was well liked and Uriel would gain nothing from besting him.

But he could not take back the deed and must endure the consequences. A shadow fell across him and he saw Pasanius standing over him, his face reproachful.

His friend sat beside him and said, 'You should not have done that, Uriel.'

'I know. I wish it could be undone, I truly do.'

'Learchus will hate you for this.'

'You think I should apologise?'

'Yes, but not now. You have publicly shamed him and he will refuse such an apology just now. Speak to him when we return to the fortress and his wrist has been set by the apothecaries.'

'I will do as you say, my friend. It was foolish – I was blinded by my rage.'

'At least you realise it was foolish. Perhaps they did get something through that thick farmer's skull of yours at Agiselus after all,' smiled Pasanius.

'Careful,' warned Uriel, 'or I might have to knock you flat as well.'

'You could try, farm boy, but it will take more than you've got to put me down.'

Uriel laughed, knowing Pasanius was right. His friend was a giant of a lad. Though he had just entered his fifteenth summer, Pasanius was already taller than most fully-grown men. His muscles stood out like steel cables against his tanned skin and none of the other recruits had yet bested him in feats of strength.

'Come,' said Pasanius, pushing himself to his feet, 'we should get moving. You know Clausel seals the gate at sunset and I for one do not relish yet another night on the mountains.'

Uriel nodded and stood, groaning as his muscles protested at the sudden activity. He realised he had neglected to stretch them after completing the run and cursed himself for a fool once more.

The recruits set off with Pasanius at their head, taking it in turns to help the chalk-white Learchus when he stumbled with delayed shock and pain. The boy's wrist had swollen to twice its usual size, the flesh a grotesque purple, and several times during the journey down the mountain he almost fainted. Uriel offered to help once, but the scowls of his fellow recruits had dissuaded him from offering again.

When they had reached the Fortress of Hera, Learchus had told the apothecaries he had broken his wrist in a fall and in the days that followed Uriel found a gulf developing between him and the others. The realisation of its existence was not enough to prevent it widening, however, and only Pasanius remained a true friend to Uriel in the years that followed.

IN THE TEMPLE of Correction, Uriel opened his eyes, shaking off the last vestiges of the memory and rose to his full height. He rarely thought back to his days as a cadet and was surprised he had done so today. Perhaps it was an omen, a message gifted to him by the blessed primarch. He raised his eyes and looked into he face of Roboute Guilliman, searching for a sign of what it might mean, but the dead primarch remained immobile on his throne.

Uriel felt the weight of his command heavy on his shoulders and strode across the chamber to stand before a bronze-edged slab on the curved inner wall of the temple's inner sanctum. The inner circumference of the temple was lined with enormous sheets of smooth black marble, each veined with lines of jade. Carved into the slabs with gold lettering were the names of every Ultramarine who had fallen in battle during their ten millennia history. Thousands upon thousands of names surrounded the primarch and Uriel wondered how many more would be added to it before he returned to this holy place. Would his own be one of them?

His eyes scanned down the slab before him, dedicated to the hundred warriors of the First Company who had fought against the alien horror of the tyranids beneath Macragge's northern defence fortresses, some two hundred and fifty years ago.

Uriel's eyes came to rest at a single name, carved just below the dedication to the heroic Captain Invictus of the First Company.

Veteran Sergeant Lucian Ventris.

Uriel's finger traced the carved outline of his ancestor, proud to bear his name. His accidental relationship to a hero of the Chapter had granted Uriel the right to be trained at the prestigious Agiselus Barracks, but it had been his own skill and determination not to fail that had earned his selection by the Ultramarines.

Uriel bowed, honouring his ancestor, then saluted smartly before turning on his heel and marching from the temple.

He had a company to make ready for war.

THREE

THE CLAMOUR OF hundreds of shouting voices was deafening. Judge Virgil Ortega of the Pavonis Adeptus Arbites smashed his shield into the face of a screaming man in heavy overalls and brought his shock maul round in a brutal arc. Bodies pressed all around him as he struck left and right. Hands grabbed at him as he and his squad pushed back the heaving crowd. A screaming man grasped at his black uniform and he brought his shock maul down hard, shattering the bone. Screams of pain and rage tore the air, but Ortega had only one priority, to prevent the rioters from reaching Governor Shonai. Already he could see that one of her party was down.

Enforcer Sharben fought beside him, ducking the clumsy swipe of a massive wrench and slamming her maul into her attacker's belly. Even amid the chaos of the riot, Ortega was impressed. For a rookie she was handling herself like a ten-year veteran. All around them, black-armoured judges clubbed screaming rioters back from the governor's podium.

This section of the plaza was a battlefield, as the angry workers of Brandon Gate lashed out. Against all reason and advice Governor Mykola Shonai and the senior cartel members had chosen to address a branch of the Workers' Collective in public, to reassure them that the so-called 'tithe tax' was a purely temporary measure.

Inevitably, tempers had flared and insults flew. Things quickly escalated as bottles and rocks were thrown. His men had taken most of this on their shields when, suddenly, a shot rang out, taking one of his squad in the leg.

Then everything seemed to happen at once. More shots were fired and Ortega saw one of the cartel men collapse, the back of his head blown off. He had slumped forwards, carrying the governor to the ground. Ortega didn't know if she'd been hit or where the shots had come from and couldn't spare the time to find out. All that mattered was that some bastard out there with a firearm had upped the stakes. Well if that was the way these people wanted to play this game, then Virgil Ortega was only too willing.

The governor's personal guard were backing away from the epicentre of the riot, carrying her and the cartel members away from the violence, but Ortega saw they were heading in the wrong direction. They were falling back to the gates of the Imperial palace, but the damn fools couldn't see that more rioters blocked the way. Elements of the crowd had swept around their flanks to envelop the podium. The Adeptus Arbites were holding the crowd back, and the water cannons of the crowd control vehicles were helping, but their line was bending and it was only a matter of time until the press of bodies became too great to hold. The governor's guard were heading away from the protection of the Adeptus Arbites and, as far as Ortega could see, he and his men were all that would get the governor out of this mess alive.

'Sharben!' he shouted. 'Take one man and get a crowd suppression vehicle. Pick up the governor and get her to the palace. Hurry!'

Sharben nodded, her face invisible behind the mirrored visor of her helmet, and struck out in the direction of their vehicles, taking a member of his squad with her. The remaining judges in Ortega's line backed steadily away from the crowd, the closest rioters unwilling to approach too close for fear of the shock mauls.

This current disturbance was pretty bad, but Ortega had contained riots far worse than this and could see that the waves of violence hadn't spread out too far. Those in the centre of the mass of people had no one to vent their anger upon and simply pressed forwards. If Sharben could get to the governor quick enough then this situation could still be saved.

Ortega looked along the line for Sergeant Collix and waved him over.

'Collix, I want you to hold the line here. Sharben and I are going to try to get the governor out of here.'

'Aye, sir!' shouted Collix, returning to his position.

Ortega turned and withdrew from the line, hooking his shock maul to his belt. He was unsure of Collix, but he was the most senior judge left in the line. Ortega reached up pulled down his vox-bead and patched into the governor's security net.

'This is Judge Ortega to Security Detail Primus. Remain where you are. You are heading into more trouble. We will be with you shortly. I repeat, remain where you are.'

Ortega pushed the vox-bead back inside his helmet without waiting for an acknowledgement and set off towards the governor.

He heard Collix shouting orders behind him, but couldn't make out the words. He skidded to a halt as he heard the unmistakable sound of shotgun slides being racked and turned. Cold fear gripped him. The entire line of judges had their weapons aimed into the crowd. Emperor's Throne, they were going to fire on civilians!

Ortega shouted, 'Sling those damned weapons!' but he was too late and the judges fired, point blank, into the crowd. The line of rioters convulsed, dozens of people falling dead. Gunsmoke obscured the casualties, but Ortega swore as he heard the primal shout of anger from those who had survived the shootings. The crowd surged forward and the shotguns fired again. More people fell, but there were thousands more pushing behind them. Men and women were crushed underfoot as they tripped over the bodies of the fallen and were trampled into the cobbles. The screams of the crowd turned from anger to panic.

In unison, the judges took a step forward, shotguns carried at their hips. They fired another two volleys into the crowd before Ortega reached them and screamed, 'Hold your fire! Sling your weapons! That's an order dammit! Do it now!'

The judges brought their weapons back to shoulder guard as the smoke cleared before them. Hundreds of bodies littered the ground, their bodies mangled by close range shotgun blasts. Blood streaked the cobbles of the plaza and the moans of the dying were barely audible over the screams of the panicking crowd. The rioters had fallen back for now, but Ortega realised they would be out for blood any second.

'Fall back!' yelled Ortega. 'Everybody back to the Rhinos. We're leaving – now!'.

Ortega began hauling his men back from the battle line, some of them only now appreciating the carnage their weapons had wreaked. The stink of cordite, blood and sweat filled the air and Ortega knew he only had moments before everything went to hell. The judges backed quickly towards the boxy black forms of the Rhino armoured personnel carriers, their powerful engines idling throatily. Several had been modified to mount a heavy-duty water cannon on the cupola and Ortega shouted at them to fire as a swelling roar of anger rose from the crowd.

The crowd lurched towards the judges, hungry for vengeance. The water cannon opened up, firing powerful jets into the crowd and knocking the nearest people to the ground.

But there were too many rioters and not enough cannons. The wrathful mob descended upon the judges, clubbing at them with fists and iron-shod boots. Disciplined shield drill and accurate strikes with shock mauls cleared the Arbites enough space and Ortega hauled open the armoured side door of the nearest Rhino APC, hustling his men inside. He jumped onto the running boards and ducked his head inside the armoured transport.

'We're clear! Get us the hell out of here!' he shouted to the driver. 'Find where Sharben is and link with her, she'll have the governor.'

The Rhinos began reversing, powering away from the surging crowd as the skilled drivers angled them towards the Arbites precinct. Ortega searched for Sharben and cursed as he saw the top of the crowd suppression vehicle she had commandeered in flames, not far from the armoured gate of the precinct house. The judge manning the water cannon lay sprawled over the weapon, his body ablaze. Ortega saw the left track hanging uselessly from the cogged wheel as rioters surrounded the vehicle, pressing in on its precious cargo. They rocked it from side to side in an attempt to tip it over.

Ortega slammed his shock maul on the roof of the Rhino and pointed towards Sharben's immobilised vehicle.

'Bring us alongside and stop beside it. Then get ready to go when I give you the word!'

The driver nodded his understanding and slewed the Rhino towards the stricken vehicle. Ortega hung on for dear life as the Rhino swung wildly from side to side.

'Sharben, come in,' called Ortega as they drew near the blazing tank.

'Sharben here, sir,' she replied over the vox, the strain evident in her voice. 'If you're anywhere near, we'd appreciate a ride out of here.'

'We're almost on top of you, Sharben. Hold on. Do you have the governor?'

'Affirmative.'

'Well done. Be ready for us.'

JUDGE JENNA SHARBEN felt the sweat run down her back inside her black leather armour. The heat inside the Rhino was becoming unbearable and it was only a matter of time until they baked to death. The vehicle was shaking violently and her civilian passengers were on the verge of hysteria. She muttered a quick thanks to the Emperor that Virgil Ortega was on his way. He might be a hard, humourless bastard, but he never left an officer behind.

'Judge!' snapped a man in a black suit whose name she didn't know. 'What are your plans? We must get to safety. I demand you facilitate our escape from this intolerable situation.'

She noticed a Vergen cartel pin on the man's lapel and bit back an angry retort. She took a deep breath and said, 'My superior officer is on his way with another vehicle and we will be underway soon.'

'I am sure we are quite safe, Leotas–' started Governor Mykola Shonai as the side of the vehicle tipped sickeningly upwards. Jenna realised the Rhino was finally going to tip onto its side.

'Brace yourselves!' she yelled, grabbing onto a stanchion and locking her legs around the crew bench. 'We're going over!'

The Rhino slammed onto its side with teeth-loosening force and an almighty crash. Jenna grabbed Governor Shonai's robes as she fell flailing towards the side of the vehicle and hauled her upright. She heard a muffled cheer from outside and repeated impacts on the hull. None were likely to penetrate, but the noise was deafening. The man the governor had referred to as Leotas lay unmoving, blood pouring from a deep laceration on the back of his head. The other occupants of the Rhino appeared almost as battered.

She released her grip on the stanchion and ripped a medi-pack from the crew locker, squatting beside the unmoving Leotas. She immediately saw she was wasting her time; the man's neck was broken and his skull fractured. The white gleam of bone was visible through his blood-matted hair.

'Will... will he be alright?' asked Governor Shonai, her voice quavering.

'No,' said Jenna bluntly. 'He's dead.'

Shonai's eyes widened and her hands flew to her mouth in shock.

Jenna dropped the medi-kit as she heard the rumble of a powerful engine and the crack of gunfire from outside. A powerful impact struck the immobilised Rhino and she steadied herself on the side of the interior as armoured boots thumped onto the wall that was now the roof above her.

The vox-bead in her ear crackled and she heard the clipped tones of Virgil Ortega.

'Sharben! Open the crew door, we're right next to you.'

Jenna clambered up the crew bench and spun the locking wheel, disengaging the door clamps. The door was wrenched open and weak sunlight filtered into the smoky crew compartment.

Ortega slung his maul and shouted, 'Give me the governor!'

Jenna grabbed a handful of Shonai's robes and dragged her to her feet. The governor cried out at Sharben's roughness, but allowed herself to be pushed towards the exit. Ortega took Shonai's outstretched hands and lifted her clear. He passed her onto another judge who waited at the crew door of his own Rhino, reaching back into Sharben's vehicle. The burst of fire from his Rhino's bolters had scattered the crowd from the damaged vehicle, but it was only a temporary respite.

'Come on!' he barked. 'Give me the rest. Hurry up, dammit!'

One by one, Jenna lifted the other passengers towards safety and Ortega transferred them to his own vehicle. Repeated bursts of bolter fire over the heads of the crowd kept them back as the rescue continued. When everyone was clear Jenna Sharben climbed out in time to see the Rhino carrying the governor rumbling through the gates of the Imperial palace.

'Time for us to go, Sharben,' observed Ortega as the mob closed in, howling as they realised they had been cheated of their quarry.

'Yes, sir,' agreed Sharben as they jumped to the ground and began sprinting towards the safety of the nearby Arbites precinct. Armoured pillboxes mounting more powerful water cannons hosed down their pursuers, breaking limbs with their force. More screams sounded behind the two judges, but they were clear of danger and pounded breathlessly into the defensive compound of their precinct.

The remainder of Ortega's Rhinos were laagered in the centre of the courtyard, surrounded by battered judges.

Jenna Sharben removed her dented helmet and ran a gloved hand through her short, black hair and over her sweat-streaked face as Ortega marched towards the sullen judges. She followed as Ortega dragged off his helmet and advanced towards Collix.

Virgil Ortega was a fireplug of a man, short and stocky, but who radiated power and authority. Sweat gleamed on his bald head and dripped from his trimmed beard.

'Sergeant! What the hell just happened out there? Did I give you an order to open fire?'

'No, sir,' replied Collix smoothly. 'But in the circumstances I felt that such an order would have been given had you been present in the battle line.'

'Then you show remarkably poor understanding of your superior officer, sergeant.'

'Perhaps,' admitted Collix.

'There's no perhaps about it, Collix. Our purpose is to enforce the laws of the Emperor, not massacre His subjects. Is that clear?'

'The crowd were in contravention of those laws, sir,'

'Don't play the innocent with me, Collix. I'll be keeping an eye on you'

Ortega glared at Collix for long seconds before stalking towards the precinct house. Without turning, he shouted, 'Good work out there, Judge Sharben.'

Jenna smiled at this rare praise and watched as Ortega vanished within the precinct.

She sat on the running boards of one of the Rhinos and laid her head back, letting the events of the morning drain from her. She felt pleased at her conduct today. She knew she had fought and behaved like a veteran member of the Adeptus Arbites, rather than the fresh-out-of-training, junior officer she actually was. Methodically, she reviewed her actions and could find no fault with her performance.

Yes, she had done well.

'YOU SHOULD ALLOW the palace surgeon to look at that cut, ma'am,' observed Almerz Chanda, pressing lightly at a swelling purple bruise on his own tonsured skull. He too had been pulled from the Arbites Rhino, but had only sustained a bump to the head. The gash on the governor's head was not deep and had been covered with synth-flesh by an Arbites corpsman, but this day had seen her nephew take a bullet for her and a close friend die in the chaos of the riot.

'Governor?' he said, when she did not reply.

'I'm fine,' she snapped, more brusquely than she had intended. She turned from the armoured glass of the window and smiled weakly at her chief advisor. 'I'm sorry, Almerz. I'm just...'

'No need to apologise ma'am, it has been a sad and terrible day for you.'

'Yes,' agreed Shonai. 'Poor Dumak and Leotas, they died before their time.'

Chanda nodded. 'We all feel their loss keenly, ma'am.'

'That bullet should have hit me,' said the governor. 'Dumak was only twenty. I planned to name him as my successor when he came of age next year.'

'He gave his life to save yours,' pointed out Chanda. 'He did his duty as a loyal member of the Shonai cartel. He will be remembered as a hero.'

'And Leotas, how will he be remembered?'

'As a dear friend who was taken from us by the Emperor for His own purpose.'

Governor Mykola Shonai smiled her thanks and said, 'You are a true friend, Almerz, but I wish to be alone for a moment.'

'As you wish, ma'am,' nodded Chanda, closing the door behind him as he left the governor of Pavonis to her thoughts.

Mykola Shonai turned back to the window as she felt her iron composure slipping. Her friend and ally, Leotas Vergen, was dead. Gone. Just like that. Only this morning he had been talking animatedly of his daughter's forthcoming marriage to the Taloun's son, and the dawn of a new age of co-operation between the cartels, but now he was dead and the Vergen cartel without a leader. Much as she hated to admit it, she realised his dream of co-operation would probably die with him.

No doubt the Taloun would be pleased, plotting even now to move the marriage forward in order to establish his son as de-facto head of the Vergen cartel. Of course the Vergen cartel would now do everything possible to block the union, but Vergen's daughter was known for her headstrong nature and the Emperor alone knew the ramifications of Leotas's untimely death. Shonai felt sorry that the young couple's relationship was now a political weapon, but that was politics on Pavonis, she reflected sourly.

She dismissed the couple's doomed relationship from her thoughts and looked out over Liberation Square.

By the Emperor, it was a mess. Rain had begun to fall, washing the pools of blood and detritus of battle into the sewers, but Shonai knew that her troubles would not be so easily banished. Bodies lay strewn across the cobbles, weeping groups of people gathered around fallen friends and loved ones. How could a day that had started with such noble intentions have gone so horrifyingly wrong?

Pavonis had been a peaceful planet a few years ago, largely untroubled by the strife that afflicted the rest of the galaxy. The tithes had been paid on time and periodically the young men of Pavonis would gather for the mustering of the Emperor's armies. In all respects Pavonis had been a model Imperial world. The people worked hard and were honoured for their labours. Riots were things that happened on other worlds.

But oh, how times had changed.

Crumpled parchments littered her desk, each one telling of similar scenes across the globe. In Altemaxa the workers had stormed the Office of Imperial Outlays and gutted the building with fire. Rioters at Praxedes had prevented the crew of an off-world trader from manning their vessel and looted the man's cargo. A petition from the trader for compensation was on its way to her office even now.

There had been yet another fire-bombing by the Church of Ancient Ways, killing thirty people and irreparably damaging the production facilities of two of the Vergen's manufactorum. A member of the Abrogas cartel had been stabbed in one of the Jotusburg ghettos and was lucky to have survived, though what he had been doing there in the first place wasn't clear. And near Caernus IV, yet another supply ship had been ambushed by the eldar pirates that had been plaguing Pavonis for the last six years. It had been carrying material and goods that were supposed to go some way to reducing the huge debt Pavonis owed to the Imperium in late tithes.

She felt the burden of each failure crushing her with their vast weight and wondered what she could have done differently. She had tried her best to meet the tithes required by the Administratum, but there was simply nothing more she could squeeze from Pavonis.

Her production facilities were stretched to the limit and few of those goods they could produce were actually getting through. Her 'tithe tax' had been an attempt to make up the deficit until the crisis could be resolved, but it had the people rioting in almost every major city. She had tried to explain the situation to her people, to show them that the hardships they were enduring were for the ultimate good of Pavonis, but no matter which way she turned, there seemed to be no escape from the inevitable downward spiral of events.

And here, in her own capital, she had been shot at. She still couldn't quite believe it. When the first shot had echoed shockingly around the plaza, Dumak had rushed to her side and tried to pull her to safety. She closed her eyes, trying to will the image of his exploding face from her mind. He'd fallen and carried her to the floor of the podium, his blood and brains leaking over her as he spasmed in death.

Mykola Shonai had cleaned her hair and sent her robes of office to have his death washed from them. She had changed into fresh clothes of plain blue, but imagined she could still feel the stickiness of her nephew's blood on her skin. Her heart ached for her younger sister, remembering that she had been so proud when Mykola had confided in her that Dumak would one day take over the Shonai cartel from her.

She saw priests and local apothecaries moving through the crowd, tending to the wounded or administering the Emperor's

Absolution to the dead. She offered a prayer for the souls of the departed and took a deep breath. She was a planetary governor of the Imperium and she had to keep control. But it was so difficult when everything kept slipping from her grasp, no matter how hard she tried to hold on.

She slumped in the green leather upholstered chair behind her desk, scanning the dozens of reports of violence and unrest. She gathered them together and placed them in a pile to one side. She would deal with them later. She had more pressing business to take care of: her political survival.

She smoothed down her damp grey hair and rubbed the corners of her pale green eyes dry. Her face was careworn and lined and Mykola Shonai felt every one of her sixty-two years bearing down heavily upon her. It did not matter that she had suffered loss today. She was the governor of an Imperial world and that duty did not pause for bereavement.

She pulled a long, velvet rope that hung beside her desk and stared at the sculpted bust of her great, great grandfather, Forlanus Shonai, that sat next to the fireplace. Forlanus had set up the Shonai cartel three centuries ago, building it from a single, small manufactorum to one of the most powerful industrial cartels on Pavonis. How would old Forlanus have dealt with this, she wondered?

She was spared thinking of an answer by a polite knock at the door and the arrival of four men in black suits, each with a Shonai cartel pin in their lapels. Almerz Chanda was at their head and he bowed to the governor as they filed in. Their expressions were dark and gloomy and Shonai could well understand their unhappiness.

'Well, gentlemen,' began Shonai, before they could offer her any banal platitudes regarding her loss. 'How bad is it?'

The men appeared uncomfortable with the question, none of them willing to volunteer an answer.

Governor Shonai snapped, 'When I ask a question I expect an answer.'

'This riot certainly wasn't the worst yet, ma'am,' said the newest member of her advisory staff. His name was Morten Bauer and his thin face was earnest and full of youthful exuberance. Shonai felt a stab of maternal protectiveness towards the young man and wondered if he even realised that he had joined a staff on the brink of collapse.

'Give me numbers, Morten. How many dead?' asked Shonai.

Bauer consulted his data slate. 'It's too early for firm numbers, ma'am, but it looks like over three hundred dead and perhaps twice that wounded. I'm just getting some figures in from the Arbites and it seems that two judges were killed as well.'

'That's not as bad as at Altemaxa,' pointed out an older man whose body had patently seen better days. 'The judges there lost an entire squad trying to hold the rioters.'

The speaker's name was Miklas Iacovone and he managed the governor's public relations. It had been his idea to address the Workers' Collective, and he was desperately attempting to put a favourable spin on today's events. Even as the words left his thick lips, he knew they were a mistake.

'Miklas, you are a fool if you think that we can come out of this smelling of roses by criticising another city's law enforcement officers,' snapped Almerz Chanda. 'We don't do negative campaigning.'

'I'm only trying to emphasise the upside,' protested Iacovone.

'There is no "upside" to this, Miklas. Get used to it,' said Chanda.

Governor Shonai laced her fingers together and sat back in her chair. Personally she felt Iacovone's idea had merit, though did not wish to contradict her chief advisor in public. She addressed the fourth man in her advisory staff, Leland Corteo.

'Leland, how badly will this affect us in the senate? Truthfully?'

The governor's political analyst let out a sigh and pulled at his long, grey beard. He removed a tobacco pipe from his embroidered waistcoat and raised his bushy eyebrows. Shonai nodded and Corteo lit the pipe with a pewter lighter before answering.

'Well, governor, the way I perceive it,' he began, taking a long, thoughtful draw on his pipe. 'If events continue in this way, it is only a matter of time until the other cartels call for a vote of no confidence.'

'They wouldn't dare,' said Morten Bauer. 'Who would propose such a motion?'

'Don't be foolish, dear boy. Take your pick: Taloun, de Valtos, Honan. Any one of them has a large enough base of support to survive a backlash even if the motion fails.'

'We're barely hanging on as it is,' agreed Miklas Iacovone. 'Our majority is only held together with promises of co-operation and trade agreements we've made to the smaller cartels. But we have to assume the big guns are lobbying them to renege on their agreements.'

'Spineless cowards!' spat Bauer.

'Opportunists, more like,' said Corteo. 'Who can blame them after all? We did the same thing ten years ago when we aligned ourselves with the Vergen and ousted the Taloun.'

'That was completely different,' said Bauer defensively.

'Oh come on now, boy. It's exactly the same. It's politics; the names may change, but the game remains the same.'

'Game?' spluttered Bauer.

'Gentlemen,' interrupted Chanda, before the smirking Corteo could reply. 'These petty arguments are getting us nowhere. The governor needs solutions.'

Suitably chastened, her advisors lapsed into an embarrassed silence.

Governor Shonai leaned forward, resting her elbows on the desk and steepling her fingers before her.

'So what can we do? I can't buy any more support from the smaller cartels. Most of them are already in the pocket of de Valtos or Taloun, and Honan will simply follow their lead. Our coffers are almost dry just keeping the wolves at bay.'

Corteo blew a blue cloud of smoke from his pipe and said, 'Then I fear we have to acknowledge that our time in office may soon be at a premature end.'

'I'm not prepared to accept that, Leland,' said Shonai.

'With all due respect, ma'am, your acceptance or otherwise is irrelevant,' pointed out Corteo. 'You pay me to tell you the truth. I did the same for your father and if you wish me to pretty up the facts like fat Miklas here, I can do that, but I do not believe that is why you have kept me around all these years.'

Shonai smiled, waving the outraged Iacovone to silence, and said, 'You're correct of course, Leland, but I still don't accept that there's nothing we can do.'

She pushed the chair back and rose to her feet. She did her best thinking while she was pacing and began a slow circuit of the room, pausing by the bust of old Forlanus. She patted the marble head affectionately before facing her advisors.

'Very well, Leland. If we accept that a vote of "no confidence" is inevitable, how long do we realistically have until such a motion is tabled? And is there any way we can delay it?'

Corteo considered the question for a moment before replying.

'It does not matter if we delay such a motion,' he said finally. 'There is nothing we can do to prevent it, so we must be ready to face it on our terms.'

'Yes, but how long do we have until then?' pressed Shonai.

'A month at best, but probably less,' estimated Corteo. 'But what we should be asking is what can we do to ensure we survive it when it comes.'

'Suggestions, gentlemen?' invited Almerz Chanda.

'We need to be seen to be restoring order,' suggested Morten Bauer.

'Yes,' agreed Iacovone enthusiastically, relieved to have been thrown a morsel he could sink his teeth into. 'We have to show that we are doing our best to catch these terrorist scum, this Church of Ancient Ways. I hear they bombed another forge hangar in Praxedes and killed a dozen workers. A terrible business.'

'We can promise to put a stop to the pirate activity of the alien raiders as well,' added Bauer.

Leland Corteo nodded thoughtfully. 'Yes, yes, well done, dear boy. That would allow us to potentially split our opposition. We could seek de Valtos's support on this issue. He has more reason to hate the eldar scum than anyone.'

Shonai paced around the room, her brain whirling with possibilities. Kasimir de Valtos probably would support any action that would see him revenged on the aliens who had captured and tortured him many years ago, but could he be trusted? His organisation was a serious contender for the position of Cartel Prime and Shonai knew that de Valtos had even used his war injury kudos to foster popular support amongst the workers.

She followed the logic of Bauer's proposal. The Taloun would no doubt see any overtures made to de Valtos as an attempt to divide her political opponents. He would probably try to sway de Valtos with similar promises, offering his own ships to hunt down the eldar.

If the Taloun's ships succeeded in wiping out the eldar pirates, well that was fine too. Their elimination would allow the tithe shipments to get through to the Administratum, allowing her to ease the pressure on her people and thus weather the coming months.

Shonai returned to her desk and sat down again. She turned to Chanda and said, 'It might be opportune to arrange a meeting with de Valtos. I'm sure he will be happy to hear of our determination to destroy the foul eldar pirates.'

Almerz Chanda bowed and said, 'I shall despatch an emissary immediately.'

Chanda withdrew from the room as the governor addressed her advisors.

'We need to stay on top of this situation, my friends. Today's unfortunate events have proven that we need to be more careful in how we are perceived,' said Mykola Shonai, pointedly staring at Miklas Iacovone. 'We lost face today, but not so much that we can't repair the damage. We can always shift the blame to heavy handed crowd control if need be.'

'I'll get right on it, ma'am,' promised Iacovone, eager to earn back his favour.

'Very well, Miklas. Let today be a lesson learned.'

Leland Corteo coughed, shaking his head as he removed fresh tobacco from a pouch at his waist.

'You disagree, Leland?' asked Shonai.

'Frankly, yes, ma'am. Loath as I am to agree with such a hidebound bureaucrat, I am afraid I concur with Mister Chanda regarding criticism of our law enforcement officials,' said Leland Corteo, filling his pipe with fresh tobacco. 'I believe shifting blame to the Adeptus Arbites would be a mistake. They will not take such allegations lightly.'

Further discussion on the matter was prevented by the return of Almerz Chanda, who marched straight to the governor's desk clutching a data slate. He offered it to Mykola Shonai, his face pale and drawn.

'This just came in from the Chamber of Voices,' whispered Chanda.

'What is it?' asked Shonai, reading the worry in Chanda's voice. The Chamber of Voices was the name given to the psychically attuned chamber where the palace astrotelepaths sent and received messages from off-world. In an empire of galactic scale, telepathy was the only feasible method of communication and, normally, such messages were relatively mundane.

Chanda's manner told Shonai that this was far from mundane.

'I don't know, it was encrypted by the quill servitors and requires your personal gene-key to unlock. It has an omicron level Administratum seal.'

Shonai took the slate and warily held her thumb over the identifier notch. Whatever this slate contained could not be good. She was savvy enough to realise that when the Administratum took an interest in a world as troubled as hers, it meant trouble for those responsible. And on Pavonis, that meant her.

She slid her thumb into the slate, wincing as the sample needle stabbed out and drew her blood. A collection of lights flashed on the side of the slate as the spirit within the machinery checked her genetic code against that stored in its cogitator.

The slate clicked and hummed, chattering as it printed a flimsy sheet of parchment from the scriptum at its base. Shonai ripped the message off and placed the slate on her desk.

She slipped on a delicate set of eyeglasses and read the message. As her eyes travelled further down the message, her face felt hot and her chest tightened. She reached the end of the message, feeling a heavy, queasy sensation settle in her stomach.

She handed the parchment to Chanda who swiftly scanned the message before placing it carefully back before the governor.

'Perhaps it will not be as bad as you fear, ma'am,' said Chanda hopefully.

'You know better than that, Almerz.'

Corteo leaned forward, his pipe jammed between his lips. 'Might I enquire as to the content of this message?' he asked.

Mykola Shonai nodded and said, 'Of course, Leland. It seems we are soon to receive an envoy – an adept from the Administratum who will be reviewing our failure to meet Imperial tithes and maintain the Emperor's peace. We may not need to try and keep the cartels from impeaching us before our time. The Administratum will do it for them.'

She could tell from the worried faces around the room that they all realised the significance of this adept's imminent arrival.

'That wretch Ballion must have sent word to the Imperium,' hissed Iacovone.

'No doubt at the behest of the Taloun,' cursed Leland Corteo.

Governor Shonai sighed. She had asked for more time from the Administratum's representative on Pavonis, but couldn't really blame the man, even if the Taloun had pressured him into it.

'Can this adept simply remove you from office without due process?' asked Morten Bauer.

'He comes with the highest authority,' answered Chanda solemnly.

Governor Shonai picked up the parchment once again and reread the last few lines.

'But more importantly, Almerz, he comes with the Angels of Death. He comes with the Space Marines.'

FOUR

THE ULTRAMARINES STRIKE cruiser *Vae Victus* slipped rapidly through the darkness of space, wan starlight reflecting from her battle scarred hull. She was an elongated, gothic space-borne leviathan with protruding warp vanes. The antenna atop the arched cathedral spire of the command deck rose from her centre and grew towards the powerful plasma drives at her rear.

To either side of the angular prow and bombardment cannon lay the crenellated entrances to her launch bays from where Thunderhawk gunships and boarding torpedoes could sally forth. Her entire length bristled with gargoyle-wreathed weapon batteries and conventional torpedo launch bays.

The *Vae Victus* was old. Constructed in the shipyards of Calth almost three millennia ago, she displayed the trademark design flourishes of the Calthian shipbuilders in the ornamented gothic arches surrounding her launch bays and the flying buttresses of her engine housings.

In her long life, the strike cruiser had crossed the galaxy several times over and had fought unnumbered battles against foes both human and alien. She had grappled with the tyranids at the Battle of Macragge, destroyed the command barge of the renegade flag-captain Ghenas Malkorgh, delivered the killing blow to the ork hulk, *Captor of Vice* and, more recently, destroyed the orbital defences of Thracia in the Appolyon Crusade.

Her hull proudly bore the scars of each encounter. The artificers of the Ultramarines had reverently repaired every wound, rendering the honour of her victories unto the vast spirit that dwelt within the beating mechanical heart of the starship.

THE COMMAND BRIDGE of the *Vae Victus* was a wide, candlelit chamber with a vaulted ceiling some fifteen metres high. Humming banks of glowing holo displays and ancient, runic screens lined the cloisters either side of the raised command nave, a shaven headed half-human, cyborg-servitor hard wired into each of the ship's regulatory systems. A broad observation bay dominated the front of the chamber, currently displaying a view of empty space before the ship. Smaller screens in the corners of the bay displayed the current course and speed of the ship along with all local objects picked up by the ship's surveyors.

The wide nave was bisected at its rear by an arched transept with ordnance and surveyor stations located to either side. Space Marine deck officers wearing plain hessian robes over their armour also monitored each station.

The recycled air was heavy with the fragrance of burning incense from censers swung by hooded priests and a barely audible choral chant drifted through the bridge from the raised sacristy and navigator's dome behind the captain's pulpit.

The commander of the *Vae Victus* stood atop his pulpit and fixed his hoary eyes on the lectern beside him. Tactical plots for the *Vae Victus* and Pavonis were displayed next to the chrono-display showing their projected course.

Lord Admiral Lazlo Tiberius cast his heavy lidded eyes around the bridge, searching for anything out of place, but satisfied that all was as it should be.

Tiberius was a giant, dark skinned Space Marine of nearly four hundred years who had fought in space almost his entire life. His fearsomely scarred face was the result of a close encounter with a tyranid bio-ship that had smashed into the *Vae Victus*'s command bridge during the early stages of the Battle of Circe. His skull was hairless and his skin the texture of worn leather. The moulded breastplate of his blue armour was adorned with bronze clusters of badges of honour, the gold sunburst of a Hero of Macragge at its centre.

Lord Admiral Tiberius stood with his hands clasped behind his back and studied the tactical plot with a critical eye, calculating how long it would take the *Vae Victus* to achieve orbit around Pavonis. He glanced at the corner of the screen and was satisfied to note that his estimate almost perfectly matched up with the logic engine's prediction.

He felt his estimate was the more realistic of the two, however.

Before him, robed crewmen worked over their extensive sensor runes, sweeping space before them with all manner of surveyors and augury devices. Tiberius knew that the captain of a starship was only as good as the crew he commanded. All the tactical acumen in the galaxy would count for nothing if he were given inaccurate information or his orders were not obeyed quickly and without question below decks.

And Tiberius knew he had one of the best crews in the Ultramar fleet. Proved time and again in the heat of battle, they had always performed exactly as commanded. The *Vae Victus* had been through some desperate battles, but her crew had always acquitted themselves with honour. This was in part due to Tiberius demanding that the highest possible standards be constantly maintained by every crewman upon his ship, from the lowliest deck hand to himself and his command staff. But it was also a reflection of the dedication and loyalty amongst the servants of the Ultramarines who provided the majority of the vessel's crew.

Once again they were entering harm's way and Tiberius felt the familiar exultation that they would soon be bringing the Emperor's fiery sword of retribution to His enemies. It had been a long time since the *Vae Victus* had tasted battle against the eldar and though he hated their alien ways with a zealot's passion, he was forced to admit that he had a grudging respect for their mastery of hit-and-run tactics.

Tiberius knew the devious eldar would rarely engage in a ship-to-ship fight under any but the most favourable terms since their ships were absurdly fragile and did not have the divine protection of void shields. They relied on stealth and cunning to close with their target, then blasphemous alien magicks to confound the targeting cogitators of their foes' weapons. Tiberius knew that often the first warning of such an attack was the impact of prow lances that disabled a ship's manoeuvring thrusters. After that it was academic who had the biggest guns; the eldar ship would run rings around its more ponderous opponent, taking it apart piece by piece.

Tiberius vowed that such a fate would not befall his ship.

IN THE DARKNESS of space, six hours ahead of the *Vae Victus*, an elegantly deadly craft slipped from the shadows of its asteroid base. Its segmented prow tapered to a needle point and jagged, scimitar-like solar sails gracefully unfurled, soaring from the cunningly wrought engines at its rear. Joining the engines and prow was a slender, domed command section, and it was from here that the captain of this lethal craft ruled his ship.

That captain of the graceful vessel, the *Stormrider*, now stared with undisguised relish at the return signal on the display before him. At last, a foe worthy of his talents. A ship of the Adeptus Astartes! Archon Kesharq of the Kabal of the Sundered Blade had grown tired of ambushing lumbering merchantmen, outwitting system defence ships and raiding primitive mon-keigh settlements. Kesharq cared not for the spoils of these raids, and even torturing the screaming souls aboard the captured vessels beyond the known limits of pain had grown stale to his dulled senses.

Such poor sport had not even begun to stretch the limit of his abilities.

A thin line of blood dribbled from the corners of his mouth and Kesharq tipped his head back, pulling the lifeless skin of his face taut over his skull and hooking the ragged edges over the sutures at the back of his neck. He had grander dreams than this and had begun to fear that his pact with the *kyerzak* was a mistake.

But now came worthy meat indeed.

THREE DECKS BELOW the command bridge of the *Vae Victus*, the chapel of Fourth Company echoed softly to the sounds of Space Marines at their prayers. The chamber was wide and high ceilinged, easily capable of holding the assembled battle brethren of the company. A polished, stone-flagged nave led towards a glassy black altar and wooden lectern at the far end of the chapel.

Stained glass windows of wondrous colour and majesty dominated the upper reaches of the chapel. Each window sat within a leaf shaped archway, electro-flambeaux set behind them casting ghostly illumination upon the assembled warriors. Each window depicted a portion of the Imperium's long history: the Age of Strife, the Age of Apostasy, the Emperor Deified and the Emperor Victorious. Battle honours the company had won in a dozen crusades hung below the windows, each testament to a tradition of bravery and courage that stretched back ten thousand years.

The company stood at parade rest in the flickering light of the flambeaux, eyes cast down at the smooth floor of the chapel. Each chanted a litany of thanks to Him on Earth, contemplating their holy duty to the God-Emperor.

Silence descended on the chapel as the iron bound door at the far end of the nave opened and two figures entered. The Space Marines snapped to attention as one.

The captain of Fourth Company, Uriel Ventris, marched down the wide nave, his ceremonial cape flaring. A pale, grim-faced warrior led him with a milky white cloak trawling behind.

Fourth Company's chaplain, Judd Clausel, wore midnight black power armour embossed with fanged skulls. Brass and gold trims on his cuirass and greaves winked in the dim light. His grinning, skull faced helmet was hooked to his hip belt alongside a voluminous tome, bound in faded green ork hide.

In his left arm he swung a smoking censer, aromatic herbs and sacred oils filling the chapel with the wild, intoxicating scent of the highlands of Macragge. His right fist gripped the crozius arcanum, his weapon and the symbol of office of a chaplain. The crozius arcanum was a carved adamantium rod surmounted with a glittering golden eagle, its spread wings razor edged. A grinning skull topped the crozius, its eyes jewelled and blood red.

Power palpably radiated from the man. Clausel did not just deserve respect, he demanded it. His build was enormous, bigger even than that of Uriel, and his stern, unflinching gaze missed nothing. One flinty grey eye searched every face for weakness, while his remaining eye regarded his surroundings through the soulless mechanics of a crudely grafted blinking red orb.

His skull was a shaven dome save for a gleaming silver topknot that trailed from the crown of his head to his shoulders. A thick face, heavily scarred and twisted into a grotesque parody of a smile, surveyed the Space Marines before him.

'Kneel!' he commanded. The order was instantly obeyed, the sound of armoured knees reverberating around the chamber as they slammed down in unison. Uriel stepped forwards to receive the smoking censer and the crozius. He moved behind the massive chaplain, his head bowed.

'Today is a day of joy!' Clausel bellowed. 'For today we are offered the chance to take the Emperor's light into the darkness and to destroy those who would stand in the way of His servants. We are not yet a full company again, my brothers. Many of our comrades met their deaths on Thracia, but we know that they did not die in vain. They will take their place at the side of the Emperor and tell the tales of their bravery and honour until the final days.'

Clausel extended his gauntleted fist then slammed it into his breastplate twice in rapid succession.

'De mortuis nil nisi bonum!' intoned the chaplain, reclaiming the censer from Uriel.

Chaplain Clausel strode from the altar towards the kneeling Marines, dipping his hands into the smoking umber ash. As he passed each warrior, he drew protective hexes and ritual symbols of battle on the armour of each man, chanting the Litany of Purity as he went. As he anointed the last man, he turned back to the altar and said, 'The Rites of Battle are complete, my captain.'

'We are honoured by your words, Chaplain Clausel. Perhaps now you will lead us in prayer?'

'That I will, captain,' replied Clausel.

Striding to the fore, he mounted the steps, knelt and kissed the basalt surface of the altar, mouthing the Catechism of Affirmation.

Rising to his feet, he began to chant as the Ultramarines bowed their heads.

'Divine Master of Mankind. We, your humble servants offer our thanks to you for this new day. As we steer our might to honourable battle, we rejoice in the opportunity you offer us to use our skills and strengths in your name. The world of Pavonis is plagued by degenerate aliens and riven with strife. With your grace and blessing, Imperial wisdom shall soon prevail in your name once more. For this we give thanks and ask for nothing, save the chance to serve. This we pray in your name. Guilliman, praise it!'

'Guilliman, praise it!' echoed the Space Marines.

Clausel lowered his arms and stood aside, arms folded across his chest as Captain Uriel Ventris stood before his men. He was nervous at addressing his company for the first time and he mentally chided himself for his lack of focus. He had faced the enemies of mankind for over a century and now he fretted over speaking to a company of Space Marines?

Uriel let his gaze wander over the assembled battle-brothers of his company, these greatest of men, and nodded in recognition towards the giant, bear-like Sergeant Pasanius. His friend from youth had continued to grow during their training and was, far and away, the strongest Space Marine in the Chapter. His massive form dwarfed most of his battle-brothers and, early in his training, the Tech-marines had been forced to craft a unique suit of armour for his giant frame composed of parts cannibalised from an irreparably damaged suit of Terminator armour.

Pasanius gave Uriel a tiny nod and he felt his confidence soar. The veteran sergeant had been a rock for Uriel to anchor himself to in his rise through the ranks and he was proud to call him a true friend. Behind Pasanius, he saw the regal, sculpted features of Sergeant Learchus and his compatriot, Cleander.

They had all grown far beyond any childish rivalry and had saved each other's lives on more than one occasion, but they had never become friends nor formed the bond of brotherhood that permeated the rest of the Chapter.

It irked Uriel that he still found such difficulty in connecting to his men in the way that truly great officers did. Idaeus had been a natural leader, who had frequently relied on his own solutions to fight his battles rather than turning to the holy Codex Astartes, the tome of war penned by the great Roboute Guilliman himself. He had led his men with an instinctive ease that Uriel found difficult to match. He drew himself up to his full height as he resolved he would take Idaeus's advice and be his own man. Fourth Company was his now and he would make sure they knew it.

'At ease!' he called and his warriors relaxed a fraction. 'You all know me. I have fought beside most of you for over a century. And it is with this wisdom that I say, be thankful for this chance to display our devotion to our primarch and the Emperor.'

Uriel deliberately placed his fist on the pommel of Idaeus's sword, reinforcing the fact that the company's former captain had passed it to him.

'I know that I have not been your leader long and I also know that some of you would prefer it if I was not your captain,' continued Uriel.

Uriel paused, gauging his next words carefully. 'Captain Idaeus was a great man, and the hardest thing I have ever done was to watch him die. No one grieves for him more than I, but he is dead and I am here now. I have taken the Emperor's light to every corner of this galaxy. I have fought the tyranids in burning hive ships, I have killed the dread warriors of Chaos on worlds of unspeakable horrors and I have defeated orks on barren deserts of ice. I have fought alongside some of the greatest warriors of the Imperium, so know this:

'I am captain of this Company. I am Uriel Ventris of the Ultramarines and I will die before I dishonour the Chapter. I am honoured to be part of this brotherhood and had I the choice of any warrior by my side, I could choose no better men than those of Fourth Company. Every man here and every one of our honoured dead acquitted themselves in a manner our kin would be proud of. I salute you all!'

At this, Uriel drew Idaeus's power sword from his side with a flourish and raised it high above his head.

Sapphire coils of energy coruscated along the length of the master-crafted sword, catching the light thrown by the electro-flambeaux.

The Marines rose to their feet and slammed their clenched fists to their breastplates, a deafening boom that echoed round the chapel.

'We are Ultramarines,' called Uriel. 'And no foe can stand against us while we keep faith with the Emperor.'

Uriel crossed to stand behind the wooden lectern and consulted the data slate cunningly fashioned into its surface. He did not need to read from the slate; he had memorised the details of their mission in the week spent travelling through warp space, but to have the details near was reassuring.

'We travel to a world named Pavonis and have been entrusted with the task of bringing it back within the fold of the Imperium. Pavonis has failed in its duty to the Emperor. It does not provide Him that which is His due. To rectify this situation, we have been entrusted with the protection of an adept of the Administratum who will instruct the rulers of Pavonis in the proper execution of their duty. The rulers of Pavonis appear to think they are exempt from the Emperor's laws. Together we will show them that they are not. Blessed be the primarch.'

'Blessed be the primarch,' repeated the Space Marines.

Uriel paused before continuing, wishing he knew more about this adept they were supposed to guard. He had not even met the man he had been entrusted with protecting by Marneus Calgar. Thus far, the adept had spent the entire voyage in his chambers, attended only by his entourage of scribes, clerics and valets.

Well, he would have to come out soon; the *Vae Victus* was only a day's travel from her destination.

Uriel lowered his voice as he moved onto the next point of his briefing.

'Perhaps as a result of Pavonis's leaders' failure to properly enforce the Emperor's rule, a group calling themselves the Church of Ancient Ways has been allowed to emerge. These heretics have embarked upon a campaign of terror bombings, seeking a return to the times before the coming of the glorious Imperium.'

A murmur of disbelief rippled through the ranks.

'To date, they have killed three hundred and fifty-nine servants of the Emperor and caused untold damage. They bomb His manufactorum. They kill His priests and they burn His temples. Together we will stop them. Blessed be the primarch.'

'Blessed be the primarch.'

'But, brothers, not only does the world of Pavonis suffer the evil of heretics within. No, the heretical scourge of the alien is upon Pavonis. For years now, the eldar, a race so arrogant they believe they can plunder our space and steal the chattels that are rightfully the Emperor's with impunity, have plagued this region of space. Together we will show them that they cannot. Blessed be the primarch.'

'Blessed be the primarch.'

Uriel moved away from the lectern.

'Return to your cells, my brothers. Honour your battle gear that it may protect you in the days of war to come. The Emperor be with you all.'

'And with you, captain,' said Pasanius, stepping from the ranks and bowing to Uriel.

Hesitantly at first, but witnessing Pasanius's acceptance of Uriel, the company took a step forward and bowed to their new captain before filing from the chapel.

Pasanius was the last to leave and turned to face him.

Uriel nodded his thanks to his oldest friend.

ARCHON KESHARQ NODDED to his second-in-command.

'Bring main power up slowly and be ready to activate the mimic engines on my order,' he commanded, his voice wetly rasping and ugly.

'Yes, dread archon.'

Kesharq dabbed at his weeping neck with a scented cloth, coughing a froth of bloody matter into a goblet beside him. Even speech was becoming difficult for him now and he swallowed hard, once more cursing the Life of a Thousand Pains upon the name of Asdrubael Vect.

The suppurating wounds on his neck would never seal. Vect's haemonculus had seen to that in the torture chambers beneath the palace of his kabal. Kesharq's bid for command of the kabal had been planned in minute detail, but Vect had known of his treachery and the coup had failed before it had begun.

Months of torture had followed. He had begged for oblivion, but the haemonculus had kept him always just at the brink of the death before dragging him back to their hell of infinite pain.

He had expected to die there, but Vect had ordered him released and his suit of skin sutured back to the wreckage of his musculature. He remembered Vect's beautifully cruel face smiling down upon him as he lay in a rare moment of sanity and coherence. He tried to close his eyes, to shut out Vect's gloating smile, but his eyelids had been neatly sliced off a week ago.

'You think you will die here?' enquired the supreme lord of the Kabal of the Black Heart. Without waiting for an answer, the dark eldar lord shook his head slowly and continued.

'You shall not. I will not allow you that luxury,' promised Vect, tracing his perfectly manicured nails along the exposed bone of Kesharq's ribs. 'You were a vain fool, Kesharq, boasting of your plans for my death when you must have known my spies would tell me everything you uttered before the words were even cold.'

Vect had sighed then, as though he were more disappointed than angry. 'Treachery and deceit I can understand, even forgive. But stupidity and incompetence merely irritate me. Your colossal vanity and rampant ego were your undoing and I think it only fitting that they be your constant companions in failure. I shall exile you from Commorragh, send you from our dark city and cast you into the wilderness with the prey species.'

Kesharq had not believed Vect, thinking that this was some elaborate ruse to raise his hopes that he might yet live, only to have them dashed before him.

But Vect had not lied. Less than a week later, he and the surviving members of his splinter kabal had limped from Commorragh in humiliation and disgrace. Kesharq had sworn vengeance on the house of Asdrubael Vect, but his former lord had merely laughed and the sounds of his mirth were whips of fire on his soul.

Vect would not be laughing soon as Kesharq thought once more of the prize that awaited him once he had outwitted the foolish *kyerzak*. But first he must take care of this newly arrived threat to the carefully orchestrated scheme.

The kill was so close that Kesharq could almost taste the blood of the Space Marines on his nerveless lips. He rose from his command chair and strode to the main screen, his movements as lithe as a dancer's despite the looseness of his skin and the wide bladed axe slung across his back. His segmented green armour shone like polished jade, highlighting the pallid dead skin mask of his face. Lifeless white hair, streaked with violet, spilled around his shoulders, held in place by a crimson circlet at his brow. He moistened his lidless eyes with a fine spray from a tiny atomiser and studied the view before him.

Slithering at his heels came a snapping pack of grotesque creatures, each constructed from scraps of random flesh sewn together to form a heaving mass of razor claws and fangs. These were the excrents, Kesharq's pets, shat into existence by a whim of his chief haemonculus. They swarmed around their master's legs, hissing mindless malevolence with their yellowed, venomous fangs at anything and anyone that dared come near.

The meat was almost in the killing zone and Kesharq's excitement began to mount. Blood pounded through his veins at the thought of inflicting pain on the corpse god's warriors. The corners of his mouth twitched in anticipation and his fingers tingled at the thought. Kesharq decided he would keep one alive as a pet, mewling in constant agony as he watched his comrades slowly dismembered to provide new flesh for his excrents.

'Dread archon, the prey vessel has entered weapons range,' hissed his second-in-command.

'Excellent,' smiled Kesharq beneath his skin. 'Power up the weapons and align the mimic engines.'

The enemy ship was still too far away to see through the viewscreen, but Kesharq fancied he could sense its nearness. He returned to his command chair and slipped his axe from its scabbard. He liked to tease the onyx blade of the weapon as he made each kill and keep its soul hungry for blood.

'Bring us in on his starboard forequarter with the sun at our backs,' ordered Kesharq.

He stroked the fractal edge of his axe.

'PERMISSION TO COME aboard the bridge, lord admiral?'

Tiberius turned from the lectern to see two robed men standing at the entrance to the command bridge and fought to mask his annoyance. Civilians on his bridge were something he tried to avoid, but this adept carried with him the highest seal of the Administratum and it would be impolitic to refuse his request.

Tiberius nodded his approval and descended from his pulpit as the robed duo shuffled their way up the cloister steps to the command nave. One of the pair was a venerable ancient in thick robes who walked with an ivory cane while the other was a man perhaps in his forties with an unremarkable face and bland features. Tiberius reflected that the man looked like every other faceless adept of the Administratum he had ever met.

The older man looked unimpressed by his surroundings, but the bland faced man positively radiated enthusiasm.

'Many thanks, lord admiral. Most kind of you to allow us onto the bridge, your sanctum, your crow's nest if you will. Most kind.'

'Is there something I can do for you, Adept Barzano?' asked Tiberius, already weary of Barzano's incessant barrage of words.

'Oh please, lord admiral, call me Ario,' replied Barzano happily. 'My personal scribe Lortuen Perjed and I merely wished to see the bridge of your mighty starship before we arrived at Pavonis. What with being so busy so far, we haven't had much of a chance to admire our surroundings.'

Barzano marched down the nave towards the viewing bay, which at present displayed the diminutive disc of Pavonis and the flaring ball of her sun.

Barzano examined several of the servitor-manned stations as he passed. He turned back and indicated that Tiberius and Lortuen Perjed should follow him.

The scribe shrugged and set off after his master, who was bent over a monitor station, waving his hand before the blank, expressionless face of a servitor. The lobotomised creature ignored the adept, its cybernetically altered brain incapable of even registering his presence.

'Fascinating, absolutely fascinating,' he observed, as Tiberius joined him. 'What does this one do?'

Controlling his impatience, Tiberius said, 'This station monitors the temperature variance in the plasma engine core.'

'And that one?'

'It regulates the oxygen recycling units on the gun decks.'

But Barzano had already moved on towards the surveyor stations through the arched transept, where Space Marine officers worked alongside the motionless servitors.

A few faces turned towards him as he entered, but Barzano shook his head, saying, 'Don't mind me. Pretend I'm not here.' He stood over a stone-rimmed plotting table in the centre of the chamber and rested his elbows on the side, studying the wealth of tactical information displayed on the embedded slate.

'This is truly fascinating, lord admiral, truly fascinating,' repeated Barzano.

'I thank you for your interest Adept Barzano, but–'

'Ario, please.'

'Adept Barzano,' continued Tiberius. 'This is a vessel of war, it is not–'

'Lord admiral,' interrupted Philotas, Tiberius's deck officer.

Tiberius hurried over to the bewilderingly complex array of runic display slates that the deck officer operated from.

'You have something?'

'New contact, lord admiral. Sixty thousand kilometres in front of us,' said Philotas, adjusting the runes before him and squinting at the readout before him, 'I have just detected a plasma energy spike on the mid-range auguries.'

'What is it?' asked Tiberius quickly. 'A ship?'

'I believe so, lord admiral. Bearing zero-three-nine.'

'Identify it. Class and type. And find out how it managed to get so damned close without us detecting it before now!'

Philotas nodded and bent to his controls once more. Ario Barzano studied the tactical plot on the central table and pointed to the blip that represented the unknown contact. Rows of numbers scrolled down the slate beside it, an exhaustive array of information regarding the unknown vessel.

'This is the contact?' he asked.

'Yes, Adept Barzano, it is,' snapped Tiberius. 'But I do not have time to instruct you in the finer points of starship operations just now.'

'Lord admiral?' called Philotas.

'Yes?'

'I have identified the unknown contact's engine signature, Lord Admiral,' confirmed the deck officer. 'It is the *Gallant*, a system defence ship out of Pavonis.'

'TARGET APPROACHING LANCE range, dread archon.'

Kesharq ran his tongue across his teeth, tasting the stale blood congealed there and shivered with barely controlled excitement. Yes, the fools were taking the bait, believing the *Stormrider* to be one of their own.

'Divert main power to the lance batteries and hold it in reserve. I wish to deliver a killing blow with one strike.'

'Yes, dread archon.'

TIBERIUS STRODE BACK to his captain's pulpit and said, 'Communications, contact the *Gallant* and pass my compliments to her captain.'

'Yes, lord admiral.'

The captain of the *Vae Victus* stared at the viewing bay, hoping to see the outline of the system defence ship, but the flaring corona from the star at the system's centre prevented him from seeing much of anything. He turned back to surveyor control and felt his temper fraying as he watched Barzano standing over the data entry booth of one of his ship's logic banks.

'Adept Barzano?' asked Tiberius.

The adept waved a dismissive hand, too intent on the slate before him and Tiberius decided he had had enough of Adept Ario Barzano. Adept of the highest clearance or not, nobody showed the commander of a starship that kind of disrespect. Tiberius descended from his pulpit – as Barzano suddenly hurried from surveyor control to meet him.

'Lord admiral, raise the shields and power up the weapons!' ordered Barzano, his voice infused with sudden authority.

Tiberius folded his arms across his massive chest and looked down into the adept's tense face.

'And why should I do that, Adept Barzano?'

'Because,' hissed Barzano urgently, 'according to the Ultima Segmentum fleet records, the governor of Pavonis reported the *Gallant* destroyed with all hands five years ago, lord admiral.'

Tiberius felt the blood drain from his face as he realised the implication and the scale of the danger his ship and crew were in.

'Hard to starboard!' he shouted. 'Raise void shields and build power in forward liner accelerators!'

'FIRE!' SHOUTED ARCHON Kesharq as he saw the massive prow of the Space Marine vessel begin swinging to face them. The ship shuddered as the forward lance batteries hurled deadly pulses of dark energy towards its prey. In a heartbeat they had closed the gap. The viewscreen flashed as colossal amounts of energy smashed into the strike cruiser and exploded with unbelievable force.

A bright halo exploded around the *Vae Victus* as the first impacts overloaded the vessel's void shields. The following bolts detonated on the armoured prow of the ship, sending plumes of fire and oxygen flaring from her stricken hull.

To see so much destructive power unleashed at such close range was truly exhilarating and Kesharq roared in triumph.

Even at this range, he could see that the damage the pulse lances had inflicted was horrendous. Metre-thick sheets of adamantium had been peeled back from the starship's structure like tin foil and jagged tendons of steel hung limp from the shattered section of the prow where they had struck.

Jets of freezing oxygen crystallised as they spewed from the ruptured hull, blast doors struggling to contain the breach. Kesharq knew that hundreds must have died in the initial blast and many more would soon have followed them screaming into hell as their compartments suddenly vented into space.

Kesharq laughed.

'Bring us about and move around to their rear quarter. Disable their engines.'

THE BRIDGE OF the *Vae Victus* heeled sideways, flooring the entire command crew as the massive explosion rippled its force along the ship's structure. Secondary blasts followed quickly behind, the detonations sounding like hollow thumps from the bridge.

Warning bells tolled and the command bridge was bathed in red as the strike cruiser went to battle stations. Emergency teams battled fires and tended to the wounded as steam, smoke and flames burst from shattered conduits and monitor stations. Dozens of servitors slumped lifeless from their chairs.

Tiberius picked himself up from the deck, a deep gash in his cheek. The blood had already clotted and he shouted, 'Damage report! Now!'

He ran to the ordnance station, wrenching the targeting servitor from the panel. It was dead, the ashen flesh burned and black and its controls shattered. The logic engines struggled to determine the extent of their hurt, but Tiberius already knew they had been grievously wounded. Not a fatal wound yet, but still a serious one.

'Void shields overloaded and we have hull breaches on decks seven through to nine,' shouted the deck officer. 'Prow bombardment cannon are temporarily offline and main launch bay took a hit. We were lucky. The last few blasts only grazed us, lord admiral. Your turn into the fire saved us.'

Tiberius grunted, feeling unworthy of such a compliment and returned to his command pulpit. Barzano's warning had come not a moment too soon and it was that which had saved the ship. Barely had the shields come up before the *Vae Victus* shuddered as the enemy struck.

Tiberius glared at the viewing bay, angry with himself for being caught out, watching as a fluid black shape, its graceful mainsail rippling in the solar wind, slid from the concealing flare of the sun and slipped out of sight around their starboard flank.

'Eldar!' cursed Tiberius. Where in the nine hells had that ship come from? How in the name of Guilliman had it fooled their surveyors and auguries?

'Surveyor control! Give me a full amplification sweep of the local area. Tell me what in the name of holy Terra is out there! Starboard broadside batteries fire at will!'

Philotas nodded, hurriedly relaying the lord admiral's orders.

'And someone stop that damned bell ringing!'

The bridge was suddenly quiet as the sacristy bell fell silent. The hiss of damaged machinery, the crackling of sparks and the insensate moans of wounded servitors were the only sounds. He felt the vibrations of the starboard batteries opening fire, but without proper ordnance control, doubted they would hit anything.

Tiberius mopped the congealed blood from his forehead as Ario Barzano staggered towards the captain's pulpit, supporting the slumped form of his scribe. Perjed was bleeding from a cut to the head, but it was not deep and once Barzano had deposited the venerable scribe on the cloister stairs, he ran back to surveyor control.

Tiberius shouted over to the adept, 'My thanks, Adept Barzano, for your timely warning.' He then called up the tactical plot onto his lectern, but the display was cluttered with anomalous readings and the close range surveyors were picking up dozens of return signals. Cursed alien magicks! Any one of them could be the eldar raider.

He had to save his ship, but what could he do with such confused information? But a bad decision was better than no decision.

'Helm control, hard to starboard and fire all batteries. Get us some distance from this bastard! We need space to manoeuvre.'

'No, lord admiral!' yelled Barzano from the tactical plot table. 'I believe we face a ship of the eldar's dark kin. I have read of such vessels and we must not move away from him.'

Tiberius hesitated, unused to being contradicted on his own bridge, but the adept had been proven correct so far and seemed to know more about the capabilities of the enemy ship.

'Very well, Adept Barzano. Time is short, what would you have me do?'

'We must close with the enemy, barrage him with firepower and hope to strike a lucky hit through his holofields.'

'Do it!' snapped Tiberius to his helm officer. 'Fire port manoeuvring thrusters and come to new heading zero-nine-zero!'

KESHARQ WATCHED THE damaged ship turn about its axis on the viewscreen before him. The ruptured prow was swinging around rapidly and, he suddenly noticed, was getting closer. He cursed as he realised that someone on board that vessel must be aware of his ship's capabilities.

He pointed to the viewscreen and shouted, 'Keep us behind it, curse your souls!'

The bridge shook as the explosions of heavy battery fire burst around the ship. The enemy gunners could not pinpoint their location, but with such weight of fire, it would only be a matter of time until they were hit. And the *Stormrider* was not built to take that kind of punishment.

The *Vae Victus* was struggling to match their turn, but such a contest could have only one winner.

'Prow torpedo bays ready to fire, dread archon!'

'Full spread,' screamed Kesharq. 'Fire!'

'INCOMING TORPEDOES, lord admiral!' warned Philotas.

'Emperor damn them to hell! Hard to port! Defensive turrets open fire!'

'Broadside batteries lock onto the torpedoes' origination point and fire!' shouted Barzano.

'Weapons control, do as he says!' confirmed Tiberius.

The bridge swayed violently and Tiberius gripped the edge of the pulpit as the *Vae Victus* reversed her turn.

SIX TORPEDOES STREAKED towards the *Vae Victus*, alien targeter scrambling systems pumping out a distortion field that made it extremely difficult for their prey to intercept them. At such close range, and flying through such heavy fire, it was inevitable that some of the torpedoes would not get through and two exploded as the broadside gunners found their mark. Another was deceived by the radiation flaring from the damaged prow and flashed harmlessly below the *Vae Victus*. The last three closed unerringly on the strike cruiser and into range of the ship's close defences.

'THREE TORPEDOES DOWN!' yelled Philotas hoarsely.

'That's still three left,' said Tiberius. 'Take them out!'

'Close-in defensive turrets targeting now!'

The giant viewing bay showed the dark of space, painted with bright smears of explosions and the icy contrails of the incoming torpedoes. The entire bridge crew could see the weapons hurtling towards them and every man felt that the warheads were pointed right between his eyes.

The crew held their breath or muttered prayers to the Emperor as the *Vae Victus*'s last line of defence opened fire.

EACH CLOSE-IN TURRET was manned by a servitor equipped with its own auguries which allowed it to independently track the torpedoes as they neared. The torpedoes were programmed with evasive manoeuvres, but it was in their final stage that they were most vulnerable. As they began to slow for final target point acquisition, their speed bled off to a level where they could not evade effectively and one of the torpedoes disintegrated in a spray of high-velocity cannon fire.

A single shell from the defensive turrets clipped another torpedo. The grazing impact was not solid enough to destroy the torpedo, but knocked its internal gyroscope off track. Its guidance system now believed the *Vae Victus* was directly above it and altered course to roar upwards for nearly three hundred kilometres before exploding.

The last torpedo completed its final manoeuvre and closed for the kill.

Every gun brought their fire to bear on the projectile and, at a range of less than two hundred metres, they brought it down.

Hundreds of shells ripped into the torpedo, which detonated in a huge ball of fire and shrapnel. However, the wreckage was still moving at incredible speed and burning shards of the torpedo slammed into the hull, destroying a close-in defence turret, shredding a surveyor antenna and collapsing a number of external statuaries.

The torpedo attack was over.

* * *

TIBERIUS SAGGED AGAINST the pulpit as he watched the last torpedo die and knew he had never seen a sweeter sight. A ragged cheer of relief burst from the throats of the bridge staff along with fervent prayers of thanks.

'Well done, lord admiral. We did it,' sighed Barzano, limp with relief and drenched in sweat.

'This time, Ario,' cautioned Tiberius. 'We were lucky, but let's not break out the victory wine just yet.'

He shouted over to his deck officer. 'What of our return fire?'

'Engaging now,' said Philotas.

'Good,' said Tiberius with a vicious grin. 'Time to show that we still have teeth.'

KESHARQ COULD NOT believe the evidence of his own eyes. The torpedo spread had been defeated! The odds against such a thing was unthinkable. As he contemplated the sheer unfairness of it all, the bridge lurched sickeningly, pitching him to the ground. The massive vibrations of nearby explosions caused the ship to shudder violently. Lights flashed and smoke billowed from smashed machinery.

'Dread archon, we have been hit!' shouted his second in command.

'Yes, thank you for that perceptive insight,' sneered Kesharq. 'And if I am killed, be so good as to point it out. How badly have we been damaged?'

The dark eldar lord picked himself up. A flap of his skin hung from his throat, exposing his wetly glistening anatomy beneath. Impatiently, he pushed it back around his neck as his underlings ran to obey his orders.

Information came at him in a barrage, each morsel more serious than the last.

'We have lost power to the holofields.'

'The mainsail has been damaged and some of the cable stays have been severed.'

'Hull integrity lost on the tormentor deck. The prisoners awaiting torture are all dead.'

Kesharq knew that this battle was over for now. Stripped of the protection of her holofields, the *Stormrider* was too exposed and would be an easy target for its enemy's gunners. The prey had proved worthy indeed and he would not make the mistake of underestimating this foe again.

'Disengage!' he ordered. 'We will return to our lair and effect repairs to the ship. This meat will wait for another day.'

'ELDAR VESSEL IS retreating!' shouted Philotas, and Tiberius released a pent-up sigh of relief.

'Very well,' said Tiberius. 'Set course for Pavonis and when we are in range of secure communication, inform fleet control of the eldar's ability to masquerade as Imperial vessels.'

'Yes, lord admiral.'

Tiberius rubbed a calloused hand across his skull. They had been caught off-guard by the eldar and had been taught a painful lesson in humility. He tapped at his lectern and assigned himself thirty nights of penitent fasting and tactical study for his failure to anticipate the attack before climbing down to the buckled command nave.

Ario Barzano squatted by the base of the pulpit, wiping blood clear of Perjed's brow and smiled as Tiberius knelt beside him.

'Well done, lord admiral. Your quick manoeuvring saved us.'

'Let us not mince words, Adept Barzano–'

'Ario.'

'Very well... Ario. Had it not been for your warning we would all now be dead.'

'Possibly,' admitted Barzano. 'But I'm sure you'd have guessed what they were up to soon enough.'

Tiberius raised a sceptical eyebrow and said, 'How is it a man of the Administratum knows so much of alien vessels?'

Barzano grinned impishly. 'I have been many places, Lazlo, met many interesting people and I am a good listener. I pick up things from everything I see and everyone I meet.'

He shrugged and said, 'In my position, a great deal of esoteric things come my way and I make sure that I digest them all. But come, lord admiral, the real question is not how I know anything, but how did our enemies know where to find us? I am assuming you brought us in away from the normal shipping lanes.'

'Of course.'

Barzano raised his eyebrows. 'Then how did they know we would be here? My signal went only to the governor of Pavonis.'

'Do you suspect her of being in league with the eldar?'

'My dear lord admiral, I am a bureaucrat. I suspect everyone,' laughed Barzano before becoming serious. 'But you are right, the allegiance of the governor is one of many concerns I have.'

Before Tiberius could ask any further questions, Lortuen Perjed groaned and raised a liver spotted hand to his forehead. Barzano helped the scribe to his feet and bowed briefly to Tiberius.

'Lord admiral, if you will excuse me, I should take Lortuen to see my personal physician. Anyway, it was most educational to visit your bridge. We must do this again some time, yes?'

Tiberius nodded, unsure of this glib tongued adept. And the more he thought about it, the more he suspected that Barzano had expected the attack on the *Vae Victus*. Why else would he have come to the bridge at this point, for a tour? And when things had suddenly exploded into deadly action, Barzano had certainly known his way about the bridge of a starship.

Sourly, he wondered what other surprises were in store for him on this voyage.

FIVE

THE OCTAGONAL SURGICAL chamber was cold, the breath of its occupants misted before them. The two figures in charge of the procedure moved with a silky elegant poise through the shadowed chamber. The light was kept low, as the Surgeon's eyes were unaccustomed to brightness and it was widely reckoned that he did his best work in near-darkness anyway.

A channelled metal slab was bolted to the floor in the centre of the chamber, surrounded by arcane devices festooned with scalpel blades, long needles and bonesaws. The chamber's third occupant, a naked human male, lay unmoving atop its cold surface. There were no restraints holding him there. The Surgeon needed total freedom of movement of the body in order to work and the drugs would keep the subject from moving.

The Surgeon had administered the precise amount to achieve such an effect, yet not so much as to prevent him from feeling something of the procedure.

Where was the art if the Honoured could feel nothing?

The Surgeon wore an anonymous red smock and pulled on thick, elbow length rubberised gloves, the fingers of which ended in delicate scalpels and clicking surgical instruments.

His assistant watched his fastidious preparations from the shadows with a mixture of languid boredom and reverence.

She had seen the Surgeon's skill with his instruments many times before, and though the things he could do were wondrous, she was more interested in her own pleasures. The Surgeon nodded to her and she span, naked, towards the slab on her tiptoes, a wicked leer splitting her full red lips.

She gripped the edges of the table and pushed herself upwards and forwards, lifting her legs slowly until she was completely vertical. She walked astride the prone human on her hands then propelled herself into the air, twisting on the descent to land astride the figure.

She could see the fear of the procedure in his eyes and smiled to herself. It was always the fear that aroused her. Aroused her and repulsed her. That this human ape could think that she, who had learned the one thousand and nine Pleasures of the Dark, could actually enjoy this. Part of her was filled with self-loathing as she realised once again that she did, and it took an effort of will not to plunge her envenomed talons through his pleading eyes and into his broken mind. She shuddered, the man mistaking it for her pleasure, and leaned forwards, trailing her tongue along his exposed chest and feeling the skin pucker beneath her. She worked up to his neck and gently bit on the skin, her sharpened teeth penetrating his skin and tasting the bitter flavour of his bad blood.

He moaned as her teeth moved up his face, feathering razor kisses along the line of his jaw. Her long, blood red nails trailed up his ribs, leaving smoking, poisonous tracks in their wake. Her thighs tightened over his hips and she knew he was ready. The blood was singing in his rotten veins.

She looked over her shoulder and nodded to the Surgeon. Even though the human could not move, she sensed the terror rise up in him. The woman vaulted gracefully over his head, landing with a gymnast's grace behind the slab, spitting the blood that coated her teeth onto the floor. The Surgeon pressed the first of his bladed digits against the man's belly. Expertly, he opened him up, paring back the skin and muscle like the layers of an onion.

The Surgeon worked for another three hours, dextrously unravelling every centimetre of the man to the bone, laying his flesh and organs open in gory ribbons of meat. How easy it would be to just continue with the opening and take it on to his skull, leaving him a screaming, fleshless skeleton. The temptation was great, but he resisted it, knowing that Archon Kesharq would visit a thousand times such misery on his own frame were he to let the kyerzak die too soon.

Humming alien machinery of rubber tubing, hissing bellows and gurgling bottles of blood surrounded the procedure, gently feeding the still-living cadaver with life preserving fluids. A loathsome metallic construction, like a serrated gallows, swung upwards and over the table, supporting a glossy, beetle-like organism that pulsed with rasping breath. Fine, chitinous black needles stretched from its distended belly and worked at each flensed slab of flesh. Moving too quickly to be seen by the naked eye, they stripped diseased, stringy matter from each organ and hunk of meat, weaving new translucent strands of organic matter in their place.

As the throbbing, eyeless thing finished with each segment of flesh the Surgeon would gently lift it back onto the body and meticulously rework it onto the subject's frame until he was once again whole.

Only the head remained unopened, his mouth moving in a soundless scream of pain and revulsion. The razor gallows lowered the glistening creature onto the man's face, its fleshy underside undulating warmly over his skin. The black needles extended once more from its body, slithering across his cheeks and working their way into his skull through the nose, ears, mouth and eyes. Threads of agony wormed through his brain as each nerve, capillary and blood vessel was stripped out and renewed.

Finally it was done. The grossly swollen organism was lifted from the subject's head and deposited on a wide metal tray at the end of the slab. The Surgeon lifted a narrow bonesaw as the creature began convulsing, its colour fading from lustrous black to a necrotic brown. Before it rotted away to nothing, the Surgeon split it across the thorax with the saw and removed a dripping yellow egg sac. It would be needed to grow another organism for the next time.

The Surgeon nodded to the naked woman who sashayed back to the slab and raised the man into a sitting position. His movements were slow and awkward, but she knew that his discomfort would soon pass. He gathered his clothing and sullenly pulled a short, blue velvet pelisse with silver stitching around his shoulders. He picked up a bronze tipped ebony cane and painfully shuffled towards the chamber's door.

Without turning, he snapped, 'Well? Are you coming?'

She cocked her head to one side, her venomously beautiful features twisting into a sneer of contempt. He turned to face her, as though sensing her loathing of him.

His eyes locked on hers with a mixture of hatred and arousal and she could see from his beseeching eyes that he had suffered greatly. She was glad, and guessed that it would take at least six of the one thousand and nine Pleasures of the Dark to placate him this time.

It was such a shame that human understanding of such things was so limited.

SIX

URIEL RESTED HIS head against the thrumming internal wall of the gunship, his hands clasped in prayer before him as they began the final approach to Brandon Gate, the capital of Pavonis.

Every man under Uriel's command sat in reverent silence, his thoughts directed to the glory that was the Emperor. At the far end of the crew compartment, Adept Ario Barzano sat with his small army of followers and Uriel shook his head slowly. How many servants did one man need?

All his years of training at the Agiselus barracks had hammered discipline and self-reliance into Uriel, and it was strange to see a man with someone to perform his every menial task for him. From the earliest age, children of Ultramar were taught to live a life of discipline, self-denial and simplicity.

Barzano was listening intently to the man he had introduced as Lortuen Perjed, nodding vigorously at whatever the old man was telling him. Adept Perjed was wagging his finger under Barzano's nose as though he were giving him a stern lecture and for a second Uriel wondered exactly who was in charge.

He dismissed the adept from his thoughts and stared out of the thick viewing block set in the side of the gunship as the last filmy clouds vanished from sight and the primary continental mass of Pavonis was laid out before him like a map.

Uriel's first impression of Pavonis was one of contrasts.

Amid the vast green and open landscape, dozens of sprawling manufactorum covered scores of square kilometres in all directions, complete with material bays, warehousing and transportation nodes to link them together. Vast cranes and yellow lifting machinery crawled through these industrial hubs, passed by lumbering rolling stock laden with fuel and supplies for the ever hungry forges. Smoke-belching cooling towers filled the air with clouds of vapour and a yellowish smog clung to the ground, coating the buildings in a filthy ochre residue.

But ahead of them, further out from the manufactorum and set amid a swathe of forest at the foot of some high mountains, Uriel could see a well-designed estate of white stone buildings and guessed that this must belong to the one of the ruling cartels that oversaw production on Pavonis. The Thunderhawk passed over the estate, startling a herd of lithe, horned beasts and passing close enough for Uriel to make out the marble columned entrance of the largest building.

The estate was soon lost to sight as the gunship roared along the line of a fast flowing river and, as the gunship rounded a rocky bluff, Uriel could see the marble city of Brandon Gate on the horizon. The gunship gained altitude and gave the city a slow circuit, allowing Uriel to look down into the star-shaped city below him. Clustered round its defensive, arrowhead bastions, black and smoking manufactorum towns sweltered and bustled in the day's heat while the interior of the city lay indolent and relaxed within, the polished white marble of the buildings radiant in the midday sunshine.

The architecture of the city was comprised of a mixture of old and new: ancient, millennia old structures abutting steel and glass domes and crystal towers. The streets were cobbled, lined with statuary and tall trees.

At the centre of the conglomeration of marble and glass lay the Imperial palace of the governor of Pavonis. A wide cobbled square stretched before the palace gates, its circumference marked by yet more statuary. The palace itself rose high above the streets below, its white towers and crenellated battlements designed in the High Gothic styling popular several thousand years ago. Bronze flying buttresses supported a massive fluted bell tower embellished with a conical roof of beaten gold and studded with precious stones.

Uriel could see from the bell's great, rocking motion that it was tolling, but could not hear it over the roaring of the Thunderhawk's engines.

The many buildings that made up the palace complex stretched over a huge area, encompassing a leafy park, athletics pavilion and a small lake. It was clear that the rulers of Pavonis liked to live well. How much, Uriel wondered, would they be willing to sacrifice in order to keep such a state of affairs? How much might they have already sacrificed?

In addition to the aesthetics of the palace, Uriel's practiced eye took in the many gun emplacements worked cunningly into the building's structure and the entrances to underground launch bays. The palace, and indeed the entire central city, would be a formidable bastion to hold in the event of an insurrection or war.

The gunship began slowing and descending towards the blinking lights of a landing platform set within a ring of tall trees just outside the palace walls. A small observation building and fuel tank, protected by raised blast shielding, sat at its edge.

Uriel snapped his fist against the release mechanism of his restraint harness as their altitude dropped to ten metres, the rest of the Space Marines following suit, and snatched his boltgun from its housing.

Pasanius and Learchus stalked the length of the crew compartment as the green disembarkation lamp began flashing.

'Everybody up! Be ready to debark, secure the perimeter.'

While the sergeants prepared the men for landing, Uriel knelt before the small shrine set in the alcove next to his captain's chair and bowed his head, speaking the Prayer of Battle and Catechism of the Warrior. He gripped the hilt of his bequeathed power sword and rose to stand at the head of the armoured crew ramp at the front of the gunship.

With a decompressive hiss and squeal of hydraulics, the ramp quickly lowered, slamming onto the landing platform. Even before it was fully down, the two squads of Ultramarines swept out from the gunship and moved to perimeter defence positions. Their bolters were held at the ready as their helmeted heads scanned left and right for possible threats.

'My goodness, they're keen aren't they?' clapped Barzano over the shrieking of the Thunderhawk's engines as they powered down.

Pasanius hefted his massive flamer as Uriel rolled his eyes and marched down the crew ramp after Barzano.

As the blast shields at the platform's edge lowered, a plump, red-faced man dressed in the plain black robes of an adept and carrying a geno-keypad emerged from the observation building.

An entire squad of bolters turned on the man, who squealed and threw his hands up before him.

'Wait! Don't shoot!' he pleaded. 'I'm here to meet Adept Barzano!'

Barzano, Lortuen and Uriel stepped onto the platform as two Ultramarines moved to flank the man and escort him towards their captain. The man was sweating profusely, dwarfed by the armoured giants either side of him.

Barzano stepped forward to greet the florid-faced man, extending one hand and placing the other on his fellow adept's shoulder.

'You must be Adept Ballion Varle. Good morning to you, sir. You already know me, Ario Barzano, we don't need to go over that, but these fine fellows are from the Ultramarines.'

Barzano guided Varle towards Uriel and waved a hand towards Uriel in a comradely gesture. 'This is Captain Uriel Ventris and he's in charge of them. They've come to make sure that everything here goes swimmingly and hopefully put the kibosh on some of the troubles you've been having here, yes?'

Adept Ballion Varle nodded, still looking up in wonder at the expressionless faces of the Space Marines' helmets, and Uriel doubted he was taking in more than one word in three that Barzano was saying.

Barzano slipped his arm over Ballion's shoulder and pressed his thumb onto the geno-keypad the trembling adept carried. The machine clicked and chattered, finally chiming with a soft jingle. Varle managed to tear his eyes from the giant warriors and glanced at the keypad.

'Well, at least you know that I'm no impostor,' smiled Barzano. 'You received my message then?'

'Ah, yes, adept. I did, though to be honest, its contents were rather confusing.'

'Not to worry though, eh? Everything will sort itself out, no need to fret.'

'Yes, but if the governor finds out I knew you would be arriving early and didn't tell her... she'll...' trailed off Varle.

'She'll-?' prompted Barzano.

'Well, she won't be pleased.'

'Excellent, then we're off to a good start.'

'I'm sorry, I don't understand, Adept Barzano,' protested Varle.

'No need to apologise, no reason you should understand. Games within games, my dear chap.'

Lortuen Perjed coughed pointedly, tapping his cane on the metal crew ramp and stared at Barzano, who waved his hand dismissively. 'Pay no mind to me, my dear fellow, I'm rambling. Do that a lot whenever I meet someone new. Now, to business. I think we'll pay a visit to the Imperial palace first, what do you think?'

'I think that the governor won't be expecting you so soon.'

'Then again...' mused Barzano, pointing to a gap in the trees where a cobbled road led towards the city walls. Uriel watched as an open-topped carriage drawn by a quartet of trotting horses made its way along the road towards the edge of the landing platform.

The carriage was borne aloft on anti-grav technology similar to that used by the Chapter's land speeders and its lacquered sides bore a heraldic device depicting a garlanded artillery shell.

Uriel knew that such technology did not come cheaply and that this conveyance must have cost a small fortune.

The horses, surely an affectation of tradition, came to a halt in a cloud of dust and a tall, rakishly handsome man clad in a black suit and blue velvet pelisse with an elaborate feathered bicorn hat clambered down from the carriage and hurried over towards the Thunderhawk, his full features smiling in greeting.

Lortuen Perjed moved to stand beside Barzano and Uriel, his emaciated frame appearing skeletal beside the armoured bulk of the Space Marine captain.

'Vendare Taloun,' whispered Perjed. 'His family cartel produces artillery shells for the Imperial Guard. Governor Shonai ousted him ten years ago and now he leads the opposition to her in the Pavonis senate. Rumour has it that he engineered the death of his brother after they were deposed in order to become family patriarch.'

'Is there any real proof?' whispered Barzano before Taloun reached them.

'No, not as yet.'

Barzano nodded his thanks without turning and stepped forward to greet the new arrival. Uriel noticed a frightened look cross Ballion Varle's face and stood beside Barzano, his hand straying to his sword hilt.

Vendare Taloun bowed elaborately to Barzano and Uriel, doffing his hat and sweeping it behind him. As he stood erect once more Barzano gripped his hand and pumped it vigorously up and down.

'A pleasure Lord Taloun, an absolute pleasure. The name's Ario Barzano, but of course you know that. Come, let us take your magnificent coach into the city, eh?'

Taloun was taken aback by Barzano's manner, but recovered well.

'Certainly, adept,' smiled Taloun, indicating his hovering carriage. 'Would any of your companions care to join us? I believe we can accommodate another one or two.'

'Uriel and Lortuen will join us I think. Adept Ballion, be a good chap and have some food and drink brought to the fellows here will you? Very good!'

As Barzano and Vendare Taloun strode towards the carriage, Lortuen Perjed whispered up to Uriel, 'Well at least we know not to trust Ballion.'

'What do you mean?' asked Uriel as he watched the rounded adept make his way dejectedly back to the observation building where he emerged with a long cape and longer frown.

'How else do you think the Taloun knew to come and greet us?'

Uriel considered the question. 'You suspected you could not trust him and still told him our time of arrival?'

'Adept Barzano felt it was likely that the local adept was in the pocket of one of the local highborn. At least this way we know whose.'

Seeing Uriel's surprise at his candour, Perjed smiled indulgently. 'It's common enough on worlds like these out here in the eastern fringes where a planet might go for decades without official contact from the Administratum.'

'Not in Ultramar,' declared Uriel fiercely.

'Perhaps not,' agreed Perjed. 'But we're not in Ultramar any-more.'

JENNA SHARBEN SMASHED her shield into the man's yellow-stained face and pushed him back into the crowd. The holding cells in the back of their Rhinos were already full. More were on their way from the precinct, but for now all the two lines of judges could do was lock shields and keep the crowd back from the roadway that led to the palace gates.

Nearly five hundred people had gathered since the palace bell had begun ringing but the great, dolorous peals were sure to bring more. She cursed whoever had thought to ring the damned thing. It had been used in the early days of Pavonis's history to gather the members of its senate, but now it was only rung out of tradition.

A damn stupid one at that, reflected Jenna as she pushed the crowd back with her shield. She knew full well that the cartel senators were all contacted directly when required for an assembly. All the bell summoned now were lots of disenfranchised workers who were angry at the very people who would soon be passing this way towards the palace.

'Keep those people back!' shouted Sergeant Collix from behind the line of judges.

What did he think they were doing, wondered Jenna? Enjoying a quiet discussion with scores of furious workers? She had heard the talk around the precinct about the massacre he'd caused in Liberation Square and how he had apparently only stopped the shooting when Virgil Ortega had ordered the judges to cease fire and fall back. What other mistakes might he make and how many people would pay for it?

She realised that this line of thinking was dangerous and tried to push it away as another man reached to grab the top of her shield. She smacked its top edge sharply across his nose and he dropped screaming to the ground.

The pitch of the crowds yelling changed and she risked a glance over her shoulder, seeing a horse-drawn hover carriage approaching the gates. The crowd pushed forward and she grunted as its weight bent the judges' line back.

She dug in her heels and pushed back.

* * *

SOLANA VERGEN RECLINED in the padded leather couch of the skimming carriage and examined her moist eyes in a small compact, pondering if they looked suitably grief-stricken. Satisfied that she presented the perfect image of a grieving daughter, beautiful but also teasingly vulnerable, she ran an ivory and silver brush through her long, honey blonde hair as she peered through the velvet-draped window onto the brightness of Liberation Square.

She gave a yawn, seeing more of the tiresome workers lining the road, yelling at her carriage as she passed towards the palace gates. Really, what did they hope to achieve? Then she noticed that many of them were wearing the green and yellow overalls of the Vergen cartel. Why weren't they at work in the manufactorum? Didn't they realise that they were working for her now?

Just because her father had foolishly got himself killed last week did not mean that people could just swan off work whenever they felt like it. She made a mental note to contact the local overseer and have him gather names of all those who had been absent today. To teach them all a lesson she would dismiss them and the overseer for allowing such indiscipline amongst the workforce.

They would all soon see that she was not the soft touch her father had been.

Remembering her father, she pouted as she thought of the condescending crocodile tears Taloun had shed with her after the riot that had seen her father die. Did the man really think that her marriage to his idiot son was anything more than one of convenience? No doubt he thought to install his son as puppet head of the Vergen cartel, but he had reckoned without Solana Vergen.

She already had contacts in the other cartels who would be only too pleased to listen to some of the things her fiancé had sobbed to her as they lay in the darkness after satisfying his baser urges.

Her father's advisors had been horrified at the idea of her taking over the reins of production, but for the life of her she could not imagine why. The head of the Shonai cartel was a woman and governor of the entire planet, for goodness sake! She pulled her pelisse tighter and rested a silk-gloved hand on the edge of her carriage as she pondered the future.

Yes, the Vergen cartel was definitely going to see some changes.

TARYN HONAN TAPPED his fat, beringed fingers in a nervous tattoo on the window of the carriage, feeling the uncomfortable vibration of his carriage's wheels with the cobbles on his ample backside.

He cursed again that he had not been allowed to spend his own cartel's money to invest in an anti-grav carriage. And it was an investment, couldn't the committee see that? It was so humiliating to arrive at the palace on a clattering wagon rather than on a smooth, prestigious conveyance like the ones used by Taloun and de Valtos.

One day he hoped to be as successful as them and have the respect and admiration of the lower cartels. He resolved to watch them closely at this gathering of the senate. Whichever way Taloun and de Valtos went, so too would he. They would be sure to recognise him as an equal if he continued to support their politics. Wouldn't they? Or would they think him spineless, following their lead simply to curry favour? Taryn Honan chewed his bottom lip and wondered what the committee would do.

But his thoughts turned petulant as he pictured them behind the long, oaken desk shaking their humdrum heads as they turned down yet another exciting business venture he had brought before them.

It was so unfair that he alone of the cartel leaders had to answer to a committee. He knew the others all laughed at him because of it, even the tiny, one-manufactorum cartels who could barely afford a seat on the senate.

So he had made a few mistakes. Who in business had not?

Yes, a few trade deals had not gone nearly as well as he might have hoped, and, yes, there had been the unfortunate business of the boy-courtesan who had accessed his credit slate and run up a mammoth debt before fleeing Pavonis on one of the many off-world freighters. But was that any reason for the committee to strip him of executive power and install themselves as omnipotent masters of his finances?

Honan fervently hoped the boy had been aboard one of the ships raided by the eldar and tortured in all manner of sordid ways. That brought a smile to his fleshy face and he licked his rouged lips at the thought, picturing the boy's debasement at the hands of eldar slavers.

He gripped his ebony cane tighter.

KASIMIR DE VALTOS yawned, wincing as his lungs burned with the bitter smog in the air and closed his eyes as his anti-grav carriage smoothly carried him towards the palace. Briefly he wondered what the Shonai bitch could want now, but dismissed the thought as irrelevant. Who really cared what she wanted any more? He smiled as he wondered if it was perhaps to announce her absurd proposal to hunt down the eldar raiders. Did she really think that his cartel could be bought so easily or that the Taloun would not see through her transparent ploy in a heartbeat?

If she thought they were going to play so easily into her hands, then she was even more stupid than de Valtos had given her credit for.

Mykola Shonai may have been a worthy political adversary once, but now she was just a tired old woman. She was barely hanging onto power by her fingertips, not realising that there was a queue of people waiting to stamp on them.

And Kasimir de Valtos was first in line.

He withdrew a silver tobacco tin from beneath his pelisse, pulling out and lighting a thin cheroot. He knew they were bad for his lungs and laughed bitterly at the irony.

After the eldar had finished with him on their infernal ship all those years ago, a breath of fog could sometimes cause his lungs to seize up, but he was damned if he was going to let that stop him from doing exactly what he pleased.

He always had done and always would do, and damn anyone who tried to stop him.

VENDARE TALOUN SMILED, exposing a row of perfect teeth, and Uriel was reminded of the fanged grins of the hissing hormagaunts he'd killed on Ichar IV. Uriel had only met the man ten minutes ago, but already did not like him.

'So, Adept Barzano, Ballion Varle tells me that your ship was attacked during your journey. A bad business indeed. The governor must do more to prevent such atrocities.'

Uriel noticed Taloun was cleverly not trying to hide the fact that Varle had told him of their early arrival, guessing that

Barzano must have already known. He wondered if Taloun thought that Barzano could be bought as easily.

'Yes, my dear Taloun, a bad business,' agreed Barzano. 'We were indeed attacked, but saw the rogues off sharpish.'

'That is good to know,' nodded Taloun. 'We have heard such tales about these despicable aliens.'

The man smiled at Uriel, patting his armoured knee. 'But now the brave warriors of the Ultramarines are here, we have nothing to fear, yes?'

Uriel inclined his head, unimpressed by the man's over-familiarity.

'I thank you for your vote of confidence, Guilder Taloun,' replied Uriel, using the local form of address for one of the cartel chiefs. 'By the Emperor's grace we shall rid you of these blasphemous aliens and return peace to Pavonis.'

'Ah, would that it were that simple, my dear Captain Ventris,' sighed Taloun, 'but I fear that Governor Shonai has led us down too ruinous a path for the simple elimination of some bothersome raiders to save our beloved world's economy. Her tithe tax hurts us all, and none more so than myself. Why, only two days ago I was forced to dismiss a thousand people from my employ in order to lower costs and improve margins, but does the governor think of people like me? Of course not.'

Uriel masked his contempt for the man's selfishness and allowed his words to wash over him.

'And what of the extra manpower she promised us to protect the manufactorum from the Church of Ancient Ways? I have lost over seven thousand man-hours of production to their bombs!' continued Taloun, warming to his theme.

Uriel wondered how many actual men he had lost or if he even cared.

'Perhaps, Guider Taloun,' suggested Uriel with steel in his voice, 'we might leave all this talk of politics for the senate chambers and just enjoy the journey?'

Taloun nodded in acquiescence, but Uriel could see annoyance briefly flare behind his eyes. Taloun was obviously a man unused to being put down by those he perceived as his political inferiors.

Uriel ignored the man and studied the landscape as it sped past them. The city walls were high and sloped inwards towards an overhanging rampart. He could see grenade dumpers worked into the machicolations and power field generators studded along its length. From his readings on Pavonis, Uriel knew that virtually everything would have been produced locally by one or other of the family cartels. The cities of Ultramar did not need such technological trinkets to defend themselves. No, they had stronger defences. Courage, honour and a people that embodied the best examples of all human nobility.

Trained from birth and educated in the ways of the Blessed Primarch, they would never break, never surrender and never submit to such unnecessary luxuries.

Uriel was startled from his bombastic reverie by a pointed cough from Perjed as they moved through the bronze gates of the city.

When seen from ground level the buildings on the inside edge of the walls were much less impressive, functionally constructed, with little or no ornamentation. The buildings of Macragge, while simple, were cunningly constructed to provide a solid, dependable structure as well as presenting something of aesthetic value. He realised that the boxy constructions of Pavonis were designed to be as cost effective as possible and lamented the fact that those who held the purse strings so often hamstrung the architect's art. Here and there, Uriel saw men and women cleaning the building walls of a filmy, ochre residue, the inevitable fallout of living so close to heavy industry. He noticed that all the cleaners wore white overalls so as to be less visible.

The carriage sped effortlessly along the cobbled streets, passing smartly dressed inhabitants in black who doffed their feathered hats as the coach passed. The peals of the palace bell echoed through the affluent streets.

Taloun waved to the passers by and Uriel was struck by his confident, easy manner.

'You are well known in these parts?' asked Barzano.

'Yes, indeed. I have many friends within the city.'

'I take it that the majority of these friends are cartel members?'

'Of course. The common people generally do not venture within the walls of the city. It's the tolls, you see. Most of them cannot afford to come inside. Especially now, what with the governor's tithe tax squeezing every last coin from them.'

'People have to pay to enter this part of the city?'

'Why, yes,' replied Taloun, as though any thought of any other possibility was ridiculous.

'And how much is this toll?'

Taloun shrugged. 'Not sure exactly. Cartel members are exempt from its payment of course, but I contribute a small amount from the yearly profits towards my comings and goings.'

Barzano leaned forwards and waved his hand over the edge of the carriage. 'How then are the city's parks maintained? The buildings cleaned? Who pays for that? The Imperium?'

'No, no, no!' explained Taloun hurriedly. 'I believe a portion of general taxes go towards their upkeep,'

'So in other words,' mused Barzano slowly, 'the populace all contribute towards this lovely place, but cannot enjoy it unless they pay for the privilege once more?'

'I suppose that's one way of looking at it,' replied Taloun haughtily. 'But no one complains.'

'Oh, I don't know,' pointed out Uriel, nodding towards the angry mob gathered before the black gates of the Imperial palace. '*They* don't look too happy about it.'

JENNA WATCHED THE latest carriage approach the palace gates and rolled her eyes as she saw that this one was open-topped. Didn't these fools realise what was happening on the city streets? Those carriages that had already passed had been pelted with bottles and cobbles torn up from the square and only by the Emperor's grace had no one been injured.

'How can you do this?' screamed a soot-smeared man in Jenna's face. 'Don't you know you're helping prop up a corrupt regime of thieves and liars?'

Sergeant Collix was suddenly at her side and slammed his shock maul into the man's face. The man collapsed, blood spurting from his shattered jaw and Collix dragged him over the line of judges. The sergeant hauled the insensible man's bleeding body towards the Rhinos.

True, the man's words had been illegally subversive, but she realised that there was the very real possibility he was right.

Barely five years out of the Schola Progenium and her Adeptus Arbites training only completed six months ago, such concerns were far above Jenna's head. Her superiors would decide if the rulers of Pavonis had become criminally incompetent and remove them from office should that prove to be the case.

She tensed her leg muscles, ready to push the crowd again, but suddenly realised there was no need as the people before her took a collective step backward, staring in wonder at something behind her. Making sure there was nobody threatening nearby, she spared a hurried glance over her shoulder.

A splendid hover carriage swept by, but it was the blue armoured giant sitting along with the Taloun and two men she didn't recognise that claimed Jenna Sharben's attention.

She had never seen a Space Marine in the flesh before, but had seen the devotional placards and posters on her homeworld of Verdan III. Never had she imagined that the outlandish proportions they ascribed to Space Marines could actually be real. She recognised the alabaster white emblem on his shoulder guard as belonging to the Ultramarines and felt a flutter of unreasoning fear as the enormous warrior glanced over at her.

The carriage raced through the palace gates and the Ultramarines warrior was lost to sight. She shook herself free of her awe at the Space Marine's size and turned back to the crowd, ready for more trouble.

But such a physical reminder of the Imperium's power had robbed the crowd of any further desire for troublemaking and slowly it began to break up. First in ones and twos, then in greater numbers as word of the enormous champion of the Emperor's arrival spread to those at the rear of the crowd who hadn't seen him. A few die-hard demagogues tried to keep the crowd together with attempts at fiery rhetoric, but they were soon clubbed to the ground and dragged towards the holding cells of the Rhinos.

'Did you see the size of him?' declared the judge next to her. 'The Space Marines are here!'

Yes, thought Jenna Sharben, the Space Marines are here.

But did that mean things had just got better or worse?

THE DOME OF the Pavonis Senate Chambers of Righteous Commerce was cast from solid bronze, its inner face lined with a rich patina of age and smoke. Beneath the dome, the circular chamber was tiered and filled with shouting members of the Pavonis cartels. The tier nearest the red and gold chequered floor was reserved for the heads of the twenty-four cartels, though the burgundy leather seats were rarely fully occupied except at the beginning of the financial year.

Sixteen of the positions were currently occupied. The heads of the six most profitable cartels – the Shonai, the Vergen, the de Valtos, the Taloun, the Honan and the Abrogas – were all in attendance, making ostentatious displays of friendship.

Behind them sat the members of their families or those who could claim some relation by marriage or adoption.

Finally, in the highest tier, at the rear of the chamber, sat the equally vocal members of each cartel who could not claim a blood tie to its owners, but nevertheless had signed exclusive contracts of loyalty to its charter. This was by far the largest tier in the chamber and its segregated members shouted venomously at one another despite the repeated calls for order by the bewigged Moderator of Transactions. These were the hangers-on and opportunists who sought social advancement through their association with the cartel of their choice. Uriel noticed Adept Ballion Varle sitting shiftily in the section reserved for supporters of the Taloun.

Guests and those without formal written remit to be part of the chamber's activities were permitted to sit in the bare wooden benches of this tier and it was from here that Ario Barzano, Lortuen Perjed and Uriel Ventris watched the dealings below.

Uriel could feel the eyes of many of the upper tier spectators upon him and forced himself to ignore them as he listened to proceedings on the floor below.

'Can't see or hear a damned thing from here,' grumbled Barzano, straining over the brass rail of the tier.

'I believe that is the idea,' observed Perjed acidly. 'Many worlds in the galactic east are notoriously reluctant to allow observers to participate in their government. Even observers as... ah, influential as you.'

'Is that so?' snapped Barzano. 'Well, we'll see about that.'

Uriel could understand Barzano's frustration about being placed here, but thanks to his genetic enhancements, he could hear and see perfectly well from their lofty position.

'Now who's that big fellow in black?' asked Barzano pointing to a corpulent man in the centre of the chamber banging a long polearm topped with a bronze sphere.

'That is the Moderator of Transactions,' answered Lortuen Perjed. 'He acts as the chairman of senate meetings, approves the agenda and decrees who may or may not speak.'

'Doesn't look like he's doing a very good job of it. What in blazes is he saying anyway?'

'He is appealing for quiet,' said Uriel.

Barzano and Perjed stared at him for a second before remembering his enhanced senses.

'Still, it won't do, Uriel,' snapped Barzano. 'It won't do at all. You might be able to hear, but I don't want to find out what's happening secondhand. No offence to you of course, my dear fellow.'

'None taken,' assured Uriel. 'First-hand battle information is always more reliable.'

'Exactly so. Now come on, let's get out of this perch and a bit closer to the action.'

Barzano led the way down the stone steps towards the lower tiers. A few muscular bailiffs in fur lined robes and bicorn hats with golden chains of office around their necks tried to bar their way with black staffs tipped with bronze. Uriel could see that they carried the cudgels like they knew how to use them and guessed that some senate meetings required breaking up when the 'discussions' became overly heated. One look at the massive Ultramarines captain soon convinced them that discretion was the better part of valour, however, and within minutes, Barzano, Perjed and Uriel were ensconced in the padded leather seating behind the heads of the cartels.

The Moderator of Transactions tapped his cane on the tiled floor and stared pointedly at the three interlopers in his senate chambers. The bailiffs behind them shrugged. Heads were turning to face them and a pregnant hush fell over the crowded hall as they waited what steps the Moderator of Transactions would take.

Uriel folded his massive arms and stared back at the sweating man. The tension was broken when Vendare Taloun stood and waved his cane in the direction of the Moderator.

'Moderator, might I be permitted to address our guests?'

The man scowled, but nodded. 'The floor recognises the Honourable Vendare Taloun.'

'Thank you. Friends, fellow cartel members and traders! It is with great pleasure that I welcome Adepts Barzano and Perjed and Captain Uriel Ventris of the Ultramarines as our guests here today. These honoured visitors from the Emperor have come to our troubled world to see what can be done to remedy the terrible hardships we have been forced to endure these last few, painful years. I feel it is only good manners to welcome them to this, our humble assemblage and extend every courtesy during their stay on Pavonis.'

Applause and jeers greeted Taloun's words in equal measure as Perjed leaned over to whisper to Barzano and Uriel. 'Very clever. He infers that it was his influence that brought us here and thus he is seen as a statesman with a greater perspective than the governor while at the same time avoiding criticising her directly.'

'Yes,' agreed Barzano, his eyes narrowing. 'Very clever.'

As the jeering, clapping and calls for other potential speakers continued, Uriel studied the other members of the cartels sitting in the front tier. The bench nearest the moderator bore the governor of Pavonis and her advisors. A thin, acerbic faced man stood behind the governor and sitting beside her was an older man with an enormous grey beard, smoking a pipe. Both men were whispering urgently to her.

Uriel liked the look of Mykola Shonai. Despite the chaos of the senate chambers, she comported herself with dignity and he could see she had great strength in her.

As Taloun sat down, Uriel noticed a white haired man seated near him whose scarred, burned face had the unhealthy pallor of synth-flesh. This man seemed uninterested in speaking and stared with undisguised hatred at governor Shonai.

'That's Kasimir de Valtos,' whispered Perjed, noticing the direction of Uriel's stare. 'Poor chap's ship was attacked by the eldar pirates. Apparently they did all manner of horrible things to him before he escaped.'

'What sort of things?'

'I don't know. "Horrible" is all my records mention.'

'What does his cartel produce?'

'Engines and hulls for Leman Russ battle tanks and heavy artillery pieces mainly, though I think that much of that is overseen by his subordinates.'

'Why do you say that, Lortuen?' asked Barzano.

'Administratum records for this world have listed Guilder de Valtos as applying for no less than seven Imperial permits to lead archaeological expeditions throughout the system. Many of the finest pieces in the Pavonis Paymaster's Gallery have come from his own private collection. He is quite the patron of the arts and has a passion for antiquities.'

'Really? It seems we share an interest then,' chuckled Barzano.

Uriel wondered exactly what that meant as Perjed threw his master a sharp look, and also pondered why Barzano himself did not know these facts. He nodded towards a bearded man with a ponytail who sat slumped on the bench close to de Valtos and Taloun. He could see that the man's eyes were glazed and even over the bodily odours of the hundreds of individuals in the hall, Uriel could detect the faint aroma of a soporific emanating from the man, possibly obscura.

'What about him, who is he?'

Perjed squinted along his nose and sighed in disappointment. 'That, Captain Ventris, is Beauchamp Abrogas, and a more sorry specimen of humanity you will be hard pressed to find this side of the Ophelian Pilgrim trail. He is a waster who could barely spell his own name if you handed him the quill and wrote half the letters for him.'

The bile in Lortuen Perjed's voice surprised Uriel and the old man seemed to realise this. He smiled weakly and explained, 'My apologies, but I find the squandering of an individual's Emperor-given talents such as this wasteful. And if there is one thing the Administratum hates, it is waste, my dear captain.'

Uriel turned his attention back to the floor of the chamber where a modicum of order had been restored. The moderator was pointing his sphere-topped staff at a fat man in a powdered white wig that cascaded across his shoulders as a shrill voiced woman with long blonde hair yelled at the moderator.

Uriel raised a questioning eyebrow to Perjed, who shrugged. 'She sits in the seat normally reserved for the Vergen, so I can only assume she is his daughter. I know nothing about her,' admitted the adept.

The woman would have been attractive, thought Uriel, had her face not been set in a permanent sneer of self-righteous indignation. She gripped the rail before her and tried to make herself heard over the shouts of the other members.

'I demand senate chambers recognise my authority to speak in the name of the Vergen cartel!' she spat. 'As the daughter of Leotas Vergen I demand the right to be heard.'

The moderator of transactions blatantly ignored the woman as two bailiffs moved to stand before her. The moderator turned away and said, 'The floor recognises the... Honourable Taryn Honan.'

A few bawdy laughs greeted this last comment from the high tiers along with balled up agenda sheets. The man appeared flustered at the reaction and puffed out his considerable chest before loudly clearing his throat and speaking in a high pitched, nasal voice.

'I think I speak for all of us when I join with Guilder Taloun in welcoming our honoured guests to Pavonis, and I for one wish to extend to them the full hospitality of my country estates.'

'Has the committee approved that, Honan?' shouted a voice from the opposite side of the hall. Applause and laughter greeted the joker's comment and Uriel noticed Guilder Taloun rubbing the bridge of his nose in exasperation, as though embarrassed by the support of Honan.

Guilder Honan sat back in his seat and rested his hands on his belly, bewildered and shamed by the laughter at his expense. The shrill voiced woman again began yelling at the moderator as he stamped the staff onto the tiles and shouted, 'If you are quite finished, gentlemen, today's first order of business is an Extraordinary Motion tabled by the honourable Guilder Taloun.'

Across the chamber, the governor of Pavonis surged to her feet.

'Moderator, this is intolerable! Will you allow Guilder Taloun to hijack proceedings like this? I called this assembly of the senate and the right of first voice is mine.'

'An Extraordinary Motion takes precedence over the right of first voice,' explained Taloun patiently.

'I know the conventions of procedure!' barked Shonai.

'Then can I assume you will allow me to continue, governor?'

'I know what you're doing here, Vendare. So just get on with it, damn you.'

'As you wish, Governor Shonai,' replied Taloun courteously. Vendare Taloun pushed himself to his feet and spread wide his hands, making his way to the centre of the chequered floor and taking hold of the staff offered to him by the Moderator of Transactions.

Once divested of the staff, the Moderator of Transactions consulted a data slate and said, 'Guilder Taloun, I notice that your submitted motion does not bear a title. Under article six of the conventions of procedure, you are required to fill subject form three-two-four dash nine, in triplicate. Can I assume that you will do so now?'

'My profound apologies for the absence of a title, but I felt that to announce the topic of my motion would be to cause unnecessary bias had its subject matter become common knowledge before my raising it. Rest assured I shall complete the said form immediately following this assembly.'

The moderator nodded in acceptance and yielded the floor to Vendare Taloun.

He rapped the staff sharply on the floor.

'Friends, we live in troubled times,' he began, to sycophantic applause.

Taloun smiled, accepting the applause graciously and raised his hands for silence before continuing.

'Seldom in our proud commercial history have we faced such threats as we do today. Vile alien raiders plague our shipping, the Church of Ancient Ways bomb our manufactorum and kill our workers. The business of trade has instead become the business of survival as costs rise, taxes bite harder and margins shrink.'

Obsequious nods and shouts echoed around the hall as Taloun began to pace the floor, jabbing with the staff to accentuate his words, and Uriel recognised a powerful orator in Vendare Taloun.

'And what does our vaunted governor do about this crisis?' demanded Taloun.

Heated shouts of 'nothing' and other, less savoury comments roared from the assembly as Taloun continued. 'There is not one amongst us that does not suffer under her financially oppressive regime. My own cartel groans under the weight of Governor Shonai's tithe tax as I know others do too. Brother de Valtos, you yourself were attacked by these despicable alien raiders who plague us so, and tortured most horribly. And yet the governor does nothing!

'Sister Vergen, your own dearly beloved father was murdered a stone's throw from where we sit. And yet the governor does nothing! Brother Abrogas, your own blood relative was nearly murdered on the streets of his hometown. And yet the governor does nothing!'

Solana Vergen was too startled by Taloun's acknowledgement of her loss to respond in a suitably grief-stricken manner, while Beauchamp Abrogas did not even register that he had been named.

'Our world is under siege, my friends. The vultures gather to pick our carcass clean. And yet the governor does nothing!'

Thunderous applause greeted Taloun's words and Uriel could see the governor's two advisors practically holding her down as Taloun turned to address the moderator of transactions directly. The chamber suddenly fell deathly silent as the assembly waited for what Taloun would say next.

'Moderator,' he announced formally, 'I table a motion that the senate cast a vote of no confidence in Governor Shonai and remove her from office!'

SEVEN

MAGOS DAL KOLURST, tech-priest of the Tembra Ridge deep-bore mine, checked the map on his data slate for the third time to make sure he was in the right place. The glow of the display threw his face into stark relief and cast a flickering green halo around him in the darkness of the mine. He glanced above him, checking that the line of glow-globes and electrical cable was intact and connected to the power transformer. He leaned closer to the transformer, hearing the reassuring hum that told him it was operational.

Yes, everything seemed to be in order. The proper obeisance had been made to the Omnissiah and he had checked that all the correct cabling was connected.

So why was he standing alone in the sweltering darkness of the mine, with only the glow of a data slate and his shoulder lamp to illuminate his surroundings?

He checked the map one more time, just to make sure he was in the right place. Shaft secundus, tunnel seventy-two, junction thirty-six. Kolurst knew he was in the right place, and couldn't understand why there was no light here, when everything told him this part of the mine workings should be lit up as bright as day.

He sighed as he realised he would have to request another generator, knowing that Overseer Lasko wasn't going to like that, what with times being so hard and the cartel clamping down on costs. It was the third generator they'd gone through in as many weeks and Kolurst just couldn't understand what was going wrong with them. He and his fellow tech-priests had hooked up each one correctly, blessing them with the Prayer to the Omnissiah and striking the rune of activation upon their surface. Each generator would be fine for a few days, maybe a week until the same thing kept happening.

One by one the transformers would stop feeding power to the glow-globes and from the depths upwards, the mine would slowly revert to darkness. Kolurst had checked each transformer again and again and found the same thing. They were supplying power, but none of it was being routed where it was required. The power was there, but where was it going?

Kolurst jumped as he heard a soft, rustling noise behind him.

He spun, directing his lamp where the sound had come from.

There was nothing there, just a soft susurration of sand hissing from a crack in the wall. Kolurst released the breath he'd been holding and wiped the sweat from his brow. He turned back to the transformer and shook his head. He began to–

There it was again. Kolurst shone his lamp into the darkness. He panned the beam back and forth, jerking it quickly as he caught a flash of movement at the edge of the light.

Something gleaming skittered out of sight round a bend in the tunnel.

'Hello?' he called, fighting to keep the tremor from his voice. 'Is someone there?'

There was no answer, but he hadn't really expected one.

Slowly, he edged towards the turn, craning his lamp further and further into the darkness. He heard a soft tapping, as of thin metal rods clicking together.

He jumped as his data slate crackled, and he closed his eyes, fighting for calm. He was letting the foolish stories the mineworkers were telling get to him. Their stupid superstitions had spooked him and he tried to dismiss them as the delusions of overactive imaginations.

That was all very well on the surface, but here, ten thousand metres below ground, it was a very different matter indeed.

Sweat trickled from his brow and dripped from his nose. It was nothing, just some…

Some what?

He glanced at the slate and gave it a perturbed tap as the display began to fade. Soon the display was dead and he cursed the ill-fate that had seen him assigned to this wretched place rather than one of the cartels' manufactorum.

The sound came again and he shivered, despite the dry heat of the deep mine. He slowly backed away in the direction of the elevator shaft as the skittering noise began growing in volume.

He swallowed hard. His heart was beating a desperate tattoo on his ribs.

The shoulder lamp flickered, its weak glow fading.

Suddenly, Kolurst could see movement at the edge of its beam, dozens of tiny, glittering reflections carpeting the floor of the mine. He took another step backwards.

And the movement followed him.

Abruptly, the light from his lamp failed completely, plunging him into utter darkness.

Magos Dal Kolurst whimpered in terror and turned to run.

But they had him before he managed more than two paces.

EIGHT

THE SENATE CHAMBER erupted. Many had expected Taloun's words, but to hear them said so baldly was still a shock. A hundred voices all shouted at once and Uriel noticed that the governor sat calm and immobile, as though a long-feared event had finally transpired.

Taloun stood silently in the centre of the floor, the speaker's staff held before him like a weapon. The moderator shouted for calm as bailiffs moved through the crowd, quieting the more vocal members of the upper tiers with sharp blows from their cudgels.

Taloun raised his hands in a mute appeal for quiet and slowly the shouts of approval and denial died away, to be replaced by an excited buzz. He tapped the staff on the floor and asked, 'Who amongst the heads of the families will second my motion?'

Kasimir de Valtos rose from his seat with a feral grin of vindication and rested his pale hands on the railing. Uriel noticed that these too were the mottled white of artificial skin and he saluted the man's courage at having escaped his alien torturers.

'I, Kasimir de Valtos, will second the honourable Taloun's motion.'

Taloun bowed deeply. 'My thanks, Guilder de Valtos.'

Jeers and boos came from the tiers behind the governor.

The moderator retrieved his staff and waved it above his head as Taloun made his way back to his seat. He rapped his staff sharply on the floor.

'A motion of no confidence has been tabled and seconded by two members. To decide whether such a vote shall indeed be cast, I ask the heads of the cartels to indicate their support or otherwise for this motion.'

The moderator moved to his chair of office and pulled on a long velvet rope, exposing a large display slate behind a wide curtain on the rear wall of the chamber.

'This should be interesting,' whispered Barzano. 'Now we'll see who's in bed with who.'

Slowly at first, the icons of the family cartels began appearing on the slate.

Barzano nudged Perjed, who began copying the votes onto his own slate. De Valtos and Taloun's icons were, unsurprisingly, the first to appear in favour of the vote with Shonai's vote against the motion following closely. The Honan icon appeared next to Taloun's to mocking laughter from the upper tiers.

A gasp of surprise echoed around the chamber as the Vergen icon flashed up in favour of the vote. As the icon appeared, the men behind Solana Vergen desperately began waving towards their cartel's scion and shouting at her to listen to reason.

'My, my,' breathed Perjed. 'Now there's an upset.'

'In what way?' asked Barzano.

'Well, the Vergen have been allies of the Shonai for nearly ten years ever since they allied to win the election from the Taloun. Leotas Vergen and Governor Shonai were rumoured to be very good friends indeed, if you take my meaning. It seems that Leotas Vergen's daughter does not intend that friendship to continue.'

Governor Shonai stared with undisguised anger at the smug, smiling face of Solana Vergen, her fury clear for all to see.

A wadded up agenda smacked the top of Beauchamp Abrogas's head and he sat up suddenly, pressing a button at random on his voting panel. The Abrogas icon appeared beside the governor's and its members let out a collective sigh of exasperation in the foolishness of their leader.

With the votes of the major players cast, the smaller cartel heads began allocating their votes, having seen which way the political wind was blowing. Eventually all the votes were cast and the result was clear. The Shonai cartel had lost.

Lortuen Perjed nodded as he entered the last cartel's vote into his slate.

'The governor has lost this round and the matter will now be thrown open to a full vote of the entire senate, though this will largely be a formality since I doubt any of the cartel members will vote against their commercial masters.'

'So the planetary governor has been overthrown. Just like that?' asked Uriel.

'Not quite,' grinned Barzano, rising from his seat.

'What are you doing?' demanded Lortuen Perjed.

'I'm going to stretch my legalistic muscles. Uriel, come with me.'

Perjed gripped Barzano's robe and hissed, 'This is hardly fitting behaviour for an adept of the Administratum.'

'Exactly,' smiled Barzano with the glint of mischief in his eyes.

URIEL FOLLOWED ADEPT Barzano down the last few steps to the chequered chamber floor, easily lifting aside a startled bailiff who blocked their way. Barzano pushed open the wooden swing gate and strode into the centre of the chamber. An astonished hush descended on the chamber at his audacity and the sheer physical presence of an Imperial Space Marine. The Moderator of Transactions stood incredulous below the voting slate, his face red with fury.

His annoyance at having the normal order of business disrupted overcame his common sense and he advanced on Barzano, spluttering in indignation.

'This is completely out of order, sir! You cannot flout the regulations that govern our lawful assemblage in this manner.'

'Oh, I think I can,' smiled Barzano, pulling the red seal of the Administratum from his robes and holding it above his head for the chamber to see. Uriel kept a wary eye on the senate bailiffs, though none appeared willing to rise to the defence of the senate's regulations.

Barzano placed the seal back in his robes and addressed the assembly of Pavonis.

'Good day to you all. My name is Ario Barzano and I come here in the name of the Divine Emperor of Mankind. It is my task to set this world back on the path of righteousness, to stamp out the corruption and troubles that plague your world. I come with the highest authority and the strength to enforce the Administratum's will.'

Uriel could not help but notice worried glances passing between several of the cartel heads as the word 'corruption' was mentioned. Barzano swept his arms wide in a gesture that encompassed the entire senate chamber.

'Consider this vote on hold, gentlemen. And ladies,' added Barzano with a nod to Solana Vergen, who fluttered her eyelashes at the adept. Angry voices were raised, but died away as Barzano stood beside Uriel's armoured bulk.

'Now if you will excuse me, my learned friends, the governor of Pavonis and I have a great many things to discuss. Good day to you all.'

Barzano bowed deeply and indicated that Lortuen Perjed should join him on the floor. The old man shuffled out to meet Barzano and Uriel, his face a deep red. As he reached them, he gripped Barzano's arm and whispered, 'That was entirely inappropriate.'

'I know,' answered Barzano, pulling free of Perjed's grasp and marching over to the governor's seats.

Mykola Shonai sat dumbfounded at this unexpected development and numbly rose to her feet as Barzano approached.

'You have my thanks, Adept Barzano. I had not expected you until later this evening.'

Barzano winked and leaned in close to the governor, 'I like to make an entrance, Governor Shonai, but don't thank me yet, this is not a reprieve. It is merely a stay of what may still inevitably happen.'

Governor Shonai nodded, understanding the distinction, but grateful for the lifeline nonetheless.

'I thank you anyway.'

'Now, before your Moderator of Transactions has an apoplectic fit, I suggest we all retire to somewhere a little less public?'

'Agreed.'

ARIO BARZANO AND Lortuen Perjed sat in the governor's chambers while Uriel stood at ease behind them. Governor Shonai sat behind her desk with Almerz Chanda and Leland Corteo either side of her. Smoke from Corteo's pipe layered below the ceiling, circulated by a leisurely spinning fan.

'I have to say, adept,' began Mykola Shonai, 'that I had not expected you to allow me to remain in office.'

'I still may not, Governor Shonai, 'that decision remains to be taken.'

'Then why did you not just allow me to fall to Taloun's vote?'

Almerz Chanda leaned forwards. 'Surely, governor, it is enough for now that the adept did not?'

'No, Almerz, it is not. Well, adept? Why?'

'I liked the look of you, and I could tell Uriel did too,' explained Barzano. Uriel had not thought he had been so obvious in his appraisal of the governor and his respect for Barzano's powers of perception raised a notch.

'Besides, my dear lady, from what I could see of the other potential candidates, you appeared to be the least, how shall I say...?'

'Slimy, deceitful and untrustworthy?' she suggested.

Barzano laughed. 'Yes, something like that. But on a more serious note, we dislike upsetting the stability of a world too much if we can at all avoid it. Replacing you at this juncture would have achieved little of value.'

'So in other words, this may only be a temporary arrangement?'

'Exactly. I will be blunt, governor. You have failed in your duties as an Imperial commander. The tithes that are the right and proper duty of the Emperor have not been forthcoming and your inability to maintain the peace on this world has resulted in my despatch to rectify the situation.'

'It is certainly true that we have been having our fair share of problems, but past circumstances have–'

'Past circumstances do not interest me, Governor Shonai,' snapped Barzano and Uriel was surprised at the vicious tone that edged his words. Perjed appeared concerned also and leaned forward in his seat as Barzano continued.

'What does interest me, however, is your lack of progress in eliminating this Church of Ancient Ways, an organisation that sounds dangerously like a cult to my way of thinking. What also interests me is the inability of your system defence ships to hunt down the eldar raiders that attacked our ship and caused the deaths of a great many servants of the Emperor. But what concerns me most of all is the fact that you did not feel it necessary to report any of this to the Imperium. An explanation of these circumstances would be most edifying.'

'What would you have me tell you, adept? The Adeptus Arbites and our own local security forces have tried to stamp out the Church of Ancient Ways, but they are like shadows and we can find no clue as to how they are being supplied with their weaponry,' snarled Shonai. 'As to the eldar raiders, our ships are ready to be mothballed; there is not one amongst them less than two thousand years old. How would you have us fight them?'

Barzano smiled as the governor finished her tirade and sat back in his chair, apparently satisfied with her answer.

Mykola Shonai placed her hands, palm down, on her desk. 'I admit it was… unwise not to have come forward sooner regarding our troubles, but I believed we could deal with them internally. If I am guilty of anything, it is that I placed too much faith in my own abilities to manage this crisis.'

'Yes,' agreed Barzano. 'But I do not believe your administration is quite beyond redemption. I propose that we put aside past mistakes for now and work to resolve the current situation as quickly as possible. You agree?'

'Of course,' said the governor quickly. 'What can I do to help?'

'The first stage in any operation is information gathering and to facilitate my researches, I shall need complete access to the data files you have in the palace logic engines and cogitators. And of course that includes all your own private files.'

'Outrageous!' stormed Almerz Chanda. 'You overstep your mark, sir!'

'Really? You have things in the files you would rather I not see, Mister Chanda? Records of bribes placed, illegal dealings with xenos and the like?' joked Barzano, though Uriel wondered how much of the question was in jest.

'Certainly not,' blustered Chanda. 'But it is a huge breach of protocol to have the governor's personal files rummaged through as though she were a common criminal.'

Mykola Shonai reached up and placed a soothing hand on Chanda's arm.

'It's alright, Almerz, I have nothing to hide. Adept, you shall have all that you require. What else do you need?'

'Since I do not particularly wish to be seen to be choosing sides amongst the cartels by accepting any offers of accommodation which I am sure will soon be forthcoming, I will require a suite of rooms in the palace for myself and my entourage. At present they are waiting at a landing platform on the edge of the city. I would appreciate it if you could send word to them along with adequate transport to convey them and my effects to the palace.'

'It shall be done at once,' assured the governor, nodding to Chanda. He bristled at such a menial task, but bowed and left the room. 'Anything else?'

'Yes. As I will no doubt be dealing with the local security forces during my investigations I shall be requiring a liaison with the Adeptus Arbites. Contact them and have them assign me an officer.'

'They won't like that much,' noted Leland Corteo.

'I don't much care whether they like it or not, just make sure it happens.'

Leland Corteo flinched at Barzano's tone, but nodded and scratched an entry in his notebook.

'Right, that should take care of matters on the domestic front. Turning our attention to the question of the eldar raiders, I propose that the *Vae Victus* commence patrol operations in the local area as soon as possible. Uriel? I think it best if you appraise the governor of any assistance you will be requiring.'

Uriel snapped to attention and stepped forward. 'To be fully effective, we shall require complete annotated dossiers on every settlement raided and ship attacked, complete with crew manifests and payload records. Also, a system map recording the exact time and location of each attack. From this it will be possible to obtain a central locus of attacks and devise an efficient patrol circuit.'

'I shall see to it personally, Captain Ventris.'

Uriel nodded and stepped back.

'When can you begin patrol operations, Uriel?'

'The Tech-marines are ministering to the ship as we speak and as soon as the requested information is transferred to the *Vae Victus* we can begin.'

Barzano rubbed his chin thoughtfully. 'Excellent. I want you to return to the ship and hunt down these deviants. I cannot stress enough the importance I attach to this task, captain.'

'Return to the ship? Adept, I was entrusted with your personal safety and I gave my word to Lord Calgar that you would come to no harm.'

'And I shall not, for you shall leave me Sergeant Learchus's squad as a bodyguard. Unless you have any reservations regarding his ability to protect me?'

'Of course I have not, Learchus is a proven veteran of many campaigns. I trust him absolutely.'

'Then I share your trust also.'

Suddenly Uriel realised how cunningly Barzano had manoeuvred him. Learchus was a great warrior and would die before allowing the adept to come to any harm, and to relieve him of this duty would be to insult his honour. Uriel had sworn to Marneus Calgar that he would protect Barzano, but to remain with the adept would mean that his men would go into battle without their captain. Reluctantly, Uriel realised that as captain of the Fourth Company he had to be able to trust the officers appointed beneath him.

He bowed to Barzano. 'You have a fine bodyguard in Sergeant Learchus and his warriors. He comes from a family of honour and will not fail you.'

'And nor will you, I'm sure, Uriel.'

'Not while my body draws breath,' the Space Marine assured the adept.

ARIO BARZANO RUBBED his eyes and leaned back in his chair as he felt the onset of a splitting headache. His researches had been fruitful, but he was growing weary of the catalogue of betrayals, double crosses and plain, human unpleasantness he had unearthed in the last two days. He pushed himself away from the desk and poured himself a strong measure of uskavar, the local drink of choice on Pavonis.

The chambers the governor had allocated his entourage were dim, the candles having nearly burned down to rippled puddles of wax. He lit another batch as he sipped the strong liquor and pondered exactly how he was going to combat the Church of Ancient Ways. Mykola Shonai had not lied when she had said that they were like shadows. In fact clutching a shadow would be easy compared to learning the whereabouts of this group.

The sect had first appeared seven years ago when a massive explosion destroyed one of the Honan's manufactorum, the resulting fire ripping through the nearby supply depots and causing untold damage. It had been put down to poor safety controls until a coded communiqué had arrived at the governor's office denouncing the financial greed of Pavonis's rulers and vowing the continuance of the bombings.

Soon, every cartel had suffered at the hands of the terrorists and the security forces had been powerless to prevent the atrocities from continuing. Nearly four hundred people had died thus far and, while on a galactic scale, such numbers were inconsequential, Barzano knew that each life was a link in a chain that would one day unravel if he and his ilk could not prevent such acts.

The local security forces on Pavonis had had little success in apprehending the terrorists, and Barzano was not surprised. He had quickly realised that their organisation was a farce. Funded by the cartels, they were no more than private security groups who protected their paymasters' interests and maintained a policy of brutal discipline on the workers, but nothing else. The few, small Adeptus Arbites garrisons scattered across the planet could do little other than enforce the Emperor's laws in the heart of the cities. In the shantytowns and worker districts that surrounded the manufactorum, the only law was that decreed by the cartels.

And they were little better than criminals themselves from what Barzano could tell. A more devious nest of scheming vipers he had scarce encountered – outside his own organisation, he reflected with a wry grin. Each of the cartels had, at one point or another, allied with one other in return for short-term goals and profits, before reneging on their contracts and supporting yet another cartel. It appeared that this was a quite normal state of affairs and it depressed Barzano immensely to think that, as the forty-first millennium drew to a close, humanity still could not put aside its differences when virtually every alien race in the galaxy was bent on its destruction.

Across almost every system in the galaxy, orks slaughtered and pillaged their way at random, and he viciously suppressed his memories of the wartorn world of Armageddon. And this close to the eastern fringes, he knew it was only a matter of time until the expanding borders of the Tau Empire reached Pavonis.

Yes, the galaxy was a hostile place, and only united through stability could the Imperium of Man hope to survive. Any other course of action was folly of the worst kind and he had sworn an oath to ensure that its stability was preserved. What had the rulers of Pavonis done to preserve the sanctity of the Emperor's realm?

He returned to his chair and activated the display terminal. The corner of the display blinked with yet another message, but he ignored it, knowing it would be another invitation to sample the hospitality of one of the cartels. Invitations to dine, to hunt, to drink and partake in other, less savoury, pastimes had come in from the every one of the commercial houses. He had politely declined them all.

He scrolled down the information he had collated over the last two days.

Of the smaller cartels, he had found nothing more than the usual round of alliances, counter alliances and pact breaking. The leaders of the larger cartels were a much more interesting cast of rogues, however.

Beauchamp Abrogas spent his time destroying his central nervous system with illegal drugs and squandering his family's fortune.

Taryn Honan was a fat fool, who spent fabulous sums on courtesans and would have a hard time managing a room full of lobotomised servitors.

He didn't know much about Solana Vergen, but had sensed the falseness of her grief over the death of her father. And changing her cartel's vote so spectacularly in the senate chamber did not bode well for the stability of her personality.

De Valtos spent most of his time locked away at his estates or chasing after antiques scattered throughout the system. Even a blind man could see the hatred and bitterness he harboured towards the governor, though Barzano could find no direct cause for that rancour. That definitely warranted further investigation. There was also the tangible link between de Valtos and the dark eldar, but Barzano understood it was not the sort of link that would engender co-operation. He had been tortured almost unto death aboard the alien vessel and, despite all the odds against such an occurrence, survived.

Barzano had discounted Mykola Shonai at the start of his investigations. He had felt no deceit from her upon their meeting and, in any case, her second, six-year term as planetary governor was almost at an end and the constitution of Pavonis forbade her to serve a consecutive third. She had nothing to gain and everything to lose by prolonging the current state of affairs. Ario Barzano knew that this fact alone could not discount her from his suspicions; he had exposed traitors with far less motive than Shonai. But affairs such as these had been his daily bread for too many years now and he fancied that he had a talent for spotting a liar, and Mykola Shonai did not seem like one to him.

Truth be told, he admired the woman. She had tried her best for her world. But he knew that simply trying one's best was not good enough on its own. Effort had to be coupled with results and the results on Pavonis spoke for themselves.

But the Taloun...

That was a different story. Defeated twice in the elections by the combined power of the Shonai and Vergen cartels over the last ten years, Vendare Taloun had everything to gain. Whenever he approached problems such as these, he always began by asking the same question. Who has the most to gain? In the chaos of terrorist activities, alien pirates and political upheaval, Taloun's cartel stood out amongst all the others.

It had suffered less than the others in the bombings with the possible exception of the Shonai, and Barzano had long ago accepted the truth that there was no such thing as coincidence in this existence. The synchronicity of timing in the arrival of the eldar raiders and the emergence of the Church of Ancient Ways spoke of an orchestrating hand to him. Taloun had already displayed his cunning and Barzano knew that the serpentine paths of his mind were easily capable of devising such a scheme.

He pushed himself away from the terminal and finished his glass. He had an early start tomorrow and wondered what else he might uncover. He had told his Adeptus Arbites liaison to dress in civilian clothes and suddenly wondered if she actually owned such things. She looked like the kind of person who lived for her calling and he smiled, realising that they were very much alike then.

Barzano heard the low voices of his Ultramarine bodyguards outside his chambers and spared a thought for Uriel Ventris. It was unfortunate that he could not tell Uriel the truth, but Barzano knew that if he had done so, he might very well have had a problem with the Space Marine captain.

He looked over to the secure safe in the wall, hidden behind the portrait of a man called Forlanus Shonai, where he had secreted the box.

He fought the urge to open it and examine the thing it contained.

For the sake of the Pavonis he prayed that he would not need to.

URIEL COULD SEE that it irked Lord Admiral Tiberius to have a system pilot aboard his vessel, but knew the admiral was canny enough to accept its necessity. The quickest route Uriel and Tiberius had plotted towards Caernus IV, site of the most recent eldar attack, took them directly through a wide asteroid belt and, without local knowledge of the safe routes through, they would surely come to grief.

Six tense hours had passed with the pilot expertly guiding them through the maze of enormous asteroids and Uriel prayed to the Emperor, Guilliman and all the saints that they would be through soon.

The system map provided by Governor Shonai had proved to be extremely useful, marking the location of every attack of the eldar raiders. Uriel had not appreciated the scale of the raids until he had seen the map; just over a hundred attacks in just six years. Almost every attack had seen a settlement utterly destroyed or a vessel crippled and its crew slaughtered. Uriel's admiration for Kasimir de Valtos had grown as he contemplated the courage and determination it must have taken for him to engineer his escape from these despicable aliens.

'Helm control, come right to heading zero-two-five, thirty degrees down angle,' called the system pilot. 'Come on, my beauty, we can fit you through there.'

Uriel glanced up from the plotting table in surveyor control towards the viewing bay and blanched as he saw the gap in the gently spinning asteroids the pilot was aiming for. He held his breath, watching as the two giant rocks, each bigger than the *Vae Victus* by several million tonnes, slid past the ship. Uriel saw Tiberius gripping the edge of the captain's pulpit tightly, his knuckles white and his face lined with worry. He had only reluctantly allowed a pilot with local knowledge to direct his ship, but had drawn the line at allowing him to do so from his pulpit.

'Do you have to fly so close to these damned rocks?' snapped Tiberius, his patience with the pilot finally fraying. 'If you even graze one of them, we'll all be sucking vacuum.'

The pilot, a native of the Altemaxa forges by the name of Krivorn grinned, exposing yellowed stumps of teeth.

'This?' he scoffed. 'Ha! I'm takin' it easy on you boys. This is the easy route. I coulda taken you along Derelicts' Alley. Then you would've seen some flying.'

'Derelicts' Alley?' quizzed Uriel. 'That's not marked on this chart of yours.'

'Nah,' agreed Krivorn. 'It's just a name I came up with after I nearly lost a ship there once.'

'You nearly lost a ship!' exploded Tiberius.

'Yeah, weren't my fault though,' protested Krivorn. 'We was flyin' along, happy as an ork in fungus, when all of a sudden this damn great hulk appears outa nowhere! I swear, one minute it weren't there, the next, we're losing power and hauling hard to starboard on full reverse.'

'I expect you made a navigational error, pilot.'

'Me? No, my lord, I checked the surveyors not a second before and it weren't there. Helm control come to new heading three-two-four, ten degrees up angle.'

'So what was it?' asked Uriel, unnerved by Krivorn's lackadaisical helm directions.

'Never did find out, but I reckon it was one of them space hulks you always hear about,' replied Krivorn. 'And I ain't the first to have seen it, neither. Lot of space-farers say they seen it around the Pavonis system. They calls it the half-moon ship on account of its shape. Helm control come to new heading zero-zero-zero, all ahead level.'

Uriel knew of such derelict vessels, wrecks lost in the warp, destined to become ghost ships, forever plying the icy depths of space.

No one could predict their movements and their appearances were completely at random, as capricious fate vomited them from the immaterium. The thought that there might be such a ship in the vicinity filled Uriel with nothing but loathing.

'Look, enough of this damn nonsense,' said Tiberius. 'How long until we are through this asteroid belt and reach Caernus IV?'

Krivorn smiled his gap toothed grin and bowed deeply to Tiberius. 'We just came through the belt, my lord. At current speed and heading, we'll be in orbit around the planet in roughly an hour. And you're welcome.'

KASIMIR DE VALTOS felt his guts contract again and vomited a froth of viscous, blood-flecked matter into the bowl of the commode. Sweat beaded his brow and painful cramps locked his belly in their powerful grip. His vision blurred as another surge of black vomit burned along his throat and into the pan.

Those damned aliens. Every day his body rebelled against the foul toxins with which they had poisoned him. Only daily infusions of intense purgatives kept the most debilitating effects at bay and even then it was only marginally less painful.

He hauled himself up from the floor of his ablutions cubicle and pulled his bathrobe tightly about his slender frame. He splashed water onto his face as the last of the wracking spasms faded. De Valtos swilled ice-cold water around his mouth in a futile attempt to clear away the acidic taste and dried himself with a silk towel. He ran an ivory comb through his albino white hair.

He stared into the mirror and wondered how his life had taken such a turn. The answer came easily enough. It had begun the day his expedition had discovered the caverns beneath the ruined city on Cthelmax and the inscriptions of the heretic abbot, Corteswain. If only he had not translated the inscription there. If only he had not followed their dire words of prophecy.

If only he had not encountered the eldar.

But follow them he had, and this was what it had led him to. He raised a pallid, blotched hand to his face and prodded the nerveless synth-flesh that covered his skull, knowing that he touched his face only by the reflection before him. Once, he had been considered handsome and had courted the finest beauties of Pavonis, but no longer. The white-hot blade of an alien torturer had seen to that.

He had considered suicide many times after his encounter with the eldar, but had lacked even the courage for that. The lure of Corteswain's words had too firm a hold on his soul and de Valtos realised that hope was indeed the greatest curse of humankind.

Why else would he continue down this path if not for hope?

De Valtos tossed aside the towel and stepped into his private bedchamber. The room was mirrorless and spartanly decorated, with none of the finery many would have associated with the leader of such a wealthy cartel. He removed his robe and strolled naked into his walk-in dresser, selecting his favourite midnight blue suit, the one with the narrow lapels and high collar. He donned the suit, the scar tissue the eldar torturer had gifted him pulling painfully tight across his chest and arms. His guest would be arriving soon and he did not want to be late.

No matter that he despised him and every petty small-minded thing he believed in.

No matter that scant years ago he had believed those same things himself.

Times had changed since then and his responsibilities had grown far beyond profit and loss, production and labour. He selected the black, carnodon-skin shoes to wear with his suit and sat on the end of his bloodstained bed as he slipped them on his feet and straightened his suit coat.

He heard the chime from the vestibule and knew that his guest had arrived. Right on time as usual. Fully dressed, de Valtos moved to the head of his bed and gathered up the bloody knives that lay scattered about the mutilated human carcass on the mattress, careful to avoid the sticky pools of blood that had collected.

He placed his items of torture in a black, leather case and slid them under the bed, feeling the familiar sense of disappointment as he stared at the corpse. This one had not even come close to satisfying his urges and he knew he would soon need to procure another fleshy canvas on which to exorcise his demons.

He pictured Solana Vergen on the bed and his heart raced with eagerness.

De Valtos turned on his heel and exited his chambers, descending the wide marble staircase to the vestibule and his guest.

He saw him below, nervously shuffling from foot to foot.

Almerz Chanda looked up at the sound of de Valtos's footsteps.

Kasimir de Valtos smiled.

* * *

JENNA SHARBEN FELT acutely uncomfortable out of her judge's uniform and wished for the hundredth time that Virgil Ortega had not assigned her to baby-sit this infernal adept. She wore a functional, close-fitting blue tunic with loose sleeves and an internal holster, where an autopistol nestled under her left armpit. She stood at parade rest in the adept's chambers and examined his quarters.

She prided herself that she could tell a lot about a person by the way they lived: their tastes, their likes and dislikes, whether they were a stickler for order or whether they liked to live in a constant state of disarray.

Her brow creased at what the varied signals the man's quarters were telling her. A dozen books stacked on the desk were arranged in alphabetical order though they had clearly not been part of the room's furniture, yet a pile of clothing lay untidily pooled on top of the bedcovers. A gunmetal grey footlocker had been placed at the bed's foot, securely locked by a geno-keyslot, while on the desk was an open journal with all the adept's hand-written notes. A half drunk decanter of uskavar sat next to the journal, alongside a crystal glass containing last night's dregs.

What kind of man was this adept?

'Seen enough?' asked a voice from the far end of the room and she started, her hand involuntarily reaching for her gun. A man in stained overalls, in the red of the Taloun cartel, slouched against the wall, chewing on a piece of tobacco. He was unshaven and rough looking, with three days' worth of growth on his round chin.

Jenna opened her mouth to ask the man his business here when she suddenly realised that it was the adept she had introduced herself to the previous evening. The change was quite remarkable.

'I have now,' she said, as the adept ambled towards her.

Barzano smiled. 'Today I am going to be Gulyan Korda, technician secundus, Smeltery three-six-two of the Taloun. What do you think?'

Jenna was speechless. Had she not known differently, she would have sworn the adept was a native of Pavonis. He had the accent, the clothes and the same apathetic slouch the manufactorum workers effected. His hair had been slicked back and she could see that his cheeks were now fuller.

As though reading her mind, Barzano withdrew two wads of cheek padding and winked before replacing them in his mouth. 'You think I'd pass for a local?'

'Without a doubt,' assured Jenna. 'Though why would you want to?'

'Well, I hardly think that given the local climate of unrest and the unpopularity of the current administration, anyone is going to open up to an off-worlder, let alone one from the Administratum. Do you?'

Jenna could see he had a point, then suddenly his insistence on her wearing civilian clothes made sense to her. He wanted to go outside and mingle with the workers. And she was to be, what – a bodyguard, a guide? Both?

'Just what are you planning, Adept Barzano?'

'Oh, just a little jaunt into the worker areas outside the city walls. Nothing too strenuous, I promise.'

Barzano indicated the books and data terminal. 'It's all very well getting information from these, but I always think that you get the best raw data from the ground up. Don't you? Yes, today Gulyan Korda, recently dismissed from the service of the Taloun, will be mingling with similarly minded malcontents and discussing the terrible state of affairs the governor has led us to.'

'And what will be my purpose there?'

'You, my dear, are my bodyguard,' whispered Barzano, obviously enjoying this new role immensely. 'You see when Gulyan left the employ of the Taloun, he took some rather incriminating records with him.'

'He did?'

'I think so. Yes, in fact I'm almost certain he did.'

'And what would that incriminating information concern?'

'Haven't a clue,' chuckled Barzano. 'Something juicy though, I'm sure.'

'What about the Space Marines outside? You're not going to be able to pass unnoticed with two armoured giants following you about everywhere.'

'Oh I know that, but they're not coming.'

'And how are you going to get out of the palace without them?'

'Simple, they won't see me,' promised Barzano. 'They'll see you and a rather disreputable looking fellow in overalls heading outside and believe that the slugabed adept is still within. Believe me, it's easier than you think.'

Jenna Sharben shook her head.

'I really don't think that this is such a good idea,' she said.

NINE

URIEL STARED AT the scorched human wreckage lying on the small cot bed and wondered how, in the name of all that was holy, this man could still be alive. The instant he had laid eyes upon the poor, tormented soul, he had called for the company apothecary to minister to the young man. The physician of this settlement had done what he could, but his skills were no match for the horrendous damage done to his body.

Apothecary Selenus gently lifted the man's leg, unwrapping bandages soiled with seeping blood and pus, and applied soothing balms to the scraps of seared flesh that still clung to his wasted frame. The apothecary worked by the light of a dozen sputtering candles and the sickening stench of atrophied, burned meat filled the room with choking pungency.

Caernus IV was the site of the most recent attack by the eldar raiders and information provided by the governor had indicated that one person had survived the butchery.

Looking at the man, whom the town's alderman had called Gedrik, Uriel felt nothing but pity at his survival.

They had come to this world to glean information from a living eyewitness, and Uriel had a strange sense that it was vitally important he talk to Gedrik.

Sergeant Pasanius leaned close to Uriel and whispered, 'Will he live much longer, do you think?'

Uriel shook his head. 'Selenus says not, but this one is a fighter. By rights he should be dead already. Something has kept him alive.'

'Like what?'

'I do not know, Pasanius, but the town's alderman tells me that he would not allow their physician to grant him the Emperor's Peace. He kept saying that he was waiting for the angels. That he had a gift for them.'

'What does that mean?' scoffed Pasanius. 'The pain must have made him delusional.'

'No,' whispered Uriel. 'I believe he was waiting for us.'

'For us? How could he know we would be coming?'

Uriel shrugged. 'It is said that those who feel death's touch yet live are sometimes granted visions and wondrous powers by the Emperor. His survival is a miracle and perhaps that is reason enough to believe it.'

Pasanius looked unconvinced. 'I always said living underground on Calth all these years couldn't be good for you, captain. You really think that just because this poor wretch is not dead means that he was touched by the Emperor himself?'

'Perhaps, I don't know. They say the blessed Saint Capilene lived for three days after the bullet that killed her entered her heart, that the Emperor would not allow her to fall until she had led the troops to victory against the Chaos-scum on the shrine world that now bears her name. I can't give you a sound explanation, my friend, but my gut tells me that something has kept him alive for a reason. I can't explain it, I just have a feeling.'

'Now you are starting to sound like Idaeus,' grumbled Pasanius. 'I always knew that when he had "one of his feelings" it meant we were heading for some real trouble.'

Apothecary Selenus rose from the bed and bowed to Uriel. 'Brother-captain, there is no more to be done for him. I have applied unguents that will prevent evil vapours from infecting the wound and dressed them as best I can, but it is wasted effort. He will die soon. Nothing now can prevent that.'

'You have done all that you can, brother,' said Uriel. As Selenus moved past Uriel, he placed his hand upon the apothecary's shoulder guard and said, 'Remember, Selenus, helping those in need is never wasted effort. Rejoin the men; I would speak with the boy now. I believe he has waited for us and that he has a message for me.'

Selenus nodded. 'As you wish, brother-captain.'

The apothecary ducked his head below the lintel and left the stinking room. Uriel and Pasanius approached the bed and knelt by the Gedrik's head.

Uriel removed his helmet, setting it on the tiled floor, and ran a hand across his scalp. He leaned in close to Gedrik, trying not to breathe in the awful scent of cooked human meat.

The young man's eyes fluttered as he felt Uriel's nearness and his chest heaved, drawing in a great sucking breath.

Gedrik's head lolled towards Uriel. His cracked and swollen lips leaked a clear fluid as he formed his words.

'I knew you would come,' he hissed, the words barely audible.

'Yes, we came. I am Uriel Ventris of the Ultramarines.'

Gedrik nodded, a weeping smile creasing his lips. 'Yes. I saw you when I stared into the night yet to come.'

'You saw me?' asked Uriel, throwing a puzzled glance towards Pasanius.

The practical-minded sergeant merely shrugged, his disbelief plain.

'Yes – you and the Death of Worlds. Light and Dark, two avatars of the same angel.'

Uriel struggled to make sense of the man's words. Death of Worlds, Light and Dark?

Was Pasanius right? Had the boy been driven insane by the things he had seen and the pain he had endured?

'Do you know why you were attacked?' pressed Uriel. 'Can you tell me anything about who did this to you?'

'They came for the metal... The machine man ripped out its heart and now it dies.'

Uriel was mystified. Caernus IV was an agri-world. According to the Segmentum records, there were no metal deposits worth mining here. Certainly none worth slaughtering an entire community for.

'I don't understand, Gedrik. What machine man? A cyborg? A servitor? What metal?'

'The metal that flows. It dies now. My sword... I forged it myself. Now it dies.'

Pasanius lifted a leather scabbard from beside the bed and gripped the wire-wound hilt of the weapon. He pulled a rusted sword from the scabbard and held it close to the candlelight.

Uriel and Pasanius shared an amazed look as they beheld the blade of the sword. Its outline exuded a faint bluish radiance, dimly illuminating the room's interior. Only the very edges of the blade remained silver, for a throbbing vein of leprous brown buried in the heart of the sword pulsed with a loathsome necrotic life. Worm-like tendrils of blackness infested the translucent metal and Uriel could see them slowly spreading throughout the weapon. He ran his gauntlet across the flat of the blade and flakes of dead metal fluttered to the floor.

'Gedrik, what is happening to the sword?'

'It dies. The white-hair and the machine man came and killed the Hill of the Metal, and now it all dies. They killed Maeren and Rouari,' wept Gedrik. 'I don't know why – we would have shared it.'

'The white-hair? Did he come with the machine man?'

'Yes. The machine man, the priest of machines.'

Uriel and Pasanius reached the same conclusion together. A priest of machines could mean only one thing. But an adept of the Machine God, a tech-priest of the Adeptus Mechanicus working with aliens? The very thought was preposterous.

'He can't mean–' began Pasanius.

'No, surely not,' agreed Uriel. 'Gedrik, I think you may have been mistaken.'

'No!' hissed Gedrik, shaking his head feebly on the stained pillow. 'The angel you serve bade me pass on these words. The Death of Worlds and the Bringer of Darkness await to be born into this galaxy. One will arise or neither, the choice is in your hands.'

'What does that mean? Did the... angel tell you what it means? Please, Gedrik.'

Gedrik sighed and his breath rasped in his throat like a dead thing. His head rolled back on limp tendons.

He whispered, 'Please, bring a priest. I want to make confession...'

Uriel nodded and said, 'Sergeant Pasanius. Fetch Chaplain Clausel, a servant of the Emperor awaits his ministrations.'

The sergeant bowed and left the death room as Uriel sat with the dying man. His mind was reeling with the possibility of a priest of the Machine God working alongside the eldar. Who could have imagined such a thing? And the Death of Worlds, the Bringer of Darkness. What were they?

Uriel heard the massive footfalls of Chaplain Clausel and turned to face the scarred warrior-priest.

'He has served the Emperor well, brother-chaplain. Hear his confession and, if he so desires, administer the Finis Rerum. I shall await you outside.'

'It shall be done, my captain.'

Uriel gazed into the death mask of bandages that was all that remained of the young man's face and snapped to attention, slamming his fist into his breastplate.

'Gedrik of Morten's Reach, I salute your bravery. The Emperor be with you.'

Uriel about turned, ducked through the doorway and left the building.

Pasanius and thirty warriors of the Ultramarines awaited him in the centre of the settlement. Beyond the edge of the settlement, Uriel could see the boxy form of their Thunderhawk gunship. Clusters of frightened townspeople watched from the township's edge.

Pasanius had collected his flamer, its bulk slung across his back, and now marched towards him.

'We're ready to move out, captain. Just give the word.'

'Very good, sergeant.'

'Can I ask you something, captain?'

'Of course, Pasanius.'

'Did you believe him? About the angel, I mean?'

Uriel did not answer Pasanius immediately. He stared into the mountains surrounding the settlement. They soared into the clouds; the achievements of mankind insignificant beside their majesty. It was said that a man's life was a spark in the darkness, and that by the time he was noticed, he had vanished, replaced by brighter and more numerous sparks.

Uriel did not accept that. There were men and women who stood against the darkness, bright spots of light that stood in defiance of the inconceivable vastness of the universe. That they would ultimately die was irrelevant.

It was that they stood at all which mattered.

'Did I believe him?' repeated Uriel. 'Yes, I did. I don't know why, but I did.'

'Another feeling?' groaned Pasanius.

'Aye.'

'What do you think he meant? The Death of Worlds and Bringer of Darkness? I do not like such concepts. They cannot bode well for the days to come.'

'Who knows? Perhaps Adept Barzano can shed more light on the subject when we return to Pavonis.'

'Perhaps,' grunted Pasanius.

'You do not like him?'

'It is not for me to criticise an adept of the Administratum,' replied Pasanius stiffly. 'But he is not like any quill-pusher I have ever met.'

The black-armoured form of Chaplain Clausel emerged from the town's small infirmary and rejoined the captain of Fourth Company.

'It is done, my captain. His soul is with the Emperor now.'

'My thanks, chaplain.'

Clausel bowed and moved to stand beside the rest of the men.

'What are your orders, captain?' asked Pasanius.

Uriel looked back at the infirmary and said, 'Fetch the boy, sergeant. We leave for Morten's Reach and will bury him with honour in his home.'

'I STILL CAN'T believe it, Kasimir. She should be out on her ear and I should be sitting in the palace,' fumed Vendare Taloun. 'All those years of negotiation with the smaller cartels wasted. Wasted!'

Kasimir de Valtos handed his fellow cartel head a crystal glass of uskavar and sat across from him in the wood-panelled drawing room of his estate house in the Owsen Hills. Taloun took the glass without looking up and continued to stare into the roaring fire in the marble hearth.

'She'll be gone soon enough, Vendare. She cannot hold on forever.'

'The bitch should be gone *now!*' roared Taloun hurling his glass into the fire, where it exploded into shards. 'Emperor damn her soul. We were so close. What does it take to get rid of her? We had every one of the smaller cartels in our pocket and even allowing for that buffoon Abrogas we still had a clear majority.'

'Well, if she won't fall, she can be pushed,' offered de Valtos.

'What are you talking about? We got a vote against her, but that damn Barzano pulled the rug from under our feet. Damn him, but I thought him to be a foppish numskull.'

'The adept is not a problem.'

'Really?'

'Indeed. Should he prove troublesome, we can dispose of him at our leisure.'

'Don't be foolish, Kasimir. You can't just kill an adept of the Imperium.'

'Why not?'

'Are you serious?'

'Deadly serious,' assured de Valtos. 'And in any case, who will miss him? He is merely one of millions of feather-licking scribes.'

'That Ultramarines captain might have something to say about his vanishing.'

'Do not concern yourself with him, my dear Taloun.'

'I am still not sure about this, Kasimir.'

'Is it any worse than what we plan for the Shonai cartel? Your tanks as well as my guns await in the mountains, Vendare.'

'That's completely different, Kasimir. We do that for the good of Pavonis.'

De Valtos laughed, a hollow, rasping sound, utterly devoid of humour. 'Don't play the innocent with me, Vendare Taloun. I know too much of your dealings. Your idiotic son has a loose tongue and his future wife has one even worse. She wags it in all the wrong places to all the wrong people.'

Taloun flushed and rose from his chair to pour himself a fresh glass of uskavar. His hands shook and the glass clinked as he poured a generous measure of the amber spirit from the decanter.

'Whatever you think you know is a lie,' he said finally.

'I believe you, Vendare,' soothed de Valtos, smiling at Taloun's back. 'But there are many people who would enjoy seeing the Taloun cartel, and especially you, fall. And you know how allegations can stick to a man's reputation, even though they may later be proved false. Just look at what happened when you allowed word to leak out about the Honan and his... liaisons.'

'But that was all true.'

'Admittedly, but my point is no less valid. It would be a shame if certain allegations regarding your brother's death were to enter the public domain. It would mean the termination of our arrangement as I could not be seen to be allying with a man guilty of fratricide.'

'Alright, dammit, Kasimir. You've made your point. So what do you intend?' asked Taloun, returning to his seat.

'Simple,' explained de Valtos. 'We proceed as planned.'

RAIN FELL IN an ever-increasing deluge as the mud-caked Thunderhawk passed low over the roofs of the destroyed township of Morten's Reach. The screaming engines threw up huge sprays of muddy water as the aerial transport touched down in the central square of the settlement, steam hissing from the hot exhausts.

Barely had the landing skids touched down before the engines rumbled throatily and the armoured doors slid back on oiled runners. Three squads of Ultramarines efficiently debarked and fanned out through the town. Two sprinted to the settlement's perimeter as the third, led by Uriel, moved towards the burnt out shell of a building that had obviously once been a temple.

Uriel swept his boltgun left and right. The rain cut visibility dramatically and even his power armour's auto-senses were having a hard time penetrating the greyness.

He could discern no movement or signs of life in the settlement and the evidence of his own sense told him that there had been nothing living in this place for many weeks.

'Sector Prime, clear!' came a shout over the vox-net.

'Sector Secundus, clear!'

'Sector Tertiarus, clear!'

Uriel lowered his weapon and slid it into the restraining clip on his thigh.

'All squad sergeants converge on me. Keep perimeters secure,' he ordered.

Seconds later, Uriel's sergeants, Venasus, Dardino and Pasanius, his flamer sputtering in the falling rain, gathered at the foot of the temple stairs.

'I want this place searched from end to end, house-to-house. Assume all locations are hostile and report in the moment you find anything.'

'What are we looking for, captain? Survivors or victims?' asked Venasus.

'Anything out of the ordinary. There may be some clue as to what the eldar are doing in this system. If there is, I want it found.'

Uriel indicated the weapon impacts on the blackened walls of the temple behind him. 'Servants of the Emperor died here and I want to know why.'

URIEL REMOVED HIS helmet and tipped his head back, allowing the rain to flow across his face, then spat a mouthful of water into the mud. He slicked his short, black hair back as examined the splintered remains of the temple doors, running his free hand across the burnt timber and impacts of small arms fire.

He slid out his combat knife and dug the point of the weapon into a small impact crater and worked the tip back and forth.

Something dropped from the wood into his hand and he lifted it closer to his face. His cupped palm swam with rainwater, but Uriel could clearly see a long splinter of jagged violet crystal. There were scores of these embedded in the wall and, from their grouping, Uriel could tell they had come from one shot.

The tactical briefings he had digested on the eldar had told that they favoured weaponry that fired a hail of monomolecular, razor-edged discs of metal. But there had been other weapons, described as belonging to a darker sub-sect of these aliens, which fired just this kind of ammunition.

Some texts codified this sub-sect as a divergent split of the eldar race, but to Uriel they were all the same: vile aliens that required cleansing in the holy fire of his bolter.

He levered aside the doors and entered the temple, fighting down his rising fury at such desecration. The stench of scorched human fat still clung to the burnt timbers and Uriel pushed his way through to the front of the church where a blackened statue of the divine Master of Mankind lay half buried under a smashed pew. He pulled the statue clear and, though it was heavy, lifted it from the rubble.

At the open rear of the temple he saw a muddy hillside with a number of simple grave markers hammered into the ground at its base. He splashed down from the temple, still carrying the statue, sinking calf deep in the mud. Uriel was saddened at the sheer number of graves. The people who had discovered and cared for Gedrik must have dug them for the people of Morten's Reach.

'Pasanius,' called Uriel over the vox-net. 'I am behind the temple. Bring me the boy's body from the gunship. He should be buried here with his people.'

'Acknowledged,' hissed the voice of the veteran sergeant.

Uriel rested the rescued statue before him and awaited Pasanius's arrival silently in the rain.

Sergeant Pasanius marched slowly around the temple carrying the bandage-swathed body of Gedrik, the green plaid of Caernus IV wrapped around his waist and his sword laid across his chest. An honour guard of Ultramarines followed the massive sergeant as he approached the mass grave.

Uriel nodded to his friend and turned to the warriors who stood behind him.

'Find a grave marked with the name Maeren. We will bury him with his woman.'

The Ultramarines fanned out through the rain, scanning the names on the wooden cross pieces on the grave markers and, after a few minutes' searching, found the grave of Gedrik's wife and child. An honour guard dug in the muddy earth until the body of the young man was finally laid to rest in the soil of his home.

Uriel marched through the graves to where the ground began to rise, intending to plant the statue of the Emperor into the soft earth to watch over His departed flock. He lifted the statue high above his head and rammed it down into the earth, where there was a dull, mud-deadened clang of stone on metal.

Uriel pulled the statue clear, laying it to one side as he dropped to his knees and scraped away the mud at his feet.

Perhaps half a metre down, the ground changed from soft, sucking mud to a wet, flaked metal. He cleared more of the mud away, revealing a rust pocked plate of metal.

'Sergeant!' he shouted. 'Get over here and bring your squad with you. I think we may have found the Hill of the Metal the boy spoke of.'

HALF AN HOUR later, the Ultramarines had cleared a vast swathe of the hillside of mud, and Uriel was amazed at the scale of what lay beneath. A strata of rusted metal lay beneath the hillside, its translucent depths awash with the same evil brown tendrils that had infested Gedrik's sword.

'Guilliman's blood!' swore Dardino when the hillside was revealed. 'What is it?'

'I have no idea,' answered Uriel. 'But whatever it is, the eldar obviously thought it was worth dying for.'

Uriel and Pasanius clambered up the slope towards a triangular depression in the centre of the otherwise flat surface of the metal. Metal crumbled beneath their armoured boots and each footfall was accompanied by squealing groans. The corrosion was converging upon the central point and Uriel knew that soon there would be nothing left. He and Pasanius squatted by the depression in the metal's surface.

The interior of the depression was lined with sockets and hanging wires that trailed into the depths of the metal.

The exact purpose of the niche was a mystery, but it had obviously contained something roughly cylindrical, which had been removed. Was this what had caused the metal to die? Ancient script surrounded the niche and Uriel traced the outline of the strange alien letters with his finger.

'Can you read it?' asked Pasanius.

'No, nor would I want to. These sigils are obviously alien in origin and their blasphemous meaning is best left undisclosed. But we should record them for those whose purpose is to delve into such mysteries.'

Uriel wiped the rusted metal and mud from his armour. 'Get a sample of this and we'll take it back to the *Vae Victus* with us. Perhaps the techs will be able to identify this substance and decipher this script.'

Uriel scooped a handful of mud and metal up in his hands, letting the ooze drip slowly from his fingers. 'I don't like it, Pasanius. Whenever xenos start acting out of character it worries me.'

'What do you mean? Out of character?'

'Well, look at this place. Every body is in its grave, perhaps two hundred people, enough to populate a settlement of this size, agreed?'

'Agreed.'

'And you checked the remains of the dwellings, was anything taken?'

'Hard to tell, but no, I don't think so. It looks like everything was burned to the ground rather than plundered.'

'Exactly my point. Why didn't they take prisoners? Have you ever known eldar raiders leave people behind when they could be taken for torture and slavery? No, these aliens came to this place for one thing only – whatever was in that metal.'

'And what do you think that was? A weapon of some kind? Maybe something of holy significance to them?'

'That's what worries me, old friend. I don't know and I can't even begin to guess either. I'm beginning to think that we may have more to deal with than a simple case of alien pirates.'

They returned to the foot of the hill and marched to the centre of the destroyed township. Rain fell in drenching sheets and Uriel welcomed it, allowing its cold bite to cleanse his skin of the evil sensation he had felt while standing at the hillside.

A piece of a puzzle lay before him, yet he could not fathom its meaning. The eldar obviously had good reason to risk Imperial retribution by attacking one of the Emperor's worlds, and he knew that these aliens would never undertake such action without good reason.

Before he could ponder the matter further, he was interrupted by a burst of static from the vox-net connection to the *Vae Victus*, and Uriel heard the excited tones of Lord Admiral Tiberius.

'Captain Ventris, return to the ship immediately. Repeat, return to the ship immediately.'

'Lord admiral, what is the matter? Has something happened?'

'Indeed it has. I have just received word that system defence ships encountered a vessel with an anomalous engine signature around the eighth planet some two hours ago and fired on it.'

'Somebody obviously listened to our warning then. Did they destroy the alien vessel?'

'No, I do not believe they actually hit her, but they have driven it in our direction. We are almost directly in its flight path, captain. The alien vessel cannot know we are here. We can spring our own ambush on these bastards.'

Uriel smiled, hearing the admiral's anticipation even over the distortion of a ship-to-shore vox-caster.

'How long before you can get back here, Uriel?'

'We can be ready to depart in less than a minute, Lord Admiral. Transmit the surveyor data to the Thunderhawk's avionics logister.'

'Hurry, Uriel. They are moving fast and we might not get another shot at this.'

'We shall be seeing you shortly. Ventris out.'

Uriel replaced his helmet and faced his warriors.

'The foe we have come to fight approach our position and we have a chance to avenge those who fell to their traitorous attack. Honour demands that we accept this challenge.'

Uriel drew his power sword and shouted, 'Are you ready for battle?'

As one, the warriors of Fourth Company roared their affirmation.

ARIO BARZANO RECLINED on his bed, sipping a glass of uskavar and scanning through a sheaf of papers delivered to his chambers by a grim-faced Sergeant Learchus. Barzano had endured the full wrath of the sergeant when he and Jenna Sharben had returned to the palace chambers after their excursion into the manufactorum districts of the city.

The pair had hit a few beerhalls and alehouses, but had learned nothing much more than the fact that there was whispered talk of a mass demonstration planned. Most of the talk had been aimed simply at deriding the planetary rulers and the general miserable lot of the workers. After three fruitless hours, they had decided to cut their losses and return to the palace.

The situation on Pavonis was in many ways more serious than he had imagined. There was more going on here than simple piracy and population unrest.

He put down the papers and swung his legs out onto the floor, rubbing the bridge of his nose and sighing deeply. He pushed himself to his feet and shuffled towards the table where a system map had been spread out over the detritus of his evening meal. Dimly he could hear the persistent scratching of quills and the low prayers of his retinue of scribes. Lortuen Perjed was with them, directing their researches and collating their scrivenings, and Barzano felt a smile touch his lips at the thought of the old man. He had been stalwart support these last few weeks and Barzano doubted he could have come this far without his help.

He returned his attention to the map and set his glass down on a curling corner.

A line of blue ink recorded the course of the *Vae Victus* and Barzano wondered if this one ship would be enough. He quickly dismissed the thought. If they could not prevent the Bringer of Darkness from returning then the entire Ultima Segmentum battlefleet would not make a difference.

The prospect depressed him and he refilled his glass.

'Shouldn't you go easy on that?' asked Lortuen Perjed, appearing from the shadows. 'It's quite strong, you know.'

'I know, but it is rather good,' replied Barzano, pouring another glass.

Perjed accepted the drink and sat on the edge of the bed. He sipped the drink, his eyes widening at its potency.

'Yes, quite strong,' he confirmed, taking another swallow. Barzano slumped into the chair before his display terminal and retrieved his glass from the map.

'So what are you still doing up anyway, Lortuen?'

The old adept shrugged. 'Not much else to do at the moment.'

'True,' agreed Barzano. 'I dislike playing a waiting game.'

'You used to enjoy it. Waiting until your prey made a mistake and played right into your hands.'

'Did I? I don't remember.'

'Yes, in the old days you were quite the patient hunter.'

'The old days,' snorted Barzano. 'How long ago were they?'

'Oh, a good few decades ago.'

'A lot's changed since then, Lortuen. I'm hardly the same man any more.'

'My, you are in a sour mood tonight, Ario. Was it not Saint Josmane who said that any service of the Emperor should be rejoiced in?'

'Yes, but I'll bet he never had to do the things we've had to.'

'No,' admitted Perjed, 'but then he was a martyr and got himself killed, Emperor rest his holy soul.'

'True,' laughed Barzano, 'a fate I'd be happy to avoid if I can.'

'That goes for me too,' agreed Perjed, raising his glass.

Barzano rubbed the heel of his palm against his temple and squeezed his eyes shut.

He reached over the desk and picked up a small glass jar of white capsules.

'Are the headaches bad?'

Barzano nodded without replying, swallowing two of the capsules with a mouthful of uskavar. He shook his head and stuck out his tongue at their vile taste.

'It is worse than before. I have felt it ever since we landed, something vast and older than time, pressing in on my skull.'

'Then perhaps you should go easy on the uskavar. It can't help.'

'On the contrary, my dear old friend, it is the only thing that helps. To blot everything out in a haze of alcohol is one of the few pleasures I have left to me.'

'No, that's not the Ario Barzano I have served for thirty years speaking.'

'And just who is that anyway? For I no longer know. The adept, the hive ganger, the courtier, the rogue trader? Who is the Ario Barzano you have served for all those years?'

'The servant of the Emperor who has never once faltered in his duty. Maybe you no longer remember who you are, but I do, and it pains me to see you do this to yourself.'

Barzano nodded and put down his glass with exaggerated care.

'I am sorry, my friend. You are correct of course. The sooner we are done here the better.'

'There is no need to apologise, Ario. I have served many masters in my time and almost all were harder work than you. But to change the subject, has there been any more contact with the *Vae Victus* and Captain Ventris?'

'Not since they arrived at Caernus IV, no.'

'Do you expect them to be able to stop the eldar?'

'I think if anyone can, it will be Uriel. I do not believe he is a man who gives up easily. He was a protégé of Captain Idaeus, you know?'

'Yes, I remember reading the report from Thracia. Was that why you picked him?'

'Partly, but he has something to prove and that's the kind of man I want on my side when it all comes down to the final scrap.'

'And you are hoping that some of Idaeus's unconventional thinking may have rubbed off on Uriel?'

'Hoping?' laughed Barzano. 'My dear Lortuen. I am counting on it.'

* * *

URIEL WATCHED THE blips indicating the incoming eldar ship and the *Vae Victus* on the Thunderhawk's augury panel and the ghostly green lines that connected their approach vectors. It was going to be close; the alien vessel was approaching at high speed and they had still to return to the *Vae Victus* to refuel. The question was: did they have time?

He pointed towards the glowing panel and said, 'How long until we can rendezvous with the *Victus*?'

The pilot checked the augury panel. 'Twenty-six minutes, captain.'

Twenty-six minutes. Add another fifteen to refuel, eight if they refuelled hot, with the engines still turning over in the launch bay. The Codex Astartes strictly forbade such a dangerous practice, but time was of the essence here and he could not afford to waste it. But then the *Victus* only had this one operable Thunderhawk and if it blew up in the launch bay...

'Can we reach the eldar ship without refuelling?'

'No, sir.'

Uriel swore. They were unlikely to get a better shot at the eldar than this, but they were hamstrung by distance and logistical necessity.

If only the eldar could be made to turn towards them.

'Quickly, patch me through to the lord admiral!'

The co-pilot opened a channel to the *Vae Victus*.

'Admiral, this is Captain Ventris, I do not believe we have time to reach you and refuel before the eldar will be beyond our reach.'

'What are you talking about?' stormed the voice of Lord Admiral Tiberius from the command bridge. 'You have to refuel, you don't have enough to reach the eldar if you don't.'

'I know that, Admiral, but if we return to the *Vae Victus* we will miss our chance to take the fight to them on their own ship. You can retrieve us when we're done.'

The vox link crackled as Tiberius considered Uriel's proposal. The admiral's tone was cautious when he finally answered.

'I do not consider this wise, Captain Ventris. You may be correct, but it goes against everything in the Codex Astartes regarding ship operations.'

'I know that, but it is the best chance we have to cripple them. If we can get on the bridge we can do some serious damage. If you can drive them towards us with some well aimed battery fire, we can manoeuvre more effectively to get a better breaching position.'

'Very well, Captain Ventris, but I shall be noting in my log that I disapprove of your flagrant disregard for the words of the Blessed Primarch.'

'That is your right and privilege, admiral, but we can discuss this at a later date. The enemy approaches.'

ARCHON KESHARQ CRADLED his axe, its blade sticky with the blood of the deck officer responsible for the maintenance of the holofields and ground his teeth in anticipation. The raid on the last site indicated by the *kyerzak* had been absurdly easy. The stupid mon-keigh had thrown themselves on his mercy, not realising that he had none to give. He had ripped their souls screaming from their bodies and stolen that which they had removed from the asteroid.

It was unfortunate that some of the lumbering ships of the mon-keigh had been so close, but Kesharq had not been worried. They were no match for the *Stormrider* and he had arrogantly steered a course through them, trusting to his holofields to confound their primitive weapons. And so they had until damage suffered during their engagement with the Astartes vessel had caused the holofields to fail. He knew he could stay and fight. The *Stormrider* could easily defeat these vessels, but they carried the final piece of the key now and its worth was far greater than a few moments of hollow glory. The crewman responsible for the failure of the holofields had been executed and his replacement was working to repair them even now.

Thinking of the prize that lay in his hold, Kesharq pictured the form of Asdrubael Vect, weeping and begging for his life before he destroyed him.

He could taste his vengeance on Vect in the blood that coated his teeth and knew that this was the most critical time. The *kyerzak* would try and rob him of his prize, but his continued existence was only due to Kesharq allowing the Surgeon to practise his art upon his flesh. Kesharq knew that this alone would not be enough of a threat to prevent him from trying. He already knew that the *kyerzak*'s electro-priest they carried had made several attempts to distil an antidote to the toxin that daily ravaged his master's body.

Kesharq knew he would not be successful. Before his disgrace by association, the Surgeon had been known as one of the finest Venomists of the Kabal and the threat of his lethal creations was the bane of every Archon's food table.

No, the *kyerzak* would not be successful and soon he would allow the Surgeon to torture the pitiful figure to death over the course of the coming months.

He glanced up at the viewing screen, calculating how long it would take to reach Pavonis.

Not long. Not long at all.

'DO YOU HAVE him, Philotas?' whispered Lord Admiral Tiberius, as though shouting would somehow alert the alien vessel that sat in the centre of his viewscreen.

'Yes, lord admiral, the alien ship appears to be without its disruption shields. Broadside batteries are establishing a firing solution now.'

'Excellent.'

Tiberius drummed his fingers on the wood panelling of his pulpit and chewed his bottom lip. He did not like Uriel's method of war. Despite the sense of it, it railed against everything he had learned after centuries of combat in space. Everything the Blessed Guilliman had set down in the holy tome, the Codex Astartes, avowed that ships should go into battle with their full complement of craft and no ship should launch boarding actions without first having disabled close-in batteries.

He did not like it, but he could see that Uriel was right. To return to the *Vae Victus* would mean their best chance at destroying the alien vessel would slip away. To launch an assault against an enemy's bridge was the dream of every boarding party and, if successful, would usually mean the capture or death of the enemy captain.

He did not like it, but he would go along with it.

'Broadside battery commanders report they have a firing solution. Target vessel has entered weapons' range.'

Firing at a vessel at this range would be unlikely to inflict many hits, but then that was not the plan. Were he to wait much longer, the alien craft would in all likelihood detect them and evade. All he had to do was spook the alien captain and drive him towards Uriel's approaching Thunderhawk, its engine emissions masked by the close proximity of the planet's atmosphere.

'On my command, order battery gunners to open fire. Then engage engines in full reverse and fire starboard manoeuvring thrusters. I want him driven over the polar-regions and into Captain Ventris's path.'

'Yes, lord admiral.'

URIEL SQUINTED THROUGH the pilot's canopy, but could see little other than the flaring discharges of the planet's atmosphere washing over the Thunderhawk's hull. The feed from the *Vae Victus* gave them the position of the eldar vessel and if it would just move a little closer they would have him.

Tech-marine Harkus intoned the Chant of Dissolution upon the Thunderhawk's boarding umbilical and the shaped breaching charges that would blast their way through the alien vessel's hull. Chaplain Clausel led the Ultramarines in prayer, blessing each warrior's gun and blade. Uriel had ordered chainswords issued to everyone, knowing that the fighting was sure to get close and bloody. Uriel rejoined his men and drew his power sword, bowing to receive the chaplain's blessing.

'DREAD ARCHON! I am detecting an energy build-up three hundred thousand kilometres directly in front of us!'

Kesharq hurried over to the warrior who had spoken and stared at the sensor returns in horror.

There was no mistaking the energy signature. An enemy ship was building power in its weapon batteries and preparing to fire.

'Hard to port, take us low over the planet. Lose him in the atmosphere!'

'BROADSIDE BATTERIES OPEN fire!' ordered Tiberius. 'Engage a reverse port turn!'

The enormous vessel shuddered as the entire port broadside unleashed a hail of fire upon the eldar vessel. Tiberius gripped the edge of the pulpit as the mighty war vessel began turning to face its foe and bring its prow bombardment cannon to bear.

They might not be doing this by the book, but by the Emperor, they were going to do it with their biggest guns.

* * *

EACH BROADSIDE BATTERY hurled explosive, building-sized projectiles towards their target. But at such extreme range, most flew wide of the mark, detonating hundreds of kilometres from the *Stormrider*. Some shells exploded close, but caused no real damage save peppering the hull and mainsail with spinning fragments.

The ship nimbly altered course, its needle-nosed prow sweeping left and diving hard towards the planet's atmosphere. More shots were fired and a vast explosion blossomed above the ship's position as the strike cruiser's bombardment cannon entered the fray.

The *Stormrider* was an obsidian dart, knifing through the atmosphere of Caernus IV, its superior speed and manoeuvrability carrying it from the guns of its enemy.

The *Vae Victus* tried to match the turn and follow the *Stormrider*, but she was nowhere near as nimble as her prey.

The eldar vessel slowed as it angled away from Caernus IV. At this point, a ship was effectively blind as its sensors realigned from the fiery journey through the upper atmosphere.

As the *Stormrider* cleared the atmosphere, a streak of blue flashed upwards and settled in behind the tall sails of the graceful ship. The Thunderhawk's powerful cannons stitched a path of fire across the rear quarter of the vessel, blasting off bladed fins and barbed hooks.

Before the eldar ship could react, the Thunderhawk swooped in across its curved topside. Drill clamps fired from the gunship's belly, burrowing into the wraithbone hull of the *Stormrider*, and dragging the lighter assault craft down hard onto the eldar ship.

TECH-MARINE HARKUS TRIGGERED the firing mechanism of the boarding umbilical and shouted, 'Fire in the hole!' as he detonated the shaped breaching charges at its end. Even through the armoured deck plates of the Thunderhawk, Uriel could feel the tremendous blast. He spun the locking handle and wrenched open the circular hatch that led through the umbilical towards the breach in the eldar vessel's hull.

Speed was essential now. Hit hard and hit fast.

'Ultramarines! With me!' he bellowed and dropped through the boarding umbilical.

* * *

URIEL HIT THE deck of the alien vessel and rolled aside as the next Ultramarine warrior slammed down behind him. He sprang to his feet and drew his power sword and bolt pistol in one fluid motion. He swept his pistol around the room as he took in his surroundings, a low-ceilinged room stacked with round containers.

He thumbed the activation rune on the hilt of his sword and the blade leapt with eldritch fire just as a pair of crimson-armoured warriors charged through an oval shaped doorway. Their armour was smooth and gleaming, adorned with glittering blades, and they carried long rifles with jagged bayonets.

'Courage and honour!' screamed Uriel, launching himself at the eldar warriors.

He smashed his power sword down on the first alien's collarbone, shearing him from neck to groin. The other alien stabbed with its bladed rifle and Uriel spun inside its guard. He hammered his elbow into his attacker's face, pulverising its helmet visor and breaking its neck.

He spared a glance behind him as more of the Ultramarines dropped through the hull breach. Pasanius was there, the blue-hot burner of his flamer roaring and ready to incinerate the enemies of the Emperor.

Uriel raised his power sword and yelled, 'The bridge!'

He sprinted through the doorway, finding himself in a narrow, shadowed corridor, with smooth walls that tapered to a point above his head.

A strange, truly alien aroma filled his senses, but he could not identify it. Two curving passages radiated forwards, their ends disappearing from sight.

Uriel picked the left hand corridor, and charged down its length.

He shouted, 'Pasanius with me! Dardino and Venasus take the right.'

Uriel heard the beat of footsteps from up ahead and saw dozens of the armoured warriors charging to intercept him. They carried the same bladed rifles and Uriel could see a number of larger, more dangerous weapons amongst their ranks.

Raising his flamer, Pasanius shouted, 'Get down!'

Uriel dropped and felt the whoosh of superheated promethium as it washed over him down the corridor. Alien screams echoed from the glassy walls as the liquid flames cooked their bodies within their armour and seared the flesh from their bones.

Uriel pushed himself to his feet and charged forwards, hurdling the burning corpses and leaping amongst the eldar. His sword slashed left and right and where he struck, aliens died. With a wild roar, the Ultramarines followed their captain, swords hacking and cutting amongst the aliens. Screaming, chainsaw-edged blades ripped through the flexible armour plates and flesh of the aliens with ease.

Chaplain Clausel bellowed the Canticles of Faith as he smote the aliens with his deadly crozius arcanum.

Uriel felt a close range blast of splinter fire impact on his arm. He ignored it, his armour absorbed the blast. Another blast slammed into his helmet and he snarled, spinning and beheading his attacker.

The last of the eldar died; the corridor had become a stinking charnel house.

None of the Ultramarines had fallen, though several bled from minor wounds. Pasanius fired short bursts of flame along a bend further down the corridor, deterring any counterattack.

Uriel opened a vox-channel to his other squads.

'Dardino, Venasus. What's your status?'

Venasus answered first, his voice steady and controlled despite the sounds of fierce battle raging around him. 'Strong resistance, captain. We have encountered what looks like a major defence point. Dardino is attempting to flank the aliens. I estimate six minutes until we overwhelm them.'

'Make it four! Ventris out.'

Gunfire spat towards the Ultramarines, ricocheting from the walls and filling the air with whickering splinters. The same type of splinters Uriel had dug from the church wall on Caernus IV.

Pasanius was on the ground, a dark, smoking hole punched in his shoulder guard. Uriel could hear the sergeant's cursing over the vox-net as the big man dragged himself away from the bend in the tunnel, never once releasing his grip on his flamer. Uriel could hear the sounds of more aliens moving to intercept them and thumbed a pair of frag grenades from his belt dispenser.

The weight of fire began to intensify and Uriel knew they had to keep pushing on lest the assault be halted in its tracks before it had even begun.

He rolled around the corner and fired two shots from his bolt pistol. The heavy crack-thump of bolter ammunition was reassuringly loud compared to the aliens' weaponry. A pair of aliens fell, their chests blown open by the mass-reactive shells as Uriel flipped both frags down the corridor. He fired twice more before diving back into cover as the grenades detonated simultaneously, hurling bodies through the air in the fiery blast.

Uriel leapt to his feet and dragged Pasanius upright.

'You ready for this, old friend?'

'More than ever, captain,' assured Pasanius hefting the flamer.

Uriel nodded and spun around the corridor, bolt pistol extended before him.

'For the Emperor!'

The Ultramarines followed Uriel as he pounded towards a crimson door, embossed with intricate designs of curving spikes and blades. Even from here he saw it was heavily armoured.

Cross-corridors bisected this one and Uriel could hear the sounds of battle from elsewhere in the ship. Red armoured figures dashed along parallel corridors and he shouted to watch the rear. With so many cross-corridors, there was a very real possibility of being outflanked and surrounded.

He slammed into the door and smashed it from its frame.

Uriel charged through the door, battle-hungry Ultramarines hard on his heels. They entered a vast, high-roofed dome and Uriel grinned with feral anticipation as he realised they must be on the command bridge at last. An ornate viewscreen dominated the far wall, with wide, hangar-like gates to either side. Iron tables with black leather restraint harnesses stood in a line, alongside racks of horrendous, multi-bladed weapons.

In the centre of the chamber, standing atop a raised command dais, was a tall, slender alien wearing an elaborately tooled suit of armour, similar to that of his warriors, but coloured a deep jade. He wore no helmet and his violet-streaked white hair spilled around his shoulders like snow. His skin was a lifeless mask, devoid of expression, and a thin line of blood ran from his lips. He carried a gigantic war axe, its blade stained red.

Dozens of aliens filled the room, heavily armoured warriors, hefting long, halberd-like weapons that pulsed with unnatural energy.

The room reeked of death and terror. How many souls had met their end in this desolate place, wondered Uriel?

He had no time to ponder the question as the wide doors to either side of the viewscreen slid open. A horde of near naked warriors, both male and female, riding bizarre skimming blades and carrying long glaives, swept from each door.

Bolter shots felled half a dozen, but then they were amongst the Ultramarines, slashing and killing with their weapons. Uriel saw Brother Gaius fall, severed at the waist by the bladed wing of one of the flyers. His killer looped overhead as Gaius's body collapsed in a flood of gore.

Uriel put a bolt round through the whooping alien's head, watching with grim satisfaction as his limp body plummeted to the ground. The shrieking blade-skimmers spun high in the air, coming around for another pass.

Bolter rounds exploded amongst them as Dardino and Venasus led their squads into battle. Uriel shot dead another flyer as Venasus moved to stand beside him, his armour slick with alien blood.

'My apologies, captain. It took us five minutes.'

Uriel grinned fiercely beneath his helmet. 'I know you'll do better next time, sergeant.'

A skimmer exploded as Pasanius's flamer gouted a vast stream of liquid fire over its rider and fresh gunshots echoed through the dome. The vox in Uriel's helmet crackled to life as the Thunderhawk pilot patched into his personal link.

'Captain Ventris, we will have to pull back soon. The alien vessel is increasing in speed and we will not be able to maintain the umbilical for much longer. I suggest you begin falling back, before I am forced to disengage the docking clamps.'

Uriel cursed. He had no time to acknowledge the pilot's communication as he smashed a leather-harnessed warrior from his sky-board and rammed his sword through his belly. He saw the jade-armoured, albino warrior cutting a path towards him and wrenched his sword clear.

Some shapeless mass writhed around the warrior's legs, but Uriel could not discern its nature in the gloom. A trio of the skimming warriors swooped in towards Uriel. He blasted two from their boards with well-placed bolter fire and beheaded the third. The jade warrior cut down two Ultramarine battle-brothers with contemptuous ease as they tried to intercept him.

Uriel shouted at his warriors to stand fast.

'This one is mine!'

From the icons on his helmet visor, Uriel could see that seven of his men were dead, their runic identifiers cold and black. His breathing was heavy, but his stamina was undiminished.

A space cleared around the two warriors as battle continued to rage throughout the bridge. The shapeless forms around the alien's legs resolved into clarity and Uriel was horrified as he clearly saw the heaving mass of creatures that hissed and spat beside the alien leader. A repulsive, horrifying and piteous agglomeration of thrashing, deformed flesh, sewn together in a riot of anatomies, writhed at the alien's feet. Each one was unique in its nauseating form, but all hissed with the same lunatic malevolence, baring yellowed fangs and jagged talons.

Uriel extended his sword, pointing the tip at the alien leader's chest.

'I am Uriel Ventris of the Ultramarines and I have come to kill you.'

The alien leader cocked his head to one side before speaking. His voice rasped, unused to forming human words.

'You are nothing but a mon-keigh, an animal, and I shall feed you to the excrents.'

Uriel brought his sword back to the guard position as the boiling mass of loathsome creatures surged forwards, their shrieks both terrifying and pitiful. He slashed his sword through the first beast, stinking pus jetting from its soft body as the blade easily sliced through its flesh. He stabbed another, but there were simply too many to kill.

Fangs snapped shut on his calf and Uriel grunted as he felt hot pain lance through him as venom pumped into his bloodstream. His sword hacked the beast's fanged appendage from the mass of its form, splattering him with its internal fluids.

Kesharq stepped forward and swung his axe in a crushing arc, hammering the wide blade into Uriel's chest.

Uriel had seen the blow coming and hurled himself back, robbing the impact of much of its force. He rolled, slashing wide, a terrible screeching from another excrent his reward. He kept rolling as Kesharq's axe hammered into the deck.

He leapt upright parrying another blow from the axe. The impact rang up Uriel's arm, but he could tell that there was little strength behind the blow. This alien was relying on the weight of the axe to do his killing. He thundered his fist into the onyx shaft of the axe and barrelled into the slender alien.

The warrior dodged Uriel's shoulder charge, slipping around the Space Marine's side and hammering the weapon into his shoulder.

The blade tore a great gouge from Uriel's armour, skidding upwards and clipping the edge of his helmet. Uriel staggered, dizzy from the impact, but raised his sword in time to parry a lighting reverse cut to his head.

Another of the excrents fastened its jaw upon Uriel's leg. He stamped his armoured boot down on its head, pulping the skull in a mash of bone and brain. Flames licked around him and a shrill screeching and stench of scorched meat filled the air as Pasanius turned his flamer upon the horrific creatures. The pilot's icon on his visor flashed urgently.

Kesharq spun his axe in a dizzying series of loops and twists, the blade a glittering web of silver. He slowly advanced on Uriel, his dead face remaining utterly immobile.

'I was wrong to think of you as worthy meat,' rasped Kesharq. 'The *kyerzak* was a fool to fear you.'

Uriel feinted with his sword, then reversed the direction of his cut, but Kesharq had anticipated the blow and parried with the shaft of his axe. The blade reversed and hammered into Uriel's side, biting deep into his armour. Hot agony flooded him and he could feel blood streaming from his body.

Bloody froth gathered at the side of Kesharq's mouth. Uriel roared and dropped his sword, gripping the axe blade lodged in his side as Kesharq attempted to pull it clear.

Uriel snatched his bolt pistol from his side and swung it to bear on Kesharq's head.

The alien moved with preternatural speed, but even he was not fast enough to completely dodge a bullet.

The bolt tore into the side of Kesharq's cheek, gouging a chunk of his pallid flesh from his skull, but the range was too close for the bolt to fully arm itself and it detonated well past the alien's head.

Kesharq howled in pain and fell back, releasing his grip on the axe. Uriel dropped to his knees as Kesharq stumbled back to his armoured warriors.

Uriel felt hands grasp at his shoulder guards. He weakly raised his pistol, but lowered it when he saw that it was

Pasanius. The massive sergeant gripped the alien axe lodged in his side and pulled it clear in a welter of blood, before dragging his captain to his feet.

'We have to get out of here now!' hissed Uriel.

Pasanius nodded and began shouting orders to his squad. Uriel bent to retrieve Idaeus's sword and joined the rest of his warriors as they began to withdraw towards the Thunderhawk. The bodies of the fallen were carried with them.

Uriel knew they must not leave the honoured dead in this blasphemous place. Apothecary Selenus would remove the progenoid glands that would allow their precious gene-seed to be returned to the Chapter.

None of the alien warriors seemed willing to give chase, however, and Uriel had a fleeting glimpse of the alien leader staring at him with undisguised hatred before he was lost to sight.

THE ULTRAMARINES FELL back in good order to the Thunderhawk and disengaged from the hull of the eldar vessel. The pilot deftly swung the gunship about on its axis and feathered the thrusters until the fuel tanks eventually ran dry. The eldar ship soon vanished in the darkness, its engines rapidly carrying it away from the battle.

The gunship drifted powerless for another hour before being recovered by the *Vae Victus*.

By then, Selenus had tended to the wounded and Chaplain Clausel had intoned the Litany of the Fallen upon the dead.

The *Vae Victus* picked up the engine trail of the eldar ship. Though fast, the Ultramarines strike cruiser could not hope to match the speed of the alien craft, but as the carto-servitors plotted its course, it seemed they would not need to.

The alien vessel was on a direct course for Pavonis.

TEN

GUNNER HARLEN MORGAN ran his hand along the flank of the vast, sixty-tonne tank and smiled as he pictured himself one day riding at the head of an armoured column of such mighty war machines. The tank was a Conqueror pattern Leman Russ, though he reluctantly conceded that the armour and technical specification of this locally produced model was inferior to those fabricated on the Conqueror's original production forge world of Gryphonne IV.

His commander, Major Webb, was lounging high on the cupola of the tank, smoking a stinking cigar, while the tank's loader, Mappin, fixed a pot of caffeine for the crew. The driver, Park, lay half-concealed by the track assembly as he attempted to fix a leaking fuel line.

Slatted sunlight filtered through the camo-netting overhead and, despite their altitude this high in the mountains, the air was still warm. He handed a ration pack up to the major who nodded his thanks and tore the foil container open, grimacing with distaste at its contents.

Morgan sat down, cross-legged, and leaned back against the earthen berm the tank was concealed in, dropping another couple of ration packs beside Mappin and Park.

'You took your bloody time,' grumbled Mappin.

'You can go and get the food next time,' he replied and began to eat.

The meal consisted of some bread, cheese and an ambiguous-looking meat product. Morgan sniffed it and was still none the wiser.

The others began eating, tearing into their food as Trooper Park finally pulled himself out from under the tank and picked up his own ration pack. He stared at it suspiciously and tossed it aside.

'By all that's holy, I'll be damn glad to get on the move and get some real food in my belly,' groused Park, unscrewing the cap from a battered hip flask he produced from within his oil-stained overalls.

'Do you ever stop complaining?' asked Mappin between mouthfuls of bread and the gluey, brown meat from the ration pack. Park took a slug from his flask and offered it to Mappin, who shook his head, but picked up Park's ration pack.

'No. Do you ever stop eating, you fat bastard?' countered Park. 'This uskavar's all I need to get me through the day.'

'Yeah, we know,' laughed Morgan, 'we've seen you drive.'

Trooper Park made an obscene gesture with both hands and said, 'Up yours, boy. Food's for lightweights anyway.'

Morgan shut out the bickering banter of his crewmates, it was a familiar ritual come mealtimes, and turned his attention to the rest of the concealed bunker complex in the Owsen Hills. From here the camouflage the tanks were concealed in looked flimsy and unconvincing, but he guessed that from the air or down on the dusty plains far below, it must look pretty good. Well, no one had discovered them yet, had they?

Their tank's berm overlooked the country estate of their heroic leader far below. A collection of marble-faced buildings, it represented more wealth than he could possibly imagine. Herds of horned stag ran wild in the grounds and a great deal of activity seemed to go on in the dark of night. He'd borrowed Park's infra-goggles and watched whole troops of men dispersing throughout the countryside.

Sensibly, he'd not mentioned this to the major.

Soldiers with shoulder-launched missiles and bipod mounted autoguns were placed around the eastern perimeter of the complex, standing ready to defend them from attack, though the major had assured them that such an attack was pretty unlikely.

But they'd all had a scare when that boxy blue gunship had roared past them last week. Everyone had run scared like panicked kids and it had been a wake up call to the men stationed here that they must be vigilant at all times.

Scores of troopers wandered about the plateau beneath the camo-net: gunners, loaders, drivers and mechanics, all the kinds of men you'd need to keep a force like this ready for action. When that action might come, Morgan didn't know, but the major had assured them it would be soon.

Altogether Morgan knew there were three hundred and twenty-seven armoured vehicles concealed on the plateau and within the mountainside. Basilisks, Griffons, Leman Russ, Hellhounds and various other patterns. He'd counted them once, when his crew had pulled patrol duty. The numbers and types sounded impressive, but Morgan had studied enough about armoured vehicles to know that these were inferior copies of Imperial forge world constructions.

That didn't matter though.

United, they were stronger than adamantium. Faith in the justice of their cause would be their armour and belief in their destiny would be their weapon.

Morgan smiled, remembering the words of Colonel Pontelus of the Pavonis Defence Force (Brandon Gate), which had brought him here. The colonel had spoken passionately about the treachery of the Shonai cartel, how it had traitorously allied itself with like minded individuals within other cartels to squeeze every last shred of money and dignity from the working man. Why, her tithe tax was nothing more than an attempt to line her own pockets before she was removed from office.

Morgan had been unsure at first, seeing the Taloun cartel pin on his commander's uniform jacket. He knew that the Taloun and Shonai were political enemies, but Pontelus's words had struck a nerve in the young tank officer. Together they would fight for their freedom from the oppressive regime of the Shonai.

Morgan understood that freedom had to be paid for and that the price was patriot's blood. He was a patriot and was more than ready to stand up and be counted. The Shonai were dragging Pavonis down and the governor's policies had become unacceptable.

Governance without freedom was tyranny by another name and he was unwilling to live one more day under the governor's yoke.

No more would the sons of Pavonis be forced to work as slaves in the sweltering manufactorum of corrupt cartels. Progressive thinkers like the Taloun and de Valtos knew that men of courage and honour needed to stand up for what they believed in, and Morgan's heart swelled.

He knew he was such a man.

ELEVEN

THE SUN ROSE further in the sky above Brandon Gate, baking the streets with its relentless heat. Despite the lateness of the year, the temperature remained high and the city below sweltered in unseasonal warmth. The towering cooling stacks of the manufactorum were bare of their gaseous halos and the hammering machineries sat idle in their hangars.

A bustling sense of purpose held sway over the city below, as thousands of people filled the streets of the outer manufactorum districts, slowly converging on the white walls of the financial and administrative heart of the city.

Vast columns of men, women and children gathered ready to march. Almost every local manufactorum and business had shut down, either by choice or simply because its workers were now on their way to Liberation Square. The transport networks had shut down and the only rail routes still functioning were those ferrying more workers in from the outlying regions to join the demonstration.

There had been fears amongst the demonstration's organisers that the news of the Space Marines' arrival would dissuade people from attending, but, perversely, the reverse seemed to be true. There was a festive mood to the crowd. Families walked, hand in hand and, scattered throughout the swelling crowd, musicians played stirring, patriotic songs to lift the hearts of the people. Colourful flags and banners flapped in the light breeze, displaying the heraldry of various branches of the Workers' Collective and proclamations of unity.

Here and there, bands of self-appointed route-marshals distributed placards bearing uplifting slogans and helped direct the motion of the crowd. Tens of thousands of people choked the streets, forming a steadily moving mass of humanity united in a common cause.

Security personnel displaying lapel badges of various cartels lined the frontages of buildings owned by their masters, but did nothing more to interfere with the demonstration's progress. Unsurprisingly, there were none from the Shonai cartel on the streets. Every now and then, laughing members of the crowd walked up to them, exhorting them to join the march. Sometimes it worked, sometimes it didn't, but there was no hostility evident either way.

As the crowd continued to grow, its organisers began to realise that the demonstration march was taking on a whole new aspect. It had changed from a show of united strength to a tremendously dangerous enterprise. Such a mass of people on the city streets, despite their peaceful nature, made this day's events perilously close to what might be considered outright rebellion. It would take only the slightest provocation for the planetary officials to regard it as such and use lethal force to break it up.

They had already proved that they were willing to take such measures. The newly sanctified Hall of Martyrs bore the names of those who had found that out the hard way and the march organisers cast nervous glances around them for the forbidding black-armoured forms of the Adeptus Arbites.

But there was no obvious signs of the judges yet, for they were marshalled beside their precinct house, deployed around the wrought iron gates of the governor's palace and at the approach streets to Liberation Square.

The march picked up speed as the streets widened on the approaches to the marble inner walls, converging upon the heart of the city from every compass point. The wide toll gates on the walls were abandoned, the gates open, their keepers unwilling to face this marching leviathan.

Ranks of Brandon Gate's ordinary citizens followed the workers, some in organised bands, some merely individuals wanting to show their support. Helmeted labourers, men in dirty overalls and plain working clothes mingled with those in bicorned hats and fine black suits that would have cost most workers a year's salary.

The march passed through the city gates, slowing slightly as the people funnelled through the gates and along wide, tree-lined boulevards. Pride shone from every face, along with a passionate determination that their voice would at last be heard. There was little anger, those more agitated members of the crowd having been calmed by the marshal teams.

All in all, the Workers' Collective demonstration was off to a good start.

GOVERNOR SHONAI WATCHED the numberless mass of people as it trod the cobbled streets of her capital and felt a shiver of apprehension, wrapping her arms tightly about herself. She had tried to guess the numbers of the crowd, but had long since given up. The numbers pouring into the city were endless. Already, thousands had spilled into Bellahon Park on the inner face of the walls, trampling delicately cultivated topiary and splashing in the shallow lake where priceless varieties of fish were bred by the palace biologis.

All the predictions regarding the threatened demonstration had told her that it could not occur. There was no organising power behind the people. Each branch of the Workers' Collective was too busy squabbling amongst themselves to organise much of anything, let alone a demonstration of any magnitude.

Well, this looked like a demonstration to her. Looking over the thousands of people thronging her city, she vowed never to listen to the predictions of her analysts again.

Was this the end, she wondered? Had the collective mass of the population simply decided that they had had enough? No, she decided. If she was to be removed it would be by the ballot or the bullet.

This was simply another entry in her list of events she would have to endure.

Her meeting with Barzano had given her some hope that she could see out the remainder of her term in office with a little dignity and perhaps set a more peaceful course for her successor, but it seemed as though even that was to be denied her.

She had not seen the Administratum's representative since he had first arrived with the Ultramarines, though the palace had been turned upside down by Sergeant Learchus when Barzano had gone missing. It turned out he and his Arbites liaison had made an excursion into the manufactorum districts, but Shonai was at a loss to understand why. There was nothing there except shabby worker bars and smoke stained hab units. She could not imagine an adept having any business in such places.

Shonai wondered if the adept had had any contact with Captain Ventris as she had since heard that the eldar raiders had attacked another outpost, this time an archaeological site. Apparently system defence ships had fired on the alien craft, and at least three captains were claiming they had hit it. She knew that was unlikely, but it was concrete proof that her administration was now taking a pro-active stance against the raiders.

The plan to enlist de Valtos's support in her aggressive policy towards the eldar and split him from the Taloun had come to naught. Her envoy to the de Valtos cartel had returned with a polite thanks from Kasimir de Valtos, but nothing concrete in offers of aid.

After the events in the Chamber of Righteous Commerce, she wasn't surprised.

To compound matters, her morning briefing had included a report from the judges that had made her groan in frustration.

Last night, the Adeptus Arbites had arrested Beauchamp Abrogas, running half-naked through the seedier end of the northeastern manufactorum district. Screaming nonsensical babble, he had been brandishing a loaded gun and taking pot shots at passers-by. Apparently he had wounded several people, and when the Arbites finally apprehended him, they discovered him raving and out of his mind on opiatix, a highly addictive and proscribed narcotic.

At present Beauchamp was languishing in a cell beneath the Arbites precinct house and would remain there until his family arranged to have him released. Shonai guessed they would let him sweat in the cells for a few days before coming for him.

There was a polite knock at her chamber door.

She shouted to her visitor to come in and glanced round to see Almerz Chanda enter, his hands clasped behind his back. She returned her attention to the scenes beyond the window. People were still entering the city.

'So many, Almerz,' whispered Shonai.

'Yes,' agreed Chanda.

'I want no trouble today, is that understood? It will take only the slightest provocation for these people to degenerate into a mob and tear the city apart.'

'I am assured that the judges are taking a hands-off approach, ma'am.'

'Good.'

'After last week's events, I am sure they are aware of today's sensitive nature.'

Governor Shonai nodded, watching as the square before the palace gates began filling.

By the Emperor, they'd better be.

YET MORE EYES watched the crowd from the upper storey of a marble building set within a low-walled garden with entirely different sentiments. Nine men worked with the quiet hustle of professional soldiers, stripping from plain grey uniforms and changing into black leathers and carapace breastplates. They carefully removed jangling dog-tags as well as any other identifying items and placed them in a canvas pouch.

Their command post was set up in a plain summer-house belonging to the Honan cartel. Dustsheets covered the furniture and the place reeked of abandonment. It was perfect.

No one spoke as another two men entered the room, the first talking softly on a portable vox-caster carried by the second.

The leader of this group, a man named Amel Vedden, handed his subordinate the vox handset and observed the thousands of people streaming into the city. He remained unimpressed. In this situation numbers meant nothing; he had sufficient force to break this demonstration into pieces.

Any idiot could break up a crowd. The key was to strike quickly and with maximum violence, so that the survivors were left stunned and unable to respond in any meaningful way.

But he did not want to break up this demonstration, he wanted it transformed from the sleeping giant into a rampaging monster, and that was even easier.

Vedden was a professional and disliked leaving anything to chance. To that effect, he had stationed another ten men downstairs with flame units and assault weapons, and the roof had been cleared, ready for their extraction by ornithopter.

His vox operator gathered up the canvas bag of dog-tags as Vedden turned to his men, now all clad in the threatening black carapace armour of Adeptus Arbites judges. Most carried automatic combat shotguns, but two carried bulkier, drum-fed grenade launchers. The slow-moving crowd was now almost in the noose of Liberation Square and he knew it was time for action.

He picked up his own shotgun and the ten 'judges' turned on their heels to leave the room.

FROM THE SAFETY of one of the gold-roofed palace towers Jenna Sharben, Ario Barzano and Sergeant Learchus also watched the gathering crowd. Learchus could see that the Arbites woman was unhappy about being here; she wanted to be down on Liberation Square with her comrades and he could understand that.

At first, he had been resentful of being left behind on Pavonis, but when Captain Ventris had explained the oath he had sworn to Lord Macragge, Learchus understood the honour and trust the captain had placed in him.

That did not make it any easier to know that he was denied the honour of battle. Still, as the Blessed Primarch was fond of saying, 'What the Emperor wills, be sure it will seek you out.'

From here they had a prime spot from which to observe the people of Pavonis voice their discontent. The animated singing and music were a muted, tinny sound through the armoured glass.

It did not sit well with Learchus that a populace behaved in this way. Where was their discipline and pride in working for the betterment of society? This kind of mass demonstration would never have occurred in Ultramar, there would have been no need for it.

On Macragge, you had discipline thrashed into you at an early age at the academies and woe betide the boy who forgot the lessons of youth.

The Arbites woman fidgeted constantly, straining against the glass to better observe the deployment and movement of her fellows, who were sensibly keeping a low profile at the palace gates and approach roads.

Heavy handed tactics would only incite the crowd to violence and Learchus just hoped that a cool head commanded the judges this day.

VIRGIL ORTEGA WAS sweating inside his carapace armour and, though he told himself it was the heat, he wasn't sure he sounded convincing. The sheer scale of the demonstration was unbelievable. Every report indicated that such an undertaking was far beyond the capabilities of the Workers' Collective, yet here it was in front of him.

His line of judges was solid. Every one of them had their shotguns slung and their suppression shields held in the guard position. Parked behind them, a line of Rhinos, most armed with powerful water cannon, were idling, ready to haul them out of trouble.

The mood of the crowd did not seem overtly hostile, but you could never tell with these kind of things. One second all would be well, and a heartbeat later, the smallest provocation would cause an eruption of violence. He would do all in his power to make sure that did not happen today and hoped that whoever had organised this felt the same way.

Ortega had expressly ordered his troops not to fire unless he ordered it. He glanced over at Collix. He couldn't see his face beneath the protective visor of his helmet, but had made especially sure that the sergeant had understood his orders. Ortega was keeping Collix close nonetheless.

The demonstrators had halted some fifteen paces from their line and, sensibly, were making no further move towards them.

Ortega could see that half a dozen people had climbed the statue of the Emperor in the centre of Liberation Square and were using its wide plinth as a podium from which to address the crowd. They carried bullhorns, shouting to their audience, punctuating each remark with a sweeping gesture, punch at the sky or pointed finger.

Ortega could not make out many of the words from this distance, but he could hear enough to know that there were no cries demanding the crowd rise up.

Cheers and claps greeted each statement from the orators and Ortega sighed in relief.

It seemed the people of Pavonis had nothing more troublesome on their minds.

VEDDEN'S TEN MAN squad emerged from the Honan's summer house and into one of the approach streets that led to Liberation Square. The street was jammed with people and they roughly pushed their way through with their shields. Shouted oaths followed in their wake, but the march organisers had been insistent: there must be no violence.

This was to be a peaceful show of unity before the planetary rulers, and thus the judges passed unmolested through the crowd.

They emerged onto Liberation Square, less than five hundred metres from the palace gates and the line of genuine Adeptus Arbites. Directly ahead of them, Vedden could see the statue of the Emperor and six people shouting at the crowd through bullhorns.

Vedden did not listen to the words.

'Wedge formation,' he hissed, and his men formed into an arrowhead shape, three either side of him with their shields facing outwards, and three men in the centre with their shotguns cocked and loaded.

'Let's go.'

They moved off, pushing a path towards the statue.

VIRGIL ORTEGA SCANNED the crowd, eyes alert for trouble, despite the avowed intentions of the speakers on the Emperor's statue. He'd just received check-ins from each of his squads and thus far, all was well.

A flash of movement and a ripple of shouting through the crowd caught his attention as he saw a group of judges emerge from the approach street ahead and to his left. He frowned in puzzlement.

Whose squad was that and what the hell were they doing out of position?

Ortega cycled through his vox frequencies, checking every squad's location and coming up with everyone in their proper place. Had the chief put more squads on the ground?

Instantly, he discounted that possibility. The chief was not so idiotic as to put uniformed troops in the square and not tell him.

A shiver passed down his spine, despite the day's heat, as he watched the unknown judges form a wedge and begin pushing their way through the crowd.

His eyes traced where their route would take them.

'Hell and damnation, no!'

'Sir,' inquired Collix.

Virgil Ortega dropped his shield and ran back to where the Rhinos rumbled throatily. He jumped on the front bull-bars of the nearest and lifted his helmet visor, scrambling up onto its roof.

The judge inside popped the top hatch and poked his head out.

'Sir?'

'Give me the damn loud-hailer. Now!'

The judge retreated into the Rhino, emerging seconds later with the loud-hailer handset which Ortega snatched from his outstretched hand.

He flicked the talk button and shouted, 'Attention. Attention. This is Judge Virgil Ortega, you people on the statue, get down now!'

The Rhino's loud-hailer was easily able to carry across the square, but his plea was ignored. Scattered shouts and jeers greeted his words and a few inaudible replies were hollered from the statue's plinth.

Damn them! Didn't these fools realise he was trying to save their lives?

He tossed the handset back and jumped from the Rhino's roof. Running back to the judges' line, he grabbed Collix and a handful of judges.

'Judges, form wedge on me. We have to get to that statue quickly. Come on.'

With practiced precision, the judges formed a wedge around Ortega, the twin of the one already within the crowd. Ortega knew he had to get to the statue first.

But even as they set off, he could see they would be too late.

THE SHOUTS SURROUNDING their advance through the crowd were getting louder, but Vedden ignored them. The statue of the Emperor was their objective and anyone who wasn't quick enough to get out of their way was brutally clubbed aside. A few kicks and punches were aimed at them, but their solid shields made fearsome bludgeoning weapons and soon most people were getting out of their way rather than defy them.

Vedden heard a rough voice ordering the speakers to get down from the statue, and saw a judge commander standing on the back of a Rhino shouting and waving his arms frantically.

But the cretins on the podium ignored him. They were making it too easy.

Like a pebble thrown in a pond, angry ripples of their advance were spreading outwards, as more people began stumbling back, bruised and bloody. A threatening rumbling spread as news of the judges' aggressive tactics began filtering through the crowd. The people on the statue now saw Vedden and his men approaching, and turned their attention to them.

Cries of abuse and self-righteousness were hurled at them, as the speakers denounced the criminal violence employed by the lackeys of a morally bankrupt administration.

The mood of the crowd had turned ugly, but it didn't matter, they were almost there.

A ring of heavy-set men surrounded the statue's base and there was no mistaking their threat. Vedden stopped as a wiry man with a long beard addressed him directly from the podium.

'Brother! We are doing no harm, we have assembled peacefully. Let us continue and I guarantee there will be no trouble.'

Vedden did not answer him.

He unlimbered his shotgun.

He racked the slide.

And in full view of thousands of demonstrators, shot the man dead.

ORTEGA SAW THE leader of the unknown judges unsheath his shotgun and pull the trigger as though in slow motion.

The sluggish echo of the weapon's discharge washed over him as he saw the man on the podium hurled languidly backwards against the alabaster effigy of the Emperor of Mankind. His blood splashed up the statue's thigh as he toppled over a carven foot and tumbled to the ground. His skull burst open with a sickening, wet crack on the cobbles of Liberation Square and, as his brains emptied from his cranium, time snapped back into focus.

The judges in the killer's shield wall crouched, bracing their shields on their thighs as the ones in the centre of the wedge took aim at the stunned survivors on the statue's podium. A volley of automatic shotgun fire blasted the remaining speakers from the Emperor's feet and Virgil knew that they would be lucky to live through this.

MYKOLA SHONAI SQUEEZED her eyes shut as she heard the echo of the shotgun blast and saw the man fall. That was it, she knew. There would be no coming back from this.

A final line had just been crossed and nothing would ever be the same again.

JENNA SHARBEN SURGED to her feet as the man toppled from the statue's plinth, a shout of denial on her lips. She faced Barzano, her face full of mute appeal, dumbfounded at what had just occurred. Barzano chewed his bottom lip, his fists curled.

She made to move past him, but he grabbed her arm with a strength that surprised her and his previously bland features took on a steely hardness. He shook his head.

He dragged his eyes from hers and scanned the crowd, taking in the tactical situation in Liberation Square in an instant. He turned to Sergeant Learchus.

'Sergeant, I need you down there.'

Gone was Barzano's jocular tone and in its place was a full, rich voice, obviously used to giving orders and having them obeyed.

Learchus had seen all that Barzano had, and understood the situation as well as he.

'What would you have me do?' asked the massive Space Marine.

'Whatever you can.'

VEDDEN FIRED ANOTHER volley of shotgun blasts into the crowd, relishing the screams of pain and terror he was causing. Those nearest to him frantically pushed away from the slaughter, but the press of bodies in the square was preventing them from getting out of the way quick enough.

Too bad for them, thought Vedden, pulling the trigger again.

Damn, but it felt good to be killing something, even if it was just dumb civilians. He'd wanted to have a crack at the judges themselves, but his orders were specific; only civilians. Kill as many as you can, capture one of their leaders and get back.

It made sense to capture one of the leaders. The Workers' Collective would demand that leader's release from the Arbites precinct house and the judges would truthfully claim that they were not holding anyone. Of course they would not be believed and it would be taken as another sign of the corruption rife within the planetary administration. It was perfect.

Vedden rushed forwards, stepping over the twitching bodies of the speaker's bodyguards and picked up a weeping girl, no older than twenty and roughly shucked her over his shoulder. She screamed in pain and he slammed his fist into her face to shut her up.

His men formed a rough circle and he stepped into their midst.

'We've got what we came for; now let's get out of here.'

HIS ARMOUR WAS dented in a dozen places and blood ran freely from his temple as he pushed another screaming man from his path. Ortega tasted blood and its coppery stink reeked of failure. He had failed to stop the senseless murders of the demonstration's speakers, failed to keep the Emperor's peace and now all hell was breaking loose.

He heard the hollow boom of more shotgun blasts from the far edges of the square and despaired. He hoped that none of his troops had fired these shots, but if things were going to hell elsewhere as badly as they were here, then he could not discount the possibility.

Bodies pressed in all around him and he angrily shouldered them away. This could not last much longer, it was only a matter of time until they were overwhelmed and killed. He slammed another man aside as he heard a series of cough-thumps and suddenly white smoke was clouding up in billowing geysers.

Grenade canisters of choke gas fired from the line of judges at the palace gates landed amongst the crowd, spewing caustic fumes outwards in obscuring banks of white. The canisters were landing just in front and beside his group and Ortega made a mental note to thank whoever had given the order to fire them. He slammed down his visor, engaging his rebreather.

Through a gap in the choking smoke, Ortega espied the retreating squad of murderers.

Knots of stunned demonstrators stumbled aimlessly through the clouds of smoke, eyes streaming and chests heaving. Many vomited on the cobbles or curled up in foetal balls.

The noise was incredible, like a great beast had awoken and roared. Ortega knew they were in the belly of that beast. He sprinted after the architects of this carnage, weaving round stumbling workers and leaping the dead bodies left in the killer's wake.

Collix and the six judges he had hastily pulled from the line charged after him, similarly eager for revenge. He shoulder charged a man wildly swinging a huge wrench, his eyes bloody where he'd torn at them.

Then they were at the mouth of the approach street and he could clearly see the backs of the killers as they made their way towards a plain white building.

He yelled an oath and levelled his shotgun. The range was not good and he couldn't get a good bead with his visor down.

Virgil squeezed the trigger and one of the killers fell, clutching his shoulder. Collix also fired and scored a hit, but neither of their shots were lethal and the wounded men were dragged along by their comrades.

'Come on,' he shouted. 'Before they get into cover!'

Their prey skidded to a halt and formed a disciplined firing line. Ortega was surprised, but not so surprised that he didn't drop to his knees and brace his shield before him as their enemy's shotguns fired controlled volleys down the street. The shield rocked under a terrible impact, and a fist-sized dent appeared in the metal next to Ortega's head. But it held and screams ripped the air as demonstrators who had chased them down the street were hit.

He sprang from behind his shield, and was punched from his feet as a second, unexpected volley hammered into the breastplate of his armour.

Ortega grunted, more in surprise than pain as he hit the ground. Collix rolled over to him.

'Sir? Are you hurt?'

Ortega groaned, and pushed himself upright and winced as he felt a sharp pain stab into his chest. The breastplate had absorbed the majority of the shot's impact, but it was holed, and blood streamed down its front. He was surprised at Collix's concern, but shook his head.

'Maybe a rib broken I think. Nothing serious.'

Collix hauled him to his feet and they continued down the street. Both men swore as they saw their prey dart through a thick, timber gate in a high wall that led into the grounds of a large town house.

Virgil Ortega jogged a few steps before he was forced to pull up short as the stabbing pain in his chest intensified. His vision blurred and he had to steady himself against the street wall. Collix turned.

'Come on, sir!'

'Go! I'll catch up,' he wheezed. Perhaps his wound was more serious than he had imagined. His breath heaved, a great sucking rasp.

He staggered after his men, casting a quick glance over his shoulder. There was no one else following them down the street, which surprised him, but he was thankful for small mercies. He took another step and closed his eyes as a wave of dizziness and nausea threatened to overcome him. His throat felt constricted and every breath felt like broken glass in his chest. He forced back the pain, biting his lip hard enough to draw blood and willed himself onwards.

His men had reached the gate the killers had gone through and Collix professionally directed them in breaching it. Two judges blasted its hinges as a third slammed an iron-shod boot into the lock, thundering the gate from its frame.

The roar of assault weapon fire blasted from the gateway, snatching the first judge from his feet. Collix and the others dodged back as another blast of gunfire raked through.

He lurched drunkenly up to his men, fighting for each breath and slammed his back into the wall. Collix risked firing his shotgun blind through the gateway and another hail of automatic fire sawed through in reply.

He dared a quick glance around the doorway, catching sight of at least four or five men with heavy stubbers, autoguns and a flame unit sheltering behind a sandbagged emplacement. Ortega swore. Anyone who showed their face in that doorway for more than a fleeting second was a dead man. A burst of gunfire fragmented the plasterwork around the gateway and he ducked back.

Collix and the others risked occasional shots through the doorway, but shotguns were no match for assault weapons and men who knew how to use them. A gout of fire spurted through the gate and the judges leapt back as the smashed edges of the frame were set alight, wreathing the entrance in flames.

Smoke and shadows danced around the street as cloudy tendrils of gas from Liberation Square oozed down the tributary street they occupied. Ortega thought he saw bulky shapes moving towards them, but his vision was blurring with pain and blood loss and he couldn't be sure.

They were at an impasse. To go forward was to die, but he wasn't willing to let these murdering swine get away. Another tongue of flame licked through the door, briefly illuminating the smoky street.

A shadow fell across Virgil Ortega as a massive form moved from behind him to stand in the entrance to the town house.

And the sandbagged emplacement disintegrated in a hail of thunderous gunfire. Flames whooshed through the gateway, wreathing an enormous armoured giant in a flickering orange glow.

Standing impervious in the flames, like some war-god of legend, a gigantic warrior in brilliant blue armour clutched a massive weapon that sprayed bolts through the gateway at a fearsome rate. Ortega's mouth fell open as he saw that there was not just one of these behemoths, but eight.

The giant turned its armoured visor to face him and he felt himself shrink under his gaze.

'We will take it from here, judge,' said the warrior, his voice distorted by his helmet vox.

Virgil Ortega nodded, unable to reply and waved his hand in the direction of the townhouse.

'Be my guest,' he wheezed.

SERGEANT LEARCHUS NODDED in acknowledgement towards the wounded judge and charged through the burning doorway, his bolter spitting explosive shells ahead of him. Cleander was beside him and the other Ultramarines fanned out behind him, firing from the hip. The immediate threat was neutralised, the men behind the sandbags torn apart by massed bolter shells, but there was more assault weapon fire spraying from the upper windows of the building.

From the sharp crack of the report, Learchus knew it was autogun fire, nothing that should trouble his holy suit of power armour. Flames still flickered over his chest where the promethium had gathered. He felt shots ricochet from his shoulder guard and returned fire. A scream sounded.

He hurdled the bloody ruin of the gun emplacement and slammed his armoured bulk against the door to the building. The heavy door exploded into splinters and the Space Marines were inside. He knew they had to hurry, his enhanced hearing had caught the distinctive whine of ornithopter engines approaching and that could only mean one thing.

Learchus rolled as gunfire sawed a path towards him, tearing up the floor tiles in terracotta chunks. He rose and fired his bolter one-handed, blasting a man in a judge's uniform on a set of wide stairs to rags and waved his men inside.

'The traitors will be on the roof awaiting pick-up. They must not leave this building,' ordered Learchus. The Ultramarines nodded and followed their sergeant as he took the steps upwards five at a time.

Learchus emerged into another long, tiled room, stacked with furniture covered in white sheets. Another, narrower flight of steps led up to an oblong of sunlight and he could hear the sound of ornithopter engines even louder now.

As he ran towards the opening to the roof a man rose up from behind one of the sheets, but before he could fire, Cleander put a bolt through his head. Learchus leapt up the steps and emerged onto the flat roof of the building.

AMEL VEDDEN WATCHED as the twin dots of the ornithopters drew closer, sourly reflecting that one would now be enough as he cast his eyes over the seven men who'd survived. He'd lost a lot of soldiers on this mission, but he couldn't bring himself to feel sorry for them.

But what a mission!

Who could have expected the Space Marines to get involved?

He'd be sure to ask for a damn sight more money for dealing with that unexpected threat. He still held the unconscious girl in his arms, knowing that he'd enjoy killing her as soon as they were safe.

He glanced back to the opening in the roof as he heard barks of gunfire from below.

Couldn't these bloody ornithopters hurry up? This was getting too close.

The insect-like shapes buzzed in on wide nacelles, bulbous gunpods like stingers slung under their noses, eerily tracking with the pilot's head movements as they circled the building.

Why didn't they land?

Vedden spun as he heard the thud of armoured footfalls and dragged out a pistol, pressing it hard into the girl's temple.

Five Space Marines stood with their unfeasibly large boltguns pointing at him and his men. His own men levelled their shotguns, but nobody moved.

The air seemed to stagnate, as though unwilling to pass through this unfolding drama. Even the sounds of the circling ornithopters and the baying crowd as they tore the city apart seemed strangely muted. His mouth was dry as he faced these mighty warriors and he felt a tremor begin in his arm.

These were Space Marines; what the hell was he doing? He dug deep within himself, searching for some untapped reserve of bravery and licked his lips.

Amel Vedden never got the chance to find out whether he had the courage to face down a Space Marine as it was at that point the guns of the ornithopters opened fire.

Heavy autocannon fire sprayed the roof of the building, churning up its pebbled surface and shredding human flesh. The men who had been awaiting rescue in the flyers were the first to die, ripped apart in seconds by the heavy calibre, armour piercing shells. Vedden screamed as an autocannon shell clipped him, instantly shearing his leg from his body in mid-thigh. He collapsed, dragging the girl to the ground with him.

The Ultramarines scattered, firing at the ornithopters, but their bolter rounds were ineffective against the armoured undersides of the gunships.

Learchus sprinted forward, diving to the ground to gather the girl in his arms and rolling on top of her as the ornithopter's shells ripped towards her. He supported his weight on his elbows so as not to crush the girl and felt the powerful impacts hammer into his back plate. He offered a short prayer of thanks to his armour for standing firm against the traitorous fire.

Abruptly, the weapons ceased fire and the ornithopters gained altitude, spinning away from the town house, their murderous mission complete. Bolter fire chased them, but they were soon out of range and vanished amid the hazy smog surrounding the manufactorum.

Learchus rose to his knees and pulled the girl out from under him. She was covered in blood, but how much of it was hers, Learchus was unsure. From a cursory inspection, he believed she would live.

He stood and lifted her into his arms. The man who had abducted her stared with glassy eyes at the sky, hyperventilating and clutching at the stump of his leg. He scrabbled weakly at the churned roof, whimpering for help. Cleander gave him emergency first aid, and put a tourniquet on his leg, hoping that the man would prove a good source of information if he lived.

The sounds of battle still raged from Liberation Square and Learchus could see orange flames and smoke spreading throughout the city as the people of Pavonis reacted to the day's events in the only way they knew how.

THE DESTRUCTION RAGED throughout the day, with the mob rampaging through the marble city with murder on their minds. Statuary on the main thoroughfares was toppled, beautifully maintained gardens and parks put to the torch and homes ransacked as the baser elements of the crowd sought to take advantage of the rioting.

Fires spread unchecked and whole districts were razed to the ground with no organised fire-fighters willing to risk their lives on the city streets. People huddled terrified, in their homes as screaming workers broke down doors and stole anything of value. Some of the wealthier inhabitants fought back, gunning down those who broke into their homes, but against the mob they had no chance and were torn apart, their priceless heirlooms and treasures smashed.

Saner heads in the crowd appealed for calm, walking through the streets with their arms upraised, but against the chaos of the riot, their voices went unheard.

Knowing that to venture into the city was to invite certain death, the judges had pulled back within the palace grounds, protected behind its armoured walls and defence turrets. A few rioters had attempted to storm the gates, but roaring blasts of gunfire from the bastions had cut them down mercilessly.

The judge squads stationed at the approach roads had quickly realised that they were cut off from the precinct house and had taken refuge in the nearest shelter they could find. They fought desperate sieges for hours until flyers from the palace were dispatched to carry them and the dwellings' owners to safety.

Protected by the Ultramarines, Virgil Ortega's ad hoc squad of judges had little to do but await a pick up from one of the palace's ornithopters. Slipping in and out of consciousness, Ortega experienced a momentary surge of panic as the propwash of the ornithopter roared over him, thinking that its guns were about to open fire.

Ortega and the wounded prisoner were carried away along with his judges. The aircraft could not carry the weight of eight fully armoured Space Marines, but the pilot assured Learchus that he would be back directly.

The sergeant assured the pilot that he and his men could make their own way back to the palace quite safely, and ordered him to pick up any remaining judge units holed up in the city.

Darkness drew in and the rioters had still not exhausted themselves. Red flames licked at the sky, smoke boiling from each blaze. Whole districts were shrouded in darkness, their frightened residents unwilling to advertise their presence with illumination. It would later be learned that over four thousand people had died this day, killed in the fighting, murdered in their homes or burned to death as fires raged, unchecked, throughout the city. It would be a day long mourned by Pavonis.

Slowly at first, then with greater speed as the chill of night took hold, many of the workers of Pavonis filed from the city. But a great many remained to vent their frustration on those they felt deserved it. Some felt shame at what was occurring, while others felt nothing but a sense of triumphant vindication.

ARIO BARZANO WATCHED, expressionless, as the palace physician worked on the wounded man, lifting bloody swabs and clamps from the ragged stump where his leg had once been. Barzano had seen enough combat trauma wounds to know that the man would not die.

Not from that wound anyway.

He was unconscious just now, pumped full of sedatives and pain suppressants. His limbs were held immobile by the bed's restraints as the physician worked to clamp the spurting artery. Brother Cleander's observance of battlefield triage had probably saved his life. It was a situation the prisoner would later come to regret, thought Barzano.

Judge Ortega lay on the pallet bed next to the traitor, his barrel chest swathed in bandages. Two of his ribs had been broken by the shotgun blast, one of the splintered ends puncturing his left lung. He was lucky to be alive and from the shouts and curses he'd made as the physician had tended to his wound, Barzano wondered if it was his sheer stubbornness that had kept him alive.

Jenna Sharben sat beside him, quietly describing the day's events he had missed while unconscious and the list of those judges who had lost their lives. His face remained set in stone, but Barzano could tell he was hurting.

The third patient was the girl these murdering scum had kidnapped from the Emperor's statue. Despite the vast quantities of blood on her clothes, she had come through her experience relatively unscathed. The physician had dug out a number of shotgun pellets embedded in her flesh and treated her for concussion, but other than that she was unharmed. At present she was sleeping off the last effects of a sedative.

Behind Barzano, Sergeant Learchus, Governor Shonai and Almerz Chanda waited in tense silence for the physician to finish his work. Barzano turned and strode towards them.

Barzano thanked Learchus for his courageous efforts during the chaos of the day. The Space Marine's armour was dented and blackened in places, yet he was unharmed. Then he turned his attention to the governor of Pavonis.

She had aged since he had last seen her. Her grey hair hung loosely about her shoulders and her face seemed to have acquired a whole new set of lines. Only Chanda seemed unmoved by the day's bloodletting.

'A bloody day,' offered Barzano, placing a hand on Mykola Shonai's shoulder.

She nodded, too choked to answer. Chanda had just provided her with a slate with the estimated death toll from today's violence and its scale had numbed her.

Barzano opened his arms to her and she accepted his embrace. He enfolded her shuddering body as she wept for the dead. Barzano looked Chanda in the eye.

'Get out,' he said simply.

Chanda looked ready to protest, but caught the iron resolve in Barzano's stare and departed through the infirmary door with a curt bow.

Ario Barzano and Mykola Shonai stood locked together for several minutes as the governor of Pavonis allowed the years of failure and frustration to wash through her in great, wracking sobs. Barzano held her, understanding her need to let out her burden that had been dammed for too long.

When she had finished, her eyes were puffed and red, but a fire that had been smothered there for so long had now been relit. She wiped her face on a handkerchief offered by Barzano and took a deep, cleansing breath. She smiled weakly at Barzano and straightened her shoulders, pulling her hair back into its tight ponytail.

She looked over to the bed containing the man whose leg had been blown off. Until now, her enemies had been faceless entities, robbing her of a means of striking back, but here, she had one of those enemies before her and she smiled in grim satisfaction. The man was unconscious and according to the physician would probably remain that way for several days.

But soon he would wake and the governor of Pavonis would show him no mercy.

LATER, ARIO BARZANO, Jenna Sharben, Mykola Shonai, Sergeant Learchus, Almerz Chanda and Leland Corteo gathered in the governor's chambers, a large pot of caffeine steaming on the table. Barzano poured a mug for everyone, except Learchus, who politely declined. Everyone looked haggard and weary, with the exception of Mykola Shonai, who bustled around the room with pent-up energy. She stopped by the bust of old Forlanus and smiled, patting his carved shoulder.

Corteo reflected that it was a smile of the hunter.

Shonai returned to her desk, taking a drink from her mug and leaned forwards, her fingers laced before her.

'Right, to business, people. We have one of our enemies below. What do we know about him?'

Jenna Sharben dumped a canvas bag on the governor's desk and tipped out its contents. A pile of silver dog-tags and assorted personal effects tumbled out: a lighter, a small clasp knife and other soldiers' knick-knacks.

'One of the stiffs we pulled from the house, a vox operator by the looks of things, was carrying this. We think he was left in the house while the others carried out their mission and then called for the ornithopter extraction when they got back. I guess they didn't count on their ride opening fire on them.'

'Do we know whose gunships they were or where they went?' enquired Shonai.

'I'm afraid not,' said Almerz Chanda. 'Our aerial surveillance systems were offline for scheduled maintenance at the time.'

'So we don't know where the gunships went,' cursed Shonai, 'but I take it those dog-tags tell us who the men that attacked the crowd were?'

Jenna Sharben answered. 'Yes, looks like they were all lifers in the Planetary Defence Forces. The highest rank we found was a captain and I'm betting that's the prisoner we have below.'

'Does he have a name?' asked Barzano.

Sharben nodded towards the adept. 'If he is the captain, he's called Amel Vedden, an officer in the Kharon barracks.'

'That's one of the regiments sponsored by the Taloun,' pointed out Chanda.

'Does he have a record?' asked Barzano.

'No, it's been expunged. Recently too.'

Barzano turned to Shonai. 'Who could expunge a military record like that? Only a commanding officer of a regiment has the power to do that.'

Shonai was quick to grasp the implication of Barzano's deduction.

'So now the loyalty of an entire regiment of PDF troopers is in question?'

She swore. 'That's nearly five thousand men.'

Governor Shonai pondered the situation in silence before coming to a decision.

'Very well, I'll authorise the mobilisation of more regiments to contain their base until we can be sure where their loyalties lie.'

'How long will that take?' inquired Barzano, looking over at Leland Corteo.

The old man sighed deeply and took a great draw on his pipe. 'It's hard to say, it's been decades since we needed to mobilise the PDF. The last time was in the governor's father's time.'

'Yes, but how long?' pressed Barzano.

'Perhaps two or three days. That's if enough of the soldiers answer the muster. There's a good chance a great many of them were in Liberation Square today.'

'The *Vae Victus* and Captain Ventris will return in less than three days,' added Sergeant Learchus. 'Then you will have a company of Ultramarines at your disposal, Governor Shonai.'

'Thank you, sergeant. I am most grateful for the aid provided by the Ultramarines. You do your Chapter honour.'

Learchus bowed his head, saying, 'We serve the Emperor.'

Shonai took another sip of her caffeine and said, 'So what else do we have to go on? Do we know who the town house belongs to yet?'

'We do indeed,' chimed Almerz Chanda with great relish. He produced a sheaf of papers, deeds of purchase and city records. 'It is a summer house belonging to Taryn Honan.'

'Honan?' exclaimed Corteo, almost choking on his pipe smoke. 'I don't believe it! That fat fool? Surely not?'

'It's all here in black and white,' gestured Chanda to the records.

'These are irrelevant,' put in Barzano. 'Whoever was behind this planned it carefully. They had no intention of picking up the soldiers after they had completed their mission. I hardly think that if Honan had been behind this, he would have been stupid enough to launch his attack from one of his own houses. Though it wouldn't hurt to bring him in to answer some questions.'

'So where does that leave us?' said Jenna Sharben.

'It leaves us,' continued Barzano, 'with a lot of work to do.'

KASIMIR DE VALTOS stabbed his fork through a succulent cutlet of meat and forced himself to swallow, despite the taste of sour bile in his throat.

The meat tasted of rancid maggots and he washed it down with a drink from a crystal goblet of wine. He was reliably informed that this particular vintage was amongst the most sought after in the sector, but to him it was as tasteless as vinegar.

Yet another legacy of his torture.

But that would soon be a thing of the past. Lasko had informed him that his men would soon breach the final chamber and it had taken all of his considerable willpower not to rush off and see for himself. He felt his grip on the fork tightening convulsively and hid it from sight beneath the table.

His guest said something trivial and banal. He smiled politely and mouthed something equally meaningless in reply. He couldn't hear the words; a roaring sounded in his ears and a hot dryness formed in his mouth. He took another drink of wine.

Beneath the table his fist beat a rhythmic tattoo on his thigh, the fork pricking his flesh deep enough to draw blood through his trousers. He couldn't feel it and it was only when he raised the fork to his plate once more, that he noticed the blood.

His breath caught in his throat at the sight of the sticky red liquid and his tongue flicked out to catch the ruby droplets as they ran from his hand.

His guest said something else, but the words were lost to him as he tasted his blood.

He could not feel the pain in his leg. He could feel no pain at all.

De Valtos felt his gaze being drawn towards the dining hall's ceiling, picturing the black leather case sitting beneath his bed, but he forced himself to look away.

It was too soon.

It was always that much sweeter when savoured. He forced his mind clear of blades, saws, pliers and barbed hooks, attempting to focus his attention on his guest. But it was impossible to concentrate on the mindless babble that spewed from its rouged lips. Sweat poured down his face as he forced another lump of meat down his throat.

He didn't think he could wait much longer to kill it.

He realised he no longer thought of his guest as human, and that was a bad sign. The hunger was growing in him and he pictured it naked. It was just meat, flesh to be carved, a cathartic release for the pain he could no longer feel.

To feel that pain again, he would inflict suffering and misery on its body, feeling his own pain echo its cries.

Blood dribbled down his chin and he realised he had bitten down hard on his lip. He wiped his chin as his guest pushed back its chair and walked down the length of the table towards him, false concern written across its bovine features.

It put its hand on his shoulder and he recoiled in horror at its touch.

'Are you feeling alright, Kasimir? You look awfully pale,' asked Solana Vergen.

Kasimir de Valtos swallowed, holding back his disgust and fury.

'Yes,' he managed, thinking of the black case. 'I will be.'

TWELVE

IT WAS INCREDIBLE, thought Mine Overseer Jakob Lasko. No matter how much juice they put through this damn cutter, it never, ever, got above half power. They were burning out generators at the rate of five or six a day and though the cost implications still rankled, he knew he had no choice but to replace each one as it failed. They had to breach this last barrier soon.

The chamber throbbed with the whine of the cutter and he was thankful for the ear protectors he wore. Not only did they make the shriek of the cutter bearable, but it also shut out the weird noise he'd been hearing recently. In his more fanciful moments - which weren't many - he could almost swear he could make out babbling voices amongst the noise, subtly layered and overlapping.

Damn, but he had been down in this bizarre place too long!

He cast his professional eye around the chamber. It was absolutely square, its proportions perfect to the last micron, or so his cartographers had told him. The walls were covered in a tight, angular script, etched into the smooth surface in triangular groups. What it said or meant was a mystery to him.

The only breaks in the script were four featureless alcoves, two on the east wall, two on the west. Each contained a giant, well-proportioned alabaster figure gripping a strange copper staff, edged with a patina of green oxide. What they were or who they were supposed to represent was yet another mystery he left to others.

All that concerned Jakob Lasko was breaching the door at the far end of the chamber.

So far the smooth black slab had resisted diamond-tipped drills and breaching charges. Only the lascutter had any effect, and this was making headway at the slowest pace.

Two tech-priests prayed and swung incense censers over the cutter alongside six miners armed with picks and shovels who looked like they'd rather be any place but here. Things had got so bad recently that none of the men were willing to go anywhere on their own. He couldn't blame them; the darkness and spook stories that had been spreading over the last few years about this place would give anyone second thoughts. But that was no excuse for the kind of worker turnover he was seeing here. The money was a lot better than a man would get any place else, so he figured that if a man signed on, he'd damn well better do his job properly.

Sure, there had been a few disappearances over the years, most recently that damn fool Dal Kolurst. Stupid idiot probably fell down a shaft in the dark. They may know about machines, these tech-priests, but they know damn all about real work. So far, they hadn't found Kolurst's body, but it was just a matter of time before someone tripped over his broken corpse.

He looked up as the lights flickered again and snapped an angry glance over at the chanting priests. The light was bad enough in here as it was without being plunged into total darkness.

The gem-smooth eyes of the statues in the alcoves glittered in the flickering light, and Lasko shivered despite himself. Yes, he decided, the money was good, but he'd be lying to himself if he claimed he wouldn't be damn glad when this job was over and he could get back to proper mining.

This archaeology might pay better money, but it didn't sit right on his worker's soul to put in so much work without seeing something tangible for your efforts. What had they hauled out of this place so far? Nothing but a few skeletal figures made of some weird, greenish metal.

The tech-priests had got all excited about them, but none of them had been able to tell him what they were or what kind of metal it was. Some experts they were.

Well, looking at the work at the door, he could see that the cutter had penetrated perhaps a metre. According to the tech-priests, there couldn't be too much more to go through, but Lasko would wait until they were through before breaking out the fifty year old uskavar. As rich as the boss was, Lasko didn't think he'd be willing to shell out for too many more generators and cutters. This operation must have cost a fortune already.

The lights flickered again, plunging them all into darkness for long seconds until, with a dull hum, the light swelled from the glow-globes once more.

Lasko was more relieved than he cared to admit and licked his dry lips.

What the hell could be behind this door that was so damned important?

He just hoped he got to find out soon.

THIRTEEN

TARYN HONAN STEPPED into the vestibule of Kasimir de Valtos's home and glanced through the open door that led to the dining hall. Broken crockery and fine crystal littered the floor at one end of the table. Such a shame to see such fine workmanship so thoughtlessly destroyed.

He tore his attention away from the dining hall as he noticed a lady's pelisse hung on a hook beside the front door. He licked his rouged lips and lifted the edge of the garment to his face, inhaling its sweet-scented aroma. Ah yes, he recognised this perfume as belonging to the lovely Solana. Was she here also, he wondered? Strange, he hadn't seen her carriage when he arrived.

A cough sounded from the stairs and he spun, dropping the pelisse, blushing in guilty surprise.

Kasimir de Valtos and Vendare Taloun stood on the landing watching him. Honan shuffled into the middle of the vestibule and cleared his throat as the two cartel leaders descended to meet him. He noticed that Kasimir looked flushed and in good sorts, whereas Vendare was chalk-white, as though he'd just had a profound shock.

'What are you doing here?' demanded Kasimir and Taryn flinched at the hostility in his voice.

'I told you not to come, remember?'

'Y-y-yes,' stammered Taryn, 'but I had to see you. I was summoned to the palace this morning, by the governor. The questions they asked me! I mean it was quite beyond the pale. All sorts of things. They–'

'Taryn, slow down,' ordered Kasimir, putting his arm around Taryn's ample shoulders. 'Come, let us have a seat in the drawing room before the fire and discuss this like civilised men, yes?'

Taryn nodded gratefully and allowed himself to be guided through the door opposite the dining hall.

As promised, a large fire was blazing and Taryn settled himself into a high backed leather chair as de Valtos poured three generous measures of uskavar from a bottle on an expansive drinks tray. Taloun walked quickly towards Kasimir and downed his drink in a single swallow. The two cartel leaders exchanged a hurried conversation in whispers then Kasimir sat down opposite Taryn, handing him a crystal class of amber spirit. Vendare remained standing by the drinks tray, pouring himself another drink.

'Now, Taryn. You were saying?'

He sipped his drink before beginning, to calm himself.

'Yes, it's a bad business when an influential cartel leader like myself is treated like a common criminal by a member of the Administratum. That new adept, Barzano, hounded me with all sorts of questions about my town house, you know, the one I loaned you for a time?'

Kasimir nodded, chewing on his bottom lip and Taryn noticed he seemed to be suffering from the heat of the fire, beads of sweat breaking out on his forehead.

'Are you alright, Kasimir?' asked Taryn.

'Far from it,' snorted Vendare, pouring himself another drink.

Kasimir shot him a vicious glance and nodded, saying, 'Please continue, Taryn. Do not concern yourself with Barzano, he will not be a problem for much longer. But what did he want to know?'

'Well, he claimed that the Church of Ancient Ways had used my town house to launch another of their despicable attacks. Can you imagine? From my house? Ridiculous, isn't it?'

'Not really, Taryn,' brayed Kasimir with an edge of hysteria to his humourless laugh. 'You see it's true. All of it. You're just too stupid to understand.'

Taryn opened his mouth to protest, but Kasimir cut him off. 'You have no idea what's happening on this planet, do you? Events are moving in a manner decided by me. Me! I have invested too much, lost too much, to have things messed up by a globulous waste of space like you, Taryn.'

Tears swelled in Taryn Honan's eyes at this unwarranted attack.

'Come, Kasimir, surely there's no need to say such things? We are friends after all. Aren't we?'

'Friends?' mocked Kasimir de Valtos. 'No, Taryn, we are not friends. You are just a pathetic piece of filth I stepped on on my route to immortality. And now it's time I discarded you.'

Taryn heard the sound of a door opening behind him. Kasimir raised his eyes to smile at the newcomer, but there was no warmth in the expression. Taryn desperately looked over to Vendare Taloun for support. Surely his dear friend Vendare would not allow Kasimir to talk to him in this way, would he?

But Vendare Taloun was staring open-mouthed in horror at the person who had entered the room. Taryn heard the sound of soft footfalls approaching the back of his chair, and a pale, delicately veined hand slipped onto his shoulder.

The nails of the long, thin fingers were sharp and painted black. A strong smell of disinfectant wafted from the hand.

Taryn swallowed in fear.

'Kasimir? What's going on?' he whimpered.

He twisted his bulk around in the chair to see a tall, slender figure dressed in a plain red smock and surgical mask. Only his eyes were visible above the mask and they were the deepest shade of violet. The figure's other hand slipped onto his neck, stretching his skin taut and despite his fear, Taryn felt his skin goosebump under the soft touch.

Kasimir de Valtos sat back in his chair and sipped his drink.

Taryn was about to speak when he felt a sharp stabbing pain in his throat as a massive needle slid into his neck. He winced, but instantly the pain was gone, replaced by a warm, floating sensation that infused his body, and his eyes drooped, suddenly feeling absurdly heavy. Kasimir was speaking and he had to concentrate to make out the words.

'Taryn, this is my surgeon. I think you and he should get to know one another better, don't you?'

Taryn Honan smiled and nodded dreamily as the fast-acting soporific raced through his metabolism.

The glass of uskavar slipped from his fingers and shattered on the floor.

BARZANO LEFT THE interrogation chamber, where Ortega and Sharben were interrogating the girl Learchus had rescued from the murderous judges. Governor Mykola Shonai, Almerz Chanda and Leland Corteo stood before the window to the interrogation chamber, watching the judges work. Shonai's face was granite hard, but Chanda and Corteo looked distinctly queasy at the violence they were seeing.

'Does she know anything?' asked Shonai.

'I don't think so. Nothing useful anyway. She'll give us some names and we can round them up, but she's too small a fish to know anything of real value.'

'So why all this... unpleasantness?' enquired Chanda, waving his hand at the dejected figure through the glass.

'Because you never know under which rock you'll find the pieces of the puzzle, my dear Almerz.'

Chanda frowned at Barzano's over familiarity and looked away.

'She was on the statue,' said Mykola Shonai. 'She's one of the ringleaders. She must know something.'

'Possibly,' admitted Barzano. 'She's hard-core militant. She won't break easily.'

'Do what you have to do to break her,' ordered Shonai. 'I don't care how, just find out who was behind this so I can make them pay.'

'Oh we'll find out who did this, I guarantee it,' promised Barzano. 'I believe that one of your rivals has been very clever and very subtle, using cut-outs and cells of activists to make sure that we can't just unravel their treachery with one arrest. I know how these things work. Nothing will have been written down, no record will have been made, but everyone in the loop knows about it. I should imagine that once a few events were put in motion, the demonstration took on a life of its own and required very little in the way of orchestration to get it started.'

Shonai nodded. 'All it needed was a spark to light it,' she said.

'Just so. Ably provided by Captain Vedden, curse his soul.'

'Is he conscious yet? Can we question him?'

'Not yet, no, but your physician believes we will be able to later today, though he wasn't at all happy about letting us talk to him so soon.'

'Damn him and his concerns, I want that bastard broken in half. We're close, Ario, I can feel it.'

'Come on,' he suggested, 'I could use a drink. Any takers?'

Shonai shot Barzano a hard look, but her grim expression softened and she nodded.

'Yes, why not?'

Corteo chuckled. 'Well, I've always said that it is bad luck to let a man drink on his own, so yes, I'll join you.'

'Almerz?' asked the governor.

The governor's chief advisor shook his head. 'Thank you for the offer, governor, but I shall stay here, just in case the judges learn something of value that needs to come to your immediate attention.'

As she turned to leave with Barzano and Corteo, Governor Shonai placed her hand on Chanda's shoulder with a weary smile. 'You are a good man, Almerz. Thank you.'

Almerz Chanda bowed and returned to watching the girl's questioning.

'So you've had experience in these matters before, Adept Barzano?' asked Leland Corteo, filling his pipe once more. Barzano sat cross-legged upon his bed and nodded, sipping his uskavar. An informal mood had descended upon the trio almost as soon as they had entered his chambers.

'Yes, Mister Corteo, I have. I have travelled to lots of different places and dealt with many people who believed that they were exempt from the Emperor's laws.'

'And you showed them that they were not?' put in Mykola Shonai.

'I did indeed,' smiled Barzano.

'And what will you do here once you have what you want?'

The question was casually asked, but Barzano could sense the seriousness behind the words. Briefly he considered lying to her, but realised that she deserved to know the truth.

'In all likelihood you will be removed from control of this world. Failure to maintain one of the Emperor's worlds is a crime, and your regime here can hardly be qualified as a success, can it?'

Corteo's face reddened in anger at Barzano's forthright answer and slammed his glass down on the adept's table. 'Now see here, damn you! You may be some fancy trouble-shooter from Terra, but you have no right to speak to an Imperial Commander like that.'

'No, Leland, he has every right,' whispered Shonai. 'He is correct, after all. I did fail, I let the small things mount up and tried to hide what was going on for too long. Perhaps we do deserve to be replaced.'

Barzano leaned forward, setting his drink down beside him and resting his elbows on his knees. 'Perhaps you do, but I haven't decided yet. After all, who would I put in your place? Ballion Varle? Vendare Taloun? Taryn Honan? I hardly think so, my dear governor. No, let us leave talk of dismissals for the moment and concentrate on the problem at hand.'

'Which is?' snapped Corteo, still angry at Barzano's rudeness.

'I think it is possible that persons on this planet are working with the eldar, using their piratical raids to cover up other activities while fermenting discord on Pavonis to divert attention from what their true purpose may be,' explained Barzano, leaning back against the wall. Both the governor and Corteo were speechless. The idea that their planet's troubles had been set in motion deliberately was appalling, and neither knew how to respond.

'I do not believe that the events which have occurred here could have done so without some guiding influence. There are too many coincidences, and I do not believe in coincidences.'

'But who?' finally managed Shonai.

Barzano shrugged. 'I don't know yet. That's what I'm hoping we can find out soon, for I fear events are approaching critical mass.'

'And what does that mean?'

'It means, my dear governor, that things are about to explode.'

IN A SECLUDED corridor of the Imperial palace, a shimmering point of light fluttered in the air, bobbing like a tiny balloon caught in a gentle updraught. Slowly the point of light began to expand, swirling in a lazy spiral with a violet glow. The fabric of the air seemed to stretch like a painting with an invisible weight placed at its centre, pulled insistently towards the glow.

The illuminators on the ceiling suddenly imploded as a soft moaning issued from the light, a gurgling, chittering sound that reeked of obscene lusts and eternal hunger. Four points of darkness began forming within the light, twisting and swelling like fluid cancers in its heart. The liquid shapes followed the spiral of the twisting nimbus of dirty light, their jelly-like forms gradually coalescing into more solid matter and pushing clear of the glowing mass.

Enveloped in membranous, amniotic skins, the rapidly solidifying things pushed through the light, creaking and twisting the air out of shape with the pain of their dark birth.

With a tortured shriek, the fabric of reality ripped and the four purple-red forms dropped to the stone floor as their glowing womb spiralled back on itself, vanishing with incredible speed, leaving the corridor in semi-darkness once more.

The four glistening forms lay shuddering for a few seconds only, before unfolding long, sinuous legs, envenomed spines, rippling muscle-ridged arms and fang filled maws.

Sloughing their dripping birth sacs, the creatures sniffed the air in unison, their entire existence enslaved to the one imperative their mistress had seeded them with.

To kill the prey.

TROOPERS KORNER AND Tarnin crept down the darkened corridor, lasguns held before them. There was something down here, that was for sure. Korner had heard some damn strange noises and had voxed the guard station that they were investigating.

Tarnin took the lead, noticing the shattered glow-globes and hearing glass crunch underfoot.

A slithering, dripping sound was coming from up ahead.

Without turning, he hissed, 'Korner, gimme your illuminator,' and reached behind to receive the portable light source.

He flicked on the illuminator and trained it down the corridor. He never really saw the creature that killed him.

A fluid shape launched itself from the darkness and disembowelled him with one stroke of its massive claws. Twenty centimetre talons tore him in two, and his skull was crushed with one snap of massive jaws.

Korner caught a glimpse of roaring fangs and talons, spraying blood and heard Tarnin's hideous scream abruptly cut short. He turned to run.

Something heavy hammered into his back, smashing him to the ground. His lasgun spun away. Furnace-hot breath burned his skin and he felt his uniform and flesh dissolving under the beast's paws. Korner opened his mouth to scream.

The warp-spawned beast tore his head off in a welter of gore and swallowed it whole in a single bite. It buried its bloody fangs in the trooper's back, swallowing great chunks of meat and crunching his bones as it began to feed.

A second beast snapped its lethal maw, a threatening growling emanating from its wide chest. Chastened, the bloody hound abandoned its feast and followed the leader as the four beasts padded unerringly through the palace corridors.

The prey was close.

BARZANO'S HEAD SNAPPED up. He unfolded his legs, standing with a smooth grace and glanced hurriedly at Governor Shonai, worry plain on his features. He dashed to the door of his chambers, wrenching it open and stepping into the corridor.

The two Ultramarines guards snapped to attention as the adept emerged, bolters held across their breastplates. Brother Cleander turned and looked down at the adept.

'Brother Barzano, is something amiss?'

Barzano nodded hurriedly. 'Oh, yes, very much amiss, I believe. Where are the rest of your squad?'

'At the cardinal entry points to this wing of the palace. Nothing will approach without coming past one of my battle-brothers.'

'Or through him,' muttered Barzano.

'I beg your pardon?'

'Nothing. Brother Cleander, I need you to vox everyone on duty and tell them that something extremely dangerous has penetrated the security of the palace. We are all in grave danger.'

Cleander indicated that his fellow sentry should carry out the adept's wishes and racked the slide on his bolter.

'What is happening, adept?'

'I don't have time to explain right now. Just tell all the guards to be ready for anything and shoot anyone or anything they don't recognise. Do it!'

Brother Cleander's face was hidden within his helmet, but Barzano could feel his anger at being ordered about by a lowly scribe.

'Your tone is disrespectful–,' he began.

'Damn my tone, Cleander. Just do it!' snapped Barzano as the heavy crack of boltgun fire sounded from somewhere close by. More shots followed and a ululating howl echoed through the palace corridors.

'Too late,' said Barzano.

THE THREE BEASTS raced along the corridors at a terrifying rate, speeding around corridors and evading cries of pursuit in their wake. The body of the fourth lay behind them, dissolving into a foetid pile of indigo ooze atop the armoured corpses of two Ultramarines.

The net was closing on them, but they had no thought for their own survival.

The prey was all that mattered.

BARZANO RUSHED BACK into his room and skidded onto his knees before the long footlocker at the end of his bed. He slid his finger into the geno-key as Shonai and Corteo rose to their feet. Both were panicked by his behaviour, and he couldn't blame them.

'What the hell is going on?' demanded Shonai.

The lid of the footlocker slid open and Barzano reached inside, saying, 'Remember that burning fuse you talked about earlier?'

'Yes, of course.'

'Well, it turns out it's a lot shorter than we thought. Our enemies have just raised the stakes. Here,' said Barzano, tossing each of them a pistol. 'You know how to use these?'

'Not really, no,' admitted Corteo.

'Governor?'

'No. I've never fired a weapon before.'

'Hell and damnation. Oh well, no time like the present to learn.'

Quickly he demonstrated cocking the weapons and how to reload them. 'When you fire, aim low, because they'll kick like a grox in heat.'

'But what are we supposed to be shooting at?' protested the governor. 'What's going on?'

Barzano returned to the footlocker and pulled out a slender bladed sword with an ornate tracery pattern etched along the length of the blade. He rose to his feet, a large pistol with ribbed coils around its flattened muzzle held in his other hand. Gone was his garrulous manner and in its place was a deadly earnestness.

'Our enemies have sent creatures from the depths of hell to hunt us and they will not stop until we kill them or they kill us.'

Barzano thumbed a rune on the pommel of his sword and Shonai and Corteo jumped as the weapon leapt to life, amber fire wreathing the blade in spiralling coils of energy.

'A power sword!' exclaimed Corteo in surprise. 'What manner of adept are you?'

Barzano grinned, but there was no humour evident.

'The worst kind,' he assured Corteo.

BROTHER CLEANDER COULD hear gunfire, the heavy crack of bolters and the snap of lasfire echoing from the walls as whatever was out there moved closer.

The echoes and twisting passages made it impossible to tell from which direction the foe was approaching, so Cleander covered one route while Brother Dambren covered the other. Cleander dearly wished he could charge to the assistance of the hunters, but this was his duty, defending the adept's quarters. Cleander was a citizen of Macragge and he would die before deserting his post.

The percussive blast of Brother Dambren's bolter was the first indication that their foes were upon them. Cleander spun to see three monstrous creatures charging towards them. He added his own fire to Dambren's, tearing the leading beast to shreds as the hail of mass-reactive bolts blew it apart from within.

But the beasts' speed was phenomenal and barely had the first died than the remaining two pounced. Cleander dropped as a beast leapt at him, rolling and firing as it sailed over him. His bolts missed, blasting great chunks of masonry from the roof.

He glanced around to see the second beast bite through Dambren's arm, ripping the limb clear in a flood of crimson. He had no time to go to his brother's aid as the beast before him charged once more.

Cleander fired, a single bolt punching through the creature's belly. It howled in fury, but kept coming, thundering into

Cleander's chest. The pair hammered backwards into the doorway, smashing it to splinters and tumbling into the adept's chambers.

SHONAI SCREAMED AS the door exploded inwards and one of the Ultramarines guards tumbled inside, a beast spawned from her nightmares frenziedly clawing at his helmet. Its long body rippled with iridescent light, a loathsome reddish purple with bony spikes running the length of its spine. Its massive head was horned and its fangs dripped blood. Each heavily muscled limb ended in vicious, barbed claws and its eyes were jet black, dead and unfeeling.

Barzano leapt forward, swinging his blazing sword at the hell beast before him.

Its speed was incredible for such a large creature and the sinuous head ducked below the crackling blade, leaping clear of the Space Marine it squatted upon. It lashed out with a taloned paw, narrowly missing Barzano, but tearing a splintered chunk of timber from the heavy desk.

Cleander rolled towards the beast, wrapping his powerful arms around the creature's neck. It snapped at the Space Marine, its blackened claws easily tearing through his breastplate. Blood poured from the gouges and Cleander snarled in pain as his flesh burned at the beast's touch.

'Get out the way!' yelled Barzano, aiming his plasma pistol.

Cleander ignored the adept, tightly gripping the thrashing monster, roaring his own battle cry as its fangs and claws tore his armour open. The second beast appeared at the doorway, its bestial jaws dripping with blood, and Barzano shifted his aim.

The white-hot plasma bolt punched through the creature's flank, hurling it backward. Foul ichor spurted from the wound and it slumped to the ground, its fabric swiftly un-knitting.

Cleander wrestled for his life against the last creature, vainly trying to hold its claws at bay, but he knew it was a fight he could not win. The beast was stronger than him. The hound slammed its jaw into Cleander's face, snapping his head back against the stone floor. His helmet cracked under the impact and his grip on the beast's neck loosened a fraction.

It was the only opening the creature needed. Its talons rose and fell, punching through Cleander's breastplate and tearing his ribcage apart.

Corteo and Shonai fired their pistols at the wounded beast, but neither was trained in firearms and their shots went wild.

Barzano pushed them back as Cleander's killer wrenched its talons clear of the body and lurched towards him. Its movements were slowed, but it was still capable of killing them all. His plasma pistol hummed, its energy cells still recharging and Barzano knew it was no use to him yet.

The beast reared up on its reverse jointed legs and charged.

Ario Barzano dived forwards, beneath its lethal talons.

He rolled to his knees, swinging his power sword in a low, sweeping arc.

The energised blade hacked the beast's legs out from under it and it crashed to the ground, thrashing the cauterised stumps of its thighs in fury.

Barzano sprang to his feet and stood beside Governor Shonai and Leland Corteo as the beast clawed its way towards them across the floor, its substance unravelling in smoky trails of darkness even as it neared.

Only its rapidly dissolving torso and head remained as Barzano stepped in, reversing his grip on his sword, and drove the blade down through its head.

Barzano slumped next to its fading remains, pulling the blade from the floor as Sergeant Learchus and his squad arrived.

Learchus dropped to his knees beside Cleander's corpse and bunched his fist in anger. Barzano left him to his grief, turning to face the ashen-faced Mykola Shonai and Leland Corteo. He tossed the pistol onto the bed and deactivated his sword, laying it upon the sagging remains of the shattered desk.

'You killed it,' gasped Shonai. 'How did you do that?'

'Better I show you,' replied Barzano, pulling aside the painting of Forlanus Shonai and exposing the secure safe in the wall.

He punched in a ten digit code and pulled the door open.

Inside was the box, which he removed and placed on the floor beside him.

Barzano reached back inside the safe and removed a smaller item which he handed to Shonai, who took it with an expression of fear and surprise.

She held a rectangular block of sapphire crystal, no larger than fifteen centimetres by eight and less than five centimetres deep. It was an inconsequential thing but for the symbol it encased.

A grinning skull embossed with a stylised capital 'I'.

Governor Shonai looked up into the face of a man she no longer knew.

'I am Ario Barzano,' he said, 'of the Holy Orders of the Emperor's Inquisition.'

FOURTEEN

At precisely 07:00 hours on the morning following the Workers' Collective demonstration in Liberation Square, tanks from the Kharon planetary defence barracks rolled through the gates of their base along Highway 236 towards Brandon Gate. Within twenty-five minutes, the column of forty tanks, locally produced Leman Russ Conquerors bearing the artillery shell motif of the Taloun, had reached the outskirts of the city, rumbling towards its centre and the Imperial palace.

A constantly repeating message blared from speakers mounted on each tank's hull, proclaiming that this manoeuvre was intended only to keep the peace and that people should not panic. The populace of Brandon Gate risked hurried glances through their windows as the tank column rumbled past, fearful of what this latest development might herald. The tanks passed the main population and manufactorum centres, halting only when they reached the marble walls of the inner city.

Within an hour of the Taloun's tanks taking to the streets, armoured vehicles rolled out from other PDF barracks sponsored by those cartels allied to the Taloun. Tanks bearing the crest of the de Valtos cartel mobilised from their base at

Tarmegan Ridge and infantry carriers from six other cartel sponsored bases mounted up and made for Brandon Gate.

By midday, one hundred and nineteen tanks and over seven thousand infantry were stationed outside the city limits. The hull speakers fell silent and a repeating vox signal cut across every frequency, announcing the PDF's intention to keep the peace that the governor obviously could not. However, in deference to her position, none of the tanks would enter her city until such time as their armoured might would be required. Nervous heads within the city pondered exactly what that might mean.

Despite repeated demands from Mykola Shonai, none of the mobilised PDF units withdrew from the city limits and to all intents and purposes, Brandon Gate became a city under silent siege.

As he limped through the shattered doorway to Ario Barzano's chambers, Uriel was shocked at the devastation the hell beasts had wreaked. The Thunderhawk had landed less than an hour ago and his mood was sombre as he remembered the downcast face of Learchus as he had informed him of the death of Cleander and three other battle-brothers.

Pasanius entered the room behind him, both men ducking their heads below the lintel. The massive sergeant carried a stasis vessel containing the metallic fragments from the hill on Caernus IV.

Despite the ministrations of Apothecary Selenus, Uriel's movements were still painful from the wounds inflicted by the eldar leader's axe, and the bites of his abominable pets. He would live, but his heart hungered for revenge on the dead faced warrior.

Barzano stood with his back to Uriel, resting his hands on an ancient looking box, which sat upon a splintered and sagging desk. He spoke in a low voice to Governor Shonai and Leland Corteo. Lortuen Perjed sat on the edge of the bed, while Jenna Sharben and Sergeant Learchus stood immobile at the back of the room. The sergeant had his bolter drawn and chainsword at the ready.

Barzano turned at the sound of Uriel's footfalls and the captain of Fourth Company was shocked at the change that had come over the man. Learchus had already informed Uriel of

Barzano's true identity, and, at first, he had scoffed at the idea of the adept really being an inquisitor.

But to see the man now, he had no trouble in accepting the fact. Barzano no longer stood in the stooped, slightly subservient pose of a typical Administratum adept. Dressed in a loose fitting tunic and knee high boots with a sword and pistol belted at his side, his pose was proud and erect. He stepped forwards, gripping Uriel's hand and placing the other on his elbow, single-minded determination shining in his eyes.

'Captain Ventris, my prayers are with your honoured dead. They died well.'

Uriel nodded in acknowledgement as Mykola Shonai moved to stand beside the inquisitor.

'It is good to see you again, captain,' she said. 'I also offer my prayers for your fallen brothers, and hope that no more shall fall defending our planet.'

'As the Emperor wills it,' replied Uriel, waving Pasanius forward. The sergeant placed the stasis vessel next to the box.

'So what have you brought me, Uriel? Something from the eldar ship?'

'No, it comes from one of the worlds attacked by the raiders.'

'What is it?' asked Barzano deactivating the stasis seal and lifting the lid.

'We were hoping you could tell us. It came from a hillside almost entirely composed of metal. According to the local populace and a survivor of the raid, this metal once ran like liquid and their smiths used it to fashion blades and ploughs. Though this practice had been going on for generations, the metal would somehow regenerate each shorn piece.'

Barzano's face paled visibly as he reached into the vessel and removed the fragment of faintly glowing metal. His eyes were wide as he traced his fingertips around the angular script carved in the metal.

Even as Uriel watched, the last of the glowing silver threads at the centre of the metal turned into the ruddy colour of rust and its lustre faded completely. Carefully, almost reverently, Barzano placed the metal on the desk and lifted his gaze to meet Uriel's. 'You said there was a survivor? I take it they are aboard the *Vae Victus* awaiting debriefing?'

'No. He was mortally wounded. I had Chaplain Clausel administer the Finis Rerum and we buried him in his home.'

Barzano struggled to contain his outrage at this valuable source of information being so casually squandered and simply nodded.

'Very well,' he managed finally, glancing at the locked strongbox his palm rested upon.

'Well?' prompted Uriel, pointing to the dead metal. 'What is it?'

Barzano drew himself up to his full height and said, 'This, my dear captain, is a fragment of wreckage from a starship more than one hundred million years old. It is also the reason we are here on Pavonis.'

'One hundred million years,' mused Leland Corteo. 'Surely that's impossible. Mankind only reached the stars less than fifty thousand years ago.'

'I did not say it was a human ship,' snapped Barzano.

'This has something to do with the troubles on Pavonis?' asked Mykola Shonai.

'I'm afraid so. Remember the deeper purpose I believed was behind your troubles? This is it. Someone on this planet is attempting to discover the whereabouts of the rest of this ship.'

'What could anyone hope to gain by its recovery?' asked Uriel.

'Power,' stated Barzano simply.

'Then if you know where it is, tell me the location and *Vae Victus* shall destroy it.'

'Ah, Uriel. If only it were that simple. It does not exist in this reality as we understand it. It drifts between time, forever flitting between this world and the immaterium. Would that it remain so for all eternity.'

'Why do you fear it so?'

Barzano lifted his hand from the locked strongbox, placing his thumb on the geno-key and crouched before the lock, allowing the box's guardian spirit to confirm his identity.

Finally, he punched in the thirteen-digit password into its lid and spoke the word of opening. The lid swung open and the inquisitor removed a heavy, iron-bound book with thirteen small golden padlocks securing its pages shut. The locks looked fragile, but each had been imbued with hexagrammic sigils of great power.

Barzano touched each lock in turn, whispering as though persuading the locks to grant access to the precious tome. One by one, the locks snicked open and Barzano straightened as the creaking cover of the book slowly opened without help from any human hand.

Uriel hissed and the others stepped back in alarm. Barzano took a deep breath and closed his eyes and Uriel felt a tinny, electric sensation pass through him. The book heaved, mirroring the inquisitor's breath and Uriel felt his hand involuntarily reach for his pistol. Sorcery!

Barzano extended his palm towards Uriel and shook his head.

'No, captain. I am entreating the spirit within the book to impart a measure of its knowledge to us.'

'Spirit within the book?' hissed Uriel.

'Yes. You have heard the expression that knowledge is power, yes? Did you think those were just empty words? Knowledge is indeed power, and knowledge has power.'

Seeing the book pulse like a beating heart, Uriel muttered a protective prayer. Suddenly he realised that there could only be one way that Barzano was, as he put it, entreating the book's spirit.

'You are a psyker?'

'Of sorts,' admitted Barzano, his brow knitted with the effort of speaking. 'I am an empath. I can sense strong emotions and feelings.'

The book suddenly seemed to swell and its pages fanned forwards as though in a strong wind, faster than the eye could follow. Abruptly, the book settled, its yellowed pages sighing and settling into immobility.

Barzano relaxed, opening his eyes and Uriel noticed beads of sweat on his brow. A trickle of blood ran from his nose, but he wiped it clear and leaned over the pages the book had revealed to him.

Hesitantly, Uriel, Pasanius, Shonai and Corteo approached the table.

At first Uriel could not understand what he was looking at. The pages had been scrawled by a crazed hand, hundreds of words overlapping and spinning in lunatic circles or viciously crossed out.

'What is it?' asked Shonai.

'These are some of the writings of the heretic tech-abbot, Corteswain.'

'And who was he?'

'Corteswain belonged to the Adeptus Mechanicus. He travelled the galaxy searching ancient archaeological sites for working STC systems. Instead he found madness.'

Uriel knew of the Adeptus Mechanicus's ceaseless quest for Standard Template Construct systems, techno-arcana priceless beyond imagining. Every single piece of Imperial technology was derived from the few, precious fragments of STC systems that remained in the hands of the Adeptus Mechanicus. Even the flimsiest rumour of an STC's existence prompted whole fleets of Explorators to set off in search of this most valuable treasure.

Barzano continued his story. 'Corteswain was the only survivor of an expedition to a dead world, whose name has long since been lost, in search of STC arcana. Something attacked his expedition and he claimed to have been taken to a world beyond this galaxy by a being of unimaginable power he called a god.'

'A god?' whispered Shonai

'Yes, a god. He claimed to have seen the true face of the Omnissiah, the Machine God. Needless to say, this didn't make him particularly popular within some factions of the Adeptus Mechanicus, who accused him of blasphemy. It caused a schism in their ranks that exists even today and within a year Corteswain disappeared from the omniastery on Selethoth where he had begun preaching his dogma.'

'What happened to him?' asked Uriel.

Barzano shrugged. 'I don't know. His rivals probably had him abducted and killed. But some of his writings survived, carried from the omniastery by his acolytes.'

'What does it mean? I can hardly make anything out,' said Shonai, slipping on her glasses.

'This particular passage talks of a vessel Corteswain claims he saw,' said Barzano, pointing out a barely legible scrawl in the corner of one page.

His fingers traced the outline of a badly sketched crescent with a pyramid shape sitting atop its middle.

Uriel squinted as he tried to read the words scratched into the parchment below the sketch. The same words were written again and again, at every angle, overlapping and curling back on themselves.

His eyes followed the least obscured portion of the spidery writing and he silently mouthed the words as he slowly pieced them together.

He finally grasped what the words said and the hairs on the back of his neck rose as he realised he had heard them before – from the burned lips of a man on the brink of death.

Bringer of Darkness.

Barzano glanced sharply at him and Uriel was reminded that the inquisitor could sense his emotions.

'Uriel,' said Barzano slowly. 'Do those words mean anything to you?'

Uriel nodded. 'Yes. The survivor on Caernus IV, a man named Gedrik, spoke them to me just before he died.'

'What did he say? Quickly!' hissed Barzano.

'He said that the Death of Worlds and the Bringer of Darkness awaited to be born into the galaxy and that it would be in my hands to decide which. Do you know what he meant by that?'

'No,' said Barzano, a little too quickly. 'I don't. What else did he say?'

'Nothing. He died soon afterwards,' replied Uriel, pointing to the crescent shaped sketch on the book. 'So the Bringer of Darkness is an alien starship. What can it do?'

'It can unmake the stars themselves, bleed them dry of energy and leave nothing alive in a star system. And it can do this in a matter of days. Now do you see?'

Uriel nodded. 'Then we must find it before the eldar.'

'Agreed. We must also discover who they are working with here on Pavonis,' said Barzano, pacing the room, hands laced behind his back.

'The eldar leader spoke a name as we fought, perhaps it was his accomplice.'

Barzano stopped pacing and spun to face Uriel, a look of disbelief on his face.

'He mentioned a name?' hissed Barzano. 'What? Quickly man!'

'I'm not sure it was a name. It was one of their foul words, it sounded like... *karsag*, or something like that.'

Barzano's brow knitted and he cast a glance at Shonai. 'Does that name have any meaning to you? It isn't one of the cartels here?'

'No, I don't recognise it.'

'Captain Ventris,' said Lortuen Perjed. 'Could the word you heard have been *kyerzak* perhaps?'

Uriel closed his eyes, picturing the corpse-faced warrior, recalling the sounds that rasped from his expressionless mouth. He nodded.

'Yes, Adept Perjed. I believe that it could very well have been that.'

Barzano rushed to his aide and knelt before the old man, gripping his shoulders tightly. His face was alight with excitement. 'Lortuen, do you know what that word means? Is it a name?'

Perjed shook his head. 'No, it is not a name, rather it is a term of address. Its roots are indeed eldar in origin and it is used to denote one who is to be honoured.'

Barzano released his grip on Perjed's shoulders and stood, perplexed. 'Helpful though that is, it gets us no nearer to who the eldar are working with.'

'On the contrary, Ario, it tells us exactly who we are looking for.'

'It does?' replied Barzano, 'Explain yourself, Lortuen. We don't have time to indulge your sense for the dramatic.'

'The word *kyerzak* means an honoured one, but in the writings of Lasko Pyre, he talks of how the torturers of the dark kin, beings he called the haemonculi, would tell him that he should appreciate the honour they did him, inflicting the most sublime pain they could imagine upon his flesh.'

Uriel and Barzano made the connection as Perjed continued. 'You see, the dark kin have corrupted the word, debasing its meaning to refer to one who has been honoured with their most painful artistry.'

Shonai clenched her fists and hissed the architect of her troubles' name.

'Kasimir de Valtos.'

CONSTRUCTED IN A hardened bunker in the eastern wing of the palace, orbital defence control was responsible for the monitoring of aerial and spatial traffic in the local area around Pavonis. It was heavily fortified and fully self-contained, with its own energy grid and reserve power supplies that would allow it to defend Pavonis for up to a year without primary power.

Second Technician Lutricia Vijeon sat at her control panel, sweeping the space around Pavonis for any unauthorised traffic.

Her commanding officer, Danil Vorens, sat with his back to her at the command console staring at a holo display projected from the plot before him.

Lutricia noticed a faint return on her surveyor scope and began noting the time of its appearance on her log. It had to be a ship, it was too large to be anything else. She checked the flight plans pinned beside her station to check if anything was expected in her sector of responsibility. There was nothing logged and she adjusted the runes before her to sharpen the image on her display.

It didn't look like anything she'd seen before, with its long, tapered prow and what appeared to be long sails rising from its engine section. What the hell was it?

The image swam hazily on the display, its image blurring as she tried to lock down its form. The image snapped into focus as a thick hand dropped onto her shoulder, squeezing it tightly. She started and looked up into the grim face of Danil Vorens.

'Sir, I've got this signal on the–' she began.

'I know about it, Vijeon. Everything has been properly logged. I have authorised it personally,' said Vorens, shutting off her surveyor scope.

'Oh, I see. But shouldn't we log it in the daily report?'

'No, Vijeon,' whispered Vorens, leaning close to her ear and squeezing her shoulder even tighter. 'This ship was not here and you did not pick it up on your surveyors. Understood?'

Vijeon didn't, but wasn't going to tell Vorens that.

Still, what did it matter to her?

She nodded and switched her scope to another sector of space.

Obviously Vorens had been expecting this ship.

THE ULTRAMARINES' THUNDERHAWK gunship landed in the country estates of Kasimir de Valtos in the foot of the Owsen Hills, nearly seventy-five kilometres west of Brandon Gate.

'Everyone out!' yelled Uriel, charging from the belly of the gunship, bolter at the ready.

He emerged into the late afternoon sun, seeing the splendour of de Valtos's country estates spreading before him. A large, multi-winged house sprawled in front of them, two black coaches sitting before the main entrance. The Ultramarines fanned out, forming a defensive perimeter as the gunship howled skyward on a pillar of fiery smoke.

Uriel waved Dardino's squad left and Venasus's right, leading Pasanius's towards the main doors.

The main door was already open and Uriel sprinted through into the chequered entrance hall. Ultramarines barged through the door and Uriel directed them with sharp jabs of his fist. He indicated that Pasanius and two other Space Marines should follow him and charged up the staircase, his bolter constantly searching for targets.

The upper landing was empty, a long carpeted passageway stretching left and right.

To the right, the passageway curved out of sight, while on the left it ended at a large oaken door. Something told Uriel that this house had been abandoned, but his soldier's instinct was too well honed not to treat this place as an anything less than hostile.

Uriel and Pasanius made their way cautiously down the passageway, bolters trained on the door. His auto senses could detect no noise from the room beyond, though he could smell a faint, but disturbing odour.

Uriel smashed the door from its frame, going in low and fast, Pasanius behind him, bolter sweeping left and right. Given the confines of the dwelling, he had opted for his bolter rather than his preferred flamer. Behind him, Uriel could hear the sounds of Ultramarines, kicking down doors and searching room-to-room.

The stench hit him before he realised what he was looking at on the bed.

It had once been a human being, but almost every vestige of humanity had been stripped from the corpse's frame by blades, saws, needles and flame. A golden halo of hair framed the body's head, its leering skull-face stripped of skin below the eyes, both of which had been gouged from their sockets with the bloodstained shards of a broken mirror that crunched underfoot.

Uriel's gorge rose at the sight. 'Guilliman's oath!'

Pasanius lowered his bolter, taking in the full horror of the dead woman.

'By the Emperor, who could do such a thing?'

Uriel had no answer.

Despite the horrific mutilation, Uriel recognised the features of Solana Vergen and he added her name to those for whom he would seek vengeance upon Kasimir de Valtos.

SERGEANT VENASUS LED his squad carefully through the lower reaches of the traitor's dwelling place. It was colder here, his suit of power armour registering a drop of fourteen degrees.

So far they had found nothing, and Venasus dearly hoped to find some of their enemies soon. Three of his men had died on the alien ship and there was a blood price to be paid for their deaths.

The bare stone passage led along to an iron door, padlocked shut and Venasus wasted no time smashing it from its frame with a well-placed kick. The sergeant powered through the doorway, his men following close behind. The room was in darkness, but his armour's auto senses kicked in.

He saw the gleam of metal to his left. A grinning skull face leapt from the darkness of the room. Venasus swung his bolter up and opened fire at the deathly apparition.

URIEL HEARD THE burst of gunfire from the top landing and sprinted downwards, following the stairs to the lower levels of the house. His blood pounded in his veins, hoping that there would be enemies to slay, his heart hungry for vengeance.

As he reached the source of the gunfire, he could see that he was to be denied such vengeance for now. The corridor was cold, its walls glistening with moisture.

Sergeant Venasus stood at the buckled doorway to a dimly lit room.

'Report,' ordered Uriel.

'False alarm, captain. I was first through the door and acquired what I thought was a target. I opened fire, but I was mistaken.'

'Assign yourself ten days of fasting and prayer to atone for your lax targeting rituals.'

'Yes, captain.'

'So what was it you fired upon, sergeant?'

Venasus paused before answering. 'I am not sure, some kind of metallic skeleton. I do not know exactly what it is.'

The sergeant moved aside to allow Uriel and Pasanius to enter the room. A single glow-globe cast a fitful illumination around the small room, which looked like some insane mechanic's workshop. All manner of tools lay strewn upon chipped and blackened benches, their exact use incomprehensible. In one corner of the room lay the shattered remains of Sergeant Venasus's target. As the sergeant had described, it resembled a metallic skeleton, its once gleaming surface stained with a patina of green and its limbs twisted at unnatural angles.

Another skeleton of stained metal lay propped up on an angled bench, bundles of wires running from its open chest to rows of yellow battery packs with red lettering stencilled on their sides. Panels on its chest and skull had been prised open and Uriel peered into the darkness within its grotesque anatomy. It resembled a skull in that it had eye sockets and a skeletal grin but there was something horrendously alien about this construction, as though its maker had set out to mock humanity's perfection.

The metallic form repulsed Uriel, though he could not say exactly why. Perhaps it was the loathsome malevolence that radiated from its expressionless features. Perhaps it was the metal's resemblance to the substance they had removed from beneath the hillside on Caernus IV.

'What in the name of all that's holy is this?' asked Pasanius.

Uriel shook his head. 'I have no idea, my friend. Perhaps they were the crew of the ship Barzano spoke of.'

Pasanius pointed at the machine on the bench. 'You think it is dead?'

Uriel walked over to it and wrenched the wires from the metal skeleton's chest and skull.

'It is now,' he said.

URIEL WATCHED THE temperature reading on his visor creep slowly downwards as he approached the last door. Steam hissed from the power unit on the back of his armour and he could feel a strange sense of foreboding as he neared the rusted portal.

The door wasn't shut, a sliver of darkness and stuttering light edging the frame. Wisps of condensing air soughed through from behind it.

He glanced behind him. Pasanius, Venasus and six Ultramarines stood ready to storm the room on his order. The remainder of his command were tearing the house apart from top to bottom, searching for a clue to de Valtos's current whereabouts. He nodded to Pasanius and hammered his boot against the metal of the door.

It slammed inwards, Pasanius charging through with Venasus hot on his heels. Uriel spun into the room, covering the danger zone on their blindside as the remainder of the men charged in.

Uriel heard the clink of chains and soft moans emanating from the centre of the room. His auto-senses had trouble adjusting to the flickering light and he disengaged them, activating his armour lights. The other Ultramarines followed his example and slowly the horrendous centrepiece of the octagonal room became visible.

Atop a stinking, gore-smeared slab lay a large human skeleton, the bones bloody, its former wrapping suspended above it.

Chunks of excised flesh hung from the ceiling on scores of butchers' hooks, each one set at precisely the correct height to shape the outline of the body they once enclosed. As though frozen a millisecond after his body had suffered some internal explosion, the flesh and organs of Taryn Honan hung suspended above his skeleton, each fatty slice of his body ribboned together with dripping sinew and pulsing cords of vein.

'By the Emperor's soul,' whispered Uriel, horrified beyond belief. Honan's head was a segmented, interconnected jigsaw of individual lumps of flesh, the wobbling jowls and severed chins circling his steaming brain, each still juddering in an imitation of life.

Uriel saw that his eyes still rolled in their sockets, as though the corpse continued to relive its last agonising moments and Uriel commended his tortured soul to the Emperor.

The slab of fatty flesh that contained the mouth worked soundlessly up and down like a macabre marionette controlled by some unseen master. The gently spinning meat containing the lidless eyes fluttered and Uriel watched, horrified, as they focussed on him and a low moaning again spilled from Taryn Honan's lips.

Fat tears rolled down Honan's pallid flesh as his mouth impossibly gave voice a low, anguished moan that tore at the hearts of the Ultramarines. Uriel wanted to go to the man's aid, but knew that it was beyond his, or any other man's power to save Honan. There was a terrible pleading desperation in Honan's eyes and his mouth kept flapping in a heroic effort to speak.

Uriel moved closer to the man's exploded anatomy, masking his horror at the mutilation.

'What are you trying to say?' he whispered, unsure whether the fleshy jigsaw could hear him, let alone understand him.

Honan's lips formed a pair of words and Uriel knew what the man desired.

Kill me...

He nodded and raised his bolter to point at Honan's head. The grotesque form of Honan's mouth formed more words before his eyes closed for the last time.

Uriel whispered the Prayer for the Martyr and pulled the trigger. A hail of bolts shredded the suspended chunks of flesh, tearing them from the hooks and granting oblivion to the mutilated cartel man.

Uriel let his fury flood through him in the cathartic fire of his bolter. His squad joined him, emptying their magazines in a storm of gunfire that tore the octagonal room to shreds, blasting great holes in the walls, smashing metal tray racks and utterly destroying any trace of the crime against nature, visited upon this latest victim of Kasimir de Valtos's insane schemes.

As the smoke of their gunfire dissipated, Uriel felt his breathing return to normal and lowered his weapon. Honan's soundless valediction echoed within his skull.

Thank you.

Their prey had flown.

No matter. They would hunt him down.

'Inform Inquisitor Barzano what has happened here and tell him that we are returning to the palace,' snapped Uriel. He turned on his heel and marched from the devastated room.

KASIMIR DE VALTOS reclined on the leather seats of his ground car. The vehicle was of a less traditional design than was usual on Pavonis, but since this was a time of change, it was not inappropriate, he thought.

He once again pictured the helpless face of Solana Vergen as he showed her the contents of his black leather case. He had savoured every scream and every pleading whimper as she begged for her life, not realising that she had signed her own death sentence the moment she had accepted his dinner invitation. He was only sorry that he had not had the opportunity to watch the Surgeon work on fat Honan, but his own needs and desires had taken priority.

Yes, Solana Vergen had been exquisite. Her death would keep the demons from assailing his every thought with blood and pain for a time. But he knew they would be back soon enough and that he would have to wash them away in the blood of another.

Kasimir looked up from his reverie at the other passengers in his vehicle, experiencing an uncharacteristic desire to share his good spirits.

The Surgeon sat opposite him, hands clasped in his lap and his eyes drifting over Kasimir's body, as though pondering the best method of dissecting him. He remembered all too well the pain of the last procedure to purge his ravaged internal organs and renew his polluted circulatory system.

Two could play at that game, vowed de Valtos, remembering the screams of over a hundred different victims he had practiced his own art upon. Soon there would be a reversal of roles when he was in possession of the Nightbringer. Its sleeping master would grant him the immortality he so craved and these upstart aliens would understand that they were the servants, not he.

The Surgeon's female accomplice reclined next to him, her long, ivory legs stretched languidly across the floor of the vehicle. Her eyes glittered playfully, arousing and repulsive at the same time. She blew him a kiss and he flinched as though she had threatened to touch him with her loathsome, yet sensual flesh.

Despite her proud words, her warp-spawned beasts had failed their mission, but he did not feel disappointed. He would, after all, get the chance to see Shonai's face as she realised he was the person behind all her years of misery.

He could feel his good mood evaporating as the tap, tap, tapping of the vehicle's last occupant intruded on his thoughts. Vendare Taloun studiously avoided looking at his fellow passengers, rapping his ring finger on the one-way glass of the window. He wanted to pity Vendare, but that emotion had died within him the moment the haemonculi's blades had peeled the skin from his muscles.

If anything he felt contempt for the man. His petty, small-mindedness had led him into this pact with de Valtos. How else did he think they were going to wrest control of this world from Shonai? With words and democratic process? He wanted to laugh and had to stifle the urge to erupt in hysterical laughter.

He forced himself to get a grip on his wildly fluctuating emotions, knowing that with the end in sight, he must not lose control. Control was everything.

As the car rounded a corner in the road, he caught a glimpse of the city of Brandon Gate ahead. He lifted his hand and squinted through a gap he formed with his forefinger and thumb. He could fit the image of the distant city between his digits and smiled as he pressed them closer together, imagining that the shortening distance separating them was the lifespan of Governor Shonai. He rolled his arm, noting the time on his wrist chrono patch as the Surgeon removed a long, curved device from the inside of his robes and peered intently at it. De Valtos was struck again by the delicate structure and dexterity of his finger movements.

The alien's lips were pursed together in displeasure. He replaced the device in his robes and said, 'The flesh sculpture has expired. There are enemies within the vivisectoria.'

De Valtos was surprised, but hid his reaction. If someone had discovered Honan, they must already know a measure of his plans.

No matter. Events were already in motion and nothing now could prevent their ordained path. They were almost at the shuttle platform where he would board the craft that would carry him to his destiny in the palace.

He thought of Beauchamp Abrogas in the cells of the Arbites precinct and almost laughed.

He spoke to the hateful alien woman, 'You gave the Abrogas boy the inhaler?'

She nodded, not even deigning to speak to him.

So strange that it would be a fool like Beauchamp who heralded the beginning of Pavonis's new age.

But that was in the future. There were matters afoot now that demanded his attention.

* * *

'So it has begun then?' asked Mykola Shonai.

'It certainly looks like it. De Valtos wouldn't abandon his home unless his plans were moving into their final stages.' answered Inquisitor Barzano snapping off the vox-caster and drawing his pistol and sword. He was possibly overreacting, but after the attack of the warp beasts, he was taking no chances.

His mood was foul, as he had just learned that Amel Vedden, the traitor Learchus had captured following the riot in Liberation Square, was dead.

Despite being kept in restraints the man had somehow managed to dislodge one of his intravenous lines and blow an air bolus into his bloodstream, resulting in a massive embolism and heart attack. It was a painful way to die and, though Vedden had escaped justice in this world, Barzano knew that all the daemons of hell were now rending his soul.

Scores of armed guards ringed the governor's private wing of the palace and Learchus had pulled the Ultramarines back to the inner chambers. Mykola Shonai and Ario Barzano were about as well protected as they could be.

'So what do we do now, inquisitor?' said Leland Corteo, obviously trying to hide the nervousness he felt. Barzano turned to the ageing advisor and placed a reassuring hand on his shoulders.

'Our first priority must be to ready all the loyal armed forces. Vox a warning to the Arbites and place the palace guard on full alert. Also, tell the defence commander to have each of his weapon emplacements acquire one of the tanks waiting outside the city walls. Hopefully it won't be required, but if de Valtos tries anything, I want us to be ready for him. You understand?'

'Of course, I'll see to it personally. I know the commander, Danil Vorens, and I shall ensure that your wishes are carried out.'

Corteo sped from the room, leaving Barzano, Jenna Sharben, Almerz Chanda and Mykola Shonai staring through the armoured glass of the governor's chambers over the smouldering city.

The exhaust fumes of dozens of tanks rose from beyond the walls, and Barzano knew it was just a matter of time until their guns were turned upon the walls of the palace.

'Judge Sharben?'

'What?' she asked, turning to face him.

'I want you to escort the governor to her personal shuttle. Then you are to travel with her to the *Vae Victus*.'

Mykola Shonai's face hardened, and she folded her arms across her chest.

'Inquisitor Barzano, this is a time of crisis for my planet and you wish me to flee? My duty is here, leading my people through this.'

'I know, Mykola,' explained Barzano, 'and normally I would agree with you, but our enemies have shown that they can reach into your most protected sanctum and strike at you. I am moving you to the *Vae Victus* for your own safety until I can be sure that the palace is secure. If this is the opening move in a full-scale rebellion, then logic dictates that there will be another attempt on your life.'

'But surely we are well protected here? Sergeant Learchus assures me that I am quite safe.'

'I do not doubt the sergeant's capabilities, but I will not be argued with. You are bound for the *Vae Victus*, and that is the end of the matter.'

'No, it is not,' stated Mykola Shonai. 'I am not leaving Pavonis, running like a scared child. I will not let my people down again. I will not run, I will stay, and if that puts my life in danger, then so be it.'

Barzano took a deep breath and scratched his forehead. Determination shone in Shonai's features and he saw that if he wanted her on the shuttle he was going to have to order Learchus to drag her there.

'Very well,' he relented, 'but I want your word that if things deteriorate further and it becomes too dangerous to remain here, then you will allow us to move you to the *Vae Victus*.'

For a moment, he thought she would refuse, but at last she nodded. 'Very well, if the situation here becomes too dangerous, I will accede to your request.'

'Thank you, that's all I ask,' said Barzano.

WHEN THE DOOR to his cell had opened and the surly gaoler told him that a member of his family had come to pay his fine, it was the best news Beauchamp Abrogas could remember hearing in a long time.

His head pounded with a splitting headache. He squinted as he was led along a long corridor, bright and featureless save for the bare iron doors to the cells that studded its length.

Already he felt superior to those poor unfortunates locked inside. Not for them the speedy payment of a fine, paid from bulging ancestral coffers.

His thoughts felt clearer now than they had for many months and Beauchamp vowed to go easy on the opiatix, perhaps even give it up for good.

Beauchamp was marched along some depressingly drab corridors, filed through several offices, and made to sign various forms, none of which he read, before finally being allowed to depart the detention level.

His spirits soared as he entered the elevator, carrying a bundle of his own clothes. They were absolutely filthy and he doubted whether even his faithful servants could get the stains from them.

He licked his lips as the elevator doors opened and he was again marched through a series of featureless corridors towards his freedom. Eventually, he was led to a plain room containing a chipped table and chairs bolted to the floor. A judge pushed him into one of the seats and said, 'Wait.'

Beauchamp nodded and crossed his arms, propping his feet up on the table as his former arrogance and poise began returning. Long minutes passed and he began to get restless, pacing the small room as his impatience mounted. Tired of pacing, he returned to the chair as he heard the locks on the door disengage.

A new judge entered, leading a heavyset man in long robes with a short, neatly trimmed beard. The new arrival carried a metal box and wore an Abrogas cartel pin in his lapel, but Beauchamp didn't recognise him.

The judge left the room as the Abrogas man sat opposite Beauchamp and slid the box forward across the table.

'I am Tynen Heras, my lord. I have come to take you home.'

'Well it's about time,' snapped Beauchamp irritably. He was damned if he'd show any gratitude to a servant. He pointed at the box and said, 'What's that?'

'I took the liberty of signing for your personal effects, my lord,' replied Heras, opening the box. Inside was a pile of cash, some jewellery, a deck of cards and–

Beauchamp's eyes widened at the sight of the plain black opiatix inhaler the raven-haired woman from the Flesh Bar had slipped into his pocket, just before his arrest. He smiled slyly, slipping the inhaler into his palm as he pocketed his effects. He decided he could be magnanimous after all, and nodded towards Heras.

'My thanks, Guilder Heras. You have done your leader a great service today.'

'My lord,' acknowledged Heras, lifting the empty box and rising from his chair. He circled Abrogas and rapped on the door. 'I shall return this to the officers and then we shall be on our way, my lord.'

'Yes, you do that, I am anxious to return home.'

The door opened and the man hurriedly left.

Left alone again, Beauchamp could feel the weight of the inhaler pressing into his sweaty palm and ran his hand over his stubbled chin, feeling the need grow within him.

No, he couldn't. Not here. Not in the Arbites precinct. There would be pict-recorders hidden in here.

But it was too late; the idea had taken hold.

It would be his own tiny bit of revenge on the Adeptus Arbites, to break the law within their own stronghold. The idea was too delicious to resist and he giggled suddenly, feeling an overwhelming urge to take the entire inhaler's worth of opiatix in one huge hit.

But that would be stupid; he'd be tossed back in the cells. Especially if it was as strong as the first batch that had gotten him arrested in the first place.

No, just a small draught then.

Well, perhaps a little more.

No more than half.

Beauchamp lifted his hand to his mouth, as though preparing to yawn and placed the nozzle of the inhaler against his lips. He tasted the plastic of the mouthpiece, felt the familiar anticipatory surge of pleasure just before he pressed the dispenser button and heaved in a breath.

Hot grains of opiatix surged down his throat and into his lungs.

Immediately, Beauchamp knew something was wrong.

By the Emperor, what the hell was in this?

But by then it was too late for Beauchamp Abrogas.

Blazing heat raced around his body, his nerves were on fire and shrieking agony knifed up his spinal cord. His legs convulsed spastically and his hands clawed at the table, ripping the nails from his fingers and leaving bloody trails in its surface. He screamed in agony and heaved his body from the chair, crashing into the concrete floor.

His entire body felt as though it was on fire.

Alien chemicals distilled from ingredients so lethal they were thought to be mythical now mixed with those the Surgeon's aide had given him at the Flesh Bar.

His brain felt like it was boiling within his skull. He clawed at his head, tearing out great clumps of hair. Beauchamp rolled to his knees, screeching like a banshee, every movement sending hot bolts of pain through his body. Molten lava filled his bones as he somehow managed to haul himself to his feet, slamming his body against the door.

He could form no words, but beat his body bloody, insane with the agony ravaging his nervous system.

The door opened and Beauchamp barrelled into an Arbites judge, knocking him from his feet. He ran blindly.

Shouts followed his mad dash, but Beauchamp was deaf to them as he shambled in a random direction, not knowing where he was going, but unable to stop moving.

He dropped to his knees, alien fire searing his body from within.

Shouting voices surrounded him.

When the chemical reactions churning in his bloodstream had absorbed enough of his body's fuel to reach critical mass, they achieved their final state of existence.

Pure energy.

And with the force of a dozen demolition charges, Beauchamp Abrogas exploded.

FIFTEEN

THE SHOCKWAVE OF Beauchamp Abrogas's explosive death ripped the front of the Arbites precinct house off, collapsing it in a billowing cloud of dust and smoke, and blew out the windows of every building within a kilometre of the blast.

Barely seconds had passed before the engines of the tanks idling before the walls of the marble city roared into life and surged towards the city gates. Two Leman Russ Conquerors from the Kharon barracks opened fire on the bronze gates, the heavy shells blasting them and a sizeable portion of the walls inwards. When the smoke cleared, a twenty-metre breach was visible and the armoured vehicles ground over the rubble and into the city.

Swiftly, two dozen tanks roared along the cobbled streets towards the Imperial palace while others spread out towards peripheral landing platforms, and troop carriers moved to secure strategic cross-roads and junctions that led to the centre of the city. Rebel PDF soldiers debarked from their carriers and sprinted through the manufactorum districts, seizing control of key factories and munitions stores.

There was resistance to the take-overs, and vicious battles erupted in the streets between the PDF troops and groups of workers loyal to the Shonai cartel. More fires were sparked as stray shots hit chemical containers and more than one raging inferno was ignited as the battle spread further into the manufactorum district.

Within the marble city, the lead tanks sped across Liberation Square, fanning out to avoid the gunfire from the palace turrets. Macro-cannons blasted huge craters in the square and several tanks erupted in geysers of flame as the huge projectiles smashed through their armour and detonated their ammo stores.

But as more tanks poured into the city, the servitor gunners were swamped with targets and simply could not take out enough tanks to prevent them from reaching the walls of the palace and the smoking Adeptus Arbites precinct house.

Dozens of burning wrecks littered the square, but too many tanks were penetrating the palace's defensive cover. For some reason, its energy shield had not yet activated and battle cannon shells began dropping within the walls of the planetary governor's fastness.

The defence turrets were the first targets, each tank trading shots with the palace gunners. Each defensive turret was swiftly bracketed and destroyed, crashing from the walls in bright flames.

Explosions rained down indiscriminately on the palace, buttresses and columned arcades that had stood for thousands of years blasted to rubble by the high explosive rounds, the ornate frescoes and galleries within destroyed in a heartbeat. Dark explosions mushroomed all across the gleaming structure, toppling gilded archways and blowing out stained glass windows of ancient wonder and priceless beauty.

The great bell tower cracked, twin detonations blowing out its midsection. The tower sagged and, with ponderous majesty, toppled into the palace grounds, the bell that had been brought to Pavonis by her first human colonists tolling one last time as it impacted on the cobbled esplanade and exploded into great brass shards.

Other tanks began shelling the walls of the Arbites precinct, but here they met fiercer resistance. The power fields incorporated into the precinct's walls were, thus far, holding the worst of the damage at bay, crackling and flashing with energy discharges. A few tanks attempted to lob shells over the walls and into the precinct, but their guns were incapable of elevating high enough or firing at a low enough velocity to land their shells within the judges' compound, and every shot was long, detonating within the hab units further east.

But as more shells slammed into the energy fields protecting the walls, it became clear that it was simply a matter of time until they failed and the wall would be reduced to rubble.

Both the palace and the Arbites precinct house were living on borrowed time.

Ario Barzano struggled out from under a pile a timber and plaster, wiping a trail of blood from the side of his cheek where splinters had cut him. He scrambled to his knees as yet more blasts thundered against the palace walls and crawled towards Mykola Shonai.

He dragged the governor's limp body from beneath shattered remains of her desk and pressed his fingers against her neck. He pulled her away from the wall, keeping low and out of sight from the smashed window. Swiftly he examined her, checking for any serious wounds, but finding only bruised flesh and lacerations from the flying glass.

Satisfied that Mykola Shonai was alright, Barzano crawled across the debris-strewn floor of the office to check on the room's other occupants. Jenna Sharben didn't seem too badly hurt, though she cradled her left arm close to her chest. She gave him a curt nod of acknowledgement and jerked her head towards the prone form of Almerz Chanda, who lay beneath a buckled section of wood panelling. The governor's aide groaned as Barzano threw off the wreckage.

'What happened?' he slurred.

'It seems the tanks in Liberation Square decided to try and remove the governor by more direct means,' answered Barzano, helping the bruised man against the wall. 'Are you hurt?'

'I don't think so. A few cuts perhaps.'

'Good, don't move,' advised Barzano, casting wary glances at the wide cracks in the ceiling as more rumbling explosions shook the room. He crawled to the remains of the wall where the window had once been and furtively poked his head around the ragged stonework.

Scores of Leman Russ tanks filled the square, some of them burning wrecks, but many more grinding towards the palace, their guns elevated to fire on the upper levels. The room shook, and plaster dust floated from the groaning ceiling as timber split and cracked. The lower reaches of the palace were in flames, the vaulted entrance now nothing more than a pile of fire-blackened stonework.

In the wake of the tanks came scores of Chimera armoured fighting vehicles, all heading in the direction of the palace and Arbites precinct.

He rolled back to where he'd left Mykola Shonai. She was starting to come round and he wiped blood and dust from her face.

She coughed, opening her eyes, and Barzano was pleased to note the absence of fear. Shonai pushed herself upright and surveyed the devastation wreaked in her personal chambers.

'Bastards!' she snapped, attempting to stand. Barzano kept her down as another volley of shells struck the palace a series of hammer blows.

He looked over at Jenna Sharben who knelt beside Almerz Chanda and nodded.

'We have to get out of here, Mykola. I don't think there's any doubt that things have deteriorated, is there?'

Despite the destruction around her, Shonai grinned weakly and shook her head. 'I suppose not.'

She pressed her hand to her temple and winced, 'All I remember is a terrific explosion and next thing I was lying on the floor.'

Shrugging off Barzano's helping hand, Shonai rose unsteadily to her feet and brushed her robes of office clear of dust as the door to her chambers was wrenched from its frame by a battered looking Sergeant Learchus. The giant warrior ducked into the room, followed by the two warriors Uriel had ordered remain with the inquisitor.

'Is everyone alright?' demanded Learchus.

'We'll live, sergeant,' assured Mykola Shonai, striding past Learchus and into the undamaged outer chambers, 'but we must act with haste now. Our enemy is at the gates and we have little time.'

Learchus picked up the stumbling Chanda in one arm as Jenna Sharben and Ario Barzano followed the governor's retreating back. Dozens of palace guards and soldiers ringed her, as though seeking to make up for their failure to protect her from the shelling. Suddenly Shonai stopped, her head cocked to one side and spun to face them.

'Why isn't the energy shield up?'

Barzano paused for a moment. 'That's a damn good question actually,' he said at last.

He opened a channel to his quarters and Lortuen Perjed.

'Lortuen, old friend. Is everyone there alright?'

After a long silence, Perjed finally answered, 'Yes, we're all fine, Ario. What about you?'

'We're alive, which is something, but we're getting out of here and heading for the *Vae Victus*. I want you to gather everybody and make your way to the landing platforms on the east wing roof. We'll meet you there.'

He shut off the communication and turned to Learchus, saying, 'Sergeant, I need you and your men to get to the aerial defence control room and find out why the shield isn't up. Do whatever needs to be done to raise it.'

Learchus looked ready to mount another protest, but Barzano cut him off, waving at the dozen palace soldiers. 'Don't worry about my safety, sergeant. We have enough protection here, I'm sure.'

The sergeant didn't look convinced, but nodded and handed the swaying Chanda to a pair of grey uniformed soldiers.

'I'll show you the way,' offered a young defence trooper.

Learchus grunted his thanks and the four set off at a jog towards the control room.

THE ONCE GRIM and imposing façade of the Arbites precinct house looked as though a siege titan had taken its gigantic wrecking ball to it. The entire west face had caved in, exposing plascrete floor slabs and twisted tendons of reinforcement. Huge metre wide cracks stretched from ground to roof and giant holes gaped in the building's fabric.

Casualties were high and the compound was choked with rubble and dust. Blood-covered judges pulled wounded comrades from the wreckage and dug for survivors while medics desperately tried to seal wounds and breathe life into crushed bodies.

Virgil Ortega pushed his way through the shell-shocked throng, trying to make some kind of sense of the events of the last few minutes. The precinct house was in ruins, and he tried to fathom how such a disaster could have occurred. It wasn't a shell impact; that much was certain, since the blast had exploded from within. There was no way anyone could have smuggled a bomb inside, but how else could it have happened?

Explanations and retribution could come later. If there was a later, he reflected, listening to the deafening thunder of shellfire as the traitor tanks attempted to batter their way in. Hastily he mentally reprimanded himself for that tiny heresy. He was a warrior of the Emperor, and while there was life in his body, there would be no surrender.

He grabbed every man that was fit to fight, shouting his orders to them. This was the first strike in armed rebellion, and when the walls failed, they were sure to be hit hard.

His breath came in short, painful bursts and his head pounded viciously. He'd only just discharged himself from the precinct infirmary and his splintered ribs still ached fiercely, but he'd be damned if he'd sit this fight out.

He would have preferred to mount his defence from within the precinct, but its structure was far too unstable and looked ready to collapse at any moment. Gun batteries on the crenellated battlements added some heavy punch to the defence, but many of these had been damaged in the explosion and subsequent collapse.

Satisfied that he was making all possible precautions for the defence, he returned to the huge gates of the precinct house where he'd left Collix with the vox-caster. Collix was blood soaked, his carapace armour dented and dust covered. Virgil had been pleasantly surprised at how the young officer had changed in the last few days. He had matured into a fine officer and Ortega was glad he had survived the explosion.

'Any luck?' asked Ortega.

'Nothing yet, sir. All the other precincts are off the net. We're being jammed.'

'Damn it!' swore Virgil. This was much worse than he'd feared.

'Try the PDF net,' he suggested.

'I've tried that already. It's jammed solid.'

'Well keep trying and call me if you get anything,' ordered Virgil.

Collix nodded and returned to the communications gear.

Ortega stared out over the rubble-strewn ground before him. The defensive perimeter of the precinct house extended three hundred metres from the front of the building's structure with angled walls, tank traps and concealed ditches providing a layered defence that his hastily prepared fire teams were even now rushing to occupy. But what should have been a clear field of fire was now littered with giant slabs of rock and steel. When the enemy breached the walls, they would have plenty of cover.

He glanced over to the buckled roller doors that protected the precinct's vehicle hangar. Inside, he could hear the three Leman Russ tanks the judges had available, their engines idling. Hopefully they could yet surprise their enemy.

A massive explosion from the walls and a whipcrack of blazing energy announced the failure of the walls' protective power fields, the machine spirits within them overwhelmed by the weight of fire. Seconds later a portion of the wall blasted inwards and a whole section collapsed.

This was it, the attack was coming and Virgil knew that with the limited time and resources available, he'd done as much as he could.

Now he would see if it had been enough.

DANIL VORENS LOWERED his smoking laspistol and returned his attention to the viewscreen before him. A stunned silence filled the defence control room, the technicians agog at what had just happened.

Lutricia Vijeon stared in open-mouthed horror at the corpse lying in the centre of the room with a ragged hole where its face had been. The old man had come in waving his pipe and screaming at them to raise the energy shield, cursing them all to hell for allowing traitors to defile the palace walls.

She had been surprised that Vorens hadn't already raised the shield, and was about to voice her concerns when the old man had burst in. She didn't know who he was, but understood that his clearance must be extremely high to allow him access to this command centre.

He'd raged at Vorens, who had calmly drawn his pistol and shot him in the face.

Vorens had holstered his pistol and turned his gaze upon the control centre technicians.

'Anyone else have any objections to my not raising the shield?' he asked mildly.

No one said anything, and Lutricia felt a deep shame burn in her heart. This was murder and treason. Safe within this reinforced structure, they could feel only the barest hint of the artillery bombardment that was pulverising the rest of the palace, and she muttered a brief prayer to the Emperor for His forgiveness.

DESPITE THE PRESENCE of a dozen palace defence troops, Ario Barzano still felt acutely vulnerable. The corridors shook as more tanks advanced into Liberation Square and added their guns to those shelling the palace. He could hear shouts and screams throughout the palace as its inhabitants ran to the shelters in the basement and the shuttle platforms. Mixed in with those shouts were those of invading soldiers.

He'd seen troops pouring into the palace and knew that the men here could not hope to hold them for long. Cut off from reinforcements and stunned at the horrendous casualties they had suffered so far, it would not be long until the palace was overrun.

It was imperative for him to get Mykola Shonai out of here. With her as a symbol for loyalist troops to rally around, they might yet hold this planet together before de Valtos's plan came to fruition.

Mykola Shonai held onto his arm and, behind him, Jenna Sharben helped Almerz Chanda. The governor's aide was slowing them down, his injuries apparently more serious than they had appeared.

'How much further is it to the shuttle bays?' asked Barzano, sure the shouts of attacking troops were closer than before.

'We're close. We should be there in a few minutes,' replied Shonai breathlessly.

The passageway rocked as fresh shells rained down and Barzano pulled up short as a section of the roof crashed down in front of them, burying the first six men in their group and filling the air with choking dust and flying debris.

Barzano picked himself up from the floor, cursing like a navy rating as he saw the passageway ahead was completely blocked with rubble. He hauled a gasping trooper to his feet, yelling, 'Is there another way to the landing platforms? Quickly man!'

The young soldier coughed, his face covered in a film of dust, and nodded.

'Yes, sir, back the way we came. It'll take longer, but we can still make it.'

Screams and the noise of small arms fire sounded dangerously close.

'Damn, this looks bad,' hissed Barzano.

JUDGE ORTEGA DIDN'T see the first shot to hit the precinct until it blew one of the gun batteries from the walls. He watched as the flaming wreckage tumbled majestically from the battlements and crashed to the ground, crushing a dozen members of his right flank's fire team.

The remaining batteries opened fire on the first tanks through the breach in the wall. The lead vehicle blew apart, its turret spinning high into the air. No sooner had the smoke cleared than a trio of Conquerors smashed their destroyed comrade aside and fired a volley of shells at the precinct, blasting huge chunks from the face of the building. The already unstable structure finally gave way.

Judges scattered as huge chunks of plascrete and steel smashed downwards in a deadly rain, burying the wounded personnel below utterly. Huge, rolling clouds of choking dust blinded Virgil, but he could clearly hear the roar of engines and he shouted over the continuing rumble.

'Stand to! No surrender!'

His voice was lost in the sharp bark of cannon fire as the precinct guns duelled with the enemy tanks. It was an unequal struggle, as the Conquerors would fire then swiftly displace to another position before the precinct batteries could acquire them. Despite this, all three Conquerors were blown apart before following rebel troops carrying missile launchers and mortars swiftly destroyed the judges' guns with concentrated volleys of fire.

Through the smoke and dust, Virgil could make out the shadowy forms of armoured vehicles and dived for cover as heavy lasfire from the turret of an approaching Chimera raked towards him.

He rolled upright behind one of the reinforced defensive walls and shouted to the nearest fire team, 'Chimera! Eleven o'clock!'

The two-man fire team heard his cry and swung their missile launcher to bear on the tank.

The shell slashed from the recoilless launcher, slamming into the Chimera's frontal section and exploded, severing the tracks but not penetrating its hull. The vehicle skidded and crashed into a torn slab of concrete, slewing round as the other track continued to roll. The rear ramp dropped and its crew began to disembark before the transport became their coffin.

Virgil swore as he saw the attackers clearly for the first time.

Pavonis PDF!

He'd known it must be the PDF, but to see them openly attacking his men was still a shock. His fury built within him until it threatened to burst from him in an uncontrolled frenzy, but he suppressed his rage, knowing that a cool head was required here.

Another missile sailed through the open crew door of the Chimera. The tank exploded, its fuel and ammunition cooking off and blasting from its rear like an immense flame-thrower. Burning PDF soldiers scattered, screaming from the wreck as a cheer went up from the Arbites line.

The cheer died as the unmistakable, metallic cough of massed mortar fire sounded.

'Incoming!' yelled Virgil, dropping to the ground and burying his head in his hands.

The mortar rounds landed in a string of thudding detonations and screams that rocked the compound. Most of the Arbites had managed to reach safety before the rounds landed, but those that did not were torn apart in a storm of shrapnel fragments.

Virgil burrowed further into his shelter as volley after volley impacted around them.

So long as they kept their heads down behind the walls, Virgil knew that the casualties from the mortar fire would be minimal. But equally, he knew that every second they sheltered, the PDF would be closing. Virgil risked a look over the wall, cursing as he saw four Chimeras nearing his position.

The sudden quiet as the mortar fire ceased was a blessed relief and Virgil rose to his feet, shotgun at the ready.

The six PDF troopers facing him across the wall were just as surprised as he to be facing one another.

Virgil blasted a volley of scatter shot into their midst.

At such close range, the blast felled two of the soldiers immediately and dropped a third, screaming, to the ground.

He vaulted the wall and swung his legs round, smashing his feet into the face of the nearest trooper and sending him sprawling into the remaining two. He racked the pump of the shotgun as he landed.

Before they could recover themselves, he blew each away with a blast to the chest.

A shot punched into the wall beside him. He dodged back as the wounded trooper fired his pistol again.

Virgil leapt forwards and brought the butt of his shotgun down hard on the man's head. Quickly, he made his way back behind the wall.

He looked along the length of the battling Arbites line. The situation was bad, but not beyond saving. The rebel PDF had more men and light artillery support, but Virgil had some of the most feared soldiers in the Imperium fighting for him. And the superior training, weaponry and discipline of the Arbites was now proving its worth as Virgil could see that the PDF attack had lost its momentum.

Instead of advancing, their attackers were sheltering behind their transports, sporadically firing their lasguns. He knew that to break them, they had to hit back with a strong counter-punch.

'Collix!' he shouted, 'Get over here!'

Sergeant Collix ran in a crouch towards Virgil, firing his shotgun from the hip.

'Captain?' said Collix, his breath and pulse racing with the beat of adrenaline.

'Get onto Veritas squadron, tell them we need them now! I need them to engage the enemy's right flank. If they can hit them hard enough and quickly enough we can roll up the rebel line and force them back!'

As Collix spoke hurriedly into the vox-caster, Virgil thumbed more shells into the shotgun's breech and racked the pump.

'Captain! Squadron Leader Wallas reports that only the Righteous Justice has been properly consecrated. Divine Authority and Holy Law will not be blessed and ready for some minutes yet.'

Ortega snarled and snatched the vox-caster from Collix and shouted into the handset.

'Wallas, get those bloody tanks out here right now or I'll come in there and rip your Emperor-damned heart out and feed it to you! Do you understand me?'

He didn't wait for a reply and tossed the handset back to Collix.

Seconds later, the armoured door to the vehicle hangar juddered upwards and the Righteous Justice, a venerable Leman Russ battle tank, rolled out with its guns blasting huge holes in the PDF ranks.

Two Chimera exploded in quick succession as the Arbites gunners found their marks. Small arms fire rattled from its thick armour as the Righteous Justice hosed its attackers in heavy bolter fire, dropping men by the dozen.

Virgil grinned to himself. By the Emperor, they could do it!

The PDF were scattering before the Righteous Justice's charge, unable to dent its hide. His breath caught in his throat as he saw a missile contrail spear towards the tank. The missile impacted on the vehicle's flank, obscuring it in smoke.

The tank sped clear of the explosion and Virgil could see that the hull mounted lascannon had been blown clear, but no further damage had been inflicted.

Virgil sighed in relief.

He shouted, 'Men of the Emperor, now is our time! Charge!' and again leapt the defensive wall.

The Arbites rose up and charged madly across the shattered, body-littered compound, firing as they went. Their blood was afire and the sight of the Righteous Justice smiting their foes gave them the punch to crush the traitors beneath their boot heels. The soldiers of the PDF fell back, overwhelmed by the twin blows of Righteous Justice and the screaming judges.

Virgil shot a trooper in the back and another in the chest as he caught sight of a trio of Conqueror tanks crashing over the breach in the walls. The heavy bolters mounted on their hulls sprayed the battlefield before them, the commanders' firing cupola mounted weapons and screaming at the judges.

The gunfire was indiscriminate and the bloodshed prodigious as bullets and lasers felled PDF soldiers alongside the judges.

The Righteous Justice's brief charge was brought to an abrupt close as a missile and the bright lance of a lascannon shot impacted simultaneously on its turret, igniting the battle cannon shells and blowing the tank high into the air.

The demise of Righteous Justice coincided with the arrival of Divine Authority and Holy Law. Bursting into the compound like a thunderstrike, their heavy bolter fire raked across the exposed PDF troops and their battle cannon blasted huge craters in the ground.

Virgil shouted a warning as he saw a group of PDF officers charge towards the Divine Authority. He could see one of the enemy officers was equipped with a power fist, its massive form wreathed in destructive energies that could easily tear through the armour of a tank.

The officer leapt forward, power fist raised to smash down. The lascannon mounted on the frontal section of Divine Authority fired, vaporising one of his companions, but the rest kept coming.

The driver of Divine Authority realised his danger and attempted to turn away from the charging officers, but it was too late. The first officer smashed his power fist through the vehicle's side, tearing the armoured hull wide open and peeling the adamantium skin back. The tank slewed round, smashing into a concrete wall and flattening it along with four cowering PDF troopers.

The other officers emptied the magazine of their weapons through the huge tear in the tank's side, slaughtering the crew in a hail of bullets.

Grenades burst around them as Arbites men rushed to avenge their fallen comrades, but the officers fled into the smoke of battle and escaped retribution. Virgil saw yet more Chimeras pour into the compound. Hundreds of troopers followed in their wake and shellfire from the three Conquerors blasted more judges to oblivion.

The Arbites counterattack, a fragile thing at best, faltered in the face of such horrendous bloodshed. As the death toll mounted, the Arbites' line suddenly broke, unable to withstand the terrible losses inflicted by the Conquerors.

At first Virgil was able to hold them together, but as more explosions and gunshots mowed down the withdrawing judges, the retreat became a rout.

Holy Law skidded round the smoking remains of Divine Authority and fired at will, attempting to buy the judges time to fall back. The PDF scattered before the tank as it rumbled towards the supporting Chimeras. Its lascannon fired, punching through the rear armour of one of the vehicles and destroying the engine in a gout of yellow flame, the huge blast somersaulting the Chimera into the air.

The burning wreck smashed down at an angle on a second vehicle, crushing its left track unit. The impact snapped the main drive shaft and pistoned it explosively downwards. Its engine revving madly, the Chimera was catapulted upwards. Spinning crazily, it crashed to the ground, exploding in a bright orange fireball and incinerating a score of PDF troopers.

Despite their loss, the Conquerors and the PDF were tearing the beating heart from the defence. Most of the judges had been cut down as they fled and Virgil knew the precinct house was lost.

He saw the same enemy officer who had ripped open the Divine Authority charge the Holy Law, his power fist crackling with lethal energies. Virgil fired his shotgun at the man, desperate to aid the last of his tanks, but the range was too great.

Holy Law gunned its engines. The driver had seen his brother tank torn to pieces by power fists and was in no mood to suffer a similar fate. Realising that speed was his only hope of survival, he turned towards the officer, hoping to crush the man beneath his armoured treads.

The traitor leapt forwards and slashed his power fist down at the speeding vehicle, the links of the tracks snapping beneath his grip.

The toothed, track cogs spun wildly.

Orange sparks flared and the track unit snarled as the power fist became caught in its grip.

The entire vehicle shuddered, the thrashing drive-unit dragging the struggling officer into its depths. The officer shrieked as he was jerked down. His arm ripped from its socket in a welter of blood and bone as the remains of the shattered tracks brutally pulled him under the tank's mass.

He was able to scream once more before the huge vehicle rolled over his body and crushed him utterly.

Virgil sprinted towards the remains of the precinct house, bleeding from a score of wounds. The battle was lost and now all that mattered was to try and get as many of his men to safety as was possible.

He knew that their chances were slim to say the least, but Virgil Ortega was not the kind of man to give up without a fight. Anything he could do to obstruct and hamper these traitorous scum was definitely worth doing.

But first he had to try and get out of here with some kind of fighting force at his command. They had themselves a respite for now. The surviving PDF troopers had paused in their attack, stunned at the horrific death of their commander and the bizarre destruction of the two Chimera transports. The reprieve didn't last as a fresh burst of lascannon fire destroyed the Holy Law before any of the crew could escape the disabled tank.

Virgil rounded up all the able-bodied judges he could find and shoved them towards the ruins of the precinct. If enough of the lower levels had escaped the blast, they could move through the tunnels below the precinct and make their way to the palace. He saw that Collix was amongst the survivors.

Good, they may yet have need of the vox-gear.

Virgil knew that escape was their only chance now and if they could lay their hands on the heavy weapons held in the armoury below the palace, their chances of holding out would be increased immeasurably.

He vowed they would make these damn rebels rue the day they had crossed Virgil Ortega.

LUTRICIA VIJEON'S THOUGHTS tumbled like an uncontrolled rail car as she tried to make some kind of sense out of what was happening here. Vorens had killed a man in front of everyone here, and was allowing the palace to be shelled.

Lutricia was a loyal servant of the Emperor and she knew that someone had to do something, but who? Her?

Her entire body shook with fear as she realised that she was no match for Vorens and that her superior officer would undoubtedly kill her. She was a technician, for the Emperor's sake! She wasn't trained for this sort of thing. How could she be expected to fight a man armed with a laspistol?

Sweat dripped into her eyes in a steady flow.

Everyone jumped as a dull thud echoed around the control room, sounding like a massive hammer blow on the main doors. Even Vorens looked concerned and she spun to look at the external pict-display. Her heart leapt as she saw three massive warriors clad in the armour of Space Marines. Yes! These holy warriors would end this nightmare and she felt a huge weight lifted from her shoulders at this answer to her prayers.

But the more she watched the pict-display, the more her hopes fell. The entrance to the command centre had been built to withstand the heaviest assault, and not even the power of three Space Marines could smash through the metre-thick layer of plate steel.

A flickering motion caught her eye and she watched as her display indicated an incoming aircraft. Telemetry flashed across the display as the logic engines flashed up identifying runes telling her course, speed and altitude of the new contact.

It was a Thunderhawk gunship.

She stole a furtive look at Vorens, who was grinning at the sight of the three Space Marine vainly attempting to break into the command centre. Lutricia realised she only had a few moments to seize this opportunity; Vorens was sure to notice the approaching craft soon. She struggled to think how she could turn the situation to her advantage.

A frightening calm replaced her fear as she realised what she had to do.

Like the trained professional she was, her fingers danced over the runes of her station, transmitting exact positional data of the command centre's location to the Thunderhawk. It might not be much, but it was all she could do.

She saw Vorens catch sight of the Thunderhawk on the main display and just hoped her own small contribution would be enough as he raced to activate the servitor defence routines.

BARZANO'S SMALL GROUP emerged into the sunlight of the landing platform and the inquisitor had never been more relieved to see the sky as he was now. They staggered towards a black shuttle, its engines shrieking as the pilot kept the power ready for immediate take off. Through the open side hatch, he could see Lortuen Perjed and his group of scribes.

He smiled as the welcome sight of the Ultramarines Thunderhawk gunship roared overhead.

Jenna Sharben led, dragging Mykola Shonai towards the shuttle and safety. The last palace guard helped the struggling Almerz Chanda. The governor's aide stumbled and fell to his knees as Barzano passed him. He kept going, catching up to Jenna Sharben and helping her with the governor.

A lasbolt fired, shockingly loud, even over the screaming engines of the shuttle. Barzano spun, wondering how the rebels could have caught up so soon. He unslung his rifle and dropped to his knees, trying to make sense of the scene before him.

Almerz Chanda stood over the body of the palace guard, expertly holding a smoking lasgun. He snapped off a shot at Barzano, taking the inquisitor high in the shoulder and slamming him back against the shuttle's hull.

Barzano yelled in pain and dropped his weapon. Jenna Sharben turned and was punched from her feet by an equally well-placed shot. Governor Shonai stood at the shuttle, staring in horror at Chanda as he strode across towards her.

He raised his rifle and aimed through the pilot's canopy, making a chopping motion with one hand across his throat. The whine of the engines died as the pilot powered down the engines and unstrapped himself from his bucket seat.

Chanda shot him through the canopy.

Barzano struggled to push himself upright as grey uniformed PDF troopers swarmed onto the landing platform from the palace and Mykola Shonai stood before Chanda, her face a granite mask of fury.

'Why?' she asked simply.

'You are the past,' replied Chanda. 'Weak, pathetic, clinging to your outdated loyalty to a withered corpse on a planet you have never even seen.'

'You disgust me, Almerz. To think I once called you a friend.' She slapped Chanda hard and spat in his face.

Chanda slammed the butt of his rifle into the governor's head, dropping her to the ground with blood spurting from her broken nose. But, still she stared at him with defiance and anger.

Barzano tried to ignore the pain of the laser burn on his shoulder. He knew they had failed, but he was determined to take this piece of blasphemous filth with him on the road to hell. He tried to raise his hand, to aim his digital needler, but Chanda knelt beside him and gripped his hair.

'I've wanted to do this for a long time,' whispered Chanda, slamming Barzano's head against the shuttle's hull.

'Get on with it and go,' snapped Barzano, nauseous from the impact.

'Oh, I'm not going to kill you, Ario. No, there is a... specialist in the service of my employer who I believe you have an appointment with. A surgeon of wondrous skill.'

Barzano coughed blood. 'Why can't you say his name? Does the stench of your betrayal stick in your throat? Can your tiny mind comprehend the scale of the mistake you have just made?'

Chanda laughed as PDF troopers surrounded the shuttle.

'Mistake?' hissed Chanda so that only Barzano could hear. 'I think not. You made the mistake of coming here. Soon I will be part of an immortal band of warriors, fighting alongside a reawakened god!'

Now it was Barzano's turn to laugh, though the act sent jolts of pain across his chest and pounding through his skull.

'Did de Valtos tell you that?' he smirked. 'Then you are a bigger fool than I took you for. I can sense your fear of him. If de Valtos succeeds, you will die. Your life energy will be stripped away to feed the hunger of this creature he calls a god.'

Chanda stood, his face angry, turning away and speaking hurriedly into a hand-held vox-caster he removed from his pocket. Barzano strained to hear the words over the heavy thump of laser fire and shelling, but couldn't make them out.

He looked up, hoping to see the Thunderhawk gunship hammering down on the platform and disgorging charging Ultramarines, but the aircraft was speeding into the clouds, chased by a fearsome amount of anti-aircraft fire. That explained why the energy shield hadn't been activated at least. Somehow de Valtos had managed to get one of his people into the defence control staff and prevent it from being raised. He wondered what had become of Learchus and the two Space Marines he had sent to the control centre.

Another shuttle swooped low overhead, setting down in a cloud of exhaust fumes on the far edge of the platform. The shuttle's door slid back and a small group emerged. Clutching a leather case tightly to his chest, the gloating figure of Kasimir de Valtos stepped down onto the platform. Vendare Taloun followed him, and Barzano saw he had the desperate look of a man trapped by circumstances beyond his control. Behind the cartel men came two slim and graceful figures, and Barzano felt a flutter of apprehension as he recognised the sinuous gait of the eldar.

These two aliens were from the darker sects that lived beyond the normal realms of the galaxy and he knew in an instant that it might have been better for them all if they had been killed.

The female moved with the grace of a dancer, her every gesture suggesting sensual lethality, while the male walked stiffly, hunched over, as though unused to the daylight. Both had cruel violet eyes and skin as pale as polished ivory.

The woman barely spared him a glance, but the other gave him a look of such emptiness that it chilled even Barzano's hardened soul.

Almerz Chanda handed his rifle to a nervous looking PDF trooper and Barzano could sense their unease at the sight of the eldar. None of them had expected this.

Kasimir de Valtos stood over the prone governor and smiled, savouring the moment of his triumph.

'This has been a long time coming, Shonai,' he said at last.

Barzano struggled to remain conscious, as Chanda stood before his true master.

'I have delivered them to you as I promised I would, my lord.'

Kasimir de Valtos turned to face Chanda and nodded.

'Indeed you have, Almerz. You have proved your treachery is complete.'

Barzano could sense Chanda's confusion and unease even above that of the PDF troops on the platform.

'I have done all that you asked of me, my lord.'

De Valtos inclined his head briefly in the direction of the eldar woman.

Her hand flashed to her leather belt in a blur of motion and suddenly there was a black dart embedded in Chanda's throat.

The man dropped to his knees, the skin around the dart swelling at a horrifying rate.

'My dear Almerz,' crooned de Valtos. 'You betrayed one master, why should I trust you not to betray me also? No, better it ends like this.'

Chanda scrabbled at his throat, fighting for breath. Within seconds his gurgling cries were silent as he slipped into unconsciousness, and collapsed on the ground. De Valtos addressed the eldar male, saying, 'Do with them as you see fit.'

He tapped his boot against Chanda's slumped body. 'But make sure you honour this one first.'

Barzano felt no satisfaction at Chanda's fate, merely a sickening sense of impending disaster. For if Kasimir de Valtos was truly as insane as he appeared to be, then he was about to unleash a force that not even Barzano knew how to defeat.

De Valtos turned his gaze upon Barzano and the inquisitor felt his empathic senses recoil from the pits of the man's madness.

'I know what you are doing, de Valtos,' croaked Barzano. 'And so does Captain Ventris. He knows everything I do and I promise you he will not let you succeed. Even now he will be calling for more ships and men to defeat you.'

Kasimir de Valtos shook his head.

'If you truly understand what I intend, then you know as well as I that more men and ships will achieve nothing.'

Barzano wanted to respond, but the words died in his throat.

Because he knew that Kasimir de Valtos was right.

SIXTEEN

BARZANO LISTENED TO the screams of Almerz Chanda echoing through the prison level, hoping that the torture was as painful as it sounded. It did not matter to him that an alien was torturing a human being. By betraying his oaths of loyalty to the Emperor, Chanda had given up any right for pity.

The inquisitor had no clear idea of how long they had been incarcerated, having earlier passed out with the pain from his wound. He had awoken in this cell to find himself stripped of his weapons, even the digital one secreted within the ring on his right forefinger, and the lasburn on his shoulder cleaned and bound with surgical dressing. Mykola Shonai's broken nose had been set as well. Apparently the alien surgeon did not wish to work on damaged subjects.

The prison level they were held in had been incorporated into the groined foundations of the palace, steel bars cemented into each stone archway. Each cell was furnished with a simple bed and ablutions unit bolted to the floor. As far as jails went, it was better than many he'd thrown traitors into.

Lortuen Perjed and his scribes languished in the cell opposite, and Barzano was pleased to see that none of them had been hurt in the coup.

Sharing Barzano's cell, Mykola Shonai sat in the corner, her face a mask of fury, and Jenna Sharben lay on the bed, her wound untreated. The judge had taken a lasbolt to the belly and though the heat of the shot had cauterised the wound, Barzano suspected she might be bleeding internally. She had not recovered consciousness since Chanda's treachery at the landing platform, and Barzano knew that without medical attention she would die in a few hours. It seemed she was not worth the attention of the surgeon's scalpel.

When the governor had come round, she had raged at the cell door, kicking and screaming oaths that would have made a stevedore blush.

Barzano had pulled her away, calming her with promises of rescue and retribution. He was unsure how he was going to fulfil these promises, but knew they still had options open to them.

He returned to the bed and mopped Jenna Sharben's brow with his sleeve. She was cold to the touch and her skin was grey, already the colour of a corpse.

'I promise you won't die, Judge Sharben,' whispered Barzano.

'Another promise you're not sure you can keep?' asked Shonai.

'Not at all, Mykola. I never make promises I can't keep,' assured Barzano. He placed a hand across his heart. 'I promise.'

Despite herself, Mykola Shonai smiled, 'Do you really think we can get out of here? I mean, there are at least three regiments' worth of soldiers in the city, probably over two hundred on this level alone, and the Emperor alone knows how many prowling the palace.'

Barzano winked, 'Do not forget the three Space Marines.'

'I haven't, but surely Sergeant Learchus and his men must be dead?'

'I seriously doubt that, my dear Mykola. I'm sure de Valtos would have enjoyed parading them past us by now if they were. No, I do not believe Sergeant Learchus will be an easy man to kill, and he will have found a way to communicate with the *Vae Victus*.'

'And you think Captain Ventris will attempt to rescue us?'

'I am sure that even the daemons of the warp would not prevent him.'

'It would be a virtual suicide mission to break us out.'

'Possibly,' agreed Barzano, 'but can you see that stopping Uriel?'

'No, I suppose not,' said Mykola, leaning her head back against the stonework of the cell. She closed her eyes and Barzano thought she had fallen asleep. But without opening her eyes, she said, 'This ship you think de Valtos is after – can he really get it?'

'I'm not sure. My ordo know that one of an ancient race of beings we know as the C'tan went into a form of stasis somewhere in this sector, but not exactly where. We think that the *Nightbringer* was once his, for want of a better word, flagship. There are ancient writings and hints about the ship and its master scattered throughout history, but we still know next to nothing about it. It is of a time before the ascendancy of man and little is known for sure.'

'This... C'tan, what was it like?'

'No one can say for certain. It has probably been dormant for millions of years and records are unclear to say the least. I've read every fragment I could lay my hands on concerning the Bringer of Darkness, but I still know almost nothing about it, save one thing.'

'And that is?' asked Mykola hesitantly.

'The Nightbringer is death incarnate. Its dreams are the stuff of every race's nightmares, becoming the very image of their doom. Every thought you have ever had regarding the horror of death and mortality comes from this creature. When it walked between the stars in aeons past, it left that legacy in the collective racial psyche of almost every species in the galaxy.'

'Can we defeat such a creature?'

'Do you want the truth?'

'Of course.'

Barzano waited until the echoes of a fresh clutch of screams torn from Almerz Chanda's throat had died away before answering. 'No,' he said softly, 'I do not think we can.'

THE MAJESTIC FORM of the *Vae Victus* slowly angled its massive bulk towards the surface of Pavonis, powerful energies building in her forward linear accelerators. Few men knew the awesome power of destruction the captain of a starship possessed; the power to level cities and crack continents. For all that the captains of the Imperial Navy might strut and boast of the capabilities of their ponderous warships, there was nothing that could compete with the sheer destructive speed and efficiency of a Space Marine strike cruiser.

Defence lasers periodically stabbed upwards from armoured silos far below on the planet's surface. None of the mighty guns could match the speed of the strike cruiser and though their powerful beams pierced the sky with their colossal energies, there was a desperation to the fire. So long as the *Vae Victus* remained in high orbit, the guns below were impotent.

Closer in, however, the smaller, aerial defence batteries were a different matter. Scores of such silos were scattered around Brandon Gate and incorporated into the planet's surface. Though these were incapable of harming a starship, even one in low orbit, they could shred any aircraft that came within fifteen kilometres of the city. All were crewed by lobotomised servitors, hard-wired into their weapons, and controlled from the defence control bunker secreted somewhere within the palace grounds.

While the guns cast their protective cover over the city, any airborne assault was doomed to failure.

KASIMIR DE VALTOS RUbbed the bridge of his nose, growling at the image on the vox-holo before him.

'Lasko, if you don't give me a straight answer then I will have you buried in one of your precious mines. Now tell me, in words of two syllables or less, have you breached the door yet? I do not have time to waste.'

The flickering image of his mine overseer, Jakob Lasko, appeared furtive even through the heavy distortion of the encrypted signal from Tembra Ridge nearly one hundred kilometres from the palace.

'Well, the last cutter made it through the door, but we're having trouble moving it.'

'And why is that?' pressed de Valtos, leaning forward, his features predatory.

'We're not sure, my lord. The tech-priests say that the density of the door far exceeds what should be possible for something of its dimensions. We've had to disassemble one of our heaviest rigs and transport it down the main shaft in pieces. The techs are putting the last parts together now, and once they've blessed it, we'll be ready to go.'

'When?' hissed de Valtos, incessantly rubbing at his forehead.

'Later today, I expect.'

'It had better be,' said de Valtos snapping off the link and reclining in the ex-governor's sagging leather chair. He massaged his temples and took a gulping breath before hawking a froth of black phlegm onto the floor. The pain was getting worse and the Surgeon's specialised facilities and equipment had been destroyed by the Ultramarines. There would be no more stripping his body down to its bare bones and reassembling it in its temporarily healthy form again. He had to succeed, and soon. If that damn fool Lasko could not break into the underground tomb complex soon, then he was a dead man.

But once within, he would know the twin joys of revenge and immortality.

He remembered the day he had first learned of the C'tan from the scrolls of Corteswain. Most of his fortune had since been ploughed into the search for its resting place, but the final irony was that it had been below him all this time. Surely the hand of fate was at work that it should turn out to be below the mountains of Pavonis.

It had been a revelation the day he had finally discovered the forgotten tomb, buried beneath the world when it was nothing but an uninhabited ball of lifeless rock.

De Valtos chuckled mirthlessly as he realised soon it would be that way again.

Soon he would walk in the halls of a god! Not the pitiful, dust filled corridors of Terra that was home to a rotting corpse masquerading as a god, but a living, breathing creature with the power of creation and eternal life at its fingertips.

When had the Emperor last walked among his people? Ten thousand years ago! Where was the Emperor when the Apostate Cardinal Bucharis plunged whole sectors into war in His name? Where was the Emperor when the tyranids devoured world after world?

Where was the Emperor when the eldar boarded his ship and tortured him to the brink of death? Where was He then?

De Valtos felt his fury growing and struggled to control his rage as blood dripped from where his artificial fingernails had dug into the meat of his palms. He wiped the blood clear and ran a hand through his sweat-streaked hair, fighting down his rapid breathing.

He rose and paced the shattered remains of the room, stepping over the splintered desk, broken chairs and heaped piles of plaster. His foot hit something solid and he looked down.

He smiled, bending down to pick up a cracked bust of white marble, cradling it gently in his scarred hands. He stroked his hand across the stern face of Forlanus Shonai, blood smearing the old man's patrician features, and strode to the devastated wall of the governor's private chambers.

The city below was wreathed in a pall of black smoke and dull, coughing detonations from pockets of resistance still fighting the inevitable. His tanks and troops lined every street and, though he knew it was regrettable that these men would all die, it was a small price to pay for his impending godhood.

He patted the head of Forlanus Shonai and smiled, before hurling the bust as far as he could from his vantage point. He watched it spin down through the air, finally shattering into fragments as it impacted on the cobbled esplanade below.

LORD ADMIRAL LAZLO Tiberius followed the blip representing Uriel's Thunderhawk on the surveyor plot table as it drew near the capital city of Pavonis. An air of tense expectation hung over the bridge and even the astropathic choir had fallen silent. The feeling gripping Tiberius was the same as that of going into battle, which he supposed was correct, even though they themselves were in no danger.

Captain Uriel Ventris was the one flying into harm's way along with his warriors. The astropaths on the *Vae Victus* had reported powerful sigils and hexagrammic wards incorporated into the walls of the cells and this, combined with the energy shield that now enveloped the palace, ruled out a teleported assault.

With time against them, they were going to have to do this the old fashioned way.

'How long?' he asked tersely.

'A few moments yet,' answered Philotas.

'The co-ordinates are dialled into the attack logister?'

'Yes, lord admiral, everything is prepared. The firing solution has been confirmed.'

Tiberius caught the hint of restrained impatience in his officer's voice and smiled, grimly. He already knew everything was prepared, but couldn't help wanting to make double and triple sure. Almost time, thought Tiberius, praying that the anonymous transmission Uriel had received as he had flown towards Brandon Gate earlier that day had been genuine.

The Emperor help him if it was not.

Forcing himself to return to his captain's pulpit, Tiberius gripped the edge of his lectern and addressed his crew.

'Brothers, we come now to this gravest hour and it is to realise that there is only one way that we can triumph, and that is together as one. We have only determination, and single-minded desire. Not one amongst us has proven willing to give up or accept defeat and for that I commend you.'

Tiberius bowed his head as Philotas reported, 'They are at the edge of the defence guns' lethal envelope, lord admiral.'

The lord admiral nodded. 'Gunnery officer,' he ordered. 'Fire prow bombardment cannon.'

LUTRICIA VIJEON'S HEART sank as she watched the incoming Thunderhawk gunship on her scope. The aircraft was flying nap-of-the-earth and the pilot was good, skilfully hugging the contours of the landscape.

But it was wasted effort. The command centre had been tracking them since they had entered the atmosphere and Vorens grinned with predatory glee as he paced the room, eagerly awaiting the gunship. She had seen his momentary fear as the three Space Marines appeared at the entrance to the command centre, but his mask of vicious arrogance had reasserted itself when they had vanished. Where had they gone, wondered Lutricia?

Most of the control centre staff prayed silently at their stations, only the servitors carrying on with their allotted tasks in the face of Vorens' treachery. She made to wipe a tear from the corner of her eye, blinking as she saw something detach from the icon representing the Space Marines' strike cruiser.

A second gunship?

No, the signal was too small and, as she looked closer, she saw that it was moving too fast for a gunship. Suddenly she realised what it was and where its trajectory would cause it to land.

A warning klaxon sounded as the aged defence cogitators came to the same conclusion, sounding the alert as a flurry of other blips fired from the cruiser.

Danil Vorens gripped the edge of his chair, rising to his feet with a look of pure terror creasing his features.

'No,' he hissed, watching as the salvo of magma bombs launched from the *Vae Victus* hurtled towards them, homing in on the precise co-ordinates provided by Lutricia Vijeon.

His knees sagged and Vorens collapsed back in the commander's seat.

Lutricia watched the bombs speed their way towards them, slashing down through the atmosphere of Pavonis at incredible speed. They would impact soon, wiping this facility from the face of the planet, and not even the energy field would protect them.

Suddenly calm, she rose from her station and strode to the centre of the chamber.

Danil Vorens watched her. He wept openly at the prospect of death, but made no move to stop her as she picked up the laspistol beside him. Though she had never handled a weapon in her life, she knew exactly what to do.

Lutricia Vijeon shot Danil Vorens in the heart, letting the pistol fall from her fingers as the proximity alarms of the command centre began screaming.

She turned to the main viewscreen and sank to her knees.

Lutricia smiled, an enormous sense of satisfaction flooding her. She knew she had done the right thing and offered her thanks that she had been granted this chance to serve Him.

She extended her hands and said, 'Come, brothers and sisters. Let us pray.'

The remainder of the control centre staff joined her in a small circle, weeping and joining hands as they prayed to the Emperor for the last time.

THE MAGMA BOMBS impacted within seconds of one another.

The first clutch hammered into the energy shield, overloading the field generators protecting this portion of the palace, and punching a hole. Subsequent bombs blasted through the wing the control centre was buried beneath, obliterating it in a thunderous detonation and hurling tank-sized blocks of stone high into the air. The next penetrated ten metres of reinforced rockcrete, blasting a crater almost a hundred metres in diameter.

Two bombs malfunctioned, the first corkscrewing wildly as it hit the upper atmosphere and landing at the edge of the Gresha

Forest, immolating a sizeable portion of the Abrogas cartel's country holdings. The second hit over nine hundred kilometres from its intended target, splashing down harmlessly in the ocean.

But the rest slashed into the crater and punched deep into the command centre, their delayed fuses ensuring they exploded in its heart. Firestorms flared, incinerating every living thing within and collapsing what little remained standing. A vast black pillar of smoke, pierced with volcanic flames rose from the destroyed command centre, the shockwave of its demise rippling outwards for kilometres as though an angry god had just smote the earth.

The aerial approach to Brandon Gate was suddenly wide open as servitor controlled batteries sat idle, awaiting targeting instructions that would never arrive.

URIEL LET OUT the breath he had been holding as he heard the pilot's voice over the vox.

'Guilliman's oath! Look at that!'

He'd seen the flash of the magma bombs' impact through the vision blocks, knowing that nothing could stand before the righteous fire of a starship sanctified by the Emperor himself.

'No incoming ground fire,' confirmed the co-pilot. 'Commencing our attack run now.'

The message had been genuine then, and Uriel closed his eyes, offering a prayer of thanks and blessing upon the courageous servant of the Emperor who had managed to get the co-ordinates of the defence control centre to them, thus sealing its fate.

Lord Admiral Tiberius had wanted to level the entire palace with orbital bombardment, but Uriel had resisted such a plan, knowing that the vast forces the *Vae Victus* could unleash would level everything within fifty kilometres of the palace. The greatly reduced yield on the magma bombs had struck with precisely the correct force, and though there was certain to be some collateral casualties, Uriel hoped that that they had been kept to a minimum.

They were here to save these people, not destroy them. Leave such simple-minded butchery for the likes of the Blood Angels or Marines Malevolent. The Ultramarines were not indiscriminate killers, they were the divine instrument of the Emperor's wrath. The protection of his subjects was their reason for existing.

Too many of those who fought to protect the Imperium forgot that it was a living thing, made up of the billions of people that inhabited the Emperor's worlds. Without them, the Imperium was nothing. With the Emperor to bind them, they were the glue that held His realm together and Uriel would have no part in their deliberate murder.

A chill passed through him as he remembered Gedrik's words on Caernus IV.

The Death of Worlds and the Bringer of Darkness await to be born into this galaxy...

He now understood their significance and did not relish the prospect of what they presaged.

The Thunderhawk swayed wildly as the pilot circled the palace, swooping in low through the gap in the energy shield the magma bombs had blasted. Gunfire spat from the towers, a few shots even striking the speeding gunship, but its armour was untroubled by such pinpricks.

The gunship's crew chief glanced out of the door and shouted, 'Get ready brothers! Debarkation in ten seconds!'

Uriel tensed, tapping his breastplate and bolt pistol in honour of their war spirits. Bracing himself against the side of the gunship, he drew his power sword and watched the ground hurtle towards them.

The Thunderhawk slammed into the cobbled esplanade before the palace.

Uriel shouted, 'Courage and honour!' and leapt from the gunship.

The Ultramarines echoed his war-cry and charged after their captain.

BARZANO AND SHONAI stared fearfully at the roof of their cell as the massive shockwave of the magma bombs' detonation rocked the prison level with the violence of an earthquake. Cracks snaked across the vaulted ceilings and dozens of archways collapsed, burying the cells' screaming occupants beneath tonnes of rubble.

Stone split with the crack of a gunshot and steel groaned as millions of tonnes of rock spread its load over the blasted foundations. Barzano scrambled to his feet. The bars to their cell squealed in protest, bowing outwards under the compression as the archway sagged.

'About time,' he muttered.

'What's happening?' shouted Mykola Shonai over the rumble of collapsing stonework.

'Well, to me that sounds like the opening strike in an orbital bombardment,' replied Barzano coolly, reaching into his mouth and tugging. Shonai watched him, bemused, as the juddering tremors of the bombardment continued.

'What are you doing?'

'Getting us out of here,' replied Barzano, finally pulling out a tooth with a grunt of pain. Blood dripped from the corner of his mouth and the ivory coloured tooth he held before him.

He hurried to the cell door working the 'tooth' deep within the lock and checking for any guards. Shouts echoed up and down the prison, inmates screaming to be let out of their cells and guards yelling at them to shut up.

Barzano moved quickly from the door and grabbed Shonai, the pair of them hauling the bed with Jenna Sharben towards the rear of the cell. Barzano knelt, protecting their bodies with his own.

'Mykola, close your eyes, cover your ears and open your mouth so the blast pressure won't burst your eardrums,' advised Barzano, pressing his face into Jenna Sharben's shoulder

The governor ducked down as the compact explosive that had been secreted inside Barzano's false tooth erupted, blasting the lock-plate of the cell door across the corridor. The door itself didn't move, pressed tightly into its frame by the lowering ceiling. Before the roar of the blast had even dissipated, Barzano rose to his feet and kicked his booted foot against the cell door.

It opened a handbreadth, but another kick slammed it wide and Barzano was through.

Holding his wounded shoulder, he turned back to Shonai, saying, 'Stay here and look after Sharben. I'll be back soon.'

'Be careful!' ordered Mykola Shonai.

'Always,' grinned Barzano, scooping up a fist-sized rock that had fallen from the ceiling and jogging cautiously down the corridor, keeping close to the walls. He reached a bend in the corridor, hearing panicked voices of the guards from around the corner. He could sense they were strung out, nervous and not thinking straight.

Hefting the rock, he affected his strongest Pavonian accent and shouted, 'Quick! The prisoners are escaping from their cells!'

Seconds later three men sprinted around the corner.

Barzano hammered the rock into the first guard's face, crushing his skull and dropping him to the floor. He leapt at the second man, cracking the rock against his helmet. The inquisitor threw himself flat as a lasbolt slashed the air above him, and rolled to his knees, driving his elbow up into the third guard's groin. Barzano caught the man's lasgun as he fell and cracked the rifle butt hard against his temple. The second guard tried to rise, but Barzano shot him in the face and he collapsed.

The inquisitor raised the rifle to his uninjured shoulder and scanned for fresh targets. His wound throbbed painfully and the dressing was leaking blood, but he didn't have time to spare to redress it.

He heard fresh shouts behind him and dropped to his knees as a flurry of blasts vaporised the rock walls beside him. He spun, firing a wild volley of shots, and two guards dropped screaming to the floor. Over half a dozen remained though, and Barzano rolled around the corner his first victims had come from.

Swiftly rising to his feet, he sprinted down the corridor, the shouts of the prison guards hard on his heels. Ahead, the corridor split into two passageways and Barzano ducked into the left one as another shot plucked his sleeve, leaving a painful, burning weal across his arm. The corridor was chill and dark, the glow-globes dim and barely illuminating this section.

Cell doors punctuated the corridor's length and at its end was a featureless door of rusted metal. Barzano's empathic senses felt an overwhelming aura of despair emanating from beyond this door and the magnitude of it made him stumble.

He fought through the palpable horror and pushed on, knowing he had seconds to reach cover before being shot by his pursuers. He sprinted down the corridor and launched himself feet first at the door.

It slammed open and he rolled through onto his back, grunting as the wound on his shoulder reopened. He fired back into the corridor, hearing another scream and kicked the door shut, slamming the locking bar into place.

He rose to his feet and swung the rifle to bear on the room's occupants.

The Surgeon stood beside a blood-soaked slab, working a buzzing saw into Almerz Chanda's bones.

Barzano's knees sagged and the rifle barrel dropped as he saw how the Surgeon had honoured Almerz Chanda's flesh.

URIEL DIVED INTO the cover of some rubble and sprayed the rebels' trench line with bolter fire. Explosions of red blossomed where his shots struck flesh and the screams of the wounded added to the din of battle. Despite the ministrations of Apothecary Selenus, the wound inflicted by the eldar leader pulled painfully tight with his every movement.

The entrance to the palace's prison level lay at the far end of this wide area of open ground strewn with rubble and small fires. Two bunkers of rockcrete flanked the entrance, covering every possible approach, and a slit trench ran in a troop-filled line before them, protected by recently laid coils of razorwire. Roaring blasts of gunfire sprayed from the defensive position: bright stabs of lasguns and the crack of heavy bolters.

Ultramarines poured fire over their own makeshift barricades, peppering the thick walls of the bunkers with bolts. A pair of missiles lanced out, slamming into the bunkers' thick walls, but they had been designed to withstand all but a direct artillery impact.

Concentrated bursts of heavy gunfire raked the Ultramarines' position and Uriel knew that they were running out of time; the enemy were sure to bring up heavy armour and counterattack. As formidable as the warriors of the Adeptus Astartes were, they would have no option but to fall back in the face of such firepower.

He called over his sergeants and hurriedly outlined the situation.

'Options?' he asked.

Pasanius scabbarded his bolter and hefted his flamer. 'Call in a limited strike from the *Vae Victus*, blow a hole in their line and fight through the gap.'

Uriel considered the possibility of an orbital strike. It was tempting, but unrealistic.

'No. If the targeting surveyors are even a fraction out, we could find ourselves the target or if the yield is too high, the entire prison complex might be buried beneath hundreds of tonnes of rubble.'

'Then I suppose we have to do this the hard way,' said Sergeant Venasus grimly.

Uriel nodded. Venasus was not noted for his subtlety of command, but as he considered the options, Uriel knew that the sergeant was right. They would have to throw tactical finesse out the window. Superior training and faith in the Emperor was vital, but in any war there would always come a time when the battle would have to be won by taking the fight to the enemy through the fire and meeting him blade to blade, strength to strength. That time was now.

Another burst of heavy fire blasted along their line, the PDF gunners working their guns methodically left and right, turning the area before the Ultramarines into a murderous killing ground.

'Very well,' said Uriel at last, 'Here's how we are going to do this.'

BARZANO BROUGHT THE rifle up in time to block the upward sweep of the Surgeon's bonesaw, the alien device hacking through the barrel in a shower of purple sparks. He ducked another sweep of the saw, barrelling into his slender opponent. The pair collapsed in a pile of thrashing limbs and Barzano screamed as he felt the whirring saw-blade slice across his hip, the screaming teeth scraping across his pelvis before sliding clear.

He slammed his forehead into the Surgeon's face. Blood sprayed as his nose cracked and the alien screeched in pain. Barzano rolled as the saw blade swung again, scoring a deep gouge in the stone floor. He bent to retrieve what remained of his lasgun. The weapon would never fire again, but its heavy wooden stock would serve as a bludgeon.

He backed against the door, bracing his weight against it as he felt the repeated lasblasts impact upon it. It wouldn't hold for long.

The Surgeon advanced towards him, the bonesaw spraying blood from its whining edge. The alien's face was a mask of crimson and his violet eyes were filled with hate.

Behind him, the shattered body of Almerz Chanda groaned on the slab, his bloody and raw flesh shuddering as the soporific effects of the Surgeon's muscle relaxants began to dissipate.

URIEL BRACED HIMSELF on the rubble and whispered a brief prayer to the blessed Primarch that this attack would succeed. All along the line of Space Marines, men awaited his orders. Chaplain Clausel intoned the Litany of Battle, his stern, unwavering voice a fine example to the warriors of Fourth Company. Uriel knew that he had to provide a similar example, by leading this charge himself.

The PDF gunners were firing blind now. Dozens of smoke and blind grenades had gone over the top, and billowing clouds of concealing smoke were spewing from the grenade canisters.

When he judged that the smoke had spread enough, Uriel yelled, 'Now! For the glory of Terra!' and surged from behind the cover of rubble and debris.

As one, the Ultramarines roared and followed their captain into the smoke, bullets and lasers tearing amongst them in a deadly volley. Deadly to anyone not clad in suits of holy power armour, blessed by the Tech-marines and imbued with the spirits of battle.

Immediately the Space Marines fanned out, so a concentrated burst of fire wouldn't hit them all. This was a gauntlet every man would run alone. Uriel sprinted through the clouds of white, lit by the eerie glow of flickering flames. He ran across burned bodies, patches of scorched ground, and piles of discarded battlegear. The whine of bullets and lasers surrounded him, the smoke whipped by their passing. His every sense was alert as he led the charge.

His auto-senses fought to pierce the obscuring fog of the blind grenades, the bright flashes up ahead the only clue to the distance left to cover.

One hundred and fifty paces.

Throughout the smoke he could make out the blurred shapes of his warriors, weapons spitting fire towards the rebel line.

One hundred paces.

Roars of pain sounded. Cold fury gripped him as he closed the gap.

Then the ground exploded around him, spraying him with stone fragments and flaming metal as heavy bolter fire hammered around him. A shell clipped his shoulder guard and helmet, spinning him from his feet. Another impacted on his power sword, the shell blasting the blade from the hilt in a shower of sparks.

Uriel fell, rolling into cover as his vision was obscured by red, flashing runes on his visor. Blood ran into his eyes and he wrenched the helmet clear, wiping the already clotted substance from his face. His rage built as he saw the damage done to the sword.

The hilt bore only a short, broken length of blade, the intricate traceries that contained the war-spirit within shattered and broken. His legacy from Idaeus had been destroyed, the one tangible link to his former captain's approval of his authority was no more.

Uriel angrily sheathed what remained of the blade and rose to his feet.

The smoke was thinning and he could see he were less than a hundred metres from the bunkers. He was almost there, but this close, the fire from the slit trench was telling and their charge had lost its momentum. The weight of fire was simply too heavy to advance through and live.

A sense of utter conviction gripped Uriel and he walked calmly through the hail of gunfire and knelt beside the body of a fallen battle brother, prising the chainsword from his fingers. Bullets stitched the ground beside him, but Uriel did not flinch or even acknowledge that he was under fire.

'Captain! Get down!' shouted Pasanius.

Uriel turned to the sheltering Ultramarines and shouted, 'Follow me!'

A lasbolt struck him square in the chest.

Uriel staggered, but did not fall, the eagle at the centre of his breastplate running molten. Chaplain Clausel rose to his feet, crozius arcanum held above his head.

'See, brothers! The Emperor protects!' he bellowed, his voice carrying over the entire battlefield. The massive Chaplain shouted, 'Up, brothers! Up! For the Emperor! Forward!'

Uriel pressed the activation rune of the chainsword, the blade roaring into life.

He turned back to the enemy line.

They would make it. There would be no mercy.

He began sprinting through the fire towards the foe.

BARZANO SWAYED ASIDE as the Surgeon thrust the bonesaw at his belly. He gripped his weapon arm and spun inside his guard, powering his elbow into the alien's side. He rolled forward, avoiding the reverse stroke of the bonesaw, crashing into the table of surgical instruments beside the slab and dropping all manner of scalpels and drills to the floor beside him. He could hear Almerz Chanda groaning in pain above him and snatched up a long, hook-bladed scalpel as the Surgeon came at him again.

Barzano's strength was failing and he knew that he could not last much longer. He pushed himself to his feet, the scalpel gripped tightly in his fist. The Surgeon swung the bonesaw at Barzano's head.

The inquisitor blocked the blow with his forearm, screaming as the tearing teeth of the bonesaw sheared into the meat of his arm, shrieking along the bone towards his elbow. The whining edge of the saw juddered to a halt, the teeth caught in the bone of the inquisitor's arm. Barzano swung his injured limb, complete with the embedded saw, away from his body and stepped in close, hammering the scalpel into the Surgeon's temple.

The alien staggered. Blood burst from his mouth as his knees gave way, a full fifteen centimetres of steel rammed into his brain. He gave a last sigh before toppling forward, the rattling bonesaw pulling clear of Barzano's arm.

Barzano slumped against the slab, fighting to stay conscious through the screaming agony of his shredded arm. A thick layer of skin and muscle flapped from his elbow and he forced himself not to look at the damage.

Fresh impacts slammed against the door and he bent to snatch a pistol of strange appearance from the Surgeon's belt, his every movement causing supernovas of agony to explode in his skull.

He felt, rather than saw, movement beside him and he swayed, bringing the pistol to bear.

Almerz Chanda pushed himself into a sitting position, his ruined body making one last surge before death claimed him.

His features spoke of the most hideous pain imaginable and Barzano could sense the madness the Surgeon's art had pushed the man into. But he also sensed his desperate need for atonement behind the pits of insanity.

As Barzano fought to remain upright, the door to the Surgeon's chambers finally crashed open.

URIEL HAMMERED HIS fist through a guardsman's visor, the man's face disintegrating under the blow. A lasbolt scored his breastplate, but the armour held firm and Uriel killed the shooter with a well placed bolter round. He swung his chainsword in a brutal arc, beheading another trooper and disembowelling a second. He fired his pistol into the face of a third and roared with the savage joy of combat.

The trench was a killing ground.

The wrath of the Ultramarines knew no bounds as they tore the men of the PDF to pieces, overrunning the trench with the fury of their charge. Bolt pistols fired, chainswords flashed red in the sunlight and gouts of liquid fire roasted men alive. There was no quarter given and within seconds the trench was nothing more than an open grave for the men of the PDF.

Before the impetus of the charge could be lost, Uriel yelled at his men to follow him, scrambling from the trench and sprinting onwards to the bunkers. Heavy calibre shells ripped a path towards him, but he jinked to one side, avoiding the hail of bullets. Firing as he ran, his charge carried him to within ten metres of the bunker. He could see Pasanius firing a long stream of liquid fire through the firing slit of the second bunker, the orange flames licking all around the giant warrior as he filled the enemy strongpoint with searing death.

Uriel dived and rolled to the foot of the bunker, narrowly avoiding being cut in two by a point blank burst of gunfire. His back slammed into its front wall. The bunker was a squat slab of rockcrete, protruding a metre above ground level with narrow gun slits in every side. Grenades would be useless. The bunker was sure to have a grenade sump, a protected chamber where the troops inside could dump grenades in order to negate their force.

More shots spewed from the bunker and Uriel waited until he heard the distinctive sound of a heavy bolter slide racking back empty. He held his breath, straining to hear the double click of a new belt feed of shells being shucked into a hot breech.

Uriel roared and rose up in front of the bunker, driving his chainsword through the firing slit and into the gunner's face. A bubbling scream and crack of bone sounded, and Uriel reached inside, dragging the heavy weapon through the slit.

He quickly spun the weapon and pushed the muzzle into the bunker, squeezing the trigger and working the bucking gun left and right, filling the bunker with explosive shells. The screaming from inside was short lived, but Uriel waited until the last of the shells from the belt feed had been expended and the firing hammer clicked down empty.

Uriel dropped the weapon, sweat and blood coating his features.

The bunkers were theirs and the prison complex lay open before him.

THE PRISON GUARDS burst into the torture chamber to be confronted by an apparition from their worst nightmares. Almerz Chanda threw himself forward with the last vestige of his strength, carrying the first men through the door to the ground.

Thrashing and screaming, the dying Chanda wailed in agony, the sound tearing at the nerves of everyone within earshot. Instinctively, the attackers fired. Lasbolts blasted Chanda's ravaged body, punching through him into the men beneath.

Chanda's death scream was one of release rather than pain.

The following troops tore their eyes from the horrifically mutilated man to the chamber's sole remaining living occupant. Barzano swayed, one side of his body completely drenched in blood. Chanda's death had bought him precious seconds he did not intend to waste. He aimed the Surgeon's pistol at the guards and pulled the trigger.

A hail of dark needles fired in an expanding cone, shredding the closest guards and killing them instantly. The guards behind were not so fortunate and the venom-tipped needles flooded their bloodstreams with lethal alien toxins.

Barzano staggered to the door as the guards fell back, some spasming in their death throes as the poison did its evil work, others retreating as they saw the fate of those in front. The inquisitor pushed shut the door, sliding to the floor as his strength poured from him in the wash of blood from his ruined arm.

More screams sounded from outside, gunfire and explosions. He felt something push against the door and weakly tried to hold it shut, but he could not prevent it from opening. He slumped to the floor, his vision blurring and attempted to raise the alien pistol.

Sergeant Learchus plucked the pistol from the inquisitor's hand and hurled it aside as he and two of his battle brothers entered the torture chamber along with Mykola Shonai, Lortuen Perjed and half a dozen petrified scribes. One of the Space Marines carried Jenna Sharben and gently deposited the wounded judge on the Surgeon's slab.

'See to him,' ordered Learchus, pointing at the unconscious Barzano.

Learchus activated his vox. 'Captain Ventris, we have Inquisitor Barzano. He is alive, but badly wounded. We will need to get him aboard the *Vae Victus* soon if we are to save his life.'

URIEL CHARGED THROUGH the smoking remains of the prison complex gateway, firing as he ran. The blast had killed most of the defenders on the inside; over the ringing echoes of the gate's destruction, only the moans of the dying could be heard.

His spirits had soared when Learchus had informed him of the inquisitor's safety, knowing that he had made the right decision to have the sergeant remain within the palace and break into the prison complex from above.

Learchus had Barzano, but there were several hundred men below ground. They still had to reach their brethren and pull them to safety. Pasanius poured another sheet of fire down the rough-hewn stairs that led into the darkness of the prison.

Screams boiled up from below, and Uriel once more led the charge of the Ultramarines.

LEARCHUS FIRED ANOTHER blast of bolter fire through the door, felling two guards and wounding a third. Thus far they had held off three attacks, but ammunition was low and they were running out of time. There were another two entrances to this chamber and each of the Space Marines fought desperately to hold off the waves of attackers with bolter and chainsword.

Mykola Shonai and Lortuen Perjed desperately battled to halt the flow of blood from Barzano's arm, but it was a fight they were losing. The Surgeon's blade had cut him to the bone from wrist to elbow and this place had only instruments for the taking of life, not its preservation. Barzano's flesh was ashen, his pulse weak and thready.

More and more guards hurled themselves through the doors, each time to be cut down by deadly bolts or hacked apart by shrieking chainswords. The stink of death filled the chamber.

Learchus dropped his bolter as his last magazine finally exhausted itself and charged the door as more enemies tried to force their way inside. His sword hacked the first men to death, before lasbolts hurled the sergeant from his feet. Status runes flashed red on his visor. He rolled and chopped the legs out from one man, thundering his fist into the groin of another. Bayonets stabbed at him, most sliding clear across his armoured might.

He stabbed and chopped, kicking and punching in all directions, feeling bones break with every motion of his body. Gunfire boomed as he pushed himself clear of his attackers, roaring with battle fury, a living engine of killing frenzy.

They were holding, but they could not continue to do so for long.

A BACKHANDED BLOW sent another enemy screaming into hell as Uriel and Pasanius pushed deeper into the prison complex. Uriel's helmet lay abandoned on the battlefield above them, so he followed Pasanius, the locator augers within the sergeant's helmet directing them towards Learchus.

He could hear the screams of dying men and furious battle from up ahead and sprinted round a corner to see scores of men pushing themselves forward through a wide door. Pasanius did not even wait for the order, simply engulfing the men in fire from his lethal flamer. Screams and the stench of scorched flesh filled the cramped corridor as the Ultramarines fell upon the prison guards from behind.

It was a massacre. The soldiers had nowhere to run to. Caught between the fury of Sergeant Learchus and this new assault, the survivors threw themselves at the mercy of Uriel. But there was none to be had and every soldier perished.

Uriel pushed himself into the Surgeon's torture chamber, breathing heavily and wiping blood from his face. Bodies littered the chamber and the stink of blood was overpowering.

The silence was a sudden contrast from the screaming combat of moments ago and Learchus blinked, lowering his blood-sheathed chainsword.

Uriel marched to meet Learchus and gripped his hand.

'Well met, brother,' whispered Uriel.

Learchus nodded. 'Aye, well met, captain.'

THE THUNDERHAWK ROARED upwards, chased by a few hastily converted shuttle-gunships and ornithopters. Designed to strafe slow moving ground targets, they were out of their element against the Space Marine craft and, after losing seven of their number, pulled back.

The rescue of Inquisitor Barzano had cost the lives of three Ultramarines and two of Barzano's scribes who had been killed in the crossfire raging throughout the torture chamber. Lortuen Perjed was adamant that they receive full honours upon their burial.

Before attending to the wounded, Apothecary Selenus had removed the vital progenoid glands from the bodies of the fallen Space Marines. The recovery of the precious gene-seed took precedence over normal battlefield triage.

He stabilised the inquisitor and set up a live transfusion of blood from a scribe with a matching blood type. The man expressed his willingness to be bled dry in order to save the inquisitor's life, but Selenus assured him that such drastic measures would not be necessary.

He had treated Jenna Sharben's wound and though she would be incapacitated for many days yet, she would live and suffer no long-term damage from her injury. Of the surviving Ultramarines, the majority of their wounds were largely superficial.

The battered Thunderhawk pulled into high orbit, finally making rendezvous with the *Vae Victus* and bringing her warriors home.

THE SENIOR OFFICERS of the Pavonis expedition gathered in the captain's briefing room, assembled around a circular table hewn from the slow growing mountain firs that surrounded the Fortress of Hera on Macragge.

Lord Admiral Tiberius sat with his back to the wall, below a magnificent silken banner listing the victories of his vessel and her previous captains stretching back to a time centuries before his birth. To one side of Tiberius sat the battle-weary Ultramarines, fresh from their battles on Pavonis: Uriel, Learchus, Pasanius, Venasus and Dardino. On the opposite side of the table sat Mykola Shonai and Lortuen Perjed.

Between them was an unoccupied chair and as Mykola Shonai took a sip of water, the last member of the council of war arrived, cradling his left arm in a synthflesh bandage and walking with a pronounced limp.

Uriel watched Barzano hobble into the briefing room, noting the telltale gleam in his eyes that indicated heavy stimm use. The inquisitor was obviously using medical stimulants to block the pain from his wounded arm and shoulder. He sat opposite Uriel, his face ashen.

'Very well,' began Barzano, 'I think it's fair to say that the situation is grim. Kasimir de Valtos has control on Pavonis, and at any moment could have his hands on an ancient alien weapon capable of unleashing destruction on a system-wide scale. Would everyone agree that is a fair assessment of our situation?'

No one disagreed with the inquisitor.

'What do you suggest then, Inquisitor Barzano?' asked Tiberius.

'What I would suggest is that you send a coded communication to Macragge and have a battle-barge armed with cyclonic torpedoes despatched to Pavonis.'

Uriel slammed his fist down on the table.

'No!' he stated forcefully, 'I will not have it. We came here to save these people, not to destroy them.'

Tiberius placed a calming hand on Uriel's arm. Mykola Shonai looked from Uriel to Barzano, a confused look upon her features.

'Perhaps I am missing something,' she said. 'What are cyclonic torpedoes?'

'Planet killers,' answered Uriel. 'They will burn the atmosphere of Pavonis away in a storm of fire, scouring the surface bare until there is nothing left alive. The seas will boil to vapour and your world will become a barren rock, wreathed in the ashes of your people.'

Shonai turned a horrified stare upon Barzano. 'You would destroy my world?' she asked incredulously.

Slowly, Barzano nodded. 'If it means preventing a madman getting his hands on the Bringer of Darkness, then yes, I would. Better to sacrifice one world than lose Emperor knows how many others because we shirked from doing our duty.'

'It is not our duty to kill innocent people,' pointed out Uriel.

'Our duty is to save as many lives as we can,' countered Barzano. 'If we do nothing and de Valtos succeeds in retrieving the alien ship, many more worlds will die. I do not make this decision lightly, Uriel, but I must rely on cold logic and the Emperor to guide me.'

'I cannot believe this is the Emperor's will.'

'Who are you to judge what the Emperor wants?' snapped Barzano. 'You are a warrior who can see his enemies on the battlefield and smite them with sword and bolter. My enemies are heresy, deviancy and ambition. More insidious foes than you could ever imagine and the weapons I must use are consequently of greater magnitude.'

'You can't do this, Barzano,' said Uriel. 'My men have fought and bled for this world, I will not give up on it.'

'It is not a question of giving up, Uriel,' explained Barzano. 'It is a question of prevention. We do not know where de Valtos is or how he intends to find the ship and without that information we can do nothing. If we hesitate and are too late to prevent him gaining possession of the *Nightbringer*, how many more lives will be lost? Ten billion? A thousand billion? More?'

'Surely there is something we can try to stop de Valtos?' asked Shonai. 'There are millions of people on Pavonis. I will not just stand by and hear the fate of my world discussed as though its destruction were a matter of no import.'

Barzano turned to face Shonai and said, 'Believe me, Mykola, I am not some heartless monster and I do not believe the death of even a single world to be of no import. Were there another way, I would gladly choose it. I have never been forced to destroy a world before, and if I could stop de Valtos any other way, I would.'

As Barzano spoke, the words of Gedrik echoed in his head once more.

The Death of Worlds and the Bringer of Darkness await to be born into this galaxy. One will arise or neither, it is in your hands to choose which.

'Do you really mean that, Inquisitor Barzano?' he asked.

'Mean what?' asked Barzano, his tone wary.

'About choosing another way if you could.'

'Yes, I do.'

'Then I believe there is another way,' said Uriel.

Barzano raised a sceptical eyebrow and leaned forwards, resting his arms on the tabletop, careful to avoid jarring his wounded arm. 'And what would that be, Uriel?'

Uriel sensed the criticality of this moment and mustered his thoughts before speaking.

'When I was in the home of de Valtos, and we found the two skeleton warriors in the depths of his house, I noticed the battery packs they were hooked up to had identification markings on them.'

'So?'

'They were marked with the words "Tembra Ridge" – perhaps the governor can shed some light on that,' answered Uriel.

'Tembra Ridge? It's a range of mountains roughly a hundred kilometres north of Brandon Gate. They stretch from the western ocean to the Gresha forest in the east, nearly a thousand kilometres of rocky uplands and scrub forests. It's a mining region: there are hundreds of deep bore mines along its length. Most of the cartels own title to land along Tembra Ridge. The de Valtos cartel have several.'

'If those things were unearthed from one of the mines along Tembra Ridge, is it not likely that the *Nightbringer* itself lies beneath the ground there too?' pointed out Uriel.

Barzano nodded with a smile. 'Very good, Uriel. Now if we could only pinpoint which one they came from we would truly have something to celebrate.'

Barzano's tone was mildly sarcastic, but Uriel could see he was at least considering the idea that the extermination of Pavonis might not be inevitable. The inquisitor turned to Mykola Shonai.

'How deep do these bore mines go?' he asked,

'It varies,' replied Shonai, 'but the deepest are perhaps ten thousand metres, while others are around three or four thousand. It depends on the seam that is being mined and how deep it's economically viable to continue drilling.'

'Then we find out which of the mines are owned by the de Valtos cartel and bombard them all into oblivion from orbit,' growled Uriel.

'Lortuen?' said Barzano, turning to his aide, who nodded thoughtfully and closed his eyes. His breathing slowed, his eyelids fluttering as he culled facts, figures and statistics from the wealth of information he and his scribes had gathered during their researches.

Uriel watched as the old man's eyes flickered rapidly from side to side as though reading information flashing past on the inside of his eyelids, noticing for the first time the tiny glint of metal behind his ear. The old man had been fitted with cybernetic implants, presumably something similar to those of a lexmechanic or savant servitor.

Without opening his eyes, Perjed spoke in a flat monotone, 'There are four mines along Tembra Ridge owned by the de Valtos cartel. All produce mineral ore to be refined into processed steel for tank chassis and gun barrels, but the northernmost's production level is by far the lowest. I suspect that its shortfall is being covered by over-production in the other facilities, which would account for the higher number of worker accidents reported at the other mines.'

Perjed's head bowed, his breathing slowly returning to normal, and Uriel stared triumphantly at Barzano.

'There,' he said, 'We have the location and can attack without resorting to genocide.'

'I'm afraid that this changes nothing, Captain Ventris,' said Tiberius softly.

'Why not?'

'Even at full yield on our bombardment cannon, the magma bombs will not be able to penetrate that far into the planet's crust.'

'Then we take the fight to the surface once more,' shouted Uriel. 'The Tech-marines tell me that we now have two Thunderhawks operational. I say we launch as soon as we can rearm and break de Valtos out from beneath the planet's surface by hand if need be.'

Uriel stared defiantly at Barzano, waiting to shout down any objections the inquisitor might have.

But Barzano merely nodded.

'Very well, Uriel. We'll try it your way, but if you fail, Pavonis will die. By my hand or that of de Valtos.'

'We will not fail,' assured Uriel. 'We are the Ultramarines.'

SEVENTEEN

VIRGIL ORTEGA DUCKED as another rattling blast of gunfire peppered the wall behind him, showering him with stony fragments. He slid behind the angled rockcrete barricade and ejected the spent drum magazine from the heavy stubber, slotting another one home and racking the slide.

Ortega swung the ponderous weapon back up onto the barricade as another rush of troops came at them, bracing the heavy stock hard into his shoulder and pulling the trigger. A metre long tongue of flame blasted from the perforated barrel and a deafening roaring ripped the air as hundreds of high velocity bullets churned the first wave of attackers to shredded corpses. The vibration of the gun's fire was almost too much for Ortega, his muscles straining to keep the gun steady. With such firepower, it wasn't so much a question of accuracy, but of ammunition capacity; the stubber could empty its magazine in a matter of seconds.

Of the twenty-seven judges he'd pulled from the disaster at the precinct house, eighteen were still alive. Emerging from hidden tunnels beneath the palace that not even the governor knew about, the judges had seized the armoury after a brief but fierce firefight. Surprise had been total and the Imperial armoury, designed to indefinitely withstand attack from the outside, had fallen within an hour.

It took less than that for the rebel forces to muster a counterattack and attempt to force the judges from their new refuge. Buried beneath the palace, the armoury was inaccessible to anything but infantry and, with a vast selection of powerful guns at his disposal, Virgil Ortega was proving to be a particularly troublesome thorn in the rebels' side. Without the enormous stockpiles of heavy weaponry stored in the armoury, this rebellion would be seriously deprived of firepower when the wrath of Imperial retaliation descended upon it.

He'd despatched Collix and six judges to rig as many explosives as they could find and prepare the armoury for destruction. With a bit of luck they could set some charges, make their escape and blow this place to the warp.

The corridor before him was littered with enemy dead, the mounds of corpses forming makeshift banks of cover for their attackers. Ortega worked the fire from the stubber mercilessly back and forth, firing bursts into any sign of movement. The judges on the line with him fired a mix of shotguns, bolters and stubbers, filling the air before them with death.

He could hear muffled curses and spared a glance behind him to see Collix dragging a wheeled gurney with a linked pair of autocannons fitted to a circular pintel mount. Ortega grinned. The weapon was designed to be mounted on a vehicle of some kind, possibly a Sentinel, and was far too heavy to be carried by a man.

Stuttering blasts of gunfire ricocheted from the walls, and Ortega pulled a judge down from the barricade as he slumped over, half his head blown away.

'Get a move on, Collix!' he shouted.

'Coming, sir!'

'How long until we can get the hell out of here?'

'I'm not sure we'll be able to, sir.'

'What are you talking about?'

'The detonators for the explosives are not stored here,' explained Collix. 'I should imagine in order to prevent an enemy from doing what we are attempting to do.'

Ortega swore and set down the heavy stubber, scrambling away from the barricade, careful to keep his head down as he made his way to help Collix with the massive guns.

'Then we have to find another way to set them off,' snarled Ortega.

'It could be done manually,' suggested Collix.

Ortega locked eyes with Collix, aware of what his sergeant was suggesting.

'Let's hope it does not come to that, sergeant.'

'Yes,' nodded Collix, grimly.

'Set them up here,' ordered Ortega, siting the guns to cover the barricade.

Collix halted the gurney and hauled on the brake lever, locking the wheels into position and extending the stabiliser legs. The recoil of the autocannons was sure to be enormous and Ortega wasn't sure the makeshift gun bed was up to the task.

Screams and desperate shouts sounded behind him and he cursed, seeing grey uniformed men struggling with his judges. Blood and smoke filled the passage as every man and woman fought with desperate savagery.

The judges were amongst the most disciplined, dedicated troops the Emperor could call upon, but the PDF fought with the frenzy of soldiers who had come through the fire of battle and survived long enough to exact their vengeance on their would-be killers.

Ortega snatched the shock maul from his belt and surged into the swirling melee, savagely clubbing his enemies. Collix swung a massive power glaive, effortlessly slicing a PDF trooper in two. There were many exotic weapons to choose from – power swords and great energy axes amongst them – but Ortega trusted the solid feel of his trusty maul.

He crushed a man's skull with a backhanded swing. He had depleted seven energy charges in his maul so far, but there was no shortage of ammo in this place. And even on the occasions he had been forced to use it without its shock field, half a metre of solid metal was a powerful weapon in the hands of a man who knew how to wield it.

Ortega fought back to back with Collix, cutting a swathe through the bloodied PDF troopers, crushing bones and breaking faces with their clubs and fists.

'The Emperor's justice is upon you, sinners!' shouted Collix, kicking a trooper in the groin then beheading him with a lethal swipe of his glaive. Ortega jabbed his maul into another soldier's belly, driving his knee into the man's face as he folded.

Blood sprayed and he lashed out again, knowing that they had to hold off their attackers just a little longer.

A space cleared around him and he dropped his shock maul, sweeping up the heavy stubber once more. He braced himself and squeezed the trigger, his entire body quaking with the powerful recoil. His ribs screamed painfully with each blast, and he was sure he'd rebroken them.

Heavy calibre shells ripped through the ranks of the PDF and a dozen men dropped, their thin flak vests unable to stop such powerful bullets. Ortega roared, an inchoate yell of released anger and pain.

'Death to those who defile the Emperor's laws!'

Blood gathered at the corners of his mouth and he could feel a hollow ache in his chest.

Yes, now he was sure he'd rebroken at least one rib.

Suddenly it was over.

The last of the attackers fell or turned tail and ran, broken by the ferocity of the judges' defence. Ortega showed no mercy, gunning the fleeing soldiers down as they ran.

A scant handful of soldiers made it to safety, firing back as they ran.

A lasbolt clipped Ortega's chest, spinning him around and the floor rushed up to meet him, the cold concrete slamming into his face. He felt hands upon him, dragging him back, but could see that his judges had held the barricade.

Another six of his men were down, but they had held.

For now.

URIEL AND PASANIUS sprinted uphill towards the collection of iron sided buildings on the mountain plateau. The heat in the mountains was fierce and the glare from the white stone of this region dazzling.

Behind him, the Ultramarines advanced uphill through the rocky, scrub-covered slopes of the Tembra Ridge mountains towards the deep bore mine Lortuen Perjed had named TR-701. It did not sound like a place worthy of heroic death and Uriel hoped that he was right in demanding this one last chance to stop de Valtos.

Ario Barzano waited six kilometres west of the mine in one of the Ultramarines' Thunderhawks, anxiously waiting for Uriel's signal that this was the place they sought.

The six squads of Ultramarines made their way uphill with no more difficulty than marching across a parade ground. Fire and movement teams covered the advance, as they were sure to have been spotted; the blue of their armour was too stark a contrast to the pale mountain stone for them not to have been.

Scalding jets of flammable gasses spewed from exhaust ports scattered across the flank of the mountain, venting for the fumes released by drilling at such depths, and Uriel was reminded of the restless volcanoes in the southern oceans of Macragge.

Squad Dardino advanced on the left flank, the slope of which was steeper, but these warriors had been equipped with jump packs, making light of the journey up the scree covered mountain. Squads Venasus, Pasanius, Elerna, Nivaneus and Daedalus marched on a wide, staggered front, each squad overwatching the other.

The mine complex shone in the sun, its silvered sides reflecting the light in dazzling beams. It was impossible to tell whether there were any enemy forces inside or not. Plumes of exhaust fumes rose from behind the perimeter buildings, but whether they were from armoured vehicles or the daily work of a mine was unclear.

They were now within three hundred metres of the plateau.

KASIMIR DE VALTOS followed his mine overseer, Jakob Lasko, beneath the flickering line of glow-globes. Lasko mopped his brow repeatedly, but de Valtos appeared too excited to care about the relentless heat this deep in the earth.

In their wake came a cadre of heavily armoured eldar warriors, their features invisible behind ornate crimson helmets. Between them, they carried a large silvered metal container, its lid sealed tight.

At their centre was the dread leader of the Kabal of the Sundered Blade, Archon Kesharq. Like his warriors, his face was concealed behind a visored helm, its jade surface smooth and featureless. He carried a huge war axe, and at his side sashayed the beautiful, raven-haired wych who had, until now, been the inseparable shadow of Kasimir de Valtos.

Snapping at his heels came the excrents, shambling after their master by whatever method of locomotion the Surgeon had gifted them with. They hissed and spat, uncomfortable in the hot, dark environment. Perhaps some latent, instinctual sense of their former lives spoke to them of the evil that this place contained.

Following the eldar warriors, a full company of PDF troopers brought up the rear. In their midst walked Vendare Taloun, his shoulders slumped dejectedly, wearily mopping his sodden skin with the edge of his robe.

The air was thick with dust and fumes and at regular intervals along the rocky walls, rebreather masks hung from corroded hooks alongside signs cautioning against the risk of toxic gases and explosion.

The procession made its way deeper into the mine, their environs changing from the bare rock of Pavonis to smooth walled passageways, their sloping sides tapering to a point some four metres above their heads.

Kasimir de Valtos paused in the square chamber that had contained the huge door that had barred his entry to this place for so long. Excitement pounded along his veins and he nodded respectfully to the room's four inanimate guardians in their shadowed alcoves. Their eyes glittered, but if they harboured any resentment towards the intruders they gave no sign of it.

Thick rusted flakes marked where the door had been, and de Valtos could sense the vast presence inside. His limbs began to shiver and he fought to control his sense of impending destiny. Within this place lay a sleeping god and he could feel the whisper of ages past in the musty wind that sighed from the tomb's interior.

Archon Kesharq strode up to de Valtos. 'Why do we wait, human? The prize is within, is it not?' snarled Kesharq. The alien's voice bubbled, his stilted High Gothic rendered almost unintelligible by the damage caused by Uriel's bolt round.

'Indeed it is, Archon Kesharq.'

'Then why do we wait?'

'Don't you feel it?' said de Valtos. 'The sense that we stand on the brink of greatness? The sense that once we enter this place nothing will ever be the same again?'

'All I know is that we are wasting time. The Astartes have the one called Barzano back and we should not spend any more time here than we have to. If the prize is inside we should take it and leave.'

'You have no soul, Kesharq,' whispered de Valtos.

He brushed past the alien and entered the resting place of a creature older than time.

THE FIRST ROCKET streaked towards the Ultramarines and exploded amongst the warriors of Squad Nivaneus, scything white-hot fragments in all directions. Two warriors fell, but picked themselves up seconds later.

As the echo of the explosion faded, a rippling roar of gunfire sprayed from the mining compound. Uriel sprinted into the cover of one of the wide exhaust vents and tried to estimate the numbers opposing them. Judging by the number of muzzle flashes he could see, he guessed there were around two hundred guns firing on them.

They were well positioned, covering every approach to the mine complex. Uriel smiled grimly, vindicated in his decision to attack the mine.

But now he and his men were faced with the prospect of attacking a well dug in enemy of superior numbers, uphill and over relatively open terrain. It was the stuff of Chapter legends, wonderful to hear, but a different matter entirely when you had to face such odds yourself.

His men were now in cover and returning fire. The Codex Astartes laid out precise tactics for dealing with such situations, but he had neither the numbers, equipment or time to follow such strict doctrine.

A geyser of fumes belched through the grille of the exhaust vent beside Uriel, enveloping him with acrid fumes and hot ash. He coughed and spat a mouthful of the mine's foul excreta, the neuroglottis situated at the back of his throat assessing its chemical content even as he wiped his face clear.

A burning mix of various sulphurous gasses, fatal to a normal human, but simply irritating to a Space Marine. He slid across the face of the grilled vent and gripped the hot, ash-encrusted metal. Parts gave way beneath his grip and he wrenched it clear, tossing it aside and staring inside.

A hot, mustardy stench wafted out. Uriel's enhanced vision could only pierce a hundred metres of the steaming darkness within, but he could see the passage sloped downwards at a shallow angle. He opened a vox-channel to Sergeant Dardino as a plan began to form in his mind.

* * *

'DAMN!' SWORE MAJOR Helios Bextor of the 33rd Tarmegan PDF regiment as he watched the blue armoured warriors of the Ultramarines go to ground in the rocks below his position.

He'd given the order to open fire too soon, and cursed his impatience. But who could blame him? The thought of facing the might of the Space Marines was enough to scare even the most courageous of men, and Major Bextor was not fool enough to think that he was such a man.

Though he knew he was not a man of great bravery, he was a reasonably competent military thinker and he felt the defences were as secure as he'd been able to make them. Two full companies defended the mine head alongside a mortar platoon equipped with incendiary rounds. Briefly he wondered what was so important about this place that it required defending, there had not been any open trade wars for centuries, but quickly discarded such thoughts. Guilder de Valtos had entrusted him with the safety of this place and that was enough for him.

He watched the rocks for a few minutes more, but there was no further movement from the slopes.

Major Bextor keyed in the vox frequency of his mortar platoons and said, 'Overwatch teams, commence volley fire. Targets at two hundred metres plus. Fire for effect!'

SECONDS LATER, URIEL heard the thump of mortar fire and saw the darts of shells as they rose on a ballistic trajectory. In the time it took them to reach the apex of their climb, he saw they would land short.

'Incoming!' he yelled.

The mountain itself seemed to shake with the concussive detonations. A second salvo launched before the echoes of the first had died. Whickering fragments and tendrils of phosphorescent light burst from each shell as they landed with bone-jarring force, sending storms of rock splinters flying through the air alongside the shrapnel.

Shells landed in a string of roaring booms, marching in disciplined volleys towards the Ultramarines. Uriel kept his head down as the ground convulsed with each burst of strikes.

They had no choice but to wait for Dardino's signal and take the punishment the enemy commander was dishing out. To advance forward through concentrated mortar fire into the teeth of enemy guns was tantamount to suicide and Uriel had no desire to see his command end in such a way.

Sheets of flame rose from each impact, craters blasted into the soil of the mountain spewing thick smoke from the flames. Uriel caught the stink of promethium on the air and frowned in puzzlement. Incendiaries? Was the enemy commander mad? Against lightly armoured troops, incendiaries would sow havoc and panic, but against warriors clad in power armour they were almost useless. Then he realised that the enemy commander was PDF and almost certainly had no prior experience fighting Space Marines.

Huge banks of black smoke rose from burning streams of fuel, drifting and spreading slowly in the mountain breeze and obscuring the combatants from one another. The Ultramarines had just been given the cover they sorely desired.

SERGEANT DARDINO PUNCHED his fist through the steel of the vent tube and peeled it back with powerful sweeps of his arms. Daylight flooded the rifled metal vent and he leaned out, training his bolt pistol upwards lest anyone was keeping a watchful eye on this portion of the mineshaft.

Before him, he saw a mass of cables descending into darkness and deep adamantium girders spanning the huge width of the mine, supporting lifting gear and dozens of thick-girthed vent tubes like the one he now pushed himself clear of.

He dropped onto the huge adamantium beam the vent pipe was bolted to and motioned for the rest of his squad to join him. One by one, the warriors of his assault squad clambered out onto the beam. Their armour was scorched and blackened from the mine's exhaust fumes. The status runes on Dardino's visor told him that his rebreather units were badly clogged.

They were deep within the cylindrical shaft of the mine, the sky a bright disc some five hundred metres above them. Too far for jump packs.

He edged out along the beam, trying not to look down into the impenetrable darkness of the mine, knowing that it dropped over nine kilometres. He holstered his pistol and turned to the nine men of his squad.

'There's only one way up. Follow me!' he ordered and leapt into the centre of the mine, grabbing onto the cables hanging from the lip of the crater nearly half a kilometre above them.

Hand over hand, Sergeant Dardino and his men began climbing back to the surface.

URIEL ROSE FROM cover and shouted, 'Men of the Emperor, forwards!'

He sprinted uphill, the augmented muscles of his power armour carrying him forwards at a terrifying rate. With a roar of defiance, the Ultramarines followed their captain into the smoke from the incendiary shells, leaping over burning pools of superheated fuel.

Mortar rounds continued to drop, most falling behind them, the artillerymen unable to correctly shift their fire.

Uriel could hear the snap of lasgun fire and crack of heavier weapons, but it was uncoordinated and sporadic. A shot grazed the top of his shoulder guard, but most of the fire was too high, further proof that they were up against poor opposition. Firing downhill, most soldiers tended to shoot high.

Uriel burst from the clouds of smoke, blinking in the sudden brightness. Gunfire leapt out to meet them, plucking at their armour and a handful of warriors fell, but all picked themselves up and charged onwards.

A missile lanced out and struck Sergeant Nivaneus, a veteran of the Thracian campaign, disintegrating his upper body in a burst of crimson. Autocannon fire sprayed a group of Space Marines from Sergeant Elerna's squad. Four went down; only two got back up.

One of the survivors had lost his right arm, but continued upwards, picking up his pistol with his remaining hand and firing as he ran.

'Spread out, don't bunch up!' yelled Uriel as the autocannon fired again.

MAJOR BEXTOR PUNCHED the air as the autocannon cut a swathe through the Ultramarines' ranks. He fired over the parapet into the charging warriors.

This was his first battle and he'd begun to enjoy himself immensely. They were holding off the Space Marines, though the analytical part of his brain told him that there were less coming at his position than had begun the assault.

He attributed this to his initial awe at the size and apparent power of the Space Marines, but now he had their measure and they did not seem nearly so fearsome. He would be a hero! The man who had beaten the Ultramarines. The men would tell tales of this battle in the regimental mess hall for decades to come.

Bextor reached for another energy cell, smiling at the trooper next to him.

'Soon see these buggers off, eh, son?' he joked.

The boy's head exploded, showering Bextor with blood and brains and he fell back, repulsed beyond words at the horrid death of the trooper. He lost his balance and fell from the firing step, thudding painfully into the hard-packed ground. He turned in the direction the shot had come from in time to see hulking figures clamber over the lip of the mine shaft and begin the systematic butchery of his soldiers.

Blackened giants with hideously grinning masks of fury, they struck his line like a thunderbolt, hacking men in two with great sweeps of shrieking swords or pumping explosive rounds into their bodies from roaring pistols.

He rolled onto his side, feeling blood run from a gash in his forehead, weeping in terror at these dark nightmares that had emerged from the bowels of the planet. Chattering gunfire ripped his men to pieces and swords surely forged in the heart of Chaos chopped and chopped, severing limbs and ending lives.

All around him, his men were screaming and dying. Weakly he pushed himself to his feet and picked up his fallen lasgun. Death surrounded him, but he vowed he would take one of these devils screaming into hell with him.

He heard a crashing impact behind him and spun. A black shape emerged from the smoke with a grinning skull mask, raising a golden weapon high. Bextor felt his knees sag in terror and his gaze fixed upon the winged eagle atop the golden staff the black armoured figure held.

Its red eyes seemed to shine the colour of blood as its energy-wreathed edge clove him in two.

VIRGIL ORTEGA FOUGHT through the pain of his shattered ribs as he fired around the door at the PDF troopers. The corridor outside the armoury was thick with dead bodies and smoke, both sides firing blindly into the stinking blue cordite fog in the hope of hitting something.

The twin linked autocannons had not proved as useful as they had hoped, the furious recoil tearing the guns loose from their mount and demolishing most of the barricade in a hail of explosive rounds. It had brought a brief respite in the fighting, however, as the PDF proved reluctant to advance into the jaws of such a weapon. It had taken them several minutes to realise that it was no longer a threat.

In the intervening time, Collix and Ortega pulled the last two surviving judges back into the armoury itself. With the barricade mostly gone there was no realistic way to hold the corridor.

Ortega hurled a pair of grenades around the door, ducking back as the explosion filled the passageway outside with shrapnel and screams.

Collix skidded next to him, handing him a canvas satchel filled with shotgun shells and clips of bolter ammunition for his pistol.

'At least there's no shortage of ammo,' grunted Ortega.

Collix nodded, 'Or traitorous curs to fire it at.'

Ortega grinned and pushed himself to his feet as he heard muffled shouts from beyond the armoury doors.

'There is no escaping the Emperor's justice, even in death!' he shouted to their attackers, wincing as his cracked ribs flared painfully.

They jogged back to a hastily constructed barricade of emptied ammo crates and tipped-over racking, taking up position as they waited for the inevitable next attack. A wealth of weaponry lay clustered behind the barricade along with a box of each weapon's ammunition. Lasguns, bolters, autoguns, two missile launchers, a grenade launcher, a lascannon and six heavy bolters.

It was an impressive array of guns, but with only four of them left alive, most of the weapons would remain unfired. Thirty metres behind them, their surviving compatriots worked furiously to rig the armoury for destruction. Without detonators much of the explosive stored here was useless, but the time that had been bought with Arbites' lives had not been wasted.

At key points throughout the cavern, they'd stacked opened crates of ammo and ordnance in large piles, placing a cluster of grenades in the centre of each stockpile, the pins pulled and arming mechanisms wired to the vox-caster's battery unit.

Within minutes, they should have a crude but effective method of setting off a chain reaction that would cook off every shred of ammo in the cavern.

THE CHAMBER OF the god was far smaller than Kasimir de Valtos had imagined, but the sense of power it contained was enormous. Its walls sloped inwards to a golden point above the chamber's exact centre, where a rectangular oblong of smooth black obsidian rested, magnificent in its solitude. The base of each wall was lined with rectangular alcoves, each containing a skeletal figure, identical to those his workers had pulled from the outer chamber of the tomb complex some months ago.

Even the eldar and Vendare Taloun looked impressed with the chamber, staring in wonder at this alien structure that had been buried beneath the surface of Pavonis for sixty million years.

'It's magnificent,' de Valtos breathed, moving to stand before one of the alcoves. The skeletal warrior within was as lifeless as the ones back at his house, its sheen dulled with a verdigris stain. Unlike the ones in his possession, these carried bizarre looking rifles, their barrels coated in dust. It was quite fascinating and he looked forward to learning more of these strange creatures when he was free of the shackles of mortality.

Enthralled by the rows of warriors as he was, he could not deny the diabolical attraction of the central sarcophagus and marched across the echoing chamber towards it.

It was enormous, fully five metres on its long edge, and as he drew nearer he saw that its surface was not smooth at all, but inscribed with runic symbols and pitted with precisely shaped indentations. His heart pounded as he recognised them as the same as the ones he had read beneath the ruins of Cthelmax.

The same runes he had been scouring the sector for since that day.

Channels cut in the floor radiated from the sarcophagus, each twisting in precise geometric patterns towards the wall alcoves.

Kesharq stood alongside him and raised the visor of his helmet. Despite the immobile nature of his face and the crudely stitched bullet wound on his cheek, de Valtos could see the hunger in the alien's eyes.

'You feel it too, don't you?' he whispered.

Kesharq sneered, quickly masking his emotions and shook his head. 'I merely wish to secure the device and be away.'

'You're lying,' giggled de Valtos. 'I can see it in your eyes. You want this as much as I.'

'Does it matter? Let us be about our business.'

De Valtos wagged his finger below the eldar warrior's nose and jerked his head in the direction of the silver case carried by his warriors.

'Very well. Give me the pieces you secured for me and I shall unlock the key to the weapon.'

Kesharq held de Valtos's stare before nodding curtly. The alien carried the silver box forward, depositing it before his leader. Kesharq opened the box without taking his eyes from de Valtos and said, 'How do I know I can trust you?'

'You can trust me as much as I trust you, my dear Kesharq.'

He could see the alien visibly strain to hold his hand away from his pistol, but knew that it would not dare shoot him until he had summoned the *Nightbringer* from the shadowy realm it now occupied.

Anchored to Pavonis by ancient science, it had remained a ghost ship in this sector since the day it had been lost.

De Valtos knew that today would see it reborn, and the galaxy would mourn its second coming.

COLLIX WAS DYING. Scything grenade fragments had blown out a chunk of his belly and his guts were leaking from his armour across the floor of the armoury. The sergeant propped himself against the barricade, firing a heavy bolter, though the recoil caused him to grunt in pain with each shot. Ortega's left arm hung uselessly at his side, a lasbolt having all but severed it at the elbow.

He fired and racked his shotgun one handed, shouting the Litanies of Justice at the rebel troopers as they broke themselves against their stubborn defence.

The explosives were rigged and now all that remained was to detonate them. There was no choice any more. Virgil had hoped that they could defend the place long enough for loyalist forces to relieve them, but that didn't seem likely any more.

He and Collix were all that was left. The other judges were dead, killed in the last attack, and now it was down to them.

Ortega had always wondered how death would come, and now that it was here, he found that it was not something to be feared, but to be embraced. It would bring the righteous wrath of the Emperor upon those who thought they could transgress His laws.

He could hear rebel officers gathering their men for another charge. Collix painfully dragged a fresh belt of bolter ammunition from the ammo crate into the weapon's smoking breech, his face ashen and twisted in pain. The shells kept slipping in his bloody hands and Ortega reached over to help his sergeant.

'Thanks, sir,' nodded Collix, closing the breech. 'Couldn't quite get it.'

'You've done well, sergeant,' said Virgil.

Collix heard the finality in Ortega's words and glanced over at the battery pack detonator they'd rigged.

'It's time then?'

'Yes, I think it is.'

The sergeant nodded, cocking the heavy bolter and drawing himself upright as much as his wounded body would allow. He saluted weakly and said, 'It has been an honour to serve with you, sir.'

Virgil returned the salute and took Collix's outstretched hand, gripping it firmly. He nodded over the barricade.

He smiled imperceptibly. 'You would have made a fine officer I think, Judge Collix.'

'I know,' replied Collix, 'Judge Captain within four years I thought. That was my plan anyway.'

'Four years? Six maybe. I think Sharben would have given you a run for your money in the promotion stakes.'

Collix nodded. 'Maybe, but think how my courageous actions here will help my chances for promotion.'

'Good point,' conceded Ortega. 'Remind me to mention it to the chief when we get out of here.'

'I'll hold you to that, sir.'

Both men turned serious and Ortega said, 'Just give me enough time to blow this place.'

Collix nodded, pulling the gun's stock hard against his shoulder and sighting on the wide doors to the armoury.

Virgil stumbled towards the vox-caster. The sharp crack of bolter fire and lasbolts heralded the next attack, but he did not dare look back.

Flashes of lasgun fire snapped around him, a round clipping his thigh. He yelled in pain as another bolt took him high in the back, sending him crashing to the floor. His wounded arm hit hard and he rolled, fighting to remain conscious over the agony that engulfed him.

He heard Collix shouting in anger over the storm of gunfire and willed the sergeant to give him just a little more time. He crawled towards the vox-caster, trailing a lake of blood from his ruptured body.

A massive explosion showered him with splintered wood, metal and chunks of rock. The PDF had finally managed to bring up some heavy weaponry and all that was left of the barricade was a smoking heap of mangled metal and bodies.

Troops began pouring into the armoury, galvanised by the destruction of their foe.

Ortega snarled and pulled himself forwards.

Another lasbolt struck him in the back.

He wrapped his arms around the vox-caster as a flurry of lasgun shots blasted through his armour and ripped him apart.

The last thing Virgil Ortega managed before death claimed him was to thumb the activation rune on the vox-caster, sending a jolt of power along the insulated wire towards the detonators of sixty grenades.

VIRGIL ORTEGA WAS dead before the first shockwave of the armoury's detonation even reached his body, but the results were more spectacular than he could ever have hoped.

Within seconds of his activating the vox-caster, the grenades he and his men had planted detonated the vast swathe of weapons and ammunition stored beneath the palace.

Even before the initial blasts had faded, a lethal chain reaction had begun.

Heat and vibration sensors registered the explosions and initiated containment procedures, but so rapid was the escalation of destruction that they could not even begin to cope with the vast forces Virgil had unleashed.

At first the inhabitants of Brandon Gate thought they were being bombarded again by the *Vae Victus* and waited in fear for the next salvo of magma bombs to rain down from the heavens.

The massive shockwave swept outwards through the ground with the force of an earthquake, shaking the entire city with the violence of the underground blast. Geysers of flame roared upwards from cracks ripped in the streets and entire districts vanished as the force of the explosion spread, incinerating buildings, people and tanks in seconds.

Shells streaked skyward, falling amid the city like deadly fireworks, adding to the panic and destruction. A number of cartel force commanders believed themselves to be under attack, either from newly arrived loyalist forces or treacherous rival cartels, and vicious tank battles erupted as decades of mistrust and political infighting was fought out on the streets of Brandon Gate.

Tanks from the Vergen cartel fought those of the Abrogas, who fought the de Valtos, who fought the Honan, who fought anyone who came in range. In the confusion, it took the commanders more than an hour to restore command and control, by which time over fifty tanks had been destroyed or taken out of action.

The unstable structure of the Arbites precinct house rumbled deafeningly, huge chunks of loosened rockcrete tumbling from its face as the esplanade cracked and whole sections were swallowed. PDF tanks revved their engines madly, vainly trying to escape the destruction, but too slow to avoid the tipping ground and collapsing building.

The statues in Liberation Square rocked on their pedestals, all but the effigy of the Emperor in its centre crashing into the square.

The Imperial palace shook to its foundations as forces it was never meant to endure slammed into it, disintegrating yet more of its already weakened structure. Whole wings collapsed in roiling clouds of dust, burying entire companies of PDF troopers beneath tonnes of smashed marble.

A vast crater yawned between the Arbites precinct house and the palace, a section of the defensive wall slumping downwards into the flaming hell of the destroyed armoury. Enormous flames licked skyward amid a gigantic pillar of smoke. Within seconds Brandon Gate looked as though it had been under siege for weeks.

In a single stroke, Virgil Ortega's sacrifice had denied the rebels the largest cache of weapons and military supplies on Pavonis.

* * *

URIEL STARED INTO the darkness of the mineshaft, a hundred metre wide wound on the face of the planet as the two Thunderhawks towards them. The circumference of the shaft was lined with massive cranes and cantilevered elevator gear to transport workers and materials both to and from the mine galleries below.

Huge funicular elevator cars secured to massive rails descended into the depths of the planet, each one capable of holding over a hundred men.

A winch wheel and control room, supported on a central pair of beams, hung over the pit, clusters of cables dropping into the darkness of the mineshaft.

When Dardino's infiltrators had torn into the defences from behind, the soldiers were doomed. Caught between the hammer and anvil of the Ultramarines attack they had had no chance.

He recalled the pride that had filled him as he watched his men follow him across the walls, cutting down the foe with righteous fury and holy purpose. They had followed him unquestioningly into battle and the zeal they had displayed was the equal of anything he had ever witnessed. Uriel felt humbled by the honour these men had brought to the company this day.

The lead Thunderhawk touched down in a howling cloud of dust and exhaust fumes, its front ramp dropping almost as soon as its engines began powering down.

Ario Barzano and a number of the thralls from the *Vae Victus* strode out to meet Uriel. The inquisitor's face was alight with anticipation. He had requisitioned a plasma pistol and power knife from the strike cruiser's armoury.

'Well done, Uriel, well done!' he beamed, glancing over at the mineshaft and the elevators.

'Thank you, inquisitor, but we're not done yet.'

'No, of course not, Uriel. But soon, eh?'

Uriel nodded, catching the inquisitor's confidence. He shouted over to his warriors. 'Get the rappelling gear disengaged from the gunships. Hurry!'

'Rappelling gear?' repeated Barzano. 'You can't be serious, Uriel, that shaft's nearly ten kilometres deep. It's far too deep to use ropes.' He pointed to the hulking form of the workers' elevator. 'What about that? We can use that surely?'

Uriel shook his head. 'No, the rebels are sure to have men stationed at the base of the mine. Anyone who goes down in that will either be stranded half way or gunned down the moment they hit the bottom.'

'So how do you intend to get down?'

Uriel turned the inquisitor around, marching him back to the Thunderhawk, where the Ultramarines were stripping blackened metallic cylinders from each rappelling rope.

'We shall use these,' said Uriel snapping one of the units from a rope. It resembled a plain cylinder of metal with a textured hand grip on its outside surface and a wide, toothed groove cut vertically along its length.

The device fitted snugly into Uriel's palm and as he clenched his fist the 'teeth' in the central groove snapped back inside the cylinder. As he released his grip, they clamped back into the groove.

'We use these for high-speed drops where we cannot use jump packs. We shall attach them to the lifting gear cables and drop along their length into the mine, achieving surprise on any defenders below.'

'You'll drop, one-handed, for ten thousand metres?'

Uriel nodded with a wry grin.

'And how, dear boy, do you intend that I get down?'

'You intend to come too?'

'Of course, you don't think after all that's happened I'm going to miss the chance to see you take down de Valtos do you?'

'Very well,' answered Uriel, walking the inquisitor towards the worker elevator. 'Then you will join us after we have dropped. I calculate it will take us almost five minutes to drop the ten kilometres to the bottom of the mine. Wait for that long until beginning your descent. After all, we will need a means of getting back to the surface.'

Barzano clearly did not like the idea of travelling down in the elevator car, but could see that there was no other way for him to reach the bottom of the mine. He certainly could not descend in the same manner as the Ultramarines. Reluctantly, he nodded.

'Very well, Uriel,' said Barzano, unsnapping the catch on his pistol holster, 'shall we?'

'Aye,' snarled the Ultramarine. 'Let's finish this.'

* * *

THE ULTRAMARINES WOULD descend in four waves, each following five seconds after the one before it. Uriel sat on the central beam, the massive winch wheel beside his right shoulder and his armoured legs dangling into the infinite darkness before him.

He and the first wave of warriors clambered down the beam, sliding the rappelling clamps over the elevator cables and clenching their fists around them, locking them in place, ready for the drop.

Uriel licked his suddenly dry lips as a sudden sense of vertigo seized him. He looked over his shoulder towards Ario Barzano in the worker elevator and sketched the Inquisitor a salute.

Barzano returned the salute.

Uriel checked left and right, to make sure the first wave was ready.

Taking a deep breath, he shouted, 'Now!' and dropped into the depths of the world.

THE METAL FELT warm to the touch, soft and yielding despite the fact that Kasimir de Valtos knew it was stronger than adamantium. Reverently, he lifted the first piece from the box and turned it in his hands, inspecting every centimetre of its shimmering surface. He had spent years of his life in search of these pieces and to see them now before him took his breath away.

Reluctantly, he tore his eyes from the object and turned to the sarcophagus, sensing the power that lay within and the attraction the metal had for it. He felt the object twitching in his hands and watched, amazed as its surface began to flow like mercury, reshaping itself into some new, altered form. Holding the glimmering metal before him like an offering, he took a hesitant step towards the sarcophagus, unsure as to whether he or the metal was more anxious.

The metal's malleable form settled into that of a flat, circular disc, like a cogwheel, yet with a subtle wrongness to its angles.

De Valtos could see the mirror of its form on the side of the sarcophagus facing him and knelt beside the dark oblong, pressing the metal into its surface. It flowed from his fingers, slipping easily into the perfectly sized niche. The metal liquefied once more, running and spreading in glittering silver trails across the surface of the sarcophagus, trickling along the patterns carved there.

Abruptly the glistening trails stopped, straining as though at the end of their elasticity, and de Valtos knew what he had to do next. He dragged the silver box over to the sarcophagus, hearing the metal fragments within clattering together, as though excited about the prospect of returning to the bosom of their maker.

As he lifted each piece, its structure rebelled from its original form, transforming into something new, shaping itself into the form required to fit into yet another niche on the sarcophagus's side. Working as fast as he could, de Valtos placed each piece of the living metal into its matching niche. As each piece was added, the quicksilver lines reached further around the basalt obelisk, an interconnecting web of angular lines and complex geometries.

Finally, he lifted the last piece from the box, a slender cruciform shape with a flattened, hooped top, and circled the sarcophagus, searching for its place. This final piece alone retained its initial form and he could find no similarly shaped niche in which to place it. Then de Valtos smiled, standing on tiptoe to find the metal's exact shape carved on the thick slab that formed the lid of the sarcophagus. He reached over and dropped it into place, stepping back to admire the beauty of the rippling silver structure before him. The sarcophagus lay wrapped in a glittering web, lines of the living metal interwoven across its surface and glowing with their own internal light.

'Now what?' whispered Kesharq.

'Now we wait,' answered de Valtos.

'For what?'

'For the rebirth of a creature older than time.'

'And the *Nightbringer*? What of it?'

De Valtos smiled, humourlessly. 'Do not worry, my dear Archon. Everything is unfolding as I have planned. The ship will soon be ours. And then we–'

His voice trailed away as a deep, bass thrumming suddenly tolled from the very air, like the beating of an incomprehensibly vast heart. Nervous PDF troopers raised their rifles as the pulsing rumble sounded again, louder.

'What's happening?' snapped Kesharq.

De Valtos didn't answer, too intent on the silver lines draining from the sarcophagus and running in eager streams through the channels on the floor. Liquid rivulets of silver flowed from the centre of the chamber towards the alcoves that surrounded them, four running from the chamber towards the antechamber outside.

The streams ran up the walls, spilling into each alcove.

Vendare Taloun dropped to his knees, a prayer to the Emperor spilling from his lips.

'Stand firm!' shouted a PDF sergeant, as several troopers began backing towards the door. The rumbling heartbeat pounded the air and de Valtos could feel a power of ages past seeping into the chamber as the gold cap at the apex of the ceiling began to glow with a ghostly luminescence.

Archon Kesharq gripped his axe tightly, scanning the room for the source of the booming vibrations. Kasimir de Valtos moved to stand beside the sarcophagus, placing his hands on its warm, throbbing side.

A cry of terror sounded.

He looked up to see the skeletal guardians of the tomb take a single, perfect step down from their alcoves, each warrior acting in absolute concert with its silent brethren. Were these the advance guard of the creature he had awoken?

A gleam of movement and light at the entrance to the chamber caught his eye and he watched as the four silent guardians from the antechamber entered the tomb, their movements smooth and unhurried. Each figure's androgynous features remained expressionless, but they carried their strange copper staffs threateningly before them.

A spectral light glittered within each of the tomb's guardians, pulsing in time with the booming heartbeat, yet none moved, content just to watch the intruders within their sanctuary.

With a noise like thunder, a great crack tore down the middle of the slab on top of the tomb. Questing tendrils of dark smoke seeped from within and de Valtos staggered back, falling to his knees as his mind blazed with unbidden thoughts of death and destruction. He reeled under the sensory overload of pain and suffering radiating from the sarcophagus.

Slowly, the sarcophagus began to unravel into wisps of smoky darkness.

EIGHTEEN

DEEPER AND DEEPER into the surface of Pavonis they fell, dropping past nine thousand metres and still going. Uriel saw a point of light below him and ordered the Ultramarines to begin slowing their descent.

He loosened the grip on his rappelling clamp, orange sparks flaring as the teeth dug into the thick wire cables. The speed of his depth counter's revolutions began to slow and Uriel watched as the collection of lights below him resolved into glow-globes and a lighted portion of tunnel. There were men there, looking up in confusion at the strange sight of sputtering sparks above them. Uriel didn't give them time to realise what they were seeing and released his grip on the rappelling clamp, dropping the last ten metres in free fall.

His armoured weight smashed down onto the first trooper, killing him before he knew what had happened. Uriel rolled, firing his pistol in quick bursts.

More Ultramarines dropped around him, quickly fanning out from the base of the mineshaft, pistols blasting and chainswords roaring.

There were forty troopers stationed at the bottom of the shaft, weapons trained at the elevator car from behind sandbagged gun nests. Gunfire blasted out to meet the attacking Ultramarines, bullets and lasbolts filling the air. Smoke billowed and blistering gouts of steam and exhaust gasses belched from shattered vents and the air grew dense with fumes.

Three powerful strides and Uriel was over the defences into the first gun nest, chopping left and right with his chainsword. A trooper brought his lasgun up.

Uriel hacked through the barrel, his reverse stroke chopping the man's head from his shoulders. In a bloodthirsty frenzy, he killed every enemy around him, savage joy flooding through him. He shot and cut his way through ten men before finally there were no more foes in reach. The fury and surprise of the Space Marine assault could not be resisted and within minutes the defenders were dead, their position now their tomb.

Uriel rejoiced in the bloodshed and his senses flooded with the urge to kill and destroy. He roared with primal rage, picturing the slaughter of hundreds, thousands of enemies, seeing their split-open corpses, flies and carrion feasting on their butchered flesh. Prisoners butchered and their blood drunk as a fine wine was his only desire and–

Uriel fell suddenly to his knees, dropping his pistol and sword as the horrific images continued to pour into his mind. He roared in anger, fighting against the torrent of filth that washed over him with all the mental discipline his training had granted him.

Gradually, he forced the images of death and murder from his mind, straining to keep the walls around his thoughts impenetrable. He could see his men fighting the same mental battle and shouted, 'Courage and honour! You are Ultramarines! Stand firm! These things you see are not your own. They belong to the creature we have come to slay! Fight them!'

One by one, the Ultramarines picked themselves up, dazed and repulsed by the horrifying visions that assailed them.

He voxed a swift acknowledgement to Barzano on the surface and watched the controls for the lift wink to life as the elevator began its rapid descent.

Pasanius's and Dardino's warriors moved to secure the perimeter while Squad Venasus checked the bodies of the fallen to ensure there were no survivors, though Uriel could see that this was unnecessary. The fury of their attack had been fuelled by unnatural alien desires and the men they had killed were little more than chunks of bloody meat. Uriel felt shame at the mindless violence they had unleashed, and not even the knowledge that their actions had been swayed by an alien power made it easier to bear the knowledge that the capacity for such wanton slaughter existed deep within them all.

He shook his head, whispering a mantra of steadfastness.

Now that he had time to determine the properties of their position, Uriel's enhanced senses could detect the rising levels of combustible fumes. Gunfire and explosions had shattered the venting mechanism here and the build-up of fumes, while non-lethal to a Space Marine, would eventually reach dangerous levels for ordinary humans.

Four passages radiated in the direction of the compass points. Palpable waves of horror emanated from the entrance to the eastern tunnel. Uriel could taste it on the air and within his bones, but kept the feeling at bay.

His thoughts still echoed with images of violence and death, torture and mutilation. Even if Barzano had not told him about the being that slept below these mountains, Uriel would have known immediately that this was the route they must take.

Uriel stood in the tunnel mouth, forcing the images of burned bodies, severed limbs and destroyed civilisations from his mind. They were not his thoughts. The taint of them in his head sickened him, but they steeled him to face the foe that lay ahead.

Uriel turned to face his men, pride burning through the hateful images in his head.

'Warriors of Ultramar, you have proven yourselves men of valour and strength, and we will soon face an enemy the likes of which has not been seen for uncounted years in the Emperor's realm. You can feel its presence clawing at your mind even now. But you must be strong: resist the impulses it creates within you. Remember that you are Space Marines, holy warriors of the Emperor, and that it is our duty to Him and our primarch that gives us our strength, courage and faith. This fight is not yet won. We must steel ourselves for the final test, where each of us must look within and discover the true limit of courage. Never forget that every man is important; every man can make a difference.'

Uriel raised his sword, its blooded edge reflecting the light of the glow-globes. 'Are you ready to be those men?' The Ultramarines roared in affirmation.

The high-speed elevator whined to halt at the base of the mineshaft and Uriel lowered his sword as Barzano stepped out. The inquisitor stumbled, raising his hands to his forehead. Uriel could scarce imagine what a terrible place this must be for the empathic inquisitor.

Barzano walked stiffly towards Uriel, his face lined with the strain of holding the horrific visions at bay.

'By the Emperor, can you feel its power?' whispered Barzano.

Uriel nodded. 'I feel it. The quicker we can be gone from this place the better.'

'My sentiments exactly, my friend,' replied Barzano, staring in revulsion down the eastern tunnel. He pressed the activation stud of the power knife and drew his pistol.

'Time to finish this, eh, Uriel?'

'Yes. Time indeed.'

Fighting the sickening power that pressed against their minds, the Ultramarines set off towards the tomb of the Nightbringer.

BLACKENED FINGERS SLID over the edge of the sarcophagus, long, dirt encrusted nails and shroud wrapped arms following as the Nightbringer arose from its tomb. Kasimir de Valtos climbed to his feet, smiling as the thoughts within his head shrieked with horrors he had not dreamed existed. Blood, death, suffering, mutilation and torment unknown for millions of years filled his skull; it felt so good.

The PDF soldiers fell to the ground scrabbling at their eyes, their pitiful screams rending the air as they sought to pluck out the horrific things in their heads. Vendare Taloun fainted dead away and even the loathsome eldar appeared to be in awe of the magnificent creature that was slowly revealing itself.

Kesharq gripped Kasimir's arm, his alien face enraptured.

'It's wondrous,' he breathed.

Kasimir nodded as the Nightbringer gripped the side of the sarcophagus and pulled itself upwards. Slowly its massive head cleared the edge of its tomb and Kasimir de Valtos stared into the face of death.

* * *

URIEL FOUGHT AGAINST the pulsing waves of violence that crashed against his mind, gripping his chainsword tight. From up ahead he could hear the screaming of the damned and he steeled himself for the coming confrontation. Barzano ran beside him, pale and drawn.

The tunnel dipped downwards, the rock giving way to sloping walls of smooth black obsidian. The wailing screams from ahead tore at Uriel's mind, feeding the evil that pounded relentlessly on his thoughts.

He entered a square room with two empty alcoves on either side. He could feel that the chamber beyond was the source of the evil in his head and a miasma of gritty darkness filled the air within.

There was nothing to be gained by stealth at this point; fast, lethal force was what was needed now.

Uriel charged into the pyramid-chamber of the Nightbringer, to find a scene of utter bedlam.

PDF troopers convulsed on the chamber's floor, faces bloody where nails and fingers had ripped eyes from heads. Those men still conscious beat themselves bloody with broken fists, mewling in terror at nightmares only they could see.

A ring of metallic skeletal beings advanced implacably towards a central block of dissolving black stone where a group of heavily armed eldar surrounded a jade-armoured warrior, the same one he had fought on the eldar space ship over Caernus IV. Kasimir de Valtos and a dark haired alien female sheltered in their midst.

He spared this scene but a cursory glance as he saw the huge creature pulling itself free of its stone prison. Swathed in rotted robes, it rose up from its tomb, the solid stone unravelling atom by atom and reshaping itself in a swirling black shroud.

More and more of the black stone disintegrated to form the concealing darkness of the creature. Soon all that was left was the slab of the tomb with the final piece of the metal burning brightly in its surface.

Uriel had a barely perceived vision of a gaunt, mouldering face with twin pits of yellow glowing weakly from within. There was insanity and a raging, unquenchable thirst for suffering in those eyes. A cloak of ghostly darkness hid its true form, a pair of rotted, bandage-swathed arms reaching from its nebulous outline. One limb ended in long, grave-dirt encrusted talons, the other in what appeared to be a huge blade of unnatural darkness, angled like a vast scythe.

As the creature rose to its full height, Uriel saw that it towered above the mortals beneath it; swirling eddies of darkness at its base snaking around the bodies of those not quick enough to escape its grasp.

The cloak of darkness swept two of the alien warriors up. The scythe arm flashed, passing through their armour and bodies with ease, and their withered corpses dropped, no more than shrivelled sacks of bone.

The aliens scattered as another of their number was engulfed by the vast alien. The alabaster figures with the copper staffs took their place at their master's side, their perfect faces devoid of life and animation.

'De Valtos!' yelled Barzano. 'By the Emperor's soul, do you know what you've done?'

Kasimir de Valtos screamed in triumph as the Nightbringer bloated the chamber with dark energies, filling his mind with the most wondrous things imaginable. The eldar warriors fell back towards the Ultramarines, ready to fight their way clear of this nightmare they found themselves within.

But the Nightbringer was hungry for soul morsels, the darkness around its form swelling and billowing as though plucked by invisible winds. A deep throbbing beat filled the chamber as the metallic skeleton warriors turned their attention to the interlopers within their master's chambers.

Uriel shuddered in revulsion as the skeletal creatures marched towards him, raising their strange weapons in perfect unison. He dived out of the way, rolling and lashing out at the nearest warrior, the chainsword hacking through its legs and toppling it. He sprang to his feet as the metallic warriors opened fire.

Uriel watched with horror as Sergeant Venasus shuddered under an invisible impact, the fabric of his armour peeling away in flayed layers, his flesh following with horrifying rapidity. The sergeant dropped to his knees as his musculature was revealed then stripped away until nothing but his crouching skeleton remained.

Another Ultramarine died in agony as his body was stripped, layer by layer, by the skull-faced warriors' weapons. Clawed hands grasped at Uriel, tearing at his armour, and he spun to face the metal skeleton he had just felled, the metal of its body re-knitting even as he watched.

He lashed out with his sword and put a bolt round through its ribcage. The warrior fell once more, but Uriel pounded the machine to fragments beneath his boot lest it somehow manage to regenerate once more. All around him was chaos.

Space Marines grappled with the metallic skeletons and were, for the most part winning, smashing them to the ground and blasting them apart with bolter fire. Sergeant Learchus tore one apart with his bare hands, smashing its skull to destruction against the floor.

But many of the deathly creatures simply picked themselves up once more, untroubled by wounds that would have killed a man twice over. Barzano fought beside Uriel, his glowing knife cutting a swathe through the enemy. His face was ashen and his movements slowing as the agony of his wounds began overcoming the pain balms.

The eldar fought alongside them and as Uriel kicked out at another foe, he kept a close eye on the aliens, ready to turn on them the second the machine warriors had been despatched. Their jade-armoured leader fought and killed with a deadly grace, his axe lashing out in a dizzying spiral of death. Wherever he struck a machine collapsed and each blow struck brought a screeching cry from the swirling darkness at the chamber's centre. But to Uriel it sounded more like a sound of amusement rather than displeasure.

The excrents snapped and bit, bearing their master's foes to the ground by sheer weight of numbers. The hideous alien weapons stripped great swathes of flesh from their deformed frames, but they fought on, oblivious to the ruin of their anatomy, until there was little left save scraps of torn, convulsing body parts.

Uriel fought like he had never fought before, cutting, shooting and killing with a skill he had not known he possessed. His reflexes were honed to perfection. He dodged killing thrusts and lethal blows with preternatural speed, deflecting clawed hands and shattering metal skulls with dazzling skill.

The last of the metal warriors were smashed to ruins, their gleaming limbs and bodies scattered in pieces across the chamber's floor. Uriel heaved a painful breath, his side burning where an alien rifle had stripped away a portion of his armour and flesh. Clotted blood caked his head and armour where grasping hands had ripped into him.

A strange calm settled as Space Marines and eldar faced one another across the chamber. The Nightbringer stood unmoving beside the slab of what had been the top of its tomb, the cruciform shaped piece of metal still glowing with eldritch fire.

Barzano joined Uriel, his breathing ragged and uneven. Uriel saw the wound on his arm had reopened, blood leaking through the synthflesh bandage.

Kasimir de Valtos stood in the undulating shadow of the Nightbringer, his features twisted in savage glee.

He raised a finger to point at the Ultramarines and screamed, 'Destroy them! I command you!'

Whether the words were aimed at the eldar or the vast alien and its bodyguards, Uriel did not know, but it was the eldar who leapt forwards. Their leader made straight for him, his war-axe raised high.

The Ultramarines roared and charged to meet them, the chamber ringing with the clash of arms as battle was joined once more.

Uriel blocked a cut and stepped in to hammer his fist into the side of the alien's helmet. His foe ducked, slamming the barbed haft of his axe into Uriel's belly, ripping a long gash in his armour.

Uriel gasped in pain, powering the hilt of his sword into Kesharq's back, slamming the alien to the floor. He reversed the grip on his sword and spun, hammering the roaring chain blade downwards.

His opponent was no longer there, but somersaulting to his feet and spinning his axe at Uriel's head. A burst of flaring light exploded as Barzano's knife intercepted the blow and Uriel took advantage of the alien's momentary distraction to smash his sword into his head.

Kesharq saw it coming and twisted his neck, robbing the blow of much of its power. The whirring teeth ripped off his helmet, the dented metal catching on the loose skin of his face and tearing it free in a wash of blood.

Kesharq screamed in pain, his fleshless face hideously revealed. He staggered back, regaining his balance and blocked Barzano's reverse cut, deflecting the blade away from him and hammering his axe into the inquisitor's chest.

Bones shattered as the axe clove downwards through Barzano's ribcage, exiting in a bloody spray above his hip. Barzano fell, the power knife dropping from his hand.

Uriel screamed a denial, slashing at the alien leader's back. Kesharq spun away from the blow, trapping Uriel's sword in the jagged barbs of the axe blade and snapping it with a flick of his wrist. Before he could reverse the stroke, Uriel dived forwards, over Barzano's body, and swept up the fallen inquisitor's blade in time to deflect a sweep meant to remove his head.

Kesharq came at him again. The axe swept round and Uriel blocked it with the glowing weapon he had taken from Barzano.

Kesharq advanced more cautiously now, the red mask of his bloody features a truly repulsive sight, the twitching of glistening facial muscles clearly visible. He spat a mouthful of blood and charged, axe raised to smash down.

Rather than step back, Uriel ducked low and caught the haft of the axe on his forearm, feeling the force of impact crack his armour open. He roared, spinning inside the eldar's guard and gripped his arms, slamming his body into the alien and pulling.

The momentum of Kesharq's charge carried him sailing over Uriel's shoulder and he smashed into the ground on his back. Uriel spun the power knife and drove it with all his strength through Kesharq's breastplate and into his heart. The alien leader spasmed, dark blood bursting from his throat as Uriel twisted the knife in the wound and plunged it home again and again.

Yells and war-cries echoed around him, but all Uriel could see was the ecstatic form of Kasimir de Valtos at the chamber's centre.

He wrenched the knife clear of Kesharq's corpse and stumbled towards the man who had set these events in motion.

KASIMIR DE VALTOS watched the furious battle raging around him with unabashed pleasure. To see so much blood spilt was pleasing to him, and the terrible things swarming through his head were a revelation. So much slaughter filled his mind! His entire being felt elevated as he savoured the thought that the things he was seeing and feeling were but the tiniest morsel of the bloodshed the Nightbringer could unleash.

It was still weak, its substance not yet fully formed, but incredibly powerful. Whether it was simply his nearness to the creature that empowered him with such knowledge or some deeper link he did not know. Perhaps it recognised in him a kindred spirit. Certainly it displayed none of the lethal hostility to him that it had to the eldar in its first moments of awakening.

The alien woman of Kesharq's stood behind him. He could feel the fear radiating from her in waves and it felt wonderful to drink in that emotion. She collapsed to her knees, her skin blistering and cracking as every shred of her life force was leeched from her body. She was able to scream once before the last vestiges of her existence was swallowed by the Nightbringer. Was this the beginning of his transformation into an immortal, wondered de Valtos? Was this the first of the new powers he was soon to manifest?

The violence around him felt truly intoxicating. He could feel the combined hatred and aggression of the enemies flaring bright and succulent, filling him, making him stronger. So pleasing to have such things to feast upon rather than the cold, tasteless energies that had sustained its form these millions of years.

Kasimir de Valtos blinked in puzzlement. Millions of years? Where had that thought come from? Suddenly he realised that the sensations flooding through him, the fear, the anger, the terror were not his own, but borrowed from the alien creature before him. Anger filled him as he realised he had been nothing more than a conduit for emotions that this being had forgotten over the passage of aeons it had spent locked away from the sight of man.

As though sensing his thoughts the Nightbringer slowly turned to face him, the yellow pits of its eyes burning his soul, boring into the core of what made him human.

But Kasimir de Valtos had set himself to becoming an immortal god and utter single-mindedness filled his thoughts as a creature from the dawn of time swept its darkness around him.

'Make me like you! I freed you. I demand immortality – it is my right!' shrieked de Valtos as the Nightbringer lowered its gaze to his.

He felt himself sucked into the creature's eyes, the emptiness of its stare more terrifying than anything he could comprehend.

He saw the dawn of the alien's race, the things they had done, the misery and suffering they had inflicted upon the galaxy and the blink of an eye that was the race of man.

He dropped to his knees as the sheer insignificance of his existence trembled before the unutterable vastness of the alien's consciousness. The fragile threads that were the twisted remains of Kasimir de Valtos's sanity shattered under such awful self-knowledge. This being had tamed stars and wiped entire civilisations from existence before the human race had even crawled from the soup of creation. What need had it of him?

'Please...' he begged, 'I want to live forever!'

The Nightbringer closed its clawed hand over de Valtos's head, the blackened fist completely enclosing his skull. Kasimir shrieked in terror at its touch, his flesh sloughing from his bones as it fed on his life energies.

The dark scythe slashed towards his neck.

He had a brief moment of perfect horror as he felt his own death flow through him, feeling his own terror and pain as the flimsiest morsel, barely worth feeding on, yet inflicted for the sake of the death it caused.

His head parted from his body.

The Nightbringer released its grip on de Valtos, letting his ravaged body topple to the ground. Slowly, deliberately, it turned its attention to the glowing metal fixed in the centre of its former tomb, passing its gnarled fingers over the shape.

And in space, a crescent shaped starship began to slowly drag itself from the shadowy realm it had occupied for the last sixty million years, called back into existence by its master.

URIEL WATCHED DISPASSIONATELY as the alien creature killed de Valtos. He felt nothing at his foe's death; the stakes were now far higher than personal revenge. He must somehow destroy this creature, or banish it; at least, stand against it.

The alabaster guardians stepped to intercept him, but Uriel was not to be denied. Pasanius, Learchus and Dardino joined him in his dash for the alien creature. Crackling emerald energies fired from the staff of the first two warriors. Uriel blocked the first bolt with the power knife and dodged the second. Pasanius raked one of the perfect figures with bolter fire, blasting porcelain-like chunks from its body, as Learchus drove his chainsword through its belly. A sweep of its staff smashed both sergeants from their feet, wreathing their bodies in green bale-fire.

Dardino hacked the warrior's legs from under it with a sweep of his power sword and Uriel leapt feet first at the second. His boots hammered home, but it was like striking a solid wall. The white figure rocked slightly, but did not fall, stabbing at Uriel with its copper staff. Uriel barely raised the knife in time, the power behind the blow sending hot jolts of agony up his arm. He rolled to his feet, punching the power knife through the figure's groin, slashing upwards and outwards. The alien warrior toppled, its leg severed at the hip, and Uriel ducked below the sweeping slash of yet another of the emotionless warriors' weapons.

Pasanius rose to his feet, firing at the remaining figures and punching another from its feet in a hail of white splinters. The final figure took a step back, Learchus's sword slashing at its head. Its master's clawed hand swept out and felled Learchus with a single blow. The sergeant groaned and struggled to rise.

Uriel, Pasanius and Dardino faced the awesome form of the Nightbringer, weapons drawn, feeling waves of horror breaking against them, but standing firm in the face of the enemy.

Uriel had nothing but contempt for the massive alien creature before him. The darkness of its spectral cloak billowed around its form and twin pools of sickly yellow pulsed within the darkness where its head might be.

The howling darkness of its scythe-arm lashed out, faster than the eye could follow. Sergeant Dardino grunted, more in surprise than pain as his torso toppled from his body and his legs crumpled in a flood of gore.

Pasanius opened fire, his bolts stitching a path across the swirling night of the alien's form. Hollow, echoing laughter pealed from the walls as each bolt flickered harmlessly through the enveloping darkness. The scythe licked out again and Pasanius's bolter was sheared in two perfect halves. The return stroke removed his right arm below the elbow.

Uriel used the distraction to close with the alien, slashing the power knife into the darkness. He screamed as the glacial chill of the being's substance enfolded his arm.

The creature's awful talons swung in a low arc, punching through Uriel's chest, tearing through a lung and rupturing his primary heart. He hurtled backwards, landing awkwardly across the remaining slab of the tomb, the glowing metal burning its image into the back of his armour. Pain ripped through him, deep in his chest, along his arm and within every nerve of his body. He groaned, fighting to push himself to his feet as he watched the Nightbringer begin the slaughter of his men.

INQUISITOR BARZANO WATCHED with pride as Uriel and his comrades stood before the power of the Nightbringer, despite the utter impossibility of victory. He pulled himself towards the slab even as life ebbed from his body. He could feel the flow of powerful energies flooding through the chamber, nightmarish visions the proximity of the Nightbringer was generating, and something else...

A soundless shriek, dazzling in its purity of purpose, called into the depths of space, calling the lost ship home. The living metal that shaped its form could not resist, pulled back from the realm it had been stranded in all these years.

So powerful was the summons that he could practically see the rippling waves of power radiating from where the C'tan's tomb had once stood. Or, more precisely, the glowing metal talisman buried in the slab.

His strength was all but gone, but still he tried to pull himself across the floor. He moaned as he watched Pasanius fall and Uriel thrown across the chamber, the Nightbringer's long, claws punching effortlessly through his armour.

Barzano felt the last of his strength drain from his body, but desperately held onto life. Where there was life, there was hope. He saw Uriel fight to pick himself up from the temple floor and realised he had one chance left.

URIEL ROARED WITH rage as the Nightbringer effortlessly butchered his men. Knowing that there was no chance to defeat this impossible creature, still they faced it, refusing to give in. Pasanius fought one-handed, slashing wildly at the creature as it darted about the chamber, cutting and slicing. A dazed Learchus bellowed at the Ultramarines to stand firm.

Horrid roars, like breakers against a cliff, echoed throughout the tomb and with a start Uriel realised that the alien creature was laughing at them, taking them apart slowly, painfully and sadistically.

Hot anger poured fuel on the fire of his endurance and he rose to his feet, a snarl of anger and pain bursting from his lips. He gathered up his fallen knife and hobbled forward, pulling up short as a sudden powerful imperative seized him. For a second he thought that the Nightbringer's infernal presence had breached his mind once more.

But there was a familiarity in these thoughts, a recognition.

Uriel turned to see Inquisitor Barzano staring at him, sweat pouring in runnels from his face, veins like hawsers on his neck.

The metal, Uriel, the metal! The metal...

The thought faded almost as soon as it formed within his head, but Uriel knew that the inquisitor had given his all to make sure he had heard it and he would not allow that effort to have been in vain.

He dropped to his knees at the edge of the slab, the glare of the glowing metal blinding to look at. He could feel its heat through the rents in his armour. What was he to do? Shoot it, stab it? Shouts of pain and rage from his men decided the issue.

Uriel hammered the power knife into the edge of the metal, wedging it between the stone of the slab and the glowing icon. He sensed a shift in the tortured energies filling the chamber and looked up to see the vast shape of the alien towering above the Ultramarines, two battle brothers held impaled on its claws.

He pushed down on the inlaid handle, feeling the blade bend as the metal's substance resisted him. He did not have the strength to force it from the slab.

The Nightbringer hurled the Space Marines aside, spinning with a ferocious sweep of its dark matter. Uriel felt its fury, its outrage that this upstart prey creature dared meddle in its affairs.

The alien's mind touched his with an anger that had seen stars snuffed out and Uriel let it in, feeling its monstrous rage flood through his body, feeling that rage empower him.

His own hatred for this being merged with its fury and he used the power, turning it outwards, ripping the metal from the slab with the sheer force of his anger-fuelled strength.

The metal clattered onto the floor of the tomb, the Nightbringer roaring in bestial rage as the connection to its star-killing vessel was severed, stranding it once more in the haunted depths of the immaterium. Uriel gripped the blazing metal and scrambled backwards. He snatched at his grenade dispenser as Pasanius leapt towards the creature.

A casual flick of its midnight talons sent him sprawling, but the veteran sergeant's attack had given Uriel the chance he needed. As the Nightbringer swept towards him, he held up the glowing metal, showing the hideous alien what he had fixed to its surface.

Uriel doubted the Nightbringer had any concept of what a melta bomb was, but somehow he knew that it would understand what it could do.

The creature drew itself up to its full height, spreading wide its taloned fists, the burning yellow of its eyes fixing Uriel with its deathly gaze.

Uriel laughed in its face, feeling the alien's terrible power pressing in on his skull. Visions of death tore at Uriel's mind, but held no terror for a warrior of the Emperor. He could feel the creature's consternation at his resistance.

The darkness began to swell around the creature's form, but Uriel moved his free hand to hover over the detonation rune. He smiled, despite the pain and tormented visions in his head.

'You're fast,' whispered Uriel, 'but not that fast.'

The Nightbringer hovered before him, flexing its claws in time with the boom of its alien heart. Uriel could feel its power and anger as a physical thing pressing in around him, but he could also sense something else.

Unease? Doubt?

The connection made between them by the Nightbringer granted Uriel the barest insight into the manifestation of this utterly alien being and suddenly he knew that despite the carnage it had wreaked, it was but a fraction of its true power. It was still so very weak and needed to feed. Uriel knew that every second that passed granted the Nightbringer fresh power as it fed on the strong life energies blazing in this place.

This was as close a chance as he was going to get to defeat the alien. Keeping his voice steady he said, 'This place is filling with explosive fumes and if I detonate this device, you will be buried beneath ten kilometres of rock. I don't know what you are or where you come from, but I know this. You're not strong enough yet to survive that. Can you imagine another sixty million years trapped below the surface of this world, with nothing to sustain you? You will be extinguished. Is that what you want? If you can reach into the minds of men, know this. I will destroy us all before I allow you to have that vessel.'

The pressure on his mind intensified and Uriel weakened his mental barrier, allowing the alien to see his unshakeable resolve. Its claws rose and fell, the darkness swirling around its nebulous form as its rage shook the chamber. Cracks split the walls and the red soil of Pavonis spilled through.

Uriel watched as the veil of darkness spiralled around the Nightbringer's form, sweeping up and over it like a dark tornado, gathering up the shattered remains of its guardian creatures within its furious orbit.

Uriel had a last glimpse of the Nightbringer as its yellow orbs were swallowed up by the encroaching darkness of its ghostly shroud. An alien hiss filled the chamber as the black storm shot upwards, impacting on the gold cap of the ceiling, shattering it into a thousand of pieces.

Then it was gone.

URIEL LOWERED HIS arm, his mind feeling as clear as a summer's day as the oppressive weight of the Nightbringer's horrific thoughts departed. He smiled, unable to prevent a huge grin splitting his face. He felt no desire to smile, but the sheer clarity of his own thoughts, freed from visions of murder and torture allowed no other reaction.

He put down the metal, its surface now cold and lifeless, and crawled towards Ario Barzano, who lay unmoving in a vast pool of blood. Uriel knelt beside the inquisitor, searching for a pulse, almost laughing in relief as he felt a weak beat.

'Get Apothecary Selenus!'

Barzano's eyes fluttered open and he smiled, his empathic senses also free of the Nightbringer's visions.

'It's gone?' he coughed.

Uriel nodded. 'Yes, it's gone. You held it at bay for just long enough.'

'No, Uriel, I only pointed the way. You held it off yourself.'

Barzano shuddered, his lifeblood flooding from him.

'You did well, I am proud of you all. You–' Barzano's words were cut off as a coughing fit overtook him and his body spasmed, fresh blood frothing from his chest wound.

'Apothecary!' shouted Uriel again.

'The governor...' gasped Barzano, through clenched teeth, 'Look after her, she trusts you. She'll listen to you... others will too... she will need your counsel and support. Do this for me, Uriel?'

'You know I will, Ario.'

Inquisitor Ario Barzano nodded, slowly shut his eyes and died in Uriel's arms.

HAVING GATHERED THEIR dead, the Ultramarines left the chamber of the Nightbringer. The only other survivor of the carnage was Vendare Taloun, whose unconsciousness had prevented the Nightbringer's visions from driving him insane. Uriel personally marched the man back to the elevator car at gunpoint. There was little need for force; Taloun was a broken man. It irked the Space Marine to have to hand his prisoner a rebreather mask for fear he would succumb to the fumes and escape just punishment for his treachery.

Along with their honoured dead, Uriel took the piece of metal he had removed from the alien's tomb, its glimmering surface still unblemished despite the none too tender ministrations of his power knife. It would go back to Macragge, to be sealed forever within the deepest vault in the mountains.

When his men had returned to the worker elevator that had brought Barzano to the bottom of the mine, Uriel handed Taloun over to a white-faced Pasanius and said, 'Wait.'

He returned the way he had come, picturing the faces of all the men he had lost on this mission, but knowing that their sacrifice had not been in vain.

Standing alone in the alien's tomb, he watched the earth of Pavonis pouring into the chamber, knowing that soon it would be buried once more. But Uriel needed more.

He knelt and placed a cluster of melta bombs on the slab the metal had come from and set the timers.

As he had promised the Nightbringer this blasphemous place would be buried forever under ten kilometres of rock.

Uriel turned and marched wearily from the chamber.

NINETEEN

Three months later...

VENDARE TALOUN WAS executed three months to the day after the battle at Tembra Ridge. During a very public trial, he confessed to his alliance with Kasimir de Valtos, the murder of his brother and a number of other appalling acts in his time as head of the Taloun cartel. He had been led, weeping and soiled, to the wreckage of Liberation Square, where he was hanged from the outstretched arm of the Emperor's statue.

Several more battles were fought before Imperial rule was restored to Pavonis, most between the squabbling PDF units whose cartel affiliations overcame any sense of loyalty to the cause they had supposedly been fighting for. Deprived of leadership, the cartel followers had soon reverted to their natural prejudices and suspicions.

When the deaths of Solana Vergen, Taryn Honan, Kasimir de Valtos and Beauchamp Abrogas became public knowledge, the cartels were thrown into disarray, paralysed by inaction as the scions and heirs fought for political and financial control.

The battalion commanders who had managed to retain a semblance of order amongst their units pulled back to their barracks to await whatever retribution might come their way. The tanks and soldiers of the Shonai cartel fought several actions to bring those men who had betrayed their oaths of loyalty to justice.

But when the *Vae Victus* lent her support to an attack on the de Valtos-sponsored barracks with devastating orbital barrages, the flags of surrender were raised as soon as the Shonai tanks came in sight of every other enemy stronghold. The Space Marine vessel had also hunted down the damaged eldar starship and, much to Lord Admiral Tiberius's delight, blasted it to atoms as it attempted to escape the Pavonis system.

When Mykola Shonai returned to Pavonis it was alongside Lortuen Perjed and at the head of the Ultramarines, their armour repaired and wounds dressed (though the Chapter's artificers would never be able to remove the cruciform shape burned into the back of Uriel's armour).

As she took her seat in the Chamber of Righteous Commerce after Vendare Taloun's execution there were shouts of approval and support from every section of the chamber.

URIEL SAT ON a marble bench, its surface cracked and pitted. This was the only portion of the palace gardens to have escaped the devastation of the shelling and the annihilation of the underground arsenal. Pasanius waited by the far entrance to the gardens, his bolter gripped tightly in his new bionic arm.

The grass was freshly cut, the scent of its fragrance reminding Uriel of the mountains back on Macragge. A simple headstone marked the final resting place of Inquisitor Ario Barzano. Beneath his name, a short inscription was engraved in a flowing script:

Each man is a spark in the darkness.
Would that we all burn as bright.

Uriel had carved it himself; he hoped that Barzano would have approved.

He rose to his feet as Mykola Shonai entered the garden. The wounds he had suffered fighting in the deep of the world were healing, but it would be some weeks yet before he would be fully fit.

Shonai's hair spilled around her shoulders and she clutched a small garland of flowers in her hands.

Three guards accompanied her, but kept a respectful distance as she approached the headstone.

She nodded to Uriel and knelt beside grave, placing the flowers gently beside the stone. She straightened, brushing the folds from her long dress and turned to face him.

'Captain Ventris, it is good to see you,' she smiled, sitting on the marble bench. 'Please, sit with me awhile.'

Uriel joined the governor on the bench and they sat in a companionable silence together for several minutes, neither willing to spoil this moment of peace. Eventually Shonai inclined her head towards Uriel.

'So you are leaving today?'

'Yes. Our work here is done and there are more than enough Imperial forces to maintain order.'

'Yes, there are,' agreed Mykola Shonai sadly. Imperial Guard transports had landed four days ago, the soldiers and tanks of the 44th Lavrentian Hussars turning the city into an armed camp. Ships of the Adeptus Administratum and Adeptus Ministorum had also arrived, their purpose to restore a measure of political and spiritual stability to Pavonis.

Preachers and confessors filled the streets with their words, taking renewed pledges of piety and devotion from the populace.

At the recommendation of Lortuen Perjed, the Administratum had permitted Shonai to remain as governor of Pavonis, on condition that at the end of her contract of service, she never again stand for political office. Lortuen Perjed was appointed permanent Administratum observer to Pavonis, replacing the criminally negligent Ballion Varle, who Jenna Sharben, the last surviving judge in Brandon Gate, had arrested and shot.

The rebel PDF troopers rounded up by the Shonai cartel were even now being transported onto a freshly arrived penal barge, bound for warzones in the Segmentum Obscurus.

The future of Pavonis had been assured, but it would no longer be under the autonomous regime of the cartels. The governmental system of Pavonis had been found lacking and would now fall under the watchful gaze of the Administratum.

Uriel could understand Shonai's frustration. She had come through the worst ordeal of her life and now, when they had won the final victory, everything was being taken from her.

'I did mean to come here before now,' explained Shonai, staring at the grave, 'but I was never sure quite what I would feel if I did.'

'In what way?'

'I owe my world's survival to you and Ario, but had things been different, he would have destroyed Pavonis and killed everything I hold dear.'

'Yes, but he did not. He gave his life in defence of you and your world. Remember him for that.'

'I do. That is why I came here today. I honour his memory and I will ensure that he will be forever known as a Hero of Pavonis.'

'I think he'd enjoy that,' chuckled Uriel. 'It would appeal to his colossal vanity.'

Shonai smiled and leaned up to kiss Uriel's cheek. 'Thank you, Uriel, for all that you have done for Pavonis. And for me.'

Uriel nodded, pleased with the governor's sentiment. Noticing her serious expression he asked, 'What will you do when your time as governor is at an end?'

'I'm not sure, Uriel. Something quiet,' she laughed, rising to her feet and offering her hand to Uriel. He stood and accepted the proffered hand, his grip swallowing Shonai's delicate fingers.

'Goodbye, Uriel. I wish you well.'

'Thank you, Governor Shonai. May the Emperor walk with you.'

Mykola Shonai smiled and walked away, vanishing back into the shattered edifice of the palace.

Uriel stood alone before Barzano's grave and snapped smartly to attention.

He saluted the inquisitor's spirit and hammered his fist twice into his breastplate in the warrior's honour to the fallen.

Uriel marched to the edge of the garden where Pasanius awaited his captain, flexing the unfamiliar tendons of his new, mechanical arm. The massive sergeant looked up as his commander approached.

'Still doesn't feel right,' he complained.

'You'll get used to it, my friend.'

'I suppose so,' grumbled Pasanius.

'Are the men ready to depart?' asked Uriel, changing the subject.

'Aye, your warriors are ready to go home.'

Uriel smiled at Pasanius's unconscious use of the phrase 'your warriors'. He rested his hand on the pommel of Idaeus's power sword and clenched his fist over its golden skull.

With the rebellion over, he had scoured the battlefield outside the prison complex, at last finding the broken blade. He had intended to repair the weapon, but for some reason he had not. Until now he had not realised why.

The weapon was a symbol, a physical sign of his previous captain's approval for the men of Fourth Company to follow. But now, in the crucible of combat, Uriel had proved his mettle and he no longer needed such a symbol. It had been Idaeus's last gift to Uriel and he knew that it would find a place of honour in the Chapter's reliquary.

He would forge his own sword, just as he had forged his own company in battle.

It was his company now. He was no longer filling the shadow of Idaeus or his illustrious ancestor, he was walking his own path.

Captain Uriel Ventris of the Ultramarines turned on his heel and together he and Pasanius marched towards the city walls where a Thunderhawk gunship awaited to take them aboard the *Vae Victus*.

'Come, my friend. Let's go home,' said Uriel.

EPILOGUE

SEVENTY THOUSAND LIGHT years away, the star known to Imperial stellar cartographers as Cyclo entered the final stages of its existence. It was a red giant of some ninety million kilometres diameter and had burned for over eight hundred million years. Had it not been for the billowing black shape floating impossibly in the star's photosphere and draining the last of its massive energies, it would probably have continued to do so for perhaps another two thousand.

Normally, it generated energy at a colossal rate by burning hydrogen to helium in nuclear fusion reactions deep in its heart, but its core was no longer able to sustain the massive forces that burned within.

Powerful waves of electromagnetic energy and sprays of plasma formed into a rippling nimbus of coruscating light that washed from the star in pulsing waves.

The Nightbringer fed and grew strong again in the depths of the dying star.

ABOUT THE AUTHOR

This regular Inferno! author hails from Scotland and narrowly escaped a career in surveying to work for the Overfiend, Andy Chambers, as one of Games Workshop's Warhammer 40,000 development team, working on such projects as Codex: Tau and Codex: Necrons. When not at work, he can often be found mumbling about home cinema and mucking about with cables while deafening his flatmates with the latest addition to his DVD collection.

More Warhammer 40,000 from the Black Library

THE EISENHORN TRILOGY
by Dan Abnett

IN THE 41ST MILLENNIUM, the enemies of mankind are legion, omnipresent and deadly. It is the sacred duty of the Holy Inquisition to hunt the shadows for humanity's most terrible foes – rogue psykers, xenos and daemons. Few Inquisitors can match the notoriety of Gregor Eisenhorn, whose struggle against the forces of evil stretches across the centuries.

XENOS

THE ELIMINATION OF the dangerous recidivist Murdon Eyclone is just the beginning of a new case for Gregor Eisenhorn. A trail of clues leads the Inquisitor and his retinue to the very edge of human-controlled space in the hunt for a lethal alien artefact – the dread Necroteuch.

MALLEUS

A GREAT IMPERIAL triumph to celebrate the success of the Ophidian Campaign ends in disaster when thirty-three rogue psykers escape and wreak havoc. Eisenhorn's hunt for the sinister power behind this atrocity becomes a desperate race against time as he himself is declared hereticus by the Ordo Malleus.

More Warhammer 40,000 from the Black Library

THE GAUNT'S GHOSTS SERIES
by Dan Abnett

IN THE NIGHTMARE future of Warhammer 40,000, mankind teeters on the brink of extinction, beset on all sides by relentless foes. Commissar Ibram Gaunt and his regiment the Tanith First-and-Only must fight as much against the inhuman enemies of mankind as survive the bitter internal rivalries of the Imperial Guard.

FIRST & ONLY

GAUNT AND HIS men find themselves at the forefront of a fight to win back control of a vital Imperial forge world from the forces of Chaos, but find far more than they expected in the heart of the Chaos-infested manufacturies.

GHOSTMAKER

NICKNAMED THE GHOSTS, Commissar Gaunt's regiment of stealth troops move from world from world, fighting for their very bodies and souls against the forces of Chaos.

NECROPOLIS

ON THE SHATTERED world of Verghast, Gaunt and his Ghosts find themselves embroiled within an ancient and deadly civil war as a mighty hive-city is besieged by an unrelenting foe.

HONOUR GUARD

AS A MIGHTY Chaos fleet approaches the shrine-world Hagia, Gaunt and his men are sent on a desperate race against time to safeguard some of the Imperium's most holy relics.

More Warhammer 40,000 from the Black Library

EXECUTION HOUR

A Warhammer 40,000 novel
by Gordon Rennie

AN INHABITED WORLD. An Imperial world, far from the nearest warzone. Once again, the guidance of the Powers of the Warp has served him well. Already the name and location of this new target are being relayed to the rest of the fleet. The Planet Killer is making ready to strike another blow for the Dark Gods. The doomed inhabitants could not possibly realise or understand it yet, but the hour of their appointed execution has just been set.

THE VILE AND unholy shadow of Chaos falls across the Gothic Sector at the onslaught of Warmaster Abaddon's infernal Black Crusade. Fighting a desperate rearguard action, the Imperial Battlefleet has no choice but to sacrifice dozens of worlds and millions of lives to buy precious time for their scattered fleets to regroup. But what possible chance do they have when Abaddon's unholy forces have the power not just to kill men, but also to murder worlds?

More Warhammer 40,000 from the Black Library

DEATHWING

Warhammer 40,000 stories, edited by Neil Jones and David Pringle

FULLY SIX METRES high, the creature stood on four splayed, spider-like legs of scything blades that cut the air with a deadly grace. Its vicious gash of a slobbering mouth was filled with hundreds of serrated, chisel-like teeth and its skin was a grotesque, oily texture – the colour of rotten meat. Where the metal of the dreadnought's hide was still visible, it was coloured an all too familiar shade of dark green. And upon its shoulder was the symbol of the Dark Angels. Whatever this creature was, it had once been a Space Marine.

IN THE NIGHTMARE future of the 41st Millennium, galaxies burn in the fires of eternal war. Fighting for its very survival, humanity must battle a myriad heretical alien races, but the most dangerous enemies of all are the former champions of mankind itself, perverted by the foul taint of Chaos.

THIS CLASSIC SCIENCE fiction anthology was first published by Games Workshop in the late 1980s and richly deserves its cult reputation. Now available in an expanded edition with three new tales, it includes superb dark SF stories by Dan Abnett, Storm Constantine, William King, Neil McIntosh, Graham McNeill, Charles Stross, Gav Thorpe & Ian Watson.